FALL FROM GRACE

This Large Print Book carries the
Seal of Approval of N.A.V.H.

FALL FROM GRACE

RICHARD NORTH PATTERSON

LARGE PRINT PRESS
A part of Gale, Cengage Learning

GALE
CENGAGE Learning·

Detroit • New York • San Francisco • New Haven, Conn • Waterville, Maine • London

GALE
CENGAGE Learning·

LIBRARY OF CONGRESS CATALOGING-IN-PUBLICATION DATA

Patterson, Richard North.
    Fall from grace / by Richard North Patterson.
        pages ; cm. — (Thorndike Press large print core)
        ISBN: 978-1-4104-4674-9 (hardcover) — ISBN: 1-4104-4674-3 (hardcover)
        1. Family secrets—Fiction. 2. Murder—Investigation—Fiction. 3. Martha's Vineyard (Mass.)—Fiction. 4. Large type books. I. Title.
PS3566.A8242F35 2012b
813'.54—dc23   2012006298

ISBN 13: 978-1-59413-598-9 (pbk. : alk. paper)
ISBN 10: 1-59413-598-3 (pbk. : alk. paper)

Published in 2013 by arrangement with Scribner, a division of Simon & Schuster, Inc.

Printed in the United States of America
1 2 3 4 5   17 16 15 14 13

For Al Giannini

■ ■ ■ ■

PART ONE
THE MISSING SON

■ ■ ■ ■

ONE

Sliding into the taxi, Adam Blaine told the cabbie where to drop him, and resumed his moody contemplation of his father.

The driver, a woman in her fifties, stole a glance at him in the rearview mirror. Though it was his practice in such proximity to be pleasant, Adam remained quiet. The past consumed him: he had returned to Martha's Vineyard, the home he had once loved, for the first time in a decade. Benjamin Blaine had made this possible by dying.

Leaving the airport, they took the road to Edgartown, passing woods and fields on both sides. At length, the driver said, "Forgive me, but aren't you related to Benjamin Blaine, the novelist?"

For a moment, Adam wished that he could lie. "I'm Adam. His son."

The woman nodded. "I saw you play basketball in high school. Even then you looked just like him."

It was inescapable, Adam knew: for the rest of his life, he would look in the mirror and see a man he loathed. "I'm so sorry for your loss," the woman continued quietly. "I drove him to the airport several times. Such a vigorous, handsome man, so full of life. To die like that is tragic."

Was it tragic for his mother, Adam wondered, or would release from Ben Blaine's dark vortex be an unspoken mercy? "It was certainly a shock," he responded. *But not as much of a shock,* he thought to himself, *as the last time I saw him.*

Understanding none of this, the driver said sympathetically, "I guess you came back for the funeral — I can't remember seeing you in years. Where do you make your home now?"

"Everywhere and nowhere." Adam paused, then deployed his usual cover story. "I'm an agricultural consultant in the third world, helping farmers improve their growing practices. Right now I'm in Afghanistan, on contract with the government."

Her eyes in the mirror were curious and perplexed. "Doing what, exactly?"

Adam chose a tone that implied his own bemusement. "The project's a little peculiar. I survey land, and try to encourage the locals to consider growing something other than poppies. In Afghanistan, the Taliban turns opium into guns."

Her face darkened. "That sounds dangerous."

Adam kept his voice casual. "Maybe, if it weren't so dumb. It's a dangerous place, it's true, but I'm well below soldiers and spooks on the hierarchy of risk. Why would the Taliban kill a hapless American on a hopeless mission? I'd be a waste of bullets."

Quiet now, the driver steered them through the outskirts of town. When they reached the church, the doors were shut. "I hope you haven't missed the service," she said.

Adam wondered if this mattered. In his heart, he had buried his father ten years ago. But his presence might help three people he deeply loved cope with their ambivalence. Though all had suffered at the hands of Benjamin Blaine, they lacked Adam's clarity of mind.

"I imagine I'll make the eulogy," he said, and handed the woman an extra twenty. "Can you drop my suitcase at the Blaine house?"

"Jack, or Ben?"

"Ben. Do you remember where it is?"

The driver nodded. "Sure."

Adam thanked her and got out. For a moment he gazed at the Old Whaling Church, absorbing the strangeness of his return. The deep blue sky of a flawless summer day framed the church, an imposing Greek revival with stone pillars and an ornate clock tower, all painted a pristine white. Along with the redbrick courthouse beside it, the church was the focal point of Edgartown, a place Adam thought of as the quintessential New England theme park — picket fences, manicured lawns, white wooden homes built in the 1800s. Though the church was now a performing arts center, it was the only place of worship on Martha's Vineyard, past or present, which could accommodate the hundreds of people who wished to honor a famous man. Had he foreseen his death, Benjamin Blaine would have chosen it himself.

A policeman guarded the door. On the steps reporters or curiosity seekers had clustered, perhaps eager for a glimpse of the statesmen, writers, actors, and athletes who counted themselves as Ben's friends. Standing taller, Adam strode toward them. He even moved like his father, he remembered people saying, with his father's grace and vigor. As he reached the steps, the curse of their resemblance struck again.

"Adam Blaine?" A young woman blocked his path, her look of birdlike alertness accentuated by quick, jerky movements of her head. "I'm Amanda Ferris of the *National Enquirer.*"

Despite his annoyance, Adam almost laughed in her face — this must be a slow week for Brad and Angelina, or the supposed progeny of Venusians and sub-Saharan adolescents. Instead, Adam brushed past her, ignoring her shrill question, "How do you feel about the circumstances of your father's death?"

"I'm Adam Blaine," he told the burly policeman at the center door, and stepped inside.

The interior was as Adam remembered it, bright and airy, its tall windows on three sides admitting shafts of light. As softly as he could, he walked down the center aisle toward the front, glimpsing the varied players in Benjamin Blaine's restless and protean life — a human rights activist from the Sudan; a veteran war correspondent; a retired Spanish bullfighter; an ex-president; a TV anchor; a young black man whose college education was a gift from Ben; the islanders, a more modest group, many of whom had known Ben all his life. Some of the latter, noting him, registered surprise at his presence. Adam nodded at a few — his old basketball coach, a teacher from third grade — all the while wishing that he could disappear. In the decade of his absence, he had learned to dislike standing out.

Reaching the first pew, he spotted his mother between his uncle, Jack, and brother, Teddy. He paused, glancing at the casket, then slid between Clarice Blaine and his brother. His mother remained almost perfect in appearance, Adam thought — the refined features, sculpted nose, and composed expression of an East Coast patrician, her blond hair now brightened by artifice. As he gave her a brief kiss on the cheek, her blue eyes filled with gratitude, and she clasped his hand. Then Adam felt Teddy grasp his shoulder.

Inclining his head toward his brother, Adam caught the complex smile on Teddy's sensitive face — fondness for Adam, bemusement at their circumstances. "Can you believe he's in there?" Teddy whispered. "I'm still afraid this is a prank."

Silent, Adam stared at the burnished coffin, the white cloth cover filigreed with gold. However richly Benjamin Blaine deserved the hatred of both sons, the enormity of his death was difficult to absorb — a man in his sixties, still ravenous for life, cut short in so strange a way. How many times, Adam wondered, had Teddy wished aloud to him for this moment? Yet its reality left Adam with the fruitless, painful wish that he and his father had been different, that he could feel the ache of love and loss instead of this wrenching bitterness, the painful question *Why?* for which no answer could suffice. He was back, Adam realized, and once more Benjamin Blaine had shattered his illusions. Adam had not resolved their past.

Nor would this service from the Book of Common Prayer, the touchstone of Clarice Blaine's heritage, provide balm for her sons' souls. "The trouble with Protestant funerals," a colleague had remarked to Adam after the murder of a friend, "is that they offer no catharsis." But for his mother the familiar ritual, that with which she had buried both her parents, might spread the gloss of decorum over the deeper truths of her marriage.

Standing near the casket, a young Episcopal priest recited the Burial of the Dead:

I am the resurrection and the life, saith
    the Lord;
he that believeth in me, though he were
    dead, yet shall he live;

and whosoever liveth and believeth in me shall never die. . . .

Adam believed none of it. In his recent experience, death was random, ugly, and very final, all too often the work of men whose God commanded these acts. That world, like this service, offered no transcendence. His only comfort was that the survivors loved one another, and now might find some peace.

Adam glanced at his mother, then his brother, trying to read their faces. Clarice wore her public expression, a mask of dignity she used to conceal more complicated feelings. But Teddy's dark eyes, cast now at the polished wooden floor, seemed to hold some anguished memory. At whatever age, Adam knew, some part of us is always a child, feeling pleasure at a parent's love or the wounds of a parent's disdain. The man inside the coffin had wounded Teddy long ago, too deeply to forget. From beneath the drone of the service, a memory of their father surfaced unbidden, as much about Teddy as Adam.

It was from that final summer, meant to be a bridge between Adam's first and second years at law school, after which life would become too serious to savor the days of sun and sea and wind so evocative of his youth. The summer that instead transformed Adam's life completely.

At the helm of his sailboat, Ben grinned with sheer love of the Vineyard waters, looking younger than his fifty-five years, his thick silver-flecked black hair swept back by a stiff headwind. To Adam, he resembled a pirate: a nose like a prow, bright black eyes that could exude anger, joy, alertness, or desire. He had a fluid grace of movement, a physicality suited to rough seas; in profile there was a hatchetlike quality to his face, an aggression in his posture, as though he were forever thrusting forward, ready to take the next bite out of life. "When Benjamin Blaine walks into a room," *Vanity Fair* had gushed, "he seems to be in Technicolor, and everyone else in black and white." As a boy, Adam had wanted nothing more than to be like him.

On this day, Adam enjoyed his father's enthusiasm for his classic wooden sailboat. "Well into this century," Ben had explained when he taught the eight-year-old Adam to sail, "the Herreshoff brothers designed eight consecutive defenders of the America's Cup. They built boats like this for the richest, most sophisticated families of their time

— the Vanderbilts, the Whitneys. I bought this one from your grandfather Barkley." His voice lowered, to impress on Adam the import of his next words. "To own one is a privilege, but to race one — as you someday will — is a joy. I mean for you to learn the primal joy of winning."

On this sail with Adam, fifteen years later, Ben was preparing for racing season yet again, his lust for competition unstanched. "This is the best thing in the world," he exclaimed. "Even better than hunting deer. Are you ever going to try that with me?"

Adam adjusted the mainsail, catching the wind as it shifted. "I doubt it."

Ben shot him a look of displeasure. "You're too much like your mother, Adam. But in this family you're the only game in town."

At once, Adam caught the reference. However demanding their father could sometimes be with Adam, for years Ben had treated Teddy less like a son than an uninvited guest who, to Ben's surprise and displeasure, kept showing up for dinner. But the role of favorite by default no longer gave Adam pleasure. "So Teddy's not like us," he rejoined. "So what? I can't paint, and neither can you. Only Teddy got that gene."

"Among others," Ben said flatly.

As Ben steered them starboard, gaining speed, Adam felt his own tension, years of too many retorts stifled. "Welcome to the twenty-first century," he replied. "Has it ever occurred to you that Teddy being gay is no different from you and I being left-handed? No wonder he never comes home." He paused, then ventured more evenly, "Someday people won't read you anymore. You'll be left with whoever is left to love you. It's not too late for Teddy to be one of them."

Unaccustomed to being challenged, Ben stared at him. "I know it's supposed to be genetic. So call me antediluvian, if you like. But genetics gave me a firstborn who feels like a foundling." His voice slowed, admitting a regretful note. "You like the things I like. Teddy never did. He didn't want to fish or sail or hunt or enjoy a day like this, God's gift to man. When I wanted someone to toss around a baseball with, you were like a puppy, eager to play. Not Teddy. He just gave me one of his looks."

"Did you ever care about what Teddy liked?" Adam paused, then came to the hard truth he too often felt. "Do you love me for me, Dad, or because I'm more like you than he is?"

Ben's face closed, his pleasure in the day

vanishing. "We're not the same person, for sure. But we're alike in ways that seem important. Think of me what you will, but I desire women. I've seen almost everything the world contains — wars, poverty, cruelty, heroism, grace, children starving to death, and women treated like cattle or sold into sexual slavery. There's almost nothing I can't imagine. But one thing I can't imagine is you looking at a man the way you look at Jenny. Teddy sees a man and imagines him naked, lying on his stomach. Assuming," Ben finished, "that Teddy is even the protagonist of that particular act."

In his anger, Adam resolved to say the rest. "I've always loved Teddy," he replied coldly, "and always will. But given how you feel about him, it's a good thing that he's in New York. And given how I feel about *that,* it might be good for you to remember that I'm the son you've got left."

Ben gave him a level look, deflecting the challenge. "He's in New York for now," he said at length. "It's where artists go to fail. Inside him, Teddy carries the seed of his own defeat. My guess is that he'll slink back here, like Jack did. The larger world was a little too large for him."

Listening, Adam marveled at the casual ease with which Ben had slipped in his disdain for his older brother. "Just who is it that you *do* respect, Dad?"

"Many people," Ben answered. "But in this family?" He paused, regarding Adam intently. "You, Adam. At least to a point."

Staring at his father's coffin, Adam wished that he had never learned what that point was. In kinship, he placed his hand on Teddy's shoulder.

TWO

Amid the hush that follows prayer, the priest began to speak.

In the Episcopal Church, Adam knew, by tradition there was no eulogy. But it seemed that his father could not be buried without one. Even dead, he was not a man for observing rules.

Briefly, Adam glanced at his mother, hands folded in her lap, attentive and almost watchful. What piqued Adam's curiosity was that she had assigned the eulogy to this cleric, a man far too young to have known Ben well. Clarice understood, of course, that neither his sons nor his brother cared to express public sentiments about the deceased. But that she had not enlisted one of the visiting celebrities suggested to Adam that she wished to maintain the public image of this family and this marriage. He settled in to endure a web of fictions and evasions.

A serious-looking young man with thinning hair, the priest began with the rise of Benjamin Blaine. The son of a Vineyard family whose males, for more than a century, had scraped by as lobstermen. The first Blaine to attend college, on a scholarship to Yale — an act of will, Adam knew, reflecting his father's iron resolve to be nothing like *his* father. A draftee who became a decorated veteran of bitter fighting in Vietnam. Author of the first great memoir for that war, *Body Count,* a searing depiction of combat that became a bestseller. A foreign correspondent who went to the hardest places on the globe. Then, not yet thirty, the novelist who, in the clergyman's words, "sought out the impoverished, the embattled, the victims of war or oppression, capturing their lives in indelible prose —"

And taking due credit for it, Adam thought. The travels not only fed his books but his legend — that there was nowhere Ben Blaine would not go, no danger he feared to face. He could have written the priest's next words: "He was handsome and charismatic, a great adventurer who was friend to some of the world's most famous people, and some of its most forgotten." All of whom, Adam would have said, his father saw as bit players in the drama of his life. Glancing at

Teddy as he suffered this account in silence, he mentally added Ben's family to the list.

"He never blinked at the cruelty of the world," the priest went on. "Instead, he recorded it with brutal honesty. That was the obligation he took on: to become our eyes and illuminate what he saw so that we could see." Give Ben Blaine his due, Adam conceded — he had breathed humanity into forgotten lives, touching the conscience of millions. For Adam, one of the mysteries of writing was that it could ennoble the most selfish of men, infusing their words with a compassion missing from their intimate life. For those who never knew him, Ben Blaine was his books.

In one sense this was true. Either because of his father's acute self-awareness, or, Adam suspected, complete obliviousness, Ben's fictional protagonists occupied the psychic space of their creator: aggressive men who failed or succeeded in pursuit of great aspirations. If they fell short, it was never for timidity, but because what they wanted was bigger than they were — whatever their strengths, and however deep their flaws, they were not prone to introspection. What they wanted lay outside them.

Involuntarily, Adam felt these thoughts drift into a countereulogy. A demeaning husband. A soul-searing father. A man whose appetite for attention and admiration could never be slaked. A compulsive womanizer for whom women were only mirrors in which he saw himself. Without looking at her, he grasped his mother's hand, and felt her fingers curl around his.

As he did, he became conscious of those who listened with them. Everyone knew about the women, of course. But in the niceties which attended death, the young priest no doubt would erase them. Glancing up at him, Adam composed his features into the expression of courteous attention he owed this man for his efforts. "Benjamin Blaine," the priest continued, "was not simply a world figure. He was also a husband, and a father. Together, Ben and Clarice raised two accomplished sons. And had Ben lived to see it, today would have been their fortieth anniversary."

Adam had forgotten this. Glancing at his mother, he saw tears glistening on her face, a look of grief and torment that surprised him. He clasped her hand tighter.

Seeing Ben's widow, the priest paused, then resumed in a thinner voice. "Those forty years are a tribute to the love between Ben and Clarice. But they are also a testament to her resilience and restraint, her commitment to fulfill the vows she pledged to her husband, and her resolve to raise Edward and Adam in the family to which they were born —"

A complex gift, Adam thought. But what puzzled him was the priest's reference — oblique but clear enough — to his father's infidelity. After all, mourners had buried Nelson Rockefeller, who had died making love to his mistress, without a whisper of what had New Yorkers snickering for weeks. Rockefeller's widow had wanted it that way and so, Adam had thought until this moment, must Clarice Blaine.

But the priest forged on. "All of us fail in some way. All of us are subject to temptation. All of us fall short of the glory of God —"

"Some more than others," Teddy whispered.

For Adam, this moment was another surprise — from his expression, Teddy had expected this reference to uncomfortable truths. "Ben Blaine," the priest elaborated, "was no exception. But in this last difficult and complex year, as in all the years of their marriage, Clarice stood by him —"

Filled with questions, Adam glanced at his mother. But she was staring straight ahead now, her face suddenly haggard. "It is not for us," the priest said firmly, "to know what was in Ben Blaine's heart during his final months of life, or at the moment of his death. We can only look, as did Clarice, at a life enriched by family and filled with accomplishment, great courage, loyal friends, and countless acts of generosity and grace. The rich, unquiet, and triumphant life of Benjamin Blaine."

Adam absorbed this statement in bewildered silence. Knowing his mother, he was certain that the minister said no more than she permitted. But what qualified this last year as more difficult than any other? And why, when his mother had ignored the truth for years, would she allow it to be spoken now? Except, perhaps, to have this priest publicly ennoble her victimhood.

Mired in troubled thoughts, he half listened to the ritual commendation. "Receive Benjamin Blaine into the arms of thy mercy, into the blessed rest of everlasting peace, and into the glorious company of the saints in light.

"Let us go forth in the name of Christ —"

Leaning close again, Teddy murmured, "Follow me, bro. You and I are pallbearers."

As the priest removed the cloth from the casket, six pallbearers took their places.

Besides Jack and Teddy, Adam saw Ben's longtime publisher; the senior senator from Massachusetts, a classmate at Yale and a frequent sailing companion; and a wrongly convicted death row inmate, a Mexican immigrant whose cause Ben had championed. All wore the sober looks of men who had lost a touchstone of their lives and, in mourning him, had glimpsed their own mortality. But this first clear look at his uncle surprised Adam. He had not seen Jack for three years, and he looked much older and more than a little weary: his thick dark hair was shot through with gray, the lines in his face were now seams, and the hollows beneath his eyes looked like bruises. No doubt this occasion, like his relationship to his younger brother, was fraught. But Jack regarded Adam across the casket with an affectionate gaze, his warm brown eyes conveying deep pleasure in seeing him.

Lifting the casket, Teddy nodded at his brother, as if to say *Feels like he's in there.* As the pallbearers started from the church, Adam felt his mother behind them, a silent figure in black. Then he saw Jenny Leigh.

She sat at the end of a pew, watching Adam's face. For an instant he almost stopped, just before she looked away.

So she was still on the island, Adam

thought, and had come here. She was much as he remembered her, slender and blond. Ten years ago she had possessed a smile that could fill his heart. But then, as now, there was something watchful in her eyes — as though she heard a distant, perhaps troubling, sound audible to no one else. Even at twenty, part of her had seemed forever out of reach; the last time he had seen her, they did not speak at all. Adam wondered how the years had changed her, and what she would say to him now.

Passing her, he stared straight ahead.

They bore his father through the entrance and into a bright sunlight that, to Adam, now felt incongruous. As they slid the casket into the hearse, the reporter from the *Enquirer* watched with a photographer who snapped pictures of the pallbearers. The key to all this interest, Adam surmised, had been hinted at in the eulogy.

Adam shook hands with his father's friends, expressing his muted thanks. Then he followed Jack and Teddy to a black stretch limousine in which his mother waited.

Once Adam stepped inside, the driver closed the door behind him. At last he was alone with his family.

Leaning forward, he hugged his mother,

discovering that she felt smaller. She gave him a wan look. "I'm so glad you're here. I know this is hard —" Her voice trailed off.

"It's not, Mom," Adam replied. "I came for you."

Her face softened in appreciation. "We're all glad," Jack affirmed.

Adam nodded. "How are you, Jack? Holding up okay?"

With his thoughtful air, so typical of Jack, he pondered the question. "For as long as I can remember," he said at length, "Ben was part of my life." He let the words stand for themselves, the enormity of their meaning left unspoken.

The limousine started toward the cemetery at Abel's Hill. "What's after this?" Adam inquired.

"A family meeting," Teddy said. "We took care of the mourners last night — a wake of sorts without the body, another ritual to get through. Be happy that you missed it."

In profile, his mother seemed to wince.

Silent, Adam looked out the window as memories of his youth flashed by — the dirt road to Long Point Beach, the turnoff for the Tisbury Great Pond. A life spent outdoors, cherished once, his memories curdled by his final summer. On the porch of Alley's General Store, where Adam had worked summers, islanders had gathered to watch the funeral procession. "A last obeisance," Teddy murmured. "How he would have loved it." For a moment, Adam wanted to ask about the eulogy, then considered his mother's feelings. He would talk with Teddy alone.

"A decade," Jack said to him. "Does it feel that long to you?"

"Longer."

His uncle nodded. "It's great to see you on the island. Whatever the reason." As if to say, Adam sensed, *Now you can come back.*

Teddy gave him the crooked smile Adam had loved since boyhood. "It *is* good, actually. Hope one of us doesn't have to follow Dad's lead to get you here again."

Adam took his mother's hand. Softly, he said, "I won't require that now."

The limousine reached Abel's Hill, the hearse ahead of it. In the gentler sun of late afternoon, the green sloping hills of the cemetery looked inviting, a good place to rest. Set among the pines were tombstones dating back to the early eighteenth century. Five generations of Blaines were buried here, some who died as children, as well as Lillian Hellman, until today its most famous occupant, whom Ben had memorably described as "an unspeakable harridan, as ugly

31

as she was dishonest." When moved to scorn, which was often, his father had minced no words.

They parked near a grave site shaded by trees and bordered by freshly dug earth, where the priest awaited them. This time Adam, Jack, and Teddy carried the casket with two cemetery workers, placing it on the platform the men would use to lower it into the ground. As Adam introduced himself to the priest, Robin Merritt, another car appeared. To his utter confusion, Jenny Leigh emerged.

He glanced at Teddy. But his brother's face registered no surprise. When Clarice saw Jenny, her expression warmed as it had for Adam. Tall and graceful, Jenny seemed to carry a separateness, as though creating her own space. But then she reached his mother and took Clarice in her arms.

Clarice hugged her fiercely. Ten years ago, Adam's mother had barely known her. And yet, by some alchemy of time, Jenny Leigh was here.

She kissed Jack on the cheek, then Teddy. Approaching Adam, her blue-gray eyes were grave and searching. She hesitated and then, as though conscious of the others watching, brushed his cheek with her lips. Drawing back, she said, "You look different. But then it's been quite a while."

Adam's mouth felt dry. "So it has. How are you, Jenny?"

"Fine." She glanced toward the grave. "Is this hard for you?"

"Less hard than what came before."

She nodded, briefly looking down. Then she stood beside Clarice.

The small group gathered around the grave. Looking again at his uncle and brother, Adam pondered the patterns within their family. In the last two generations, the birth order seemed to have repeated itself; Teddy, the firstborn, resembled Jack; Adam was the image of Jack's younger brother. Now they were burying Ben beside the father he had despised, Nathaniel Blaine, just as Teddy and Adam loathed the man they were burying. Both older brothers, Jack and Teddy, had been overshadowed by the younger. But there was this difference, for which Adam was profoundly grateful — whereas Ben's transcendence over Jack came with a streak of cruelty, Adam, observing that, had striven to be easier for Teddy to love. A generous spirit, Teddy had perceived this. As a brother, he was all that Adam could have asked.

Standing together with folded hands, Adam and Teddy listened as Father Merritt recited the commitment to the grave. "Almighty God, Father of mercies and giver of comfort, deal graciously, we pray, with all those who mourn: that, casting all their care on you, they may know the consolation of your love —"

When this was done, they lowered Ben into the earth. Clarice shoveled dirt on the casket, then Jack, Teddy, and Adam. He had wondered how this would feel. Now he felt nothing but the desire to be done with it.

As Adam put down the shovel, Clarice turned toward Jenny. "We're going home," she said. "Would you like to come?"

Jenny glanced at Adam, then replied with equal softness. "Adam is here now. This should be a time for family."

Looking from Jenny to Adam, Clarice nodded. Without another word, Jenny hugged her and left.

From the road, Adam saw, the photographer from the *Enquirer* was shooting pictures of his father's grave. As Adam turned to watch Jenny departing, Teddy placed a hand on his shoulder. "Just as well," he murmured. "We've got some things to tell you, and Jenny's the least of it."

THREE

For all of Adam's life, the Blaines had lived in a sprawling white frame house, set in a grassy clearing amid ten wooded acres. Built in the 1850s, it was sheltered by trees from the winds off the Atlantic, though clear-cutting had created an opening through which one could view the cliff overlooking the water. In the 1940s, a wealthy couple from Boston, Clarice's parents, had bought this as their summer home; long before Adam and Teddy had played hide-and-seek in the woods and swum off the rocky beach below, Clarice had spent the best months of her childhood in this house. As with many homes of this vintage, the porch that looked out at woods and ocean had been more generous than the rooms, a reminder that what was most compelling about the Vineyard was outdoors. Adam could still remember the summer evenings when his mother and father, like Clarice's, would sit on the porch until nightfall, talking or just listening to the crickets.

But like everything he touched, Ben had left his mark on the house of Clarice's youth. Discontented with cramped space, he had knocked down walls and added a study that his wife and sons entered by invitation only. Now the living room was large and open, filled with comfortable furniture, sumptuous Asian rugs, and mementos of Ben's travels — Asian vases, African masks, scrolls in Arabic and Hebrew, and Middle Eastern antiques acquired by dubious means. On the rough-hewn dining room table was the silver Herreshoff Cup, possessed for a season by the winner of the summer sailing competition, which Ben had claimed again in his sixty-fourth year. The home was so redolent of his father's life that Adam, entering for the first time in years, half-expected to see the man they had just buried drinking whisky in his brown leather chair.

Instead, his family sat in a room that, despite its many appointments, felt empty. Shaking off this moment of strangeness, Adam poured himself a scotch and took deeper stock of the survivors. Whenever he could, he had met them off-island, so he did not gauge them by the ten-year span of his self-imposed exile. But all three had changed since Adam had seen them last.

His mother looked smaller and more worn, her beauty now the faded handsomeness of a woman in her sixties. Though she still carried herself with an air of serenity and self-possession, a second persona seemed to peer out from behind her cornflower-blue eyes, more tentative and wounded. In Adam's mind, she had always been the master of appearances — her parents had taught her well, and she had polished her skills in the larger world as Ben Blaine's lovely and forbearing wife, hiding the pain of her marriage and, with that, its loneliness. Clarice Blaine, her son thought sadly, was perhaps the nicest person no one really knew.

Lean and angular, Teddy was an amalgam, with his mother's air of refinement, Jack's sensitive brown eyes, and a forelock of Ben's unruly black hair falling over his pale forehead. But his essence was uniquely Teddy — the artistic talent, the ironic smile with humor to match, a cover for his own hurt. The disease that had driven him back to the island, non-Hodgkin's lymphoma, had left him frailer and, it seemed to Adam, out of place. It was hard to grow up gay on Martha's Vineyard; even for adults, there was not much cushion for that among the natives. But it was worse to return to Ben's scorn and indifference. Nothing Teddy accomplished could change his father's verdict: where Adam saw a gifted painter, Ben had seen a feckless dreamer. In a just world, Adam thought, Jack would have been Teddy's father.

Jack, too, had been an artist — a sculptor. Faltering in his chosen path, he had become a woodworker, sublimating whatever frustrations he might feel in an embrace of the island's natural world. But the fraternal pattern persisted — when Jack chose to compete with Ben, as he had for years of summer sailing, far more often than not Ben won. Now Ben was dead, and Jack looked hollowed out and weary. Perhaps the saddest part of this moment for Adam was that, for all of their resentments, Ben Blaine had been the dominant figure in the lives of these three people, and in his own.

Following Adam's lead, Teddy poured a tumbler of scotch for his mother, another for himself, but none for Jack. In response to Adam's querying look, his uncle said simply, "I've stopped. It was getting me through too many winter nights."

The note of regret in Jack's voice underscored the reticence in the room. Adam looked at the three of them, Clarice sitting beside Jack on the couch, Teddy in an antique chair. Each seemed grim and subdued, as if they had much to say and no easy place to begin. Remembering Teddy's words at the grave site, Adam said to his brother, "The eulogy got my attention. What 'difficult year' are we talking about? Every year with our father was difficult."

Teddy glanced at their mother. "This one was harder," she said in a brittle voice. "Especially the last four months."

"How so?"

The trace of melancholy in her eyes did not match the asperity of her tone. "He was drinking heavily — much more than when you knew him. His behavior became very erratic, with frequent mood changes and outbursts of temper, lapses where he couldn't find the word he wanted." She shook her head. "Some of this isn't easy to describe. But there were moments when I remembered my father in the first stages of dementia."

"That seems odd for a healthy man in his midsixties." Adam pointed at the silver trophy. "Last August, he was fit enough to snare that cup after a two-month racing season. The drunken or demented couldn't do that."

A note of reproof entered Clarice's voice. "You weren't here, Adam. By December, your father was a different man. For me, perhaps the oddest thing was that his writing habits completely changed. You remember how disciplined he was."

"Sure. At his desk by seven — even hungover or sick as a dog — writing and rewriting until the cocktail hour. 'Writers should have workdays,' he used to say, 'like bureaucrats or bankers.' "

"He lost that," his mother said wearily. "His writing became frenzied, even nocturnal. I'd find him at his computer past midnight, a drink on his desk. He'd never written at night, or used alcohol as a spur."

Another remark of his father's sprung to Adam's mind: "This myth of drunken writers is romantic bullshit — all drinking ever got them was vomit on the page." It was disconcerting how much about his father came back to him now.

"None of this makes sense to me," Adam said at length. "Including his death. He must have walked a thousand times to that promontory, but never that close to the edge. He could have gone there blindfolded and not fallen off the cliff."

"Well, he did," Jack said flatly. "The next morning I found him on the rocks below in a pool of dried blood, his skull crushed."

Adam tried to envision this. "Has there been an autopsy?"

"In Boston. But we don't know the results yet. The certificate of death we needed to bury him listed the cause of death as 'Pending.' " Jack's tone became sarcastic. "If it were me, I'd have written 'Fell ninety feet before he hit a rock headfirst.' One look at him resolved all doubt."

Something was very wrong, Adam knew. Facing Teddy, he asked, "Have the police paid you a visit?"

His brother frowned. "Yup."

"About what?"

"It was pretty much the same questions for all of us. When we last saw him. What he was wearing. What we were doing when Dad must have taken his swan dive. If anyone was with us." Briefly Teddy looked at the others — Clarice with her brow knit, Jack watching Adam's face. "One thing they asked me is if I noticed a button missing on his shirt."

"Who was doing the asking — the locals or the state police?"

"The staties. The lead guy was a Sergeant Sean Mallory."

"Did they take anything?"

Biting his lip, Teddy nodded. "The clothes

41

and shoes we were wearing that night. Also samples of our DNA."

"They like to do that in a homicide investigation," Adam replied softly. "I remember it well from when I interned at the Manhattan DA's office. Please tell me you have lawyers."

The worry deepened in his mother's eyes. In a voice both vulnerable and defensive she said, "Why would we? None of us knows what happened to him."

"Come off it, Mom. These folks think someone gave Dad a shove — maybe one of you. At least they haven't ruled it out. Were any of you with someone else that night?"

Jack spread his hands. "Turns out all of us were alone. I was at home, watching the Red Sox game."

Adam looked at Teddy. "In my innocence," his brother replied, "I was painting another unsalable landscape."

"And I was reading," Clarice said tautly.

Adam looked at her, obviously shaken now, her tenuous mask of calm stripped away by his questions. He had begun to understand the agonizing delicacy of the eulogy, her need to navigate the land mines of Ben's death. A wave of sympathy overcame him — instead of a certain peace, Ben's death had brought her fresh anguish.

More gently, he asked, "Is George Hanley still the local DA?"

"Yes." Clarice shook her head, as if she felt her world slipping away. "George has been polite, but very guarded. All he'll say is that this is a police matter."

Adam looked from one to the other. "Before my legal education was aborted, I picked up some rudiments here and there. I know this was a shock, and that you've had to deal with quite a lot in very little time. But each of you needs to see a lawyer before talking to Sergeant Mallory again."

No one else spoke. Sitting back, Adam tried to read their expressions. Then he said, "I sense a very large elephant in the room, something else waiting to be said. At the church, I was hassled by a reporter from the *Enquirer,* of all places. Whatever else, my father wasn't Michael Jackson. I can't imagine that rag's demographic gives a damn that he tumbled off a cliff."

His mother turned away, face pinched. "The great man left a will," Teddy said in a monotone. "A new one."

Impassive, Adam waited. Teddy inhaled, then continued, "He disinherited Mom and me. The house, and most of Dad's estate, goes to Carla Pacelli."

Stunned, Adam tried to take this in. "The

actress?"

"The very one. Catnip for people whose lips move when they read."

Adam felt comprehension war with disbelief. "What on earth does a TV star have to do with Dad? The last I heard of her, she was coming out of rehab, her series canceled, her finances trashed, and her career in ashes."

Clarice still looked down, a study in mute humiliation. "As you'll remember," Teddy responded, "every summer the Hollywood contingent graces us with their presence. Supposedly, this particular second-tier talent came to heal herself. Instead, she took refuge in the guesthouse at the Dane place, a convenient five-minute walk from here, then she found salvation in the arms of the Vineyard's resident celebrity. Now she's about to become the owner of this house, and everything that's in it."

Turning to Clarice, Adam said, "How can that be, Mom? I thought this house was yours."

With effort, his mother looked up at him, a damp sheen in her eyes. "It would have been. But when my father went bankrupt, Ben bought it. As a favor to me, I thought."

"Who knew?" Teddy remarked. "All these years, bro, we lived here at his sufferance."

At once, Adam grasped the depth of his mother's grief and betrayal. At the moment of her husband's death, he had stripped her of everything — her past and her future. If nothing mattered to his father but his own desires, if years of loyalty and common enterprise were trifles to him, there was no way Clarice could compete with a woman barely older than Adam — an actress who, a mere two years ago, had been a stunning beauty, her aura so electric that she seemed to pop off the screen. The female embodiment of Ben Blaine's self-concept, the ultimate mirror of his ego.

In a rough voice, Adam said, "Long ago I found out that my father was a monster of selfishness. But this suggests I thought too well of him." Stopping himself, he finished quietly, "You don't deserve this, Mom."

Jack glanced at Clarice, his lined face graven with helplessness and frustration. Fighting back his anger, Adam realized that the will helped explain the interest of the state police in Ben's wife and oldest son, his victims. If given a second chance, Adam would have killed his father without remorse. "Who knew about this will?" he asked.

"Not me," Teddy answered. "And certainly not Mom. Needless to say, Jack didn't."

God, Adam wanted to say to his father, *is there no end to you?* Instead, he called upon the coldness of mind he had cultivated since leaving. "You said Pacelli gets most of the estate. Who gets the rest?"

In his driest tone, Teddy said, "There's a million for Jenny Leigh, of course. I believe that particular bequest says, 'So she can live the writer's life her talent deserves.'"

Adam stared at him. "You're joking."

"Just another act of beneficence. Apparently, our father had more regard for struggling writers than starving painters —"

"It's not Jenny's fault," Clarice interjected. "She's as shocked by Ben as we were."

At this, Jack shut his eyes, as though to distance himself from the fresh hatred he felt for his brother. "Too bad for Jenny," Adam told his mother, "because I don't think Dad can do this to you. You have property rights in his estate."

Clarice folded her hands. With quiet dignity, she said, "I once did, Adam. But I signed them all away years ago."

Adam shook his head in wonder. "He made you sign a prenup?"

"He didn't make me do anything, Adam. I voluntarily signed a postnuptial agreement, giving up any claim to the income derived from Ben's books."

46

"But that's everything we have," Adam protested. "This is Grandfather Barkley's house — my father took it, just like he took over your family's life. Except for writing, Benjamin Blaine would have been as poor as a church mouse."

"As poor as me," Jack interposed.

Adam kept watching his mother. "When did you sign this?"

Clarice hesitated. "Before you were born."

"Could I ask why?"

Clarice gazed out the window, as though into her own past, her unsipped scotch still cradled in her hands. "The books weren't mine. I trusted Ben to care for us."

To Adam, the answer was senseless beyond words. "Forgive me, Mom, but I don't recall you making bold feminist gestures, especially ones this expensive. Besides which, you helped him a myriad of ways — researching, proofreading, scheduling his appearances."

"Nonetheless," Clarice said, "it's what I did. No one regrets it more than me."

Adam rubbed the bridge of his nose, staring at the last patch of failing sunlight on the deep-red Persian rug. "When did you first hear about this will?"

"Only after he died. When the police asked how we were getting along."

"What did you say to them?"

"Not too well." Clarice's voice was hushed. "He'd never been as blatant as with this actress. It was as though he'd lost his mind."

Adam searched for a way to comfort her. "He may have, Mom. Were there any other odd bequests?"

Teddy's smile was no smile at all. "Only the one to you."

Adam laughed in bitter amazement. "An autographed picture, signed 'Love, Dad'?"

"Oh, it was much more elegant. He left you a hundred thousand dollars and an album of old photographs of a trip to Southeast Asia." A sliver of anger entered Teddy's voice. "Your bequest comes with its own valedictory, 'To Adam, who has the courage to hate.' A last poisoned dart at the rest of us, I assume. Especially me. His final way of saying that you were the one he admired, even now, and that I'm a faggot and a failure."

Adam could not argue with this interpretation, and would not insult his brother by trying. At length, he said, "He always hated that we were close. He loved competition, no matter how perverse. Ask Jack."

This seemed to awaken Jack from his trance. "There's more, Adam. In his coup de grâce, Ben made you the executor of his estate." His voice roughened. "As I understand it, you're responsible for carrying out his wishes. You now have the job of completing your mother's disinheritance."

Adam felt the expression drain from his face. For moments, as the others watched him, he did not speak. Then he stood, leaning over to gently kiss the crown of Clarice's head. Softly, he said, "This will get better, Mom. I promise."

She did not answer. Standing straighter, Adam spoke to his uncle in a wholly different voice. "Take me to the promontory, Jack. I want to see where he died."

FOUR

Adam and Jack stood at the promontory where, countless times before, the younger Adam had watched the sunset with his father.

Like the bow of a ship, the point jutted out from land over the rocky beach below, affording a sweeping view of the Atlantic on both sides. The massive rock on which they stood, embedded in hard red clay, had been polished as smooth as a table by wind and rain. When Adam was a boy, his father had organized evening picnics for his wife and sons, exulting in the elemental beauty of the sun descending toward the vast cobalt sea. One memory from Adam's last summer on the Vineyard was especially vivid — Ben at his most appealing, the nature sensualist enthralled by the gift of life. The evening was hazy, the setting sun a red ball, turning a backdrop of nimbus clouds into a panorama of brilliant orange. Grinning, Ben had told him, "This is my favorite place on earth — that rarest of things in these parts, a water view of the ocean with a western exposure. I never tire of it; every sunset is different. When I die, I hope to God someone will have the grace to scatter my ashes here."

But his mother had not done so — she had buried him in the earth, next to the father he despised, perhaps the only revenge she had left. His father had died in this place, his skull shattering on the rocks below. Another memory came to Adam — as a small child, bold even then, he had stood at the edge of the promontory, gazing down the sheer cliffside with no thought to his safety. Taking his hand in a strong grip, his father had pulled him back. In gentle rebuke, Ben said, "Don't stand so close, son. You could fall to your death. Follow my example and stay back from it." Perhaps Ben, sure-footed as he was, had said this for a child's benefit. But even on that last night, their final sunset together, his father had stood well short of the cliff.

Amid this skein of memory, another thought came to Adam — that, however subconsciously, his childish resolve to stand at its edge had been a way of showing up Teddy, who suffered from vertigo and endured these family picnics like a conscript. Odd, too, that in these memories his mother, though surely present, had left no image of herself behind.

Pensive, Adam walked to the edge. Ninety feet below, the coarse sand was covered with rocks and boulders; no one could survive such a fall. "Where exactly did you find him?" Adam asked.

Jack pointed at a group of jagged rocks. "Beside those. The last thing you'd imagine, I know."

"The very last."

"Ten years makes a difference, Adam. In me, in you — even in Ben. The man you remember wasn't the man I found there."

Adam shoved his hands in his pockets, feeling the wind on his face as he watched the sun, a red-orange disk, slice into the water. At length, he said, "Funny he died on the summer solstice, the longest day of the year. His favorite time to come here."

Jack gave him a curious look. "You sound almost sentimental."

"I'm just trying to envision what happened that night." He turned to Jack. "The state police taped off this area, I assume."

Jack inclined his head toward the hiking trail that ran along the cliff. "Only for a few hours. There's too much foot traffic here."

Adam looked around them, gauging how the police would evaluate their surroundings. Bordered by woods, the promontory would be visible only to hikers or from the waters below. The trail itself, running in both directions, headed past other homes until it meandered to the main road. The pathway from the Blaine house, trod by his mother's family and then his own, ran to the cut in the trees perhaps fifty feet to Adam's left. Peering over the rock again, Adam saw the wooden stairway to the beach, built by Ben for his sons when they were young. That night anyone could have approached this promontory from any of four directions, and likely remained unseen by anyone but Ben himself.

"They took your shoes," Adam said. "That suggests there were footprints here. What was the weather like that day?"

Jack stared at the clay, his shaggy white-tipped eyebrows raised in thought. "It had rained that morning. Anyone coming by might have left some prints."

Adam scoured the area around the rock. "Even wet, that clay is pretty hard."

"True. Anyhow, no point looking now. A few hours after I found him it started raining buckets."

Adam faced his uncle. "Tell me what you

think, Jack. Did someone give him a shove?"

Jack shook his head, less in demurral than distress. "Why would they?"

"Take your pick. Fear. Greed. Reprisal. Not to mention the sheer pleasure of it." Adam's voice hardened. "Personally speaking, I don't much care if someone helped him, or who it was. But Sergeant Mallory does."

A look of reticence entered Jack's eyes, perhaps the superstitious fear of speaking ill of the dead, or worry about the police. "Whatever Ben did, he's gone now."

Adam felt a resurgence of the anger he could never escape, stirred by the revelations of the last hours. "Gone? In a year, maybe I'll believe it. But he's as much trouble dead as he was alive, and not just because of how he died. He shafted my mother — even now Benjamin Blaine is pulling our strings. We didn't bury him at all."

Jack stared at his feet. "I wish we could," he said. "Death should put an end to hatred."

Adam shook his head. "Not for me. Not with what he's done."

After a moment, Jack met his eyes. "I know," he said in a tone of resignation. "How do you suppose *I* feel, Adam? Long before you were born, Ben was my brother."

For Adam, Jack's statement had its own complex resonance. His uncle's nature was inherently kind; despising Ben must carry its own pain. Through the prism of hindsight, Adam could see that Jack treated those who suffered as he had — Ben's wife and sons — with deep compassion, understanding all too well how they must feel. Where Ben was indifferent to Teddy's talent, Jack — who knew what it was to make things with his hands, using his eye for form and shape — encouraged him. And when Teddy wrestled with being gay, it was only Jack who listened.

This led Adam to the question of why Jack had never married. Perhaps, like Teddy, Jack was gay — for an islander of Jack's years, secrecy might have felt safer. Or perhaps sexual intimacy was not important to him. But whatever Jack's nature, Adam, too, had benefited from his uncle's care.

When Ben was away — as was frequent — Jack took him fishing or sailing or hiking, teaching him to observe the small wonders of nature. With Jack, Adam never felt that clutch in the stomach, the need to please his harshly judgmental father. In Ben's absence, Jack came to Adam's games, cheering as he played quarterback, or point guard, or center field. It was from Jack, not Ben, that Adam learned the value of positive encouragement — to cherish his achievements, to learn from his mistakes. It was Jack who taught Adam compassion for himself, and then for others. Without Jack, Adam might have become his father.

Perhaps that had been his uncle's plan. For as long as Adam could remember, the two brothers had a quietly corrosive relationship. Ben spoke of Jack with dismissive scorn; Jack did not mention him at all. It was as if Ben's family was their only bridge. When, as a teenager, Adam had wondered aloud why they seemed estranged, Jack had answered wryly, "We have temperamental differences." But gradually, through his mother and a populace that, in winter, shrunk to fourteen thousand souls, Adam had come to understand far more.

Their family of origin had been impoverished in every way. Nathaniel Blaine had been frustrated by the harshness of his way of life, all that he knew, and a deep sense of his own limitations. He was a man of volcanic anger, subjecting his wife, Amy, to a stunted and fearful existence. Both drank to excess; neither had much love to give Jack, and less after Ben was born. But Jack was gentle from birth, while Ben burned with the desire to transcend his family. The first test for Ben was Jack — quite explicitly, Ben set out not just to outstrip Jack as a student, athlete, and sailor, but to sear Jack's soul with the knowledge of his own inferiority. It was Ben who left for Yale; Ben who became the Vineyard's most famous son. Jack was known as his older, lesser brother.

Parsing these reflections, Adam glanced sideways at his uncle, Jack's gentle mien illuminated by the sun in its descent. Jack should not have been on this island — then or now. In his twenties Jack, like Teddy, had struggled for survival in New York City. Then the widowed Nathaniel Blaine, stumbling while drunk, had struck his head on the kitchen counter and bled to death on the floor. No one had found him for days; no one cared much. But he had left the home he died in, a small house near Menemsha Harbor. In a seemingly benign gesture, Ben had waived his rights of inheritance, giving Jack a home he could not replace anywhere else by selling it. And so Jack had returned to live in Ben's shadow — which, Adam thought now, was likely Ben's intention. Ben had held out a poisoned chalice, and his older brother had taken it. Even in that last fateful summer, when Adam had tipped the balance of their rivalry, he knew that the fault line in his life had cracked open before his birth. And now he had come back.

Adam became aware of his long silence. "You're right," he told his uncle. "I've been away a long time now. I remember him as he was."

Jack gave him a probing look. "Why *did* you leave?" he asked. "You changed the entire course of your life, cut off your father, and wouldn't say why. It was like you were too proud to tell us."

The tacit accusation stung. But Adam had no desire to explain his reasons, and Jack no right to know them. "Maybe I just got sick of him."

Jack raised his eyebrows. "Enough to shun him for a decade?"

"Yes. That much."

The laconic rebuff, hard for Adam to deliver, had the unexpected result of softening Jack's expression. "He got no better, Adam. Sometimes I found myself wishing that, like you, I'd stayed away."

"Why didn't you?"

Jack's shoulders slumped, as if the weight of his reasons was too great to express. "This was home," he said simply.

Adam felt a rush of affection, accompanied by the fervent wish that he could respect his uncle fully. Perhaps Ben had stamped Adam with his own harsh judgment, but he could not quell his verdict on Jack's life: *You should have left.* Instead, Adam said, "Then there's my mother. Why on earth did he marry her, and why did he stay?"

It was telling, Adam realized, that he did not ask why his mother had married Benjamin Blaine. As it was, the question made Jack frown. "The first part is easy enough to answer. At Ben's core was this raging anger that he was born into this stunted family, with no money or accomplishment. He was deeply ashamed of that, and of our parents. The shame deepened when the summer people came, enjoying their affluence and success. To scrape together some money Ben and I started working as waiters at their parties, serving them cocktails and hors d'oeuvres, then cleaning up the careless mess they made."

"That's how they met, right?"

Jack nodded. "For years, he watched your mother, the beautiful daughter of a family who took their lives for granted. No one knew that later on her father's investment firm, his inheritance, would collapse under claims of mismanagement." Jack's smile was brief and mirthless. " 'Inbreeding,' Ben told me once. 'The Barkleys' blood got thin, until everything her father had he owed to ancestors with more brains and balls.' "

The echo of his father's scorn re-ignited Adam's anger. "It didn't keep the sonofabitch from marrying the old man's daughter."

"Clarice was a prize to be won," Jack replied, "a symbol of all he wanted and never had. For a passing moment, I thought he was after your mother's best friend, Whitney Dane. But once Ben left Yale, it was his time to go after her. She never had a chance — the triumph of capturing her was too great for Ben to fail." Jack's tone grew hard. "So he pursued her, married her, and cheated on her. The ultimate proof of his superiority was that he made her parents' home his own. And now he's taken that piece of her life and given it to this actress."

Feeling the chill of this story and its coda, Adam shut his eyes. Another moment with his father came to him, again from their final summer. Jenny was off-island, and Adam had asked Ben to go fly-fishing off Dogfish Bar. With a rueful smile, Ben shook his head. "Believe me, son, I'd vastly prefer your company to the living death I'll experience tonight. But your mother insists on going to some idiot's Fourth of July party.

For reasons that are obscure to me, she actually cares about what these people think." Ben sat back in his chair, his tone confiding. "I call it high school for the rich. They go from party to party, dying for acceptance, never wondering whether it's worthwhile being accepted by whatever moron they encounter. The only amusement they hold for me is wondering who'll flatter me in the most unctuous and transparent way. Knowing full well that none of them would give a damn except for who I am.

"Time is too fleeting for that. I could spend tonight fishing with my son, or making love, or talking with a man or woman who actually has something to say, or rereading *War and Peace,* the greatest novel ever written. By midnight, both of us will be six hours closer to being dead, and only you will have anything to show for it. Just thinking about it curdles me with envy."

Adam laughed. "Have I told you Jenny's theory on summer social life?"

"These minnows justify an entire theory?"

"A small one. Jen caters parties, like you used to do, honing her skills of observation. She says that the summer social circuit is actually a game called Celebrity Pac-Man, with a scoring system based on how many famous people you can hang out with between the Fourth of July and Labor Day —"

"Celebrity Pac-Man?" Ben repeated with a grin. "As in I got 'Tom and Rita' or 'Ted and Mary' or 'Alan and Carolyn'?"

"Or 'Ben and Clarice,' " Adam responded. " 'Tom and Rita' are a ten. Whereas, I'm sorry to say, Mom and you are more like a seven —"

"I'm heartbroken."

"You should be. Anyhow, the season starts tonight, so you absolutely have to be there. I'll be thinking about you."

With a faint smile, Ben regarded his youngest son. "Your friend Jenny has some insight. I don't know whether you'll ever be a famous trial lawyer, Adam. But if you become one, let me give you some advice. I like fame, quite a lot. But you have to know how to use it." His eyes became serious, his voice penetrant. "I use it to gain things of value — access to people I respect, or whose lives or achievements interest me. I use it to gain experiences I haven't had, and learn things I didn't know. Fame is hard to win, all too easy to lose, and way too precious to squander on tonight's group of nattering hangers-on."

"So why don't you just let Mom go without you?"

"If only I could. But I'm the draw — in a marriage, sacrifices must be made." Ben paused. "This Jenny of yours sounds smart enough. Is this a serious thing?"

Adam weighed his answer. "She's still pretty young, only twenty. But it's serious enough that we're only seeing each other."

Ben gave him a speculative look. "Then I hope she's good, my boy."

Abruptly, Adam felt a flash of anger — this was a line his father could not cross. "Good at what, Dad? You make her sound like an athlete."

Watching Adam's face, Ben shrugged, his way of backing off. Adam would never give him an answer, let alone the truth: *Sometimes Jenny just goes away. Like she doesn't know where she is, or that I'm the man inside her.*

And now Jenny Leigh had become his father's heir.

Adam looked at his uncle, ashamed of his own judgment of Jack's life. This man was everything his father was not — loving, humane, and protective of Adam's mother and brother. "At the end," Adam asked, "did you think my father was crazy?"

In the failing light of dusk, he saw Jack frown. "Crazy? I don't know. I just know that he was different."

"In what way?"

"The ones your mother saw. Especially this thing with Carla Pacelli." Jack shifted his weight, seemingly uncomfortable. "I mean, you know what he was like. When it came to women, as with a lot of things, Ben had a complete indifference to other people's pain and a fierce desire to compete. Nothing was better than sticking his penis where some other man's had been —"

"I know that," Adam cut in. "But for whatever reason he always stayed with my mother. He didn't start putting girlfriends in his will, for godsakes."

"So maybe he was crazy," Jack said in measured tones. "Or maybe, in his way, he fell in love with Carla Pacelli."

"That's a complete oxymoron. Ben Blaine wasn't capable of love."

Jack met his gaze. "I think he loved your mother once. At least as much as he was capable of love."

"When?" Adam asked with real scorn. "Before I was born?"

"Yes," Jack answered. "Before you were born."

Adam folded his arms. At last, he said, "I may have left here, and he may be dead. But it's not over between us, after all. It won't be until I undo everything that bastard has done."

Jack's expression was tinged with melancholy. "How, exactly?"

Adam felt the same steel enter his soul he had felt ten years before. "I haven't worked that out yet. But trust me, Jack, I will."

FIVE

Adam found his mother in the den, his father's sanctuary. It was filled with photographs of Benjamin Blaine with world leaders, politicians, missionaries, mercenaries, and soldiers in half-forgotten wars. There was nothing of his family in it. Yet Clarice had gravitated there, sitting on the leather couch in the dim light of Ben's desk lamp, as if to search for meaning in her life with this man. Adam sensed the desperation beneath her composure — she had lost not only her inheritance but her identity as a woman. In the end, Ben had taken everything.

"What are you doing, Mom?"

"Remembering." Her voice was quiet and bitter. "Taking stock of my accomplishments. Except for this last manuscript, I took part in every one he wrote — proofreading, researching, or just telling him what I thought. And no one knew but me."

Adam sat beside her, absorbing the weight of her loss. For as long as he could remember, he had felt for her, all the more so when, still young, he had learned to decode the meaning of his father's nocturnal disappearances, the jaunty look he took on in the wake of some new conquest. The boy Adam had loved her, worried for her, and wished that he could protect her from hurt. But he did not want to be like her — despite everything, the person he admired was his father.

Now, filled with anger and pity, he did not know what to say. Instead, Clarice told him, "I'm sorry, Adam. For everything."

Adam took her hand. "He made this mess, not you. As always."

Turning, she looked him in the eyes. "I don't mean the will. The way you look at me now is all too familiar. I can see how worried you are."

"Shouldn't I be?"

"I suppose so. But that's the point — you always were." Her voice was new to him, clear and filled with reckoning. "I loved you both even more than you know. But instead of standing up for you and Teddy, what I gave you was an inconstant mother who drank too much. So you became *my* parent, helping me as best you could, while I went on pretending for others that my marriage was better than you knew it to be. And when you grew old enough to understand it all, you left in disgust."

"Only with him."

Clarice shook her head. "Not just him. I think you were smart enough to realize that on a more elevated plane, we had replicated Ben's family of origin — the acquiescent mother, the demeaning father, the sons who suffered at his hands. And, as Ben did, our youngest son broke away. The worst part for me was knowing that only he gave you the strength to do that. Because you were so much like him."

Adam felt a stab of fear, the need to protest that, like Jack, he had the ability to reflect, a concern for how his desires might impact those around him. But what he said was, "There's a biblical quote that goes something like 'When I was a child, I acted as a child. But when I became a man, I put aside childish things.' To the day he died, my father was a cruel and destructive child, with a child's self-absorption. No one else was real to him."

"There was more to Ben than that," Clarice responded. "For whatever it's worth, your rupture hit him hard. He seemed to flinch at the slightest mention of your name, like the hurt he felt was too deep to admit —"

Adam's harsh bark of laughter was involuntary. Abruptly, Clarice demanded, "Tell me what he did to you, Adam. After all this time, I have the right to know."

Adam met her gaze. "All he had to do was be himself. One day I'd had enough. It's a wonder you never got there —"

"You dropped out of law school, dammit."

"I dropped out of my life, Mom. And made another that belongs to me alone."

"Really? Is that why you're working in a hellhole like Afghanistan? It's exactly what Ben would have done."

"Not exactly," Adam responded. "Anyhow, he's dead. At the moment I'm more concerned with how he got that way."

Clarice looked at him steadily. "He was drunk, and he fell."

"That drunk? A man who could drink a half bottle of scotch and still sail his boat in a storm?"

Clarice shook her head. "The man you knew also wrote between seven and five. This may sound odd, but what frightened me most was to see him struggling to write at midnight, as if he were racing to finish. I no longer knew him at all."

"Did you read his manuscript?"

"He wouldn't show it to me." Clarice nodded toward Ben's desk. "When he finished working for that day, he'd lock it in that drawer. I can't find the key."

Adam gazed at the drawer. "Before he left that night, did he say anything?"

"Very little." Clarice stared fixedly past him, as though trying to recall the moment precisely. "He sat in this room with a bottle of scotch, brooding and silent. Then he announced in a slurry voice that he was walking to the promontory, to watch the sunset at summer solstice. Those were the last words he ever spoke to me."

"What did you say to him?"

"Nothing. I didn't know whether to believe him."

Adam took this as a tacit reference to Ben's affair with Carla Pacelli. "And that's what you told the police?"

"Yes."

"What else did they ask you?"

Clarice folded her arms, then answered in a brittle voice. "Among other things, whether that button on his denim shirt was missing. I said I didn't notice — that I wasn't in the habit of mending his shirts and sewing on his buttons."

As much as anything she had said before, this belated assertion of autonomy struck

70

Adam as profoundly sad. Gently, he inquired, "I assume they also asked if you knew about Carla Pacelli."

"Of course. That was why I didn't necessarily believe Ben was going to the promontory." Her voice lowered. "For once, he was telling the truth."

His mother, Adam realized, seemed determined to never speak Pacelli's name. "Did they ask about your relationship with Dad?"

Clarice sat straighter. "Why is that of such interest to you?"

"Because I'm interested in whatever interests the police. Please, humor me."

Clarice's lips compressed. "This is painful — particularly from a mother to a son. But yes, they asked about Ben and me in considerable detail. Such as the last time Ben and I had sex. I told them it was months ago." There was something new in her tone, Adam thought, an angry, widowed sexuality. But when she turned to him, tears glistened in her eyes. "How I wish you had at least some illusions."

Adam shook his head. "It wasn't you who took them from me. Can I ask how you found out about Ms. Pacelli?"

His mother hesitated. "Jenny told me. She saw them together on the beach."

"Nice of her."

Clarice studied his expression. In a tone of reproach, she said, "After you left, Jenny and I became good friends. She only told me when I worried aloud that Ben was going out at night, without excuses or explanation, becoming more blatant by the day. At that point she'd have had to conceal what she knew." Her voice flattened out. "In the end, Jenny did me a favor. She spared me the surprise when I followed Ben on one of his nightly jaunts, and saw him standing with a woman on the promontory."

"A woman, or Carla Pacelli?"

"It was too dark to see. But I'm sure it was her — they appeared to be having the kind of intense conversation that men and women only have when they're involved. And she'd taken the guesthouse at the Dane place, as Teddy told you. So it would have been an easy walk for her."

Adam recalled one of the minor mysteries of his mother's past — her aborted friendship with Whitney Dane. Among the affluent WASPs who summered on the Vineyard, the Barkleys and the Danes were unique among their class for living in Chilmark, which came to feature a significant Jewish population, rather than Edgartown, the traditional redoubt of their class. Through college, Adam knew, Whitney and Clarice had been intimate friends; as an adult, Whitney had become an eminent novelist, and would have been a natural peer for Ben save that Clarice, for reasons unclear to Adam, assiduously avoided her. That Carla Pacelli had landed in her estranged friend's guesthouse could only have deepened his mother's wounds. But of more immediate interest was the location of the guesthouse — from several directions, anyone could approach the promontory and not be observed. He was framing another question when, without warning, Clarice bent over, hands covering her face, shoulders trembling with soundless sobs. In that painful moment, Adam felt the pride, shame, and repression that had come to define her life. Helpless, he put his arm around her, and then his mother broke down entirely, cries of anguish issuing from deep inside her.

"Talk to me, Mom. Please."

At length, she sat up, her voice tremulous. "It's everything. Any day now, I'll wake up and she'll own our family's home, and the guesthouse where Teddy lives and paints. Neither of us will have anything." She paused, her throat working. "But it's so much more than that. Where do I put my memories of Ben when he turned them all to ashes? What can I say my life meant?

What can I believe I accomplished, with one son estranged, the other struggling? Nothing. By the end, all I hoped for was to live my life with some semblance of dignity. And now my husband of forty years has taken that from me as well, in the cruelest and most public way."

With your collaboration, Adam thought. For a long minute, he gave her the gift of silence. Then, gently, he said, "When you signed that postnup, he must have promised something in return."

Mute, Clarice shook her head.

"Why, then?"

"As I said, I thought I was going to inherit all I needed from my father. Another rude surprise."

Adam searched his inventory of family lore. "I thought Grandfather went bankrupt before I was born."

"No," she said tersely. "After."

Perhaps, Adam thought, she had been too insulated by her family's cosseted life to believe that it would ever vanish. "And you knew nothing about this new will?"

Clarice sat straighter, retrieving a semblance of her usual composure. "No. Once Father lost everything, I thought Ben would do the decent thing. As to affairs, he'd had them before."

"You didn't think this woman was different."

"No." Clarice exhaled. "It was your father who was different."

Adam watched her face in profile. It had been some time, he realized, since she had looked him in the face. "Did Dad ever threaten to leave you?"

She gave a vehement shake of her head. "Never. Nor could I leave him. Not just for my own security, but Teddy's. Once he got sick, he depended on us, both for a place to recover and for money to get back on his feet." Her voice became parched. "As for me, I had the consolation of being Mrs. Benjamin Blaine. The one he always stayed with."

And now, Adam thought, she faced the reckoning that she had never allowed herself to imagine. "I'm back," he told her. "If this will holds up, I'll give the money he left me to you and Teddy. But I mean to see that it won't."

His mother mustered a smile. Then, to his surprise, she said, "You haven't asked about Jenny."

Adam shrugged. "She's not a member of this family. Right now I'm concerned with the people who are." He stood, placing a hand on her shoulder. "I should spend some time with Teddy."

Clarice studied his face, her eyes questioning. Adam kissed her on the cheek and left.

Crossing the lawn, he saw a light in the guesthouse. Instinctively, he stopped, for a moment unable to move.

You haven't asked about Jenny.

Six

With almost cinematic specificity, Adam could still remember the crucial moments of that final summer, most of them centered on Jenny Leigh.

In early June, a week after he finished his first year of law school, Adam and Jenny had pushed off from Sepiessa Point in a double kayak, a picnic cooler between them, headed across the Tisbury Great Pond. A brisk spring wind skidded cirrus clouds across a vivid blue sky, and the whitecapped water was still cool from winter. Determinedly, they paddled toward the green shoreline ahead.

Though three years older than Jenny, Adam had known her for half his life. As a senior at Martha's Vineyard High School when Jenny had been a freshman, he had admired her poetry in the school newspaper. But it was during the previous summer that Adam had encountered Jenny at a beach party and rediscovered her as a woman he was drawn to.

Both were home from school. But where Adam was set on being a trial lawyer, Jenny had focused on the far more elusive goal of becoming a fiction writer. In Adam's mind, she seemed to have a poetic temperament — at one moment vibrant and amusing, at others inward and almost elusive, given to long silences that often ended in remarks that were both original and oblique. He had never known anyone quite like her.

For one thing, Jenny had grit. A Vineyard kid whose father had taken off and whose mother seemed barely able to cope, she had taken her future in her own hands, compiling a record of achievement that had gained her a full scholarship to UMass Amherst. But she lived in an aura of mystery that Adam found intriguing — she seldom mentioned her family and said little about her past. When Adam had asked how she imagined her future, she answered simply, "I feel like one of my stories. I'm still creating myself."

Her willingness to make such delphic remarks was an expression of trust, Adam sensed, the hope that he might understand her and help her better understand herself. When she became moody or aloof, Adam learned to ride it out, knowing that this was not directed at him. But on that sparkling afternoon, as they forged across the choppy waters, the "social Jenny," talkative and appealing, explained Celebrity Pac-Man and the point system by which the competing stalkers could calculate their ranking. "I'm not sure the famous ones even know they're playing," she observed. "They're way too secure. They're even nice to people who wait on them, like me — they'll ask you questions, honestly trying to find out who you are. The rude ones are the wannabes and name-droppers, too busy trying to puff themselves up to notice the help." She paused and then, as so often, her tenor softened. "Maybe I shouldn't be so judgmental. Being like that must be painful — needing other people's approval just to convince yourself that you matter."

Paddling briskly, Adam inquired, "Don't writers need approval? Not just from readers, but from critics."

From behind him he heard the silence of thought. "It's different. You're not with them while they're reading your story, or deciding whether or not to buy your book. You never see their faces. So it feels safer to me."

"That has a certain Jenny-logic," Adam

responded with a smile. "But rejection is still rejection. Every book out, my dad is scared that it won't sell."

"Benjamin Blaine scared?" she said with real surprise, and then pondered this. "I guess when you're that big, people notice failure — including other writers who are jealous of your success. Schadenfreude kicks in.

"I just never thought of someone like your father as being vulnerable. And then you go and tell me that every age and status has its own terrors." Suddenly, she laughed at herself. "Whatever do I live for now? Until you shattered my illusions, I thought that when I got famous I'd be a whole different Jenny. I was looking forward to getting up every morning feeling great about myself."

"Speaking for me," Adam assured her, "I think you're pretty okay now."

He expected that this compliment would please her. Instead, she answered seriously, "You're the okay one, Adam. There's something real at your core that no one will ever take from you."

He caught something wistful in her tone, a kind of guileless envy. Then she asked, "So why do you want to spend your life defending criminals?"

Adam watched an osprey fly low across

the water. "Who says they're all criminals?" he parried. "Some might actually be innocent. Others may need someone to explain them. There are reasons why we become the way we are, which often aren't apparent on the surface of our lives." He paused, then added gently, "You've told me that your father drank too much, and that your mother worked too hard to be around. But I don't know how that affected you, and it matters quite a lot to me. Because you matter to me."

Jenny's expression turned opaque. "It's all I know. So I don't think about it much."

"Your father vanished, Jenny. Wasn't that important to you?"

"No," she answered coolly. "It's only important that he's gone."

This was so unlike her that, too late, Adam sensed the wall between them. "My modest point," he temporized, "is that most people have hidden stories. A defense lawyer has to tell them in a sympathetic way."

"Even if they're murderers or rapists?"

"Even then."

Jenny fell quiet, deep within herself. They paddled in silence until they reached the shore.

They beached the kayak, and Adam led her

through the trees into a grassy clearing dappled with sunlight. Spreading a blanket, he laid out the picnic he had prepared. "How did you find this place?" she asked.

"Teddy and I found it together. When we wanted to get away, we'd paddle over here with food or books to read. Sometimes we'd camp out for the night, looking up at the night sky, listening to the wind stir the leaves and branches."

"It sounds peaceful."

Especially for Teddy, Adam thought. For his brother, this glade was more than a refuge from Benjamin Blaine. Adam still remembered the day Teddy had discovered it. One of the joys of painting, his brother had enthused, is that you can be out in the world and suddenly find yourself looking at something, the image you might create growing in your mind's eye — at those moments life becomes art, and nothing is wasted. Listening, Adam saw the world as Teddy did. When Teddy painted the glade, he gave the painting to Adam.

"It was," he told Jenny. "We both loved it here."

Jenny smiled. "So do I."

At the bottom of the cooler was a bottle of chardonnay. "A little wine?" he asked.

"Just mineral water, thanks." She hesitated, then gave him a tentative look. "I've started taking meds that wouldn't mix too well with wine. A good thing, probably. Alcohol hits me too fast, and I like it too much."

She was on antidepressants, he guessed, though perhaps her fear of alcohol came from her father. "Then I won't drink either," he told her.

They shared the picnic in companionable silence, Adam letting Jenny's thoughts drift where they would. After a while she took his hand, her fingers interlaced with his. "You're the only person who ever lets me do this."

"What, exactly?"

She looked into his eyes. "Sometimes I need to be alone. You let me be alone with you."

For Adam, there was a world of meaning concealed in those few words. Smiling a little, he said, "I just like being with you. Even when you're alone."

A new and palpable affection surfaced in her eyes. She leaned over to kiss him, her mouth soft and warm, then leaned her forehead against his. Quietly, she asked, "Would you like to make love with me?"

Taken by surprise, Adam felt a tightness in his throat. "Yes."

Wordless, she stood in front of him, eyes locking his. She took off her sweater, then her bra, the nipples rising on her small, perfect breasts. Transfixed, Adam watched her step out of her jeans, then lower her panties, exposing the light brown tuft between her slender legs. Then she turned around to show him everything before facing him again.

"Do you like me, Adam?"

He could not seem to move. "Even more than I imagined."

"Then why are you still dressed?"

He stood, peeling off his clothes, his desire for her written on every fiber of his body. She kissed him deeply, then knelt to take him into her mouth. "Not that," he murmured. "It's you I want."

"Then lie down," she said in a husky voice.

He lay on his back. With silent urgency, Jenny mounted him, eyes closing as she took him inside her body. As she began to move with him, her face went rigid, almost blank. Their rhythm quickened, drawing soft cries from inside her. When she cried out more fiercely, her body shuddering, Adam saw tears at the corners of her eyes. Then, all at once, he was beyond wondering why.

When they were spent, Jenny searched his face again, as though rediscovering its features. "Just hold me," she whispered.

Filled with tenderness and questions, Adam did that.

Breaking off this memory, Adam knocked on the door of the guesthouse. "Come on in," a mordant voice said. "Whoever you are, you can't be my father."

Adam stepped inside. Though his brother sat in front of a canvas, for a moment Adam saw neither Teddy nor his surroundings. "What's wrong, bro?" Teddy asked. "You look like you've seen a ghost."

At once, Adam shook off the illusion of having stepped into the past. "It's just that I haven't been here for so long. The last time I saw this room it wasn't an artist's studio."

That much was true. When Teddy, like Jack, had returned to the island, Clarice had pled with Ben to make the guesthouse Teddy's home. The front room had become his place of work, with painting supplies, an easel, and several half-finished canvases awaiting the artist's touch. Teddy had turned from the easel, his normally grave features displaying the engaging smile he reserved for those he cared for. Sitting on the sofa, Adam said simply, "I'm sorry about all this."

Teddy gave him a look that mingled affection and directness. "Not your fault. I know you always felt like it was, somehow. But the only one to blame is him."

Adam felt himself relax. Within their family, he realized, his relationship with Teddy was a respite, unalloyed by his own complex feelings for his mother and his loathing for the father he too closely resembled. "Did you have any idea he'd do this, Ted?"

Teddy's face hardened. "Why would I? He'd written me off when he was still alive. He just decided to save the coup de grâce for after he was gone."

"That could have been years from now," Adam objected. "Dad was the last man who could imagine his own death. Why change his will so soon?"

In the light from above, focused on Teddy's easel, Adam saw a grim smile play on his brother's lips. "Don't ask me to explain the workings of his mind. Whatever they were, he timed his departure quite badly. I'm destitute."

"Literally?"

Teddy considered him, his left elbow

propped on his knee, his face resting in his palm. "Why do you think I came back? Nostalgia? Once I got lymphoma, I hit the financial wall — I was too sick to work, my old paintings stopped selling, and I was all but uninsured. Then Brian died. In a few months, my life had become the train wreck Dad had always predicted. Mom wheedled the money from him for my treatment, then this 'safe haven' in which to recuperate —"

"But you're all right now, true?"

Teddy twitched his shoulders. "As far as I know. Except for discovering that living with him wasn't the worst part."

The quiet bitterness in Teddy echoed their mother's. "How *did* you get along with him?" Adam wondered aloud.

"Mostly by avoidance. Though it seemed to amuse him to keep me here on life support, and our mother dangling on yet another string."

The psychology of Teddy's return, with its cycle of debasement for both son and mother, was painful for Adam to contemplate. But whatever the cost, he knew what Teddy had salvaged. Since boyhood, his brother had burned with the love of painting, the one thing — beyond the sexuality their father had scorned — that defined him. His partner had died; to lose the freedom to paint would have felt like another death, his own.

Turning, Adam studied Teddy's canvas. The landscape was both unsettling and unsurprising, reflecting Teddy's originality and the seeds of his defeat. Though it portrayed Martha's Vineyard, it lacked the soothing elements prized by the purchasers of popular art: the beaches of summer, bordered by sea grass; a sailboat breaching whitecapped waves; verdant farmland and trees at the height of their foliage. Instead, Teddy's landscape captured winter — not the snowy landscape of a greeting card, but the bleak, pitiless gray of February, when short days and long nights led to drunkenness and domestic violence, families turning on one another. This was the Vineyard seen through a glass darkly, harsh and barren, its shadows distorted, its trees so stripped of life that they seemed the remnant of some terrible disaster, a nightmare terrain that would haunt anyone who saw it. Adam found it startling and unforgettable, evoking hidden truths perceived by a unique vision — and likely unsalable.

As if reading Adam's thoughts, Teddy remarked dryly, "Seems like I've got this corner of the market to myself."

Adam kept staring at the painting. "It's

astonishing, Ted — surreal yet all too real. When I was a kid, I wondered how you could do this. I still do."

Teddy smiled a little. "So do I, sometimes. It can be hard to live with."

Adam looked up at him. "And the Vineyard? Other than the obvious, how has living here been for you?"

"Solitary." His brother paused, stressing the word. "For a while I had a boyfriend — or thought I did. But then he got strange, in ways I won't bother to describe. Except to say that I didn't absorb enough of our mother's masochism." Teddy flashed a smile, interrupting himself. "Enough of that. Tell me when you're escaping Afghanistan, so I'll know when to quit worrying you'll get yourself beheaded."

The jaunty air Adam tried to conjure sat on him uncomfortably, both because it was false and because he was certain that, for Teddy, it evoked Benjamin Blaine. "There's nothing much to worry about," he said easily. "I'm doing a tiny bit of nation-building in a nation that will never get built. Given that the place is crawling with our soldiers, the Taliban couldn't care less about me."

Teddy gave him a penetrant look. "Cut the bullshit, Adam. Maybe this agrarian project you're on is as pointless as you suggest. But they still deliver the *New York Times* here. Helmand Province is the most dangerous place on earth, filled with Taliban and laden with IEDs. You could get yourself killed by accident."

Adam shook his head. "Long ago, I stopped emulating Benjamin Blaine. Assuming that his death was, in fact, an accident."

Something flickered in Teddy's eyes. "Meaning?"

"I want to know what happened the night he died."

A veil seemed to fall across Teddy's features, leaving him expressionless. "Damned if I can tell you. The bastard took his curtain call without inviting me to share the moment. Typical."

"Did you see him at all that night?"

From behind the mask Teddy watched his brother's face. "I barely saw him, period. It seemed to suit us both."

"Did you talk to anyone? In the family or outside it?"

Teddy sighed. "The police asked me all this, Adam. Truth to tell, I really can't remember. If I'd known it was his final sunset, I'd have taken better notes."

"Do you agree that he was acting strangely?"

Teddy shifted on the stool so that one side

of his face was in shadow. For the first time his voice, though level, was faintly accusatory. "As I keep reminding you, we didn't hang out together. Maybe I lived a hundred feet away, but you were the one he wanted here. For him, looking at you was like gazing in the mirror. How could he not love you? But I grew up without a father. Why do you think that changed?"

Adam became pensive. "It's just odd," he finally said. "The way he died."

"Falling off his favorite cliff? Actually, the image gives me a certain pleasure." Abruptly, Teddy turned away, speaking in a different voice, rough and low. "Listen to me. Our father dies, and all that's left to me is hollow jokes. God knows how much I wanted to love him, and him to love me. Even though I knew it was impossible."

Adam felt a wrenching sadness — not for his father, but for those whom he had harmed and would continue to harm. "We're taught to believe in archetypes," he replied. "Families are warm, parents love their children, fathers cherish their sons. But that's not how it was. Believe me, he did real damage to us both. I just resemble him too much for you to see that."

Teddy regarded him with open curiosity. "Strange, isn't it? The son he wanted was the one who cut him off."

The unspoken question lingered between them. "It was instinctive," Adam said. "Like the reflex that tells an animal when to run."

Ted gave him a look of silent appraisal. "There's something else that's odd," Adam ventured. "Carla Pacelli."

"That's odd?" An incredulous smile spread across Teddy's face. "It's classic Benjamin Blaine — a beautiful actress, thirty years younger. It would have been odd if he hadn't gone for it."

"Maybe so. But this attachment somehow feels deeper than his norm."

"I couldn't really say," Teddy responded in his driest tone. "Our father didn't confide in me about male–female relations."

Nodding, Adam looked around the room. He saw now that it made a perfect studio for Teddy, containing the elements his brother had explained to him long ago. There was wall space for his finished work, ample room for a table on rollers, its surface covered with multicolored oils and cups filled with paintbrushes. The main window faced north, admitting a steady light, and during the day the skylight would illuminate Teddy's easel. It was possible, Adam reflected, that the work Teddy could do here allowed him, at least for a time, to forget the man who owned it. And then a painting on the wall caught him up short. As stark as the others, it portrayed an image Adam had seen a hundred times before, the sun setting over the promontory from which their father had fallen to his death.

Teddy followed his brother's gaze. "A memory painting," he said evenly. "As I told the police, I haven't gone there in years."

Adam met his eyes. "Even though it's literally in your own backyard."

"Even so. Then and now, I hated that place."

Remembering the truth of this, Adam fell silent. At length, he said, "It's been a long day, hasn't it?"

Teddy still stared at the painting. "With many more to come. Maybe we can rent our family home from the newly affluent Ms. Pacelli. Though I doubt we'll have the money for even that."

The cruelty of what his father had done struck Adam anew. Then Teddy said in a somber tone, "But it has been a long day. You look depleted, bro."

He was exhausted by how far he had come, Adam realized, and not just in miles. When he stood, so did Teddy. As the brothers embraced, Teddy murmured, "I love you, Adam. Always did, always will."

Adam hugged him for an extra moment. "Me too."

Releasing his brother, Adam left. As he crossed the lawn, he saw that their mother had left the light on in his old room, a rectangle of yellow in the darkness.

Lugging his suitcase, Adam climbed the stairs, floorboards creaking under his weight.

His room was intact, a museum of the past, as though he had never left. High school trophies, a certificate acknowledging him as valedictorian of his class. A Yale coffee mug filled with pens. A family photo, four people smiling into the camera, Ben with his canine grin, Teddy standing a little separate from the others. A photograph of Ben and a marlin that the college-age Adam had labeled "Hemingway Lite." A picture of Jenny Leigh.

The remnants of another life, Adam thought, everything but Miss Havisham's wedding cake. Then he remembered that it was his father who, when Adam was not yet ten, had patiently read *Great Expectations* aloud to him from start to finish. There was something magical, he had discovered, about hearing Dickens's words in his father's rich baritone voice.

You broke my heart, you bastard.

For a moment Adam sat on his bed caught in the vortex of memory. Then he began to unpack, filling the old chest of drawers with the clothes of a much older man. When he took out the last shirt, all that remained in the suitcase was his handgun.

He did not know why he had packed the Luger. Habit, he supposed; the last six months had made him jumpy, no matter where he was, even more watchful and untrusting than before. One week ago, this gun had saved his life, or he would have died on the same day as his father. Now he concealed it under two pairs of slacks.

Turning out the light, he crawled between fresh-smelling sheets that his mother must have laundered for him. But his surroundings, at once familiar and strange, did not allow for sleep. Reviewing what his mother, uncle, and brother had told him, he wondered how much to believe.

At last, his mind weary, he drifted into the restless sleep that had become all that he could manage.

But the nightmare caught him, even here. He started awake, forehead damp, reaching for his gun before he realized where he was. Much of the dream was as before — though he could see himself, his body lay by the road, eviscerated by an IED. But this time his corpse had the graying hair of Benjamin Blaine the last time Adam had seen him.

EIGHT

The next morning, as was the family custom, Adam drove to Alley's General Store to buy the *New York Times*. The headlines were grim — the Taliban had ambushed and killed seven American soldiers in Helmand Province, and the Afghan government had descended into factional squabbling that, to Adam's jaundiced eye, reflected the corruption of all. It made the death of young Americans that much harder to accept.

Returning home, Adam passed the cemetery at Abel's Hill. Inevitably, his gaze was drawn to his father's grave, lit by shafts of morning sunlight, the grass around it a deepening green. Beside it, the solitary figure of a woman in a simple black dress bent to place flowers on his grave. Adam pulled over to the side of the road and got out, walking among the tombstones to reach the place where, only yesterday, his family had buried Benjamin Blaine.

The headstone was engraved BENJAMIN BLAINE, 1945–2011. HUSBAND OF CLARICE, FATHER OF EDWARD AND ADAM. Beneath this were the words Ben once had spoken in an interview: "I WROTE THE TRUTH AS I SAW IT." Kneeling, the woman quietly recited a prayer; though she must have heard Adam behind her, she gave no sign of this. Finally, she crossed herself and, rising, turned to face him.

Tall and slender, she looked a touch older than her age, which he put at thirty-two. On television she had been striking and exotic, an Italian-American brunette with dark, intense eyes and a vitality that made her all the more memorable. Now she had the tempered beauty of a survivor. In the last photograph Adam remembered of her, taken after her arrest, her eyes were clouded by drugs and filled with shame and confusion. But the eyes that regarded him now were clear and flecked with sadness. The faint smile at one corner of her mouth did not change them.

"You could only be Adam." Her voice was as he recalled it, smoky, with a trace of Mediterranean intensity. "Now I know how your father must have looked at your age."

She took it for granted that he knew who she was. The strangeness of the moment left him briefly silent. Then he said, "And you're Carla Pacelli. Or used to be."

The veiled insult did not change her expression. "I'm sorry if I've upset you. But the only service I could hold for him is private."

Instinctively, Adam looked toward the road. Near his car he saw a Jeep, then a woman he took to be Amanda Ferris with a photographer whose telescopic lens glinted in the sun. Facing Pacelli, Adam said, "Not too private. I think you and I just made the *National Enquirer.*"

Briefly, Pacelli shut her eyes. "I'm used to this," she said wearily, "and it's way too late to care. But I didn't mean to inflict them on you or your family."

Adam dismissed this. Perhaps she had staged her touching graveyard visit to cast herself as a woman in mourning. She was, after all, a performer, no doubt conscious that an image, if artfully created, could conceal avarice and calculation. Adam's reality was this — she had been his father's lover and the chief beneficiary of his will, heedless of the damage she inflicted on Clarice Blaine. At length, Adam said, "You were far from his only woman — just the one in the girlfriend chair when the music stopped. All I care about is what you've taken from my mother."

A moment's anger flashed in Pacelli's eyes, then died there. In the same even tone, she said, "Then there are a few things I should say to you, as clearly as I can. Whatever you choose to think, I loved your father. Except for consideration and respect, I didn't expect much in return. Nor did I ask for anything. I didn't know about the will, or request him to change the one he had. From time to time, he helped me with expenses, but that was all. I'd far prefer that Ben were still alive."

This was the defense that Adam expected, stated with the quiet command of an actress. In his estimation, Carla Pacelli had been a good one — whether feigned or real, grief was written on her face. "Nonetheless," Adam said, "his demise has worked out nicely for you."

She gave him a long, cool look. "Then I should be happy, shouldn't I. Do I seem it to you?"

Adam met her eyes. "No," he answered. "But your business is appearance, not reality, and good taste requires the appearance of sadness. I am curious, though, about the last time you saw him alive."

Pacelli looked at him with the same directness. "I'm not sure I'm ready for this conversation. You buried him yesterday; I buried him just now. That's hard for me. But if we're going to talk, would you mind sitting down? I haven't slept much lately."

With mock gallantry, Adam gestured at a swatch of grass beside his father's tombstone. After a moment, Pacelli sat, Adam beside her. When he looked toward the road again, the reporter and photographer were watching. Facing Pacelli, Adam asked, "Did you see him on the night he died?"

"No," she answered. "The last time I saw him was that afternoon."

"What did you talk about?"

She turned to him. "I'm sorry, but that's personal to me. As is everything that happened that day."

"But you told the police. I'm sure."

"Only because I had to." She hesitated, then added in a lower voice, "For obvious reasons, they were easier to talk to. Even looking at you is painful."

Were she not who she was, Adam might almost have believed her sorrow — if not her claim to be ignorant of the will. Bluntly, he asked, "Did you know my father was failing?"

Studying him, she seemed to weigh her answer. "Do you mean physically or mentally?"

"Both."

She turned away from him, regarding a patch of grass in front of them. Then she said, "It won't surprise you to know that while you were burying your father, I was consulting a lawyer. Call that cold, if you like, but the requirements of 'good taste' left me with a free afternoon. Right now, for various reasons, I'm not prepared to take this any further.

"That doesn't mean I won't, in time. You're free to try me later. We'll see how things stand then."

Carefully, Pacelli got to her feet, her face suddenly pale. She began to leave, then looked back at him again. "There *are* two more things I should say to you. Whatever happened between you and your father, he deeply regretted that. And whatever happened with Ben and your mother, I'm sorry for how she must feel."

Left unspoken was whether Pacelli meant his father's affair, his death, or the loss of his estate. The nerve of this expression of sympathy left Adam briefly silent, even as he rejected the notion of his father mired in regret. Then he asked, "Did he tell you why I left?"

Pacelli shook her head. "I asked him,

several times. But he could never talk about it."

"That much I believe."

Pacelli looked into his face. Then he turned from her and walked away. The image of her last expression, curious and intent, lingered in his mind.

Walking toward the road, he saw the reporter waiting by his car. When he reached it, she stood in front of the door, her voice and manner so feral that Adam wanted to push her aside. "Mr. Blaine," she said, "tell me what you and Carla were talking about."

For an instant, Adam felt a reflexive sympathy for Carla Pacelli. Then he looked at the reporter so coldly that she seemed to recoil. "When I want to see you," he told her, "I'll let you know."

He got in the car. The original reason for this trip, the newspaper, lay forgotten on the passenger seat. Looking back at the cemetery, Adam saw Pacelli, her head bowed, her hand resting on his father's tombstone. No doubt she thought that the *Enquirer* could use another photograph.

When Adam came through the door, his mother was in the living room. "Where were you?" she asked.

"I decided to stop at his grave."

Her mouth parted, as if to form a question, and then the telephone rang.

Clarice answered. "Hello, George," she said, her tone pleasant but reserved. "Yes, I'm all right, thank you. Please, tell me."

For a moment, she listened intently. Then her face froze, save for the bewilderment in her eyes. "I had no idea," she managed to say. "Are you sure?"

As she listened, Adam saw, she placed a hand on the chair as if to retain her balance. With great civility, she said, "Thank you, George. It was kind of you to call."

Putting down the phone, she gazed past Adam as if he were not there. "Was that the DA?" he asked.

She blinked, aware of him again. "Yes. He called about the cause of death."

"Is there something more?"

Clarice drew a breath. "Yes. Your father had brain cancer. A massive tumor, apparently."

The words hit Adam with a jolt. "Did *he* know?"

Clarice sat down. "If so, he chose not to tell me."

Looking away, she held a hand to her face. Another betrayal, Adam sensed her thinking, another secret. Then a further thought struck him: that on the night he died, Benjamin Blaine was looking at the last summer solstice of his life and, perhaps, knew that. A host of implications started running through Adam's mind, complicating or explaining his father's last few months, the shocking suddenness of his death.

Who might have known? he wondered, and thought again of Carla Pacelli.

NINE

Dr. Philip Gertz, the Blaines' family doctor, had gray hair, a thin face, and a judicious manner underscored by thoughtful blue eyes. In ten years, he had changed surprisingly little. But his office in the new Martha's Vineyard Hospital was a considerable upgrade. Waving Adam inside, he said, "I saw you at Ben's funeral. But I didn't have a chance to give you my condolences."

The remark came wrapped in a dubious tone. Evenly, Adam said, "That's all right, Doctor. When someone dies, you have the funeral, and once it's over the man is still dead. All that's left is how he treated the living."

Gertz regarded Adam closely. "And you've been all right?"

"Fine."

"Good." The doctor paused, glancing at his watch. "You said you wanted to ask me something."

"About my father. We just learned that when he died, he had a very serious brain tumor."

Gertz sat back, his face slack, then slowly shook his head. "Sweet Jesus Christ."

"You didn't know?"

The doctor shook his head. At length, he said, "Late last year he came to me complaining of headaches that disturbed his concentration. I referred him to a neurosurgeon in Boston."

"And?"

"Ben called me later to say he was fine, and that the headaches were gone."

"Did he ever see the neurosurgeon?"

Gertz's brow furrowed. "If he had, I'd have expected a report — a reputable specialist, which this man is, would have performed tests. So maybe not."

For a moment, Adam tried to enter his father's mind. "Still, I'd like this doctor's name."

Gertz wrote it on a sheet of paper. Shaking hands, he said, "Tell me what you learn. When it comes to Ben, I guess nothing would surprise me."

A redbrick Georgian structure, the Dukes County Courthouse was located next to the site of his father's funeral. Since Adam had last been on the island, the county sheriff had installed a magnetometer at the entrance and a conveyor belt on which Adam placed his keys and wallet. Passing through security, he noticed cameras pointed at him from the ceiling, attached to the wires of a new alarm system. The shadow of 9/11 had reached the island.

George Hanley's office was on the second floor, a cubbyhole jammed with file cabinets and a wooden desk covered with papers. The room was further dwarfed by the local DA himself, a burly man at least six feet four, with thick white hair, a mustache to match, and shrewd green eyes. As Hanley stood to shake hands, he gave Adam a warm Irishman's smile that did not obscure his keen look of appraisal. On top of his desk, Adam noticed, was an accordion folder marked BENJAMIN BLAINE.

"Mind if we talk outside?" Hanley asked. "The older I get, the more I resent sitting here on a day like this. How many more of these do I get? I've started to wonder."

The remark, though casual, carried a pensive undertone. Adam's father and Hanley had been friends, at least of a kind, and he supposed that, for Hanley as for others, Ben's death had left a psychic hole. "Sure," Adam said. "I'd rather feel the sun on my face and watch the passing parade. I've been away for a while."

"Which was duly noted," Hanley said good-humoredly. "This island is a small place, you'll remember."

With that, Hanley led Adam down the stairs. As they left, Adam noticed a sheriff's deputy in a room near the entrance, watching a TV monitor that showed a sequence of doors and hallways in the courthouse. As with the camera and alarm system, he filed this away.

The two men found a wooden bench between the courthouse and the Old Whaling Church. Hanley raised his face to the light, breathing in the clean fresh air. Then he cast a jaundiced eye on the tourists who jammed the redbrick sidewalks along Main Street, bobbing in and out of clothing stores, a bookshop, an ice cream dispensary. In his rumbling voice, he said, "God, I hate to see them. Then I hate to see them go. They bring the money that keeps this island afloat."

Adam nodded. "So," Hanley ventured, "I guess you've got some questions about Ben's death."

"A few."

Hanley turned to him. In the same mild tone, he said, "Frankly, Adam, I didn't know your father was of any particular concern to you."

"He wasn't," Adam answered in a clipped voice. "But the rest of my family is, starting with my mother. This has left her badly shaken. It isn't often that one loses a husband and an inheritance in the space of a few days. Nor did it help that the state police treated her like a suspect in his death."

Hanley shrugged, his expression neutral. "The state police aren't from here. Someone on the island dies under funny circumstances, they take a boat over from Barnstable — the crime lab to inspect the scene, the medical examiner to take the corpse to Boston, and someone like Sergeant Mallory to work with me and the town police. Mallory doesn't know your mother, brother, or uncle. What he does know is that this is a high-profile death with several possible explanations. Which can be summarized as 'jumped, fell, or pushed.' "

Though Adam knew this, the blunt coda carried a disturbing message — this was a homicide investigation, and Hanley and the police had reason to pursue it. "Do you have a favorite?" he asked.

Hanley's smile was less amused than deflective. "If I did, I couldn't tell you. And if I can't, Sean Mallory certainly won't. Don't even bother with him."

"But it's fair to say you've reached no conclusions?"

"That's fair to say," Hanley replied in a tone that conveyed vast reserves of patience. "If we had, we'd have closed the case or indicted someone. At some point one or the other will happen."

"Based on what?"

Hanley drew a breath. "I'm only talking to you as a courtesy, and only to the extent I can. What I will tell you is that you can expect to hear from Sergeant Mallory. For understandable reasons, he's taken an interest in your family. But then it's an interesting family, isn't it?"

For a moment, Adam watched some prototypical tourists — dad, mom, squabbling sister and brother — passing in newly acquired Martha's Vineyard T-shirts. "All families are interesting," he said. "It's just that some are less public. The medical examiner's report must be of some help."

The corner of Hanley's mouth twitched. "Not to you."

"Not even for my mother's sake?"

"I admire your mother," Hanley said firmly. "But we can't give it up while the investigation is on."

So the report was completed, Adam divined, and in Hanley's possession. "Then it's fair to say that the report doesn't preclude a homicide."

Hanley leaned forward, elbows on knees, weighing his answer. At length, he said, "In itself, a fall off that cliff doesn't tell you much. You get a severe trauma to the head, bleeding around the brain, a fractured skull, and scrapes on the face and body. None of that says why Ben fell."

"Did he land close to the cliff, or out a ways?"

Hanley laughed briefly. "Kudos for the question. But I'm not telling you anything your uncle Jack couldn't. Ben landed close to the cliffside."

"Meaning that no one hurled him into space."

Hanley's smile lingered, as though he were following Adam's thoughts. "Ben was a big man, Adam. The Incredible Hulk is not among the suspects."

"In other words," Adam persisted, "the location of the body is also consistent with accident or suicide."

"I suppose."

"Then I suppose you also know he was drunk."

"So your mother tells us. But the toxicology report isn't in yet."

"Still, he could have fallen. And now you've learned that he had brain cancer, which suggests the possibility of suicide."

Hanley's smile became bleak, his lips clamped tight. "The man I knew for fifty years would not have deprived the world of his presence. But you could posit that — unlike wars, famine, pestilence, and plague — brain cancer disheartened him a bit."

"And therefore, accident or suicide are real possibilities. I'm left to wonder why you think this could have been a murder."

"Yup," Hanley agreed laconically. "You're left to wonder. Not that I'm saying it was."

Adam watched his eyes. "But you think it was, don't you?"

Hanley fixed him with an unblinking gaze. "You know that promontory intimately. Do you believe Ben had one too many and just stumbled off the cliff? Or decided to end his life even a day before God did it for him?"

No, Adam thought. "I've no idea, George. As you point out, I hadn't seen him for ten years."

A new expression, probing and tough, entered Hanley's eyes. "Can I ask why?"

Adam had expected this. "Objection, George — irrelevant. When he went off the cliff, I was in Afghanistan. I sure as hell didn't push him."

"But there came a time when you might have wanted to, didn't there?"

Adam stared at him. "Everyone wants to know why I left, like it must be shrouded in mystery. I suggest that you consider the man you knew."

Suddenly, Hanley's expression held the merciless bleakness of a recording angel. "You know what I'm asking. Was there something about Ben, even ten years back, that might provoke someone to consider killing him?"

The way he treated all of us, Adam thought. In an even voice, he said, "Which cuckolded husband or boyfriend are we talking about? Beyond that, I haven't got a clue."

Hanley's tone and expression were unimpressed. "Even when you were in high school, Adam, they said you were the smartest guy around. You're here for your own reasons. I suspect it's the will, and the feelings it might engender among members of your family."

Adam shook his head. "You can't feel anything about a will that you don't know exists. That leaves Carla Pacelli, who had everything to gain and, as I understand it, no alibi at all."

Quiet, Hanley watched the passing parade of Vineyarders and tourists. At length, he said, "We're not going to play this game, young Mr. Blaine. You could say the same about your mother and Teddy, who got written out of the will — after all, no murderer with a motive would confess to having one. Or Jack, who everyone knows disliked Ben intensely. And if you're looking for people who gained from Ben's death, you could throw in Jenny Leigh." He turned to Adam. "I'm not saying who I think it is, if anyone. I'm merely following your logic to its insubstantial conclusion."

"So Pacelli has no alibi."

Hanley's eyes glinted. "You can think that if you like. So tell me why your father left you a hundred thousand and made you his executor."

"Oh, that's easy," Adam said in a throwaway tone. "He wanted to compete with me from beyond the grave."

Hanley's eyebrows shot up in surprise, and then he laughed aloud. "You plan to break the will, don't you."

"It's crossed my mind. Maybe it crossed his. He always liked games."

Hanley's smile faded. "Hard to believe he's dead," he mused. "I still remember him in high school. I wanted to be quarterback in the worst way. But there was Ben, always Ben. He wouldn't let me beat him out."

"He couldn't, George. That would have killed him for sure."

Hanley appraised him. After a moment, he said, "I think I've said all I care to, and you've ferreted out what you can. Any time you want to say what else is on your mind, feel free."

"I will," Adam said easily. "At the moment, all that's on my mind is using the restroom."

Briskly, Hanley shook his hand. "First floor, if you don't mind passing through security to take a piss. Too many nuts with guns, I guess."

Turning, he shuffled up the steps, his shoulders slumped, unhappy to retreat inside.

Once more Adam gave up his keys and wallet to pass through the magnetometer, then spent an obligatory minute in the men's room parsing his troubled thoughts. As he left, he glanced into the room containing the TV monitor and committed the name and make of the security system to memory.

On the courthouse steps, Adam saw a sturdy figure in the uniform of a police officer. His instant impression was of a body bound to thicken, already straining the blue shirt, its torso almost as broad as the man's thick shoulders. Then he saw the man's features — blue eyes, caramel-colored hair, a round, amiable face that hinted at perpetual puzzlement, as though something were about to surprise him. Smiling with his own surprise, Adam experienced in miniature what a high school reunion must feel like.

"Bobby?"

Bobby Towle stopped abruptly, gazing at Adam until an answering grin spread across the broad planes of his face. "Adam Blaine," he said, and gave Adam an awkward hug. "My God, how long has it been?"

"A while," Adam replied. "I think the last time was at a beach party. But you may not remember."

Bobby's grin was rueful. "I was with Barbara, right?"

"The beautiful Barbara," Adam amended. "What happened with that?"

The smile diminished. "We're still together. Married, in fact."

"Can't blame you a bit. It's Barbara I wonder about."

Bobby shifted his weight. "What about you?"

"Single. I've become a world traveler,

which gets in the way."

"Not a lawyer?"

"No."

Bobby appraised him. "At least you look the same," he said, patting his stomach. "No fat on you. Maybe a little older, and a little meaner."

Beneath his guilelessness, Adam remembered, Bobby had an instinctive gift for grasping essential truths. "Not you, Bobby. Not even in uniform. You're a cop, looks like."

"Chilmark Police." Bobby grimaced a little. "Sorry about your dad."

"Thanks." Adam paused for an appropriate moment, then rested a hand on Bobby's shoulder. "Why don't we meet for a drink somewhere. Or don't you do that anymore?"

A faint look of hurt surfaced in Bobby's eyes. "Not as much, nowadays. But, sure, I'll tip a couple of beers to keep you company."

"Great. The Kelley House still open?"

"Definitely."

"Check with Barbara, then, and give me a call."

Bobby hunched his shoulders. "Tomorrow night's fine. Say eight o'clock?"

Something was wrong at home, Adam felt sure. "You're on, Bobby. We can replay the last touchdown in the Nantucket game. You really crushed that guy."

Driving home, Adam wondered about Bobby Towle, and felt a twinge of conscience for his intentions. Sometimes that still happened, even in Afghanistan.

TEN

Promptly at six, the time once mandated by his father, Adam had dinner with his mother, Jack, and Teddy. At first he did not say much, nor did anyone mention that Clarice had prepared Benjamin Blaine's favorite dinner — lobster and Caesar salad, with a bottle of Chassagne-Montrachet.

Facing Adam across the table, Jack said, "I sense you have something to tell us."

"Several things. I read the will this afternoon. It's been a while since I studied estates and trusts law, so I'm no expert. But I think Mom can attack it."

Teddy glanced at Clarice, then told Adam dryly, "Then you'll be glad to know we're seeing a real lawyer."

"Good. So let me suggest what he might look at."

"Please," his mother interposed with a trace of humor. "I'd like to think that year at NYU wasn't completely wasted."

121

This touched a sore point, Adam knew — for his mother, the pain of his abrupt departure was deepened by his failure to pursue a career for which he seemed well suited. Facing her, he said, "First there's his behavior — whether caused by brain cancer or something else. That calls into question his mental capacity to execute a valid will." Adam looked at the others. "Before Mom sees this lawyer, all of you should write down anything he said or did that seemed peculiar —"

"Can we make things up?" Teddy interjected wryly.

Adam shrugged. "Our father did. Just remember that you lack his gift for make-believe." He faced his mother again. "Then there's Carla Pacelli. If Dad wasn't right in the head, she could have pressured him to make changes he otherwise wouldn't have."

"Maybe she did," Jack said. "But what interest would Carla have in Ben leaving Jenny a million dollars?"

Adam had pondered this himself. "None, on the surface. Probably it was his idea. But a truly clever woman might have obscured her role by suggesting Dad leave money to someone else outside the family. Anyhow, it's worth a shot. At least maybe Mom can force a settlement that gives her back the house and enough to live on.

"There also may be a problem with how Dad passed on his money. He created a trust in favor of Pacelli, taking the proceeds outside his estate and, as a result, outside the property Mom can claim a share in. Under the law, that may not hold up." Adam turned to his mother again. "Finally, there's the postnuptial agreement. Are you absolutely certain, Mom, that he gave you nothing for signing it?" He paused, concluding quietly, "Or, at least, that no one can prove he did?"

His mother flushed, then nodded stubbornly. "I'm sure."

"Then the law may protect you from yourself." Adam glanced around the table. "Then there's George Hanley. George is a smart man, and he's playing this close to the vest. But I'm pretty sure he thinks that one of you pushed my father off that cliff."

His mother's face became expressionless. "Why would he think that?" Jack demanded. "Hasn't Clarice been through enough?"

His uncle wore an expression Adam had seldom seen, angry and defensive. "It's not personal," he answered calmly. "As to the why, my guess is that George believes that one or more of you knew about this will."

"Then we'd be fools," Teddy cut in. "Unless we can break the will, his death locked in our disinheritance."

Adam stared at his brother. Since Ben's death, it was clear, the members of his family had considered their positions more deeply than they acknowledged. "A good point," Adam responded. "Assuming that murder is a rational act. But our father had a way of provoking hatred, didn't he."

For a moment, no one spoke. Studying their expressions, now quite composed, Adam felt a frisson — at the least, he sensed, someone at this table knew more than they wished to tell him. "In any event," he said, "Dad named me executor of his will. That means I'm staying for a while." His voice chilled. "He wanted to drag me into this. So now I'm in."

Clarice gave him a complex look of worry and relief. After a moment, she reached across the table, touching Adam's hand. "Whatever the reason," she said in a husky voice, "I'm glad you're not disappearing. The last time was hard enough."

After dinner, Jack sat with Adam on the porch. It felt familiar and companionable, reminding Adam of the evenings they had spent a decade ago or more, when Ben was off-island and his uncle would come for dinner. Adam always cherished them, not least for the release of tension from his father's oversized presence, the pleasant contrast of Jack's solicitude and calm. Sometimes they would talk for hours.

But this evening Jack was quiet, the coffee cup untouched beside him. Finally, he asked, "You're very worried about the police, aren't you?"

Adam weighed his answer. "I don't care if he was murdered, Jack. I just don't want anyone in this family to pay for it. He did enough harm when he was alive."

Jack studied him. "Teddy's on to something, you know. Why would anyone kill a man whose death would ruin them?"

A shadow of memory crossed Adam's mind. "Because sometimes hatred is enough. But you're right, of course — motive is important. And there are people outside this family who stand to profit from his death. Mom certainly hasn't." Adam paused to sip his coffee, eyeing Jack over the rim. "Do *you* know why she signed that postnup?"

For a moment, Jack's thoughts seemed to turn inward, and then he looked at Adam intently. "I know what your mother says. I think you should accept that. The shame she feels whenever you bring it up is painful to watch —"

"Not as painful as its consequences."

"I can see that." Jack paused. "I also understand why you'd want to help her. But will your firm allow you to stick around that long?"

"I'm not giving them a choice."

The worry in Jack's eyes deepened the gravity of his expression. "As your uncle, let me speak my piece. No matter what you say about it, I'm not happy with you going back to Afghanistan. But all of us except you got sucked into Ben's orbit. At least you escaped —"

"This is different, Jack."

"So it is. But I don't think you can change what happens here. Maybe you should go back to the life you've created for yourself. Or better, start a new one."

Adam contemplated the coffee cup, cool now in his hands. "I can't," he answered simply. "I need to bury him for good."

Before sunset, Adam climbed down the wooden stairway from the promontory to the beach. Gazing up at the cliff, he imagined the trajectory of his father's fall. Beneath it he found a rock with a faint rust-colored stain that, a week before, must have been a pool of his father's blood.

Adam closed his eyes. If someone had pushed him, they could be certain that he could not live to say who, or why. Perhaps no one but the murderer would ever know.

He sat down on a rock, contemplating a vivid sunset Ben would have loved, which now began to cast a shimmering orange glow on the darkening waters. Seeing his mother, uncle, and brother had reminded Adam, if he needed this, how deeply he loved them. But that did not mean he believed everything they said, any more than he would tell them the entire truth about himself and what he meant to do here. The last ten years had created a duality in his nature — he had learned the uses of dissembling, and how to wall off his emotions to survive. He could feel love and practice deceit in the same moment.

Glancing around him, he took out the untraceable cell phone he had not used since coming back. He punched in the number, imagining the man at his desk noting which telephone he had called on. When his superior picked up, he said, "It's Blaine."

"Where are you?"

"Still on the island. I have to stay here for a while. My father seems to have disinherited my mother."

A moment's pause. "Isn't it a little late to

change his mind?"

"There's something off here, Frank. Several things. Don't tell me a man of your broad interests doesn't read the *National Enquirer*."

Svitek laughed. "I have, actually. Sounds like your father's interests were very broad indeed. But we need you back there, my son."

The orange disk, Adam noticed, was swiftly vanishing. "They need me here much more," he replied. "While I'm gone, you've got other people to do the work."

"Starting from scratch? Come off it, Adam. We can't just clone an operative with your exceptional skills —"

"Which are?"

"Deception. Manipulation. Withholding information. Knowing whom not to trust. Getting those who trust you to take risks on your behalf. And, of course, pretending to be someone you're not." His superior's tone changed from ironic to practical. "The Afghans like you. You have a knack for inspiring confidence while telling your prey only what they need to know."

Adam's laugh was hollow. "As I consider it, Frank, those are the attributes of a sociopath."

"In our line of work we call them 'survival

skills.' " Svitek paused, his voice admitting a note of compassion. "You're hardly a sociopath, Adam — you care about people too much. That weakness aside, you're the best we have."

"By which you mean they haven't killed me yet. Despite a dead man's best efforts."

"True enough. But that makes my point, doesn't it?"

Adam's tone hardened. "Given all that, I've earned myself a leave. As you suggest, working under cover gives us certain skills. One is a gift for changing outcomes in ways that can't be seen. For the next little while, I mean to use those talents on behalf of the three people I most care about."

Svitek was silent. "You've made a commitment to us," he replied at length, "and your work is essential. Whatever you mean to do there, wrap it up in one month's time. And don't get yourself in trouble."

"I won't," Adam said flatly. "Whomever or whatever I'm dealing with, at least it's not the Taliban."

He got off, then walked to the stairway. As he looked up, the promontory was shrouded in darkness. All he could see was the moon and stars.

That night Adam could not sleep. He tried

to purge his mind and imagine himself as Benjamin Blaine in the last months of his life.

Brain cancer.

Did he know? If so, this could account for much of his behavior — in his son's estimate, Ben's deepest fear was of his own mortality. The spectre of death could explain his writing schedule — frenzied, drunken, and nocturnal — as he felt his powers flagging and his gifts slipping from his grasp. A desperate race against the last, eternal night.

The manuscript was locked in his desk.

Adam reached into the drawer for the Luger he had concealed, then attached the silencer to its barrel. Leaving his room, he crept past the bedroom where, he suspected, his mother slept as fitfully as he. Then he took the stairway to the first floor and entered his father's study, gun in hand.

Turning on the desk lamp, he found the drawer where his father kept his final work in progress. Then he aimed the gun at its lock and fired. With a pneumatic hiss, the lock vanished.

Opening the drawer, Adam put the manuscript on the desk, and sat in his father's chair. The title page read *"Fall from Grace"* and, beneath that, "A Novel by Benjamin Blaine." Then he turned to the dedication page, and his hand froze.

"For Adam," it said, "the missing son."

Fingertips steepled, Adam stared at the words. Then he turned the page and forced himself to read.

Between the ages of sixteen and twenty-three, Adam had read *Body Count* and the rest of his father's novels to that date. He had admired their force, their craftsmanship, the sturdy architecture of the narrative and the strength and vigor of Ben's prose. And so this work began. But as Adam turned the pages the writing became flatter, the scenes less fully realized. But this did not obscure the arc of the story, or lessen Adam's disquiet.

He stopped, recalling another night from their last summer as father and son.

The evening after the Fourth of July, Ben had picked up on Adam's suggestion that they go fly-fishing at Dogfish Bar.

Striped bass were nocturnal, and so Ben and Adam arrived at nightfall. The moon rose behind them, its silver light glistening on the surf at their feet. Together, they cast as Ben had taught him since the night on which, when Adam was six, his father had first awakened him to fish in darkness. Adam had not complained; he cherished this initiation into what he imagined as his father's secret world. "It's wonderful and mysterious," his father had told him, "to cast a line into dark waters, hoping to connect with something you can't see." And so Adam discovered. For years, he worked to emulate the skill and grace his father brought to the art of casting a weightless line, his stiff arm tracing and retracing the same perfect arc. Now they cast together; in the darkness, Adam knew, no one could tell the father from the son.

Behind them, he heard voices in the night. On the rise that descended to the water, four more fishermen appeared, wearing boots and carrying fly rods, their outlines backlit like some shadowy militia come to occupy the beach. When Adam tried this simile on his father, Ben replied, "I may steal that from you, son. Did you ever consider writing yourself?"

"Compete with you? No thanks."

Ben looked at him sharply. "If you're afraid of that, all the more reason to try: fear exists to be mastered, not bowed to. Still, maybe you're right — where is it written that you can do what I've done? And I can hardly blame you for choosing your own path. Thank God I didn't follow my old man like he followed his."

Though he could not see Ben's face, Adam heard a note of satisfaction mixed with dread, as though Nathaniel Blaine might still pull Ben by the collar into the life he had fought to escape. "What was he like?" Adam asked. "I can't remember much."

"Limited," Ben said flatly. "They all were. Granted, they had a certain mulish persistence that might have passed for character — through a century of lobstering, they stuck with it, no matter how hard the life. Their problem was tunnel vision. Each took those same traits of character and did the exact same thing, generation upon generation. From the age of five, I set out to be different."

Something in Ben's claim of uniqueness nettled Adam. "So did Jack," he said.

Ben laughed under his breath. "Jack? All he managed was getting out of the water."

It was always like this, Adam thought — his father determined to have him perceive his uncle as smaller than Ben himself. "He did more than that, Dad. Jack's woodworking is special. He's an artist, like Teddy."

"Yes," Ben answered tartly. "On a rock off the coast of Massachusetts, fifty square miles. This is a place to come back to, not to define the boundaries of a life. The world has too much to offer."

Adam felt the familiar stab of ambivalence mixed with admiration. His father was ever on the lookout for places that bared the nature of man at its noblest and most terrible — in Vietnam, Cambodia, Kosovo, Nigeria, the West Bank, Lebanon, the Sudan. He had embedded himself with American troops during the Gulf War, followed the Afghan rebellion against the Soviets, forging lifelong bonds with a legendary operative for the CIA. It was as though he were engaged in a worldwide game of dare — danger, tragedy, and war had always drawn Benjamin Blaine.

But equal to Ben's hunger for experience was his iron will to record it with merciless clarity. "Whatever you do," his father continued, "dream big, take risks, and work harder than whoever else is doing the same thing. Do you know why I've succeeded? Not because of talent — I've known writers more gifted than I am. But I was driven to wring every molecule out of whatever talent I possessed. Success is not something you aspire to — you have to grab it by the throat.

"There's a story about Bobby Kennedy I've always loved. When Bobby was attorney general, he set out to jail the crook who ran the Teamsters, Jimmy Hoffa. One night

Bobby worked on the Hoffa case until two a.m. Driving home, he passed the Teamsters Building, and saw the light on in Hoffa's office. So he turned around and drove back to work." Chuckling with fondness for the image, Ben concluded firmly, "There'll be people better and smarter than you, Adam. There always are. Your strength must be to want it more, and let nothing get in the way. They called Robert Kennedy ruthless. But for a few months before he died, when I joined his campaign, I knew Bobby very well, and I can tell you he was most ruthless with himself. That's how you should be."

In this story, Adam knew, lay a key to his father's psyche, part of which was his deep admiration — even love — for Robert Kennedy. But he could as easily have recounted his night on Chappaquiddick, fly-fishing in a bitter wind that drove his competitors off the beach. Ben held out until dawn, lips blue with cold, at last catching a forty-three-pound bass that set a world record. But the best example was his writing. No doubt Ben was ruthless there — Adam firmly believed he could bury his wife and sons in the morning, and write a chapter in the afternoon. No writer could steal the march on Benjamin Blaine.

Now, ten years later, Adam stared at his father's final work.

Where is it written that you can do what I've done?

Reading on, Adam felt anew the full weight of those words. Ben could not stand the thought of anyone besting him — especially Adam, the one most like him, the one he had always feared. And now this.

On the page, the language revealed Ben's deterioration. Now and again a lucid, vigorous passage evoked Benjamin Blaine as readers knew him. But the last pages were so poorly written that they resembled Cliffs Notes of the novel that might have satisfied his father. The man Adam had known would have ripped them up in disgust. Unless he had been so rushed or drunken or impaired that he had not paused to read the story of his own decline.

Adam forced himself to finish.

The story was set in the nineteenth century, its principal characters a family of lobstermen. Though incomplete, the narrative focused on the father's fraught and ultimately tortured relationship with his younger son, the subject of its most piercing passages. At times, the son resembled Adam; at other times, Ben himself. There was similar confusion between Ben's father as Adam understood him and the father Adam himself had known. Though the pages ended abruptly, marking his father's death, Adam could grasp the tragedy ahead. By the end of this novel, he understood, one of these men, father or son, was meant to kill the other.

■ ■ ■ ■

PART TWO
THE PROVOCATEUR

■ ■ ■ ■

ONE

The next afternoon, Adam met Matthew Thomson at the trailhead of the Menemsha Hills nature preserve.

His father's personal lawyer was much as he remembered him — a lean, puckish figure with wire-rimmed glasses, curly iron-gray hair, and a humorous play around the mouth and eyes that hinted at intelligence, irreverence, and an unvarnished view of humanity. The meeting place suggested Thomson's love of outdoor exertions: in his youth, he had been a distance runner, and he retained the sinewy, stringy look of someone wedded to diet and exercise. As they shook hands, Thomson said, "Jesus, you look like him. I guess everyone tells you that."

"Everyone does."

Thomson looked at him more closely. "Left you a mess, didn't he? Let's walk a little and review the wreckage."

There was something bracing, Adam found, about the lawyer's disinclination toward expressions of sentiment. He recalled his father's appraisal of Thomson: "a first-rate brain unfettered by illusions." Together, they headed into the woods, the older man setting a brisk pace.

The trail was as Adam recalled it, a winding path through oaks and maples that admitted patches of sunlight, enveloping them in a hush punctuated by the cries of birds. "I'm not a religious man," Thomson observed, "so this is the nearest I come to church, a place to reflect and appreciate what we've been given on this island." He glanced sideways. "But you're wanting to talk about what Ben took from your mother. I suppose Clarice mentioned that I was as shocked as she was."

"She did. Which makes me wonder when you last met with him."

"Concerning his estate? Not quite a year ago. We reviewed his will and decided that nothing needed to change. At that point, the estate — including the house — was worth about twelve million. Ample to provide for Clarice and preserve a chunk for Teddy when she goes."

Hearing this made Adam wish anew that he could reach back in time, changing his father's last year. "Did he say anything about another estate plan?"

"Zero. Nothing at all about Jenny Leigh — or this actress."

"If the tabloids are right, she wasn't here. Ms. Pacelli seems to work fast."

A quizzical smile surfaced in Thomson's eyes. "You're in an odd position, it seems. Your father's executor; your mother's son."

Adam breathed deeply, inhaling the crisp, tree-scented air. " 'Odd' doesn't cover it. That's why I need your best legal advice. In confidence, of course."

"All right. Your familial position may be perverse. But your legal position is simple. As executor, you're obligated to carry out your father's will, ensuring that your mother and brother get nothing at all. Which, psychologically, must be excruciating."

"Only if I let it be."

"So you may be resigning?"

"I'm considering my choices. As executor, what power do I have to investigate why he left everything to those two women?"

Thomson's keen expression deepened. "You stand in his shoes as a matter of law. So you, and you alone, can waive the privilege that prevents Ben's doctors or lawyers from revealing their dealings with him.

Including on matters pertinent to this will
—"

"In other words, my legal status is unique. Neither his lawyer nor his doctor can tell my mother anything. But I can make them talk to me."

Thomson nodded. "As I expect you've grasped, should Clarice challenge the will, her attorney would very much want to know what Ben said to his new lawyer, and how his doctors think the brain cancer might have affected his powers of reason. But these professionals can only reveal that to you. And, as executor, your duties are in direct conflict with your mother's interests. Your obligation is to work with Ben's lawyer, not Clarice's."

Adam had the strange sensation of conducting a two-track conversation — the first track what Thomson could say, the second its unspoken implications. "But it's also true, is it not, that I can gather information to determine whether and how my mother can break the will?"

"For what purpose?"

"To anticipate her strategy. So as to defend and enforce the will, of course."

"Oh, of course," Thomson said with quiet irony. "You're simply being cautious. I suppose there's nothing to stop you, as long as you're not passing information to Clarice. But, of course, you know that. Just as you know that Ben's doctor and lawyer, like me, can't reveal to your mother what they told you."

Adam smiled a little. "Just in case I visit him, what do you make of your successor?"

"Young Mr. Seeley?" Thomson said with real scorn. "Hungry, shrewd, prone to legal shortcuts, and fundamentally stupid." He paused, taking in the trees and foliage that surrounded them. "When I'm in this sacred forest, I should try to be more charitable. Let's just say that Ted Seeley underrated the difficulty of building a practice on this small island, and that your father showed his usual keen eye for human weakness. Unless hiring Seeley was Carla Pacelli's idea. I'd be curious to know if she was in the room when Ben and Seeley came up with this abortion."

With a sudden edge, Adam responded, "Whoever conceived it had an opening. Thirty-four years ago, give or take, my mother signed a postnuptial agreement renouncing any interest in my father's property — including the house she lives in. As I understand it, that particular gem was your work."

"So it was." Thomson stopped abruptly,

facing Adam. "I represented your father. Given the nature of that document, I couldn't advise Clarice on what to do — it would have been a conflict of interest. So I referred her to Ed Rogers, now deceased. Only your mother can tell you why she signed it."

"You don't know?"

"Not a clue." Thomson's speech, flat and unadorned, underscored the discomfort written on his face. "I told Rogers that I had to say in the agreement that Clarice was doing this for 'consideration' — the legal way of saying she was getting something for giving up her spousal rights. But he never told me what that was. If anything."

Pensive, Adam listened to the breeze stirring leafy branches. "What did my father say?"

Thomson pursed his lips, as though tasting something bitter. "I asked Ben why the hell she'd sign a document consigning her to economic serfdom, and why he'd want her to. His response — delivered in his most mordant tone — was that this was personal between husband and wife. And that I was his lawyer, not his priest."

Adam could imagine his father at that moment — the icy voice, the chill in his eyes that made men look away. "Did you give him any advice about it?"

"I surely did." Thomson shifted his weight, his voice becoming harsh. "Frankly, I viewed this entire episode with suspicion and distaste. Had I been Clarice's lawyer, I'd have shot her before I'd let her sign. As it was, I told Ben that this miserable agreement might not hold up in court."

Adam tried to sort through troubled thoughts. "Mom says she expected to inherit from her father. Is that how you recall it?"

Thomson's eyes narrowed, crinkling their corners. "At some point," he answered slowly. "I remember learning that Clarice's father had lost everything. But I'm not sure when that happened. If she signed this post-nup after her father's ruin — which I frankly can't imagine — then she left herself defenseless against whatever Ben might do." He gave Adam a meaningful look. "That really *would* have given her a reason to stay with him, wouldn't it? Whatever his adventures with other women."

Adam considered this. "Do you know when he bought the house from my grandfather?"

"I think that was handled by a lawyer in Boston. But the date would help pinpoint when your grandfather Barkley's fortunes went south." He shot Adam a querying glance. "You're not questioning your mother's explanation, are you?"

"As you said, I'm simply curious. Including about why you told my father that the postnup might not fly."

Thomson's probing look persisted. "A central point, to be sure, given that it's the basis for Ben giving all his money to Carla and Jenny. And, again, completely confidential except from his executor. No doubt you're simply preparing to defend your father's will against attack."

"No doubt."

A corner of Thomson's mouth curled. "In any event, under Massachusetts law, the enforceability of a postnuptial agreement is less than that of a prenup — unlike a prospective bride, Clarice gave up marital rights she already possessed. The law views that with less favor. Which, in turn, raises a critical question: Exactly what 'consideration' did your mother receive for cutting her own throat? Promoting marital harmony may not be sufficient. Certainly any subsequent change in her father's circumstances would at least get Clarice a more sympathetic hearing —"

There was a sharp sudden sound of branches cracking, a stirring in the bushes. Instinctively, Adam flinched, bending at the knees, head pivoting to look around him. Then a startled deer flashed across the trail. Catching himself, Adam stood straight again, laughing at himself. "I haven't seen a deer in years. Where I've been working, they don't have them."

Thomson gave him a swift look of appraisal. "You've been assisting the forces of international beneficence, your mother tells me."

"Attempted beneficence," Adam said, and began walking again. "On that general subject, do you have any insight into Dad's bequest to Jenny Leigh?"

"None. In all the years I knew him, I don't recall Ben mentioning her at all." Thomson seemed to ponder this, remaining silent as the trail ahead became wider, closer to the water. "Truth to tell, almost everything about his latest will bewilders me. It's a fun house mirror of the one Ben instructed me to draft less than three years earlier. Clarice was its sole beneficiary. After she died, Teddy got everything." Thomson gave Adam a reluctant glance. "You were specifically excluded, and the reason spelled out. Your estrangement from Ben."

Adam shrugged. "I never wanted my father's money, and he no longer wanted me as a son. It all makes perfect sense."

"This new will doesn't. I can't begin to explain why Ben left Jenny a million dollars, and gave you a chunk of change along with making you executor. Why would Carla Pacelli want him to do that?"

"I haven't figured that out. But one possibility is that my father lacked the mental capacity to execute a valid will. Or resist pressure from a striking and seductive woman half his age."

Thomson frowned. "Why couldn't he? It's not like Ben was a virgin. Credit all the lore about him, and he slept with every beautiful woman around but Jackie Onassis."

"Not at sixty-five," Adam rejoined, "suffering from brain cancer and abusing alcohol. Those facts might create an opening for my mother."

Thomson pondered this. "They could," he replied cautiously. "But it's more complex than you imagine. Including, I'm afraid, for you."

Two

The path cleared in front of them, opening to a vivid blue swath of sky. After a few more paces the two men stopped at the edge of a sheer cliff, reminding Adam of the promontory from which Ben Blaine had fallen to his death. For a time, they scanned the Vineyard Sound, its aqua waters dotted with sailboats and glistening in the afternoon sun.

"As you suggest," Thomson began, "your mother has two lines of attack based on Ben's mental condition. The first is that he lacked the mental capacity to understand the consequences of this new will. The second is that Carla Pacelli exerted such control over your father that he lacked independent judgment in leaving her most of his money.

"Let's take the first. Unfortunately for Clarice, to prove lack of capacity she'd pretty much have to show that Ben had the intellect of a termite. The legal standard is appallingly low: about all Carla's lawyer needs to prove is that Ben knew who he was and who was getting his money —"

"Even if he was drunk when he signed the will?"

"Even so. Drunks are assumed to be sober at the moment of signing; bipolars to be rational; people with moderate Alzheimer's to be enjoying a lucid moment. And the witnesses Ted Seeley found to watch Ben's signing — his employees, I'd expect — will swear that he reminded them of Albert Einstein. Believe it or not, the law gives their testimony great weight."

Though Adam had expected this, he found Thomson's narrative disheartening. "What about the effects of brain cancer?"

Thomson gave him a long, speculative look. "That would require expert medical testimony, wouldn't it? Most important, from the specialist in Boston that Phil Gertz referred Ben to — and who's barred from revealing to Clarice the course of Ben's treatment, or what he said and did." He paused, then added, "Unless, as your father's executor, you waived the physician–patient privilege. And why would you do that when your obligation is to see that Carla Pacelli gets Ben's money?"

Adam met his eyes. "Suppose I allowed the doctor to testify in order to rebut attacks on my father's mental state."

Thomson gave him a wintry smile. "So find out what he'd say. You'll also want the pathologist's report on the nature and extent of the tumor."

"I've asked. But George Hanley won't give it up."

"George always had a suspicious mind. When it comes to how and why Ben died, and whether someone killed him, this will doesn't help your mother and brother, does it?"

"Not at all."

"What a mess," Thomson murmured. "Back to the subject of Ben's mental state, Clarice could also use the testimony of a psychiatrist on how brain cancer might affect his powers of reason. Assuming that a shrink feels comfortable opining on a man he'd never met."

Adam had considered this. "He could base his opinion on what our family says. My mother saw him every day; Teddy and Jack often enough. They can describe excessive drinking, memory loss, slurred speech, and erratic behavior of all kinds."

Thomson looked at him narrowly. "I'm sure they can — and would. Just as Ms. Pacelli will describe a man of keen intelligence and the saintly temperament of the late pope John Paul. All of which will be regarded by the judge as self-serving bullshit." Thomson's voice became flinty. "If your mother has a prayer of showing that Ben's synapses were shot, it's through this neurosurgeon. As executor, you can stand in her way or not. I don't need to reiterate your legal obligations, or the ethical dilemma they create. You can't get caught helping her and remain as executor."

"Of course not," Adam replied blandly. "So let's move on to my mother's second line of attack — 'Carla made him do it.' What would she have to prove in court?"

Thomson sat on an old log that doubled as a bench, making room for Adam to join him. "As far as Ben's acuity goes, the standard for proving 'undue influence' is less daunting — Clarice need only show that his intellect was weakened at the time he signed the will. That shifts the burden to Carla to prove by 'clear and convincing evidence' that she didn't control Ben's actions."

"That does sound easier."

"In the abstract, sure. But 'undue influence' usually involves an old person who feels powerless without a caregiver.

Carla may have cooked Ben's favorite dinners, but he was still living with your mother. And whatever Clarice says about him now, he was still moving around in the world without the help of either woman." Thomson's speech became sardonic. "Off the cuff, I'd say this was a case of 'due influence.' It's perfectly rational for a man Ben's age to change his will so he can keep on fucking a woman who looks like Carla Pacelli. It's just not nice. If that were grounds for insanity, our asylums would be as jammed as our prisons."

Adam gave a perfunctory laugh. "Still, the man had brain cancer. Mom has to take that as far as it can go."

Thomson's voice became somber. "As desperate as she must be, I'd try anything. But there are two other areas in which Carla may have real problems.

"The first is that Seeley created trusts in favor of Carla and Jenny Leigh. No doubt his purpose was to take the money Ben gave them out of the estate, and therefore beyond Clarice's legal reach —"

"Why bother, when the will already cuts my mother out?"

"My best guess? Ben remembered me saying that the postnup might not hold up. If Clarice can break it, under Massachusetts

155

law she's entitled to one-third of Ben's estate — no matter what his will says. That's not enough for her to keep the house, but it's far better than where she is now. Frankly, this ugly ploy with the trusts bespeaks Ben's ruthless determination to leave Clarice with nothing." Thomson paused, adding slowly, "What did she ever do, I wonder, to make him hate her that much?"

Adam felt a suffocating wave of anger. "Nothing," he said curtly.

"Whatever the reason, Ben found just the lawyer to help him. Assuming he's capable of legal research, Seeley must have relied on an old case called *Sullivan v. Burkin*. That decision cited what was then settled legal precedent: that a husband in this state had an absolute right to dispose of his property as he saw fit — including creating a trust that cuts off the wife's legal interest in its assets. But our highest court found this rule so unfair that it implored our legislature to change the law.

"Given that half our legislators are crooks or cretins, they did nothing. But the opinion suggests that our courts may not uphold this trick in the future. *If* they don't, and *if* Clarice can invalidate the postnuptial agreement, she'd be entitled to one-third of what Ben gave Carla and Jenny."

"So we're back to the postnup."

"As always. But there's one more factor that may benefit Clarice. The last will I drew up deferred estate taxes until she died. If she succeeds in bringing the trust assets back into the estate, Carla and Jenny will have to pay taxes on every dime they get. That means the estate will lose almost four million dollars, potentially leaving Clarice with one-third of the eight million dollars remaining. Assuming, again, that she can bust the postnup." Thomson smiled a little. "If Carla's the schemer you believe her to be, she won't like that result one bit."

Adam thought swiftly. "What if Mom can force a settlement with Pacelli?"

"Then she'll get the full amount of the settlement without paying any estate tax. The question becomes what she'd have to give Carla in return."

"And if she can prove my father lacked the mental capacity to execute this will?"

"That would invalidate the will in its entirety — including its revocation of the prior will. Clarice gets everything; Carla, Jenny — and you — nothing. So Carla, and perhaps Jenny, will fight Clarice like tigers." Thomson shook his head. "I'd hate to think it, but perhaps Ben in his perversity hoped for that."

157

A cooling breeze touched Adam's face. "More than perhaps. It would have pleased him to imagine women fighting over his remains." His tone became crisp. "So how does Mom keep the money away from Carla until the court decides the will contest?"

"She needs to race to the courthouse claiming that the trust assets are part of Ben's estate. Once she files, the probate judge will bar Carla from taking the money and haul Ted Seeley, as Ben's cotrustee, before the court." He gave Adam a sideways glance. "What you need to do, as executor, is notify your mother that you're submitting the will for probate. If she's prepared, she'll be in court a nanosecond later. No doubt Carla knows that."

"No doubt."

Thomson's eyes became curious. "I gather you've met her. And so?"

Adam sorted out his impressions, trying to separate his emotions from the woman he had encountered. "Pacelli's not quite what I expected. She's cooler, smarter, and very self-contained. And beautiful, I'll grant you, but in a different way — tempered and subdued. With her gifts as an actress, she'll make a better impression than she deserves."

Thomson nodded, eyes narrowing as he

looked out at the water. "Whatever the reason, she made a considerable impression on Ben. That much I know."

His tone caught Adam's curiosity. "How, exactly?"

"The last time I saw him was a few weeks before he died. We were fishing off Lambert's Cove on a chilly spring night. I didn't know that he was dying — no one did, perhaps not even Ben. But he tired easily, which worried me some. To keep him company, I sat with him on the beach, sipping whisky from a flask to keep the dew off.

"It was quite dark, just the two of us in the silver light of a quarter moon. Ben got very quiet. He felt different to me, like life was weighing on him — I realize now that he'd already changed the will. Because we were old friends, and because I felt a debt to your mother, I brought up this actress." Thomson grimaced. "There'd been talk, I mentioned, enough to embarrass Clarice deeply. I asked if Ben weren't a little old for such foolishness, and whether he should place more value on the woman who'd stood by him all these years."

Adam was touched. "A good question, and an act of grace. How did he respond?"

"Strangely, I thought. He just smiled, in a way I found smug yet oddly melancholy. All he said was 'Carla has promised to make me immortal.' "

"Do you know what he meant?"

"No. It was a curious remark, I thought. Even Ben knew that no one gets out of life alive."

"A sane man would know that," Adam amended.

"True. Anyhow, too late to ask him now. He's dead, and you're his executor." Facing Adam, Thomson spoke slowly and firmly, "I don't know your intentions, and don't want to. But you know the rules for remaining as executor. You should at least appear to follow them. That means that you'll graciously accept Ben's generous bequest to you, and take no overt steps to undermine the will. Or Ms. Pacelli and Mr. Seeley will have you pilloried by the court. Still with me?"

"Yes."

"Let your mother's lawyer, Gerri Sweder, do the heavy lifting. Gerri's no one's fool. The first question she'll ask Clarice is the one I always wanted to ask — why such a clever woman signed this disastrous post-nup. On that fateful day, and ever since, I've wished that I could read your mother's mind. But she's the last of the old-line WASPs, and she holds on tight." Thomson gave Adam a long, quiet look, and then finished evenly, "With your father's demise, she's the only one who knows her reasons. There's nothing to stop Clarice from choosing her answer with care."

Adam offered no response; it was clear that Thomson wanted none. "There's one more issue," Adam said, "involving George Hanley and the state police. Suppose that someone who inherits under the will pushed him off the cliff. They get nothing."

Thomson gave him a pointed look. "Are you confessing to his murder?"

"No. Regrettably, I wasn't here."

"Then the pool of people who profit from Ben's death shrinks to two, doesn't it? Who's your favorite — Carla or Jenny?"

"Carla, naturally. She gets more money."

Thomson stared at him. "You're not joking."

Adam shrugged. "George thinks someone killed him. That it be Ms. Pacelli serves my family's interests at least two ways. It cuts her out of the will and gets George off our back. What better?"

Thomson laughed aloud. "You are a cool one, aren't you?"

"Just practical."

"Then it would help if George convicts her. To simply accuse her won't suffice. So have a care."

"Always." Adam paused. "A last detail. How would I find out the date my father bought our house from my grandfather?"

"By asking Clarice. If her memory isn't precise, ask to see Ben's papers."

"Then let me put it another way. How would Carla's lawyer determine the date without alerting my mother?"

Thomson contemplated the ground. "I gather you're thinking about the postnup," he said at length, "and your mother's reasons for signing it."

"Not very subtle, am I?"

"Subtle enough. So here's the deal. If the sale took place after 1985, which is roughly nine years after she signed the postnup, Carla's lawyer could check Massachusetts land records on the internet. If Ben bought the house before then, he'd have to slog through the Registry of Deeds in Edgartown. But eventually you'll find what you need — date, parties, and price." Thomson paused, then added, "Of course, someone might remember you were looking and wonder why. Best to ask your mother."

Adam stood. "I will. This has been very helpful."

"To whom, I wonder." Thomson remained seated, gazing at the water. "Mind if I sit for a while? I've got some thoughts of my own to sort through."

Adam thanked him, and went on his way.

When Adam returned home, he went to his room and spent a few moments on the internet. Then he found his mother on the porch, sipping iced tea as she watched the late-afternoon sun descend toward the water. She had just completed a bicycle trip around the island — even as a child, Adam had perceived that she sought distraction in strenuous exercise from whatever troubled her. Now her face had the healthy flush of exertion. But she still looked older to him, more vulnerable, with wisps of gray in her hair that seemed to have escaped the colorist. Looking up, she asked, "Did you see Matthew Thomson?"

"Not yet, no." He sat beside her. "When are you meeting your lawyer?"

"Tomorrow, at ten."

"Good. Tell her I'll be offering the will for probate on Friday, and that she should be ready to file. That should keep Pacelli from running off to Switzerland."

Her eyes filled with quiet gratitude. "Thank you, Adam."

"There's something else I'd like to be clear about. When you signed the postnup, you believed you'd still inherit from your father."

"Yes," she said with a trace of impatience. "As I recall, this is the third time you've asked that —"

"So Grandfather hadn't sold the house to Dad?"

"Why does it matter?"

Adam watched her eyes. "Because as I understand you, he sold the house after going belly-up."

"That's true. Though I can't retrieve the specific date."

"I'm more interested in the date relative to the postnup. I do know Dad bought this place before 1985, because I checked the computerized records." He hesitated, choosing his words. "When and why you signed that postnup will be a central issue in the will contest. As to that, your testimony in court requires more precision than what you tell me when we're alone. So I want you to double-check Dad's papers before you see your lawyer, and be very clear on which event came first. You don't want to be wrong about this."

His mother's face closed. "If you say so."

"I do," Adam replied flatly. "That's the first part of a conversation that, once it's over, you and I never had. The rest concerns how you answer when your lawyer asks what Dad offered you in exchange for signing."

"Exactly what I told you — nothing."

"You also told me you signed it on principle." He paused, looking into his mother's face. "I don't blame you for concealing the deeper truth for the sake of your sons. But you can't be so reticent in court."

His mother's blue eyes held confusion and alarm. "What do you mean?"

"That my father threatened you. That you were afraid of him. That you signed this agreement under duress." His tone softened. "Domestic violence is a terrible thing. All the more so because, back then, the victim saw it as a shameful secret no one outside the marriage could know. So now no one but you knows how badly my father treated you, and how endangered you felt by the consequences of refusing him. I can't know the details. But you can provide them easily. All you need is the will."

Though Clarice's mouth parted, she could not seem to speak. With quiet urgency, Adam said, "You owe him what he left you with — nothing. Your sole obligation is to save your future, and Teddy's. Are you prepared to do that?"

Comprehension stole into her eyes, and then Adam saw her make a decision, reluctance followed by resolve. "If I have to."

The quiet firmness in her tone, Adam thought, reflected the knowledge that she was cornered and must fight for her own survival. "You do," he said coolly. "And please skip the story about signing the post-nup as a feminist gesture. Not even I believe that." His voice became gentler. "Don't say anything, Mom. All I ask is that you remember everything I've said, and forget who said it."

Clarice bowed her head, briefly touching her eyes. Then she looked up at her son again. "It's been so terrible, all of it. Now you're back, my deepest wish. But the more I see you, the more I'm reminded of Ben."

Against his will, Adam felt wounded, even scared. "That's the last thing I want."

"I understand. But you're very sure of yourself, as he was. As if you can bend the world to your will."

Adam grasped her hand. "I'll be damned if I'll let my father take everything away from you. If that makes me like him, so be it."

His mother's eyes moistened. "I understand, Adam. I'm sorry if I hurt you."

He squeezed her hand and then sat back, letting a fragile peace settle between them.

THREE

At eight that evening, Adam walked into the bar at the Kelley House.

In ten years it was little changed — dim lights, wooden tables, and a bar jammed with tourists and islanders, the din of laughter and conversation bouncing off walls covered with old photographs and Vineyard memorabilia. Bobby Towle sat at a small table in the corner, looking bulky and awkward in blue jeans and a polo shirt big enough to double as a beach towel. In the instant before Bobby saw him, Adam had the affectionate thought that he looked like Baby Huey all grown up — a little bulkier, a lot sadder.

With a smile, Adam sat down. "So, pal, how've you been the last decade or so?"

Bobby mustered a smile of his own. "You know how this island is. Days pass, then years, nothing changes much. Pretty soon that's your life."

But something had changed, Adam sensed. For a guy like Bobby, being a cop, and married to the prettiest girl in their high school class, should have felt better than it appeared. Bobby ordered two beers, then asked, "And you? Seems like you just disappeared."

Adam nodded. "One day I woke up and decided to see the world. For me everything changes, every day. I don't know which is better."

The puzzlement lingered in Bobby's eyes. "Everyone thought you'd be a lawyer. Maybe marry Jenny Leigh."

Adam felt the familiar ache, the memory of a life torn asunder. "So did I," he answered. "I found out that wasn't me."

A young waitress brought two beer mugs full to the brim. Hoisting his, Adam said, "To victory over Nantucket."

Clicking mugs, Bobby replied nostalgically, "That was a game, wasn't it?"

"Yup. I'll remember the last play on my deathbed. They're two yards from the goal line, five seconds to go, a quarterback sweep away from beating us. He almost gets to the goal line. Then you knock the sonofabitch into tomorrow, and the ball loose from his hands —"

"And you fall on it," Bobby finished.

"Happiest moment of my life."

"Happier than marrying Barbara?" Adam asked lightly. "Football games are sixty minutes; marriage is supposed to last a lifetime. Or so they tell me."

Bobby's face changed, his bewildered expression followed by a slow shake of the head. "That's what I always believed." He stopped himself. "I don't much like to talk about it, Adam. With what happened to your dad, we maybe shouldn't even be having this beer."

It was another sign, if Adam needed one, that George Hanley and the state police thought someone had killed Benjamin Blaine, and had focused on a member of his family. Shrugging, he said casually, "This is the Vineyard, not Manhattan, and we're old friends. That doesn't entitle me to anything you don't want to tell me. But if it helps, I'd like to hear more about you and Barbara."

For a long moment Bobby looked down, then shook his head again, less in resistance than sorrow. "It's all just so fucked up."

Adam gave his friend a look of quiet commiseration. After a time he said, "I guess we're talking about your marriage."

Bobby puffed his cheeks. Expelling a breath, he murmured, "Barb got mixed up with a guy where she worked. At the bank."

This required no elaboration. "Sorry," Adam proffered. "That's tough to take, I know."

Bobby looked past him, seemingly at nothing. "You start to imagine them together, you know? Still, the unfaithful part I could have gotten past. But this douche bag was into crystal meth." His voice became almost hopeful. "I think that was what Barb was into, more than him."

Keep telling yourself that, Adam thought, *if it helps.* Signaling for a second beer, he asked, "Did you guys break up?"

Bobby stared at the table as though examining the wreckage of his own life. "She begged me to take her back. But by that time it had gone on way too long, and she was way too deep into meth. I had to put her in a treatment center."

It was the kind of thing Bobby would do, Adam thought — even in high school, he had been a responsible kid, stepping up when a lesser person would not. "When did all this happen?"

"She went away six months ago, to a treatment center on the Cape. She's still there." He frowned. "It sort of reminds me of the actress your dad got mixed up with. Except she had the money to get straight."

"Oh, it worked out fine for Carla," Adam said. "For her, this island became a profit center. But I guess helping Barbara gets expensive."

"Like lighting hundred-dollar bills on fire," Bobby answered resignedly.

When the waitress brought their second beers, he barely noticed her. Adam thanked her, then asked his friend, "How are you affording that?"

"I'm not. Had to take a second mortgage on the place we fixed up together. Only reason I could buy it is my granddad left me a little." A look of bleakness seeped through Bobby's stoic mask. "You haven't been here for a while. I love this place, for sure. But us ordinary folks are getting squeezed out of the real estate market by summer people with money. Not to mention we're losing work to these Brazilians and day laborers from the mainland, and property taxes keep going up. Families who've been here since time began are barely hanging on." He looked at Adam, as though recalling the difference in their circumstances. "Your dad always had plenty of money. Still, you're well out of all this. Except for what happened to him, I guess."

"More to my mother. I guess you heard about the will."

171

"Oh, yeah." The words were weighted with significance. "We've heard."

"I guess everyone has," Adam said resignedly. "How has it been working with the state police?"

"About what you'd expect. They send over this sergeant named Mallory — thinks he's a hotshot and that cops on this island are all buffoons. Not that he says that. It's more the way he's so patient and polite. Like when I was talking to Grandma after she got Alzheimer's."

Adam had to laugh. "From now on, Bobby, I'll speak very slowly and distinctly."

Bobby's grin was rueful. "It really is like that, you know."

"So how long do you have to put up with these guys?"

"As long as they keep digging."

Adam shook his head. "I can't believe that anyone killed him. I don't know why they'd think so."

"Well, they do." Bobby looked away, then into Adam's face. "Is anyone in your family getting legal advice?"

Adam feigned surprise. "They've got no reason to lawyer up. What with the will, they can't afford to anyhow."

Bobby stared at his beer. "Maybe they should try," he said in a flatter tone. "I know where they can get a second mortgage."

"Not on a house that belongs to Carla Pacelli. I'm the only one with money, and not much at that." Adam paused, then asked quietly, "How much should I worry about them, Bob?"

Bobby considered his answer. "All I can tell you," he said in a lower voice, "is there's a problem with the autopsy report."

"What kind of problem?"

For what seemed to Adam a painfully long time, Bobby concealed his thoughts behind half-closed eyelids. "How close are you to your brother, Adam?"

With difficulty, Adam summoned a look of composure, maintaining the same puzzled tone. "Teddy? We used to be very close."

Bobby seemed to inhale. "If you still are, you might ask him the last time he was at the promontory. Depending on how you like the answer, tell him to get a lawyer —"

"Bobby," Adam interrupted, "I know my brother. He hated that place."

"So he says. Problem is, he also hated your father."

"No more than I did."

Bobby shook his head. "Maybe so. But Teddy stuck around." Pausing, he glanced at the nearest table, then continued speaking under the din. "Might as well tell you what Teddy already knows. Your brother used to have a boyfriend on the island, and Sean Mallory went to see him. Seems like Teddy used to fantasize about giving your dad a shove, then watching him hit the rocks headfirst. Pillow talk, I guess."

Adam's skin went cold, and then a memory pierced his consciousness. The brothers had set up an old army tent to camp in the backyard. Teddy was twelve, Adam ten — the evening before, Teddy had refused to join the family picnic at the promontory, and Ben had mocked his fear of heights. "I guess you're made for sea level," their father had concluded. "A metaphor of sorts." Lying in the tent, Teddy repeated this, then said, "Loves those sunsets, doesn't he?"

"Yeah."

"Ever think about pushing him off that cliff?"

Teddy's tone of inquiry unsettled Adam badly. All at once, he felt the difference between them, the line of demarcation that was their father. "Not really, no."

"Because I do, all the time. Sometimes it feels like the bastard is choking me to death —"

Facing Bobby, Adam shook his head, as if to clear it. "That sounds like something a kid would say. Even at that, it doesn't sound like Teddy."

"People grow up," Bobby rejoined, "get serious about life. Maybe there's a lot he hasn't told you. Like that he called his ex-boyfriend the night your father died, leaving a message that he needed to talk."

"About what?"

"The message didn't say. But your brother sounded desperate, almost out of his mind. Not like I remember him from high school, this kind of gentle guy." Bobby stopped to stare at him. "You don't know anything about this, do you?"

"No," Adam conceded. "Nothing."

"That's pretty interesting, don't you think? Anyhow, I've made my point, and said way too much to do it. But ask yourself which neighbor of yours likes to walk that trail after dinner."

Adam searched his memory. "Nathan Wright used to."

"Tell Teddy to see a lawyer," Bobby repeated. "That's all I have to say. If you want to talk about old times, I'm happy to stick around. Or you can tell me about what you've been up to."

Bobby's misgivings were palpable, and in his last words Adam heard a plea — *Help me make this a night with an old friend.*

"Then let's switch to whisky, Bob, and do it right."

For the next few moments, waiting for two glasses of Maker's Mark on ice, Adam spun stories about Afghanistan — in his telling a strange and exotic place in which Adam was a seriocomic bit player. Over one whisky, then another, they began reprising the Nantucket game, recalling key moments in a night that made them champions of their league. "You know," Bobby said in a thicker voice, "my dad always said that next to Ben Blaine, you were the best quarterback we ever had."

Adam laughed briefly. "Funny, Bob. My dad said that, too."

At length, they got up, with Adam leaving crumpled bills on the table. Outside it had rained; the night air had cooled, and shallow pockets of water glistened on the asphalt. The two men embraced, and then drew back, looking into each other's faces.

"Good luck with Barbara," Adam said. "I hope it all works out."

Bobby's shoulders slumped. "Me too," he murmured. "I always wanted kids, you know."

"So did I," Adam replied, and realized that this was true. "A family of my own, where I made things turn out better."

Bobby looked up again. "Ask Teddy about the insurance policy," he said, and walked unsteadily toward his car.

FOUR

The next morning brought a dark, lowering sky, clouds heavy with incipient rain. Shortly before nine, Adam met Sergeant Sean Mallory at the promontory overlooking where Benjamin Blaine had fallen to his death.

Though Mallory was accompanied by another plainclothes cop — a stocky, dark-haired woman named Meg Farrell — Adam focused on her superior. Mallory was perhaps forty, with a graying crew cut, bleak blue eyes, and a long face made for tragedy, accented by a quiet, somewhat monotonal voice and an air of watchful patience. He reminded Adam of a priest in the confessional, prepared to hear the worst. In Afghanistan, he had learned to make swift judgments about men whose lives were foreign to him, knowing that an error could mean his own death. Now he assessed Sean Mallory. A dangerous man, he guessed. His one advantage was that Mallory did not know what Adam knew.

"Thanks for meeting with us," the sergeant said. "Though I'm curious about why you wanted it to be here."

"I have some questions of my own. I thought this place might bring them into focus."

Mallory nodded, then asked, "You were in Afghanistan when he died, I understand."

"That's right."

"Mind telling me what you do there?"

Standing to one side, Farrell began scribbling notes. "I'm an agricultural consultant," Adam replied, "with an outfit called Agracon." Before Mallory could continue, he said, "You've been looking into my father's death for a while, Sergeant. I'm interested in why."

Mallory's eyes betrayed a hint of surprise. "I'm sure you know we can't answer your question."

Adam cocked his head. "No law against it, Sergeant. After all, I don't have to tell you anything either. Given that you've interrogated members of my family, it's fair to ask the premise."

Mallory held his gaze, his tone level but ungiving. "Once I tell you something, I can't know what you might let slip, and to whom. It's simply human nature."

Especially since you suspect my brother, Adam thought. "I'm not asking for a list of suspects," he replied. "But before we go any further, I'd like to hear why you suspect that someone pushed my father off this cliff. As his son, and executor of his will, I have good reason to ask."

Adam watched the calculation in Mallory's eyes. "There are certain things," the sergeant allowed in the same polite tone, "we're still trying to clear up. Maybe they mean one thing, maybe another. Take one example I mentioned to your family — a button on your father's shirt was missing. Maybe he lost it in the fall. If so, we'd expect to find it on the beach. But if we found it up here, it might suggest he lost it in a struggle. Problem is, we can't find it at all. It leaves you wondering."

"Not unless you suspect someone of killing him."

Almost imperceptibly, Mallory's face became more stony. "We're keeping an open mind, Mr. Blaine."

"Adam, please. Mr. Blaine is dead."

Mallory ignored this. "On that subject, how was your relationship with him?"

"Distant, I'd say. At least in the sense that we haven't spoken since 2001. It helped preserve our relationship."

Farrell looked up from her notepad. A brief glint appeared in Mallory's eyes, the trace of a smile. "Why did you find that necessary?"

"I found it preferable," Adam replied calmly. "As to my reasons, I don't know why that's relevant. After all, I was in Afghanistan when Jack found him on the rocks. That leaves everyone else on this island a potential suspect, it seems. Including, incongruously, the members of my family. And, far less incongruously, Carla Pacelli."

Mallory did not respond; it was as though he had not heard. "Tell me about Jenny Leigh," he said abruptly.

For a split second, Adam hesitated. "What's to tell?"

"You were close to her once, I understand. You must know why your father left her a million dollars."

"Another mystery, Sergeant. After I left the island, it seems, my mother and Jenny became friends. Jenny is an aspiring writer. Maybe that's what motivated him — a random act of kindness. That happened on occasion —"

"Do you think your father may have had a more intimate relationship with her?"

Adam emitted a bark of laughter. "Like with Carla? Beats me, though I wouldn't put it past him. Still, I never heard that, and there's only so much a dying man can do —"

"He wasn't dying all his life, Mr. Blaine."

"We all are," Adam said easily, "if you care to get philosophical. But I take your point. In the last ten years, I haven't spoken to anyone on this island save my mother, Jack, and Teddy. Except at the funeral, I haven't seen Jenny in a decade. Better to ask her. Which I assume you have.

"As to the members of my family, I kept up with them through phone calls, emails, and occasional meetings off-island. If they knew what my father had done with this will, I'm sure any or all would have told me. None did."

Mallory met his eyes. "So why do you distinguish them from Carla Pacelli? In their minds, like hers, your mother stood to profit from his death."

And by extension, Adam thought, *Teddy.* He considered anew that Teddy or his mother could have feared that Ben would change the will, not knowing that he had already done so. "If they didn't know about the will," he parried, "why worry? And if they did, pushing my father off this promontory would be the dumbest thing they could do — a favor to Pacelli."

182

From his expression, Mallory had processed all this long ago, parsing the alternatives based on whatever pieces he was missing. Above the gray waters behind him, Adam noticed, the clouds were blacker, closer. Abruptly, Mallory asked, "How did you learn he'd died?"

Recalling his own reaction to the astonishing news — a sudden, surprising inability to speak — Adam was acutely aware of Farrell taking notes, watching him as she did. "My mother called me, in Kandahar."

"Did she say anything about the will?"

"Nothing."

"But she knew at that point, yes?"

"I doubt it. As I understand it, she called within hours of Jack finding his body. She was still in shock — she could barely find the words to tell me, and her voice broke when she did. I can't imagine his estate plan was foremost in her mind."

"Before that," Mallory prodded, "when was the last time you spoke to any member of your family?"

"Perhaps three weeks ago. Actually, it was an email from Teddy, exclusively focused on how I was doing. He can't imagine why I chose to work there, and he worries too much."

Saying this, Adam grasped Mallory's point

— between the email and their father's death, Teddy could have divined something about Ben's intentions, and taken out his fear and anger on a weakened man. As if to confirm this, Mallory asked coolly, "What was Teddy's relationship to your father?"

You might ask him, Bobby Towle had advised, *the last time he was at the promontory.* Looking Mallory in the face, Adam asked, "How much do you understand about Benjamin Blaine?"

"Not as much as you, Mr. Blaine. But that wasn't my question."

"Then maybe it should be," Adam retorted. "So here goes. My father was brilliant, immensely talented, extremely driven, and capable of great charm and generosity. He was also vain, self-centered, and the focus of his own world. Other people weren't real to him, simply props in the drama of Benjamin Blaine." Adam softened his voice. "Nonetheless, my mother spent a lifetime loving him. And so, despite their differences, did Teddy.

"He wasn't an easy father. With both of us, he was frequently demanding, and not uncommonly demeaning. There were times when we resented him bitterly, and Teddy had a more extravagant way of expressing that. But except in words, Teddy is the least violent man I know." Adam looked from Mallory at Farrell, waving a hand to indicate the promontory. "Not to mention that he's afraid of heights. He'd come here from time to time, but it was never his favorite place, and he never lingered. And Teddy also feared our father. I didn't. If you're looking for a family member who'd have pushed him off this cliff, I'd be the one."

Mallory stared at him. "And you know all of that remained true," he inquired more skeptically, "even though you weren't here?"

Teddy had left a footprint, Adam guessed, or Nathan Wright had seen him near the promontory on the night their father died. "True, I wasn't around. But you're asking me to imagine a different man. I've spent time with Teddy now, and he's the same. Are you familiar with Occam's razor?"

The sharp look Mallory gave him reminded Adam of a bird. "That the simplest explanation is the best."

Adam nodded. "That night my father was drunk, weakened, and very sick. Maybe he fell. Maybe he jumped — he was a dead man, regardless, and must have known it. Take your pick, Sergeant. Instead, you're questioning my family about a hypothetical murder that is medically superfluous." For a moment Adam stopped, gauging the

185

impression he intended to make on Sean Mallory, one false, one true: that he could lose control of his emotions, speaking without thought; and that he would make a compelling character witness for his brother. "One more thing," he continued, "before you decide that this was murder, and focus on Teddy or my mother. Considering the will — which is the sole motive you've got — only Carla Pacelli and Jenny Leigh stood to profit from my father's death. There's no way Pacelli didn't know she was in the will. She's the one who gained the most by giving him a shove, and it seems my mother saw her with him, in this very spot.

"But there's something else. My father was a dying man — emotional, erratic, and drinking heavily. He was fully capable of waking up and realizing that my mother deserved better than disinheritance. She'd never done a thing to him but be a loyal wife and mother. Pacelli must have known that, too. Why take the chance he'd change his mind? Only when he went off this cliff did that become impossible." Adam paused again, concluding evenly and slowly, "Too many suspects, too few reasons to settle on Mom or Teddy. But I'm sure you've thought of that."

Mallory had, Adam perceived at once —

that was why he had not arrested anyone. But he also knew things about Teddy that Adam did not. *All I can tell you,* Bobby had said, *is there's a problem with the autopsy report.* Adam needed to find out what it was.

He felt Mallory watching him. "Thank you," the sergeant said coldly. "You've been very helpful."

A dangerous man, Adam was now certain.

FIVE

Within an hour, the rain swept in from the Atlantic, heavy drops pelting the roof of Ben's house with an arrhythmic crackle that, to Adam, sounded like gunfire. He stayed in his room, calling five men and two women he needed to meet with, then scoured the internet for information about Carla Pacelli. From his window he could see the guesthouse. Now and then, he imagined Teddy painting, enveloped in the gloom of his darkened skylight, trying to lose himself in some haunting image of the Vineyard. But Adam did not seek him out. It was not yet time.

In late afternoon, the storm passed. On impulse, Adam drove to Menemsha, parking near the wooden catwalk off the dock. The small fishing village was filled with tourists shopping for curios and crowding the fish markets in search of bass or salmon or lobster. Near the end of the dock the vast sweep of Menemsha Pond narrowed to meet the ocean. Here Ben Blaine had moored his Herreshoff. To Adam, the trim wooden craft, still perfectly maintained, had an orphaned quality. Against his will, he saw his father at the helm again, tensile and alert as he sailed into a headwind from that summer ten years before. But Jack's sailboat, its near twin, had vanished from the water. Perhaps Jack had sold his. Yet Adam could still feel its tiller in his hand.

Paralyzed by memory, Adam stood there, the present erased by a sparkling day in August, an image of white sails racing to catch the wind. An hour passed, Adam half-aware of the smell of sea and salt and fish, so familiar from his past. As evening fell, he drove home, still avoiding his mother and brother, and set out from the promontory toward Nathan Wright's old farmhouse.

As arranged, the two men met where the dirt path from Nathan's place intersected with the trail along the cliff. Walking back toward the promontory, they spent the first few minutes catching up. Nate was from an old Vineyard family, the last of the property owners along the bluff who had not sold his land to summer people. A fisherman like Ben's father, he was close to seventy, the years showing in his thinning hair and weathered face, the mica stubble on his chin. In the years since Adam had left, he learned, Nate's wife had died, his four children had moved off-island. "Pretty soon," he told Adam, "I'll sell the property for as much as I can get. No doubt to some newcomer half my age, investment banker maybe, so I can put some of it in trust for the grandkids' educations. It's the way of things nowadays."

The laconic, faintly bitter coda made Adam sad. "Where will you go?"

"Maybe live with my middle son, the one with the most children. Keep me young, I hope. Gets lonely here with no one." As they reached the promontory, Nathan turned to Adam, hands in his pockets. "Times change. Only the rich can keep up with them. Or a smart man like your father."

Even Nate's voice sounded weathered, Adam thought, wearing away like the rest of him. "He wasn't so smart at the end, Nate."

Nate gave a grudging nod. "Maybe not. I don't hold with what he did to Clarice, the soul of kindness ever since she was a girl. Though I've got to say, having met Ben's girlfriend along this very trail, taken on her own she didn't seem so bad. Not flashy like I expected."

Adam gazed out at the horizon, backlit by

orange rays of sun breaking through low white clouds. "So I hear," he responded. "But an actress can play anyone. As matters stand, she's about to become your neighbor."

Nate frowned, shoulders hunched, squinting as he imagined this. "How's your mother holding up?"

"As well as anyone could — you know how she is. But his death was a shock, his will a humiliation, his funeral an ordeal. My father took way more from her than money and her parents' home."

Nate cocked his head. "Never liked him much, did you?"

"I did. Then I stopped."

"And never came back, not even to see your mother."

"Oh, I saw her. Just not on this island. I work overseas, and it's a long way from there to here."

Nate turned, gazing at the flattened rock that covered much of the promontory's surface. For a time he seemed lost in thought. Then he asked abruptly, "What's on your mind, Adam?"

"My father's death. I'm having trouble sorting out how he died and what his last few months were like. I'm hoping you can help me."

In profile, Nate squinted. "About his state of mind, can't tell you much. He pretty much went to ground."

Beneath this reticence, Adam sensed, lay something more uncomfortable. Adopting a casual tone, he inquired, "When was the last time you saw him?"

Lips compressed, Nate faced him. "I'm not supposed to talk about that. Police business, they say, and no one else's."

Silent, Adam locked into his eyes. Turning away, Nate said, "Spooky how much you favor him." Then he added slowly, "Guess there's no harm in telling you what I already told that sergeant from the mainland. God knows it's been keeping me up nights. Whatever else, Ben was your father."

"He was that," Adam agreed softly. "Whatever else."

Nate folded his arms, gazing at the promontory. "I was walking along this trail," he began. "Ben was standing here, not near the edge at all. That's another reason the idea of him falling by accident bothers me so much —"

Ben was gazing at the sun as it declined, Nate recalled, his large frame so still that Nate feared that he might startle him. Then he said, "Hello, Ben."

When at last Ben turned, Nate was taken aback. Before this he had always imagined his neighbor looking near invulnerable, even in his sleep. But this new Ben, thinner and older, seemed weary and unspeakably sad. Somberly, he said, "I can't imagine not looking at this, Nate. Can you?"

He spoke these words with utter sincerity, Nate thought, an undertone of yearning. Uncomfortable, Nate decided to make a joke of it. "Our sunsets aren't going anywhere just yet. It'll be a few hundred years before global warming swamps us all."

Ben's smile was but a movement of lips. "That's good, then. I'm pretty sure I won't live that long."

"Me neither," Nate said amiably. "Enjoy the night, my friend."

As was his habit, Nate walked another thirty minutes before turning back, the sea on one side, the edge of the woods on the other. By that time the sun had vanished, the trail so dark that Nate followed it by memory. As he neared the promontory, he thought he heard a thin cry. Like a bird or wild animal, he thought, except that its odd, tremulous note evoked human fear or laughter. It seemed less to stop than fade away, as though whatever species it came from had taken flight.

Nate stopped in his tracks, hair rising on the back of his neck. Then he began walking again. Rounding the bend, he saw a shadow on the promontory, caught by moonlight for a few swift seconds before it vanished into the shelter of the trees. All Nate knew was that it was human, either man or woman, though he shivered as if he had seen an apparition.

"I thought it might be Ben," Nate said slowly. "I didn't know he'd fallen, or that I was the last person to see him alive. Unless I was the second."

Adam's skin felt cold. "You must have heard him falling."

In the fading twilight, Nate stared down at the rocks. "God, I hope not. But maybe so. Only thing I know for sure is I'll hear that sound until I die."

And so would he, Adam realized, if only in his imagining. "Makes me wish I'd stayed with him," Nate went on, "not let Ben watch that sunset by himself. But it felt like what he wanted." He paused, then added in a musing tone, "If it weren't for your father, I wouldn't have been there at all. Or standing here with you."

"How do you mean?"

Nate faced him again. "When my youngest boy got to college, I had two ahead of him and a girl behind. So I put my place on the market. Hated to do it — my family had lived there since the 1850s, one son passing it to the next. But what choice did I have?" He shook his head in wonder. "Next thing I knew, Ben had set up a fund to cover my kids' educations. I couldn't accept it, I told him. 'What else is money for?' he answered. 'I know how my own family struggled, lobstering like yours, and what it meant for me to go away to Yale. I'm doing this as much for me as them.' "

Stunned, Adam absorbed this. "I never knew that."

"Neither of us talked about it — me out of pride, Ben out of kindness." A film of tears shone in the old man's eyes, and he placed a hand on Adam's shoulder. "He wasn't all bad, far from it. Maybe now you can hang on to that."

After Nate left, Adam climbed down the stairway to the beach.

Ten years ago, he had descended this same stairway at night, Jenny waiting for him below. Knowing this, the climb downward had not bothered him. Now it did. The distance was too far to fall.

A thin cry in the night. Adam had heard

men cry out, dying in pain or fear, the final darkness enveloping them. This must be what Nathan Wright had heard.

Now Adam heard only the echo of waves dying on rock and sand. Reaching the bottom, he rested a hand on the stone that had broken his father's fall. If he could have chosen this man's last moments, he wondered, would he have wished for this? He had no answer. It was one thing to have the right, another to have the heart.

He glanced around him, wondering if the white button from his father's shirt was camouflaged by fragments of rock and shell. No way of telling now. He climbed the stairs again, its worn wood rough on his hand, wondering if Ben's antagonist had come for him in this same way. But tonight he could imagine many things. Nearing the top, he half-expected a dark figure awaiting him on the promontory, his father or his killer.

There was no one, of course. Taking a small flashlight from his pocket, he studied the dirt near the promontory. Before the night Ben died here, rain had fallen, as it had today. In the soft dirt Adam found the partial imprints of Nate's heavy boots, then his own walking shoes, as distinct from each other as the soles themselves. Nate and Ben must have left their prints here on the night

196

his father died. And so, Adam believed now, had Teddy.

Somber, he considered his own footprint in the light. His weight had pushed up the dirt at its edge, half-exposing a buried pebble. No, he realized, not a pebble. Its edge was too round.

With thumb and forefinger, he removed his father's button from the dirt.

Why, he wondered, had the police not found this? Mallory was hardly careless; neither, he felt sure, was the crime lab. What must have happened, Adam posited, was that his father's murderer had ripped it from his shirt before one of them had stomped it beneath the muddy surface of the clay.

Pensive, he inspected the button, weighing his choices. *Maybe he lost it in the fall*, Mallory had said. *If so, we'd expect to find it on the beach. But if we found it up here, it might suggest he lost it in a struggle. Problem is, we can't find it at all. It leaves you wondering.*

Adam no longer wondered.

For a moment, he considered throwing it into the darkness, replicating the trajectory of his father's fall. A new thought stopped him — there might be fingerprints on this button, maybe damning to his brother, maybe not. Whatever the truth, Adam could not allow it to be found. Not until he knew more, or, perhaps, ever.

Adam put it in his pocket.

He knelt there for a time, considering the places Ben's killer could have come from — the beach, the trail, or his mother and Teddy's home. All directions remained possible except the one in which Nathan Wright had continued walking. But the murderer could easily have followed in Nate's path, until he or she found Benjamin Blaine on the promontory, watching his last sunset.

Slowly, Adam took the path back toward Nate's place. Near his house the line of woods ended; the Wrights' modest home, a dark outline in the moonlight, sat on a gently sloping meadow. Passing it, Adam continued toward the property where Carla Pacelli lived.

The Danes' guesthouse, too, was a short distance from the trail, commanding a view across the meadow to the Atlantic. Nearing it, Adam stopped. The kitchen window was a square of light, framing Carla's face as she washed dishes, her expression abstracted, her head a little bowed. He had seldom seen a woman look so alone.

Despite his purpose, Adam felt like a stalker, or a voyeur. Yet for moments he kept watching her face in the light, pale yet lovely. At length, she looked up, gazing toward him in the darkness. Though she surely could not see him, Adam had the illusion that she had. Her face and eyes were that still.

Turning from her, he walked back to the promontory — a twenty-minute journey on which, once past Nathan's house, she would have been concealed from view. With Nathan farther along the trail, she could have come here and returned, and no one would have seen her.

Suddenly, Adam heard a twig snap, then — for an instant — saw a dark form near the trail. Instinctively, he reached for the gun he did not have. Heart racing, he addressed the silent darkness in a clear voice. "Do you want to kill me too? That won't be quite so easy."

There was an answering sound, perhaps undergrowth rustling, perhaps only the wind. Then, he thought, a single footstep. Then nothing.

Adam released a breath. Perhaps he had been speaking to his father, or the shadow of his own fear. The night was still now.

Adam walked back toward the house, glancing from side to side. Then he checked his watch, climbed into his father's truck, and went to see Avram Gold.

SIX

Like the Blaines, Avi Gold had a home in Chilmark, and during his summers there, the renowned defense lawyer and professor had discovered a certain affinity of outlook with Adam's father. Both were to the left of center; neither avoided controversy. In his career, Gold had defended a famous baseball player on murder charges, and a glowering Russian middleweight accused of rape, triumphs sprinkled amid lesser known cases where Gold, without charge, had assisted unfortunates railroaded by the legal system. He stoutly defended civil liberties, no matter the vituperation this attracted, as well as the state of Israel at the most fractious junctures in its history. All this had earned Ben Blaine's respect.

But in Adam's brief experience of Avram Gold, he had found a crucial difference from his father: contrary to his combative public image, Gold was one of the fairest and most generous people around, a man at peace with human complexity and disinclined to harsh judgment. With enthusiasm, he had recommended Adam for law school, and encouraged him to consider criminal defense. And so, though they had not seen each other in a decade, Adam sought out Gold's advice.

Though more rain was falling, the night was temperate, and they sat on Gold's screened-in porch, the dark pool of the Atlantic visible only by its absence of light. Gold was fresh from a dinner party; among the summer crowd he was known as a great raconteur, and his days and nights were crowded — this time, however late, was what he had. Despite his evident pleasure in seeing Adam, Gold asked for no explanation of what, to him, must have seemed such an abrupt and remarkable change of career plans that some emotional breakdown lay beneath it. Nor did he probe his visitor's life now. Perched in his deck chair, Gold listened to Adam's reason for coming, his eyes behind wire-rimmed glasses alert, his lean face — the summary of generations of Ashkenazi scholars — curious and sympathetic.

For a quarter of an hour, Adam related what he knew without disclosing who or what had led him there. "Obviously," Adam said, "the DA and Mallory suspect that some member of our family caused my father's death. Among my interests is protecting them from further pain — or worse — and, with luck, persuading the police to look harder at Carla Pacelli. I need your advice, and expect to pay for it. Anything I say to you, or you to me, has to be confidential." Adam paused for emphasis. "I don't want anyone to even know we've talked. I'd prefer that the people I deal with think I'm only as smart as I am, instead of as smart as you are."

Silent, Gold nodded his acceptance, though his eyes contained a hint of amusement. "This is more than an estate problem," Adam concluded, "or even a criminal law problem. This involves my mother's and brother's future, and I mean for it to come out right. But before I start playing three-dimensional chess — hopefully, without the other players knowing what I'm up to — I need to think this through."

"Then let's start with the obvious," Gold said at once. "If the DA convicts Carla Pacelli of murder, that solves all your problems. Clarice and Teddy are off the hook, and the assets Ben left Carla go to them. And no doubt Carla has the clearest motive." His voice took on a cautionary note. "Assuming that she knew about this will —"

"How could she not?"

"You'd think that. But with Ben dead, Carla alone knows *what* she knew — if anything. Unless the lawyer who drew up the will, Seeley, can put her in the room with Ben."

"I mean to find that out," Adam replied. "Whatever way I can."

For a moment, Gold appraised him. "And then what? The best of motives is no good without evidence that Carla killed him. Okay, maybe she *was* the woman Clarice saw on the promontory with Ben — on some other night. But maybe not. And the shadowy figure your neighbor saw could have been the abominable snowman."

Despite the circumstances, Adam smiled at Gold's bluntness. "The snowman would have left a distinctive footprint. So I think we can rule him out."

"Unless *Carla* left a footprint," Gold responded, "I'm not hearing a case against her either. Granted, people do the most surprising things, including the ones we have reason to know the best. I've only met Pacelli a couple of times — understandably, she has little taste for the summer scene.

But there's a certain dignity about her, as well as a vulnerability she seems determined to conceal. She doesn't strike me as type-casting for a murderer."

"Maybe she doesn't play one at cocktail parties," Adam rejoined. "When I met her, she didn't seem like someone who'd steal my mother's husband, then leave her without a penny. But she did."

"Assuming that Carla planned any of that. But let's move on to your mother, Jack, and Teddy. None have alibis; all claim that this will was a surprise. Do you believe them?"

"It doesn't matter what I believe," Adam said flatly. "The one person who would have told them, my father, is dead. So I figure that part of their story stands."

Gold arched his eyebrows. "I have to say that I find your detachment interesting."

"Necessary," Adam corrected. "Whatever they are, my feelings about this don't do my family any good. All that matters is what can or can't be proven. Asserting ignorance of the will is helpful to them."

"To a point," Gold warned. "But motive isn't your problem here. The police have taken evidence from every other member of your family — not only their statements, but clothes, shoes, and DNA. They clearly think one or all of them are lying. If not about Ben's fall itself, then about some crucial fact."

"That's clear," Adam agreed. "Which brings us to Teddy, I'm afraid."

Gold's tone became encouraging. "I can understand how worried you are. You believe Teddy left a footprint and, if so, that he lied about the circumstances. But there's a lot left to determine. Were there indications of a struggle? How did Ben lose that button? And, critically, what does the pathologist's report say about whether someone pushed Ben off that cliff? Were there bruises or scratches on the body, and fingerprints on Ben's skin? Were there traces of someone else's DNA? And if there were any or all of these, is there some explanation more benign than murder? You just don't know."

"That's what bothers me," Adam said in frustration. "There's way too much I can't get to."

Gold shrugged. "You can always wait until Hanley makes his move. All too often, that's what defense lawyers are forced to do."

"I'm not a defense lawyer," Adam said simply. "My preference is to influence events, not wait until they overtake some member of my family."

In the dim light of the porch, Gold regarded him in silence, the only sound sheets of rain driven by the wind. "About Teddy," he said at length. "A lot of us have imagined patricide, or left an emotional message for some ex-lover. Neither makes Teddy a murderer. I'd be more concerned if you know why, as seems to be the case, he went to the one place — the promontory — he avoided while you were growing up. Do you have any idea of what could have driven him there on this particular evening?"

"No. I haven't asked him yet."

"Then consider if you want to. Anything Teddy says to you, or you to him, would be fair game for George Hanley. That means that one or both of you would have the choice of testifying about that under oath — or committing perjury."

"I understand."

"I'm sure you do," Gold answered in a tougher voice. "So let's take that problem to its logical conclusion. Suppose you find out that your father was murdered by a member of your family. Is that something you really want to know?"

Adam bent forward, chin propped on folded hands. "That depends on whether I can protect them."

Gold shook his head in reproof. "There's more to it than that," he said sternly.

"There's the psychological burden you'd carry for the rest of your life, no matter what you thought of Ben. But there's also a legal and moral problem. If one of them killed your father, what do you do? Do you let the DA charge an innocent man or woman? And if Hanley puts you on the stand, do you lie to save your brother or mother and ruin the life of someone else? Or your own?" Gold paused, then finished in a calm, emphatic tone, "When I encouraged you to enter the law, I knew you to be an unusually smart and capable young man. That's how you strike me now — though whatever life you're leading has made you as hard as you think necessary. But the road I see you choosing, Adam, is a perilous one. You can't know where it ends."

Adam felt his own apprehension. "I appreciate that."

"Then let's talk about what you can count on without placing yourself at moral hazard. Hanley has to prove that there was a murder, then identify the murderer beyond a reasonable doubt. The police don't have a witness to Ben going off that cliff — all they've got, thanks to Nathan Wright, is an unidentified person who could have pushed him. Whatever apparition Nate saw doesn't disprove that Ben fell by accident or, aware that he was dying, decided to jump. Even if your mom's or Teddy's DNA is on his body, that could have happened through normal contact — which is also true of Carla, by the way. And the cause of death, no doubt a brain hemorrhage, sheds no light on why he fell." As Gold paused, Adam could see his mind at work, the swift sequence of thoughts in his narrowed eyes. "Maybe the police have more," he conceded. "I'd like to see the crime scene workup, and the notes from their interviews of Clarice, Jack, Teddy, Carla, and Jenny Leigh. For sure I'd want that pathologist's report —"

"So would I."

"But you can't get it, can you?" Gold looked past him into the darkness, speaking with a clinical dispassion. "I always found your father's company bracing. Why wouldn't I, when he had no effect on me or those I loved? But all too often he was a selfish, callous man, heedless of anything but what he wanted. God knows how many people, at some point in their lives, were damaged by Benjamin Blaine — some of whom, if only for a moment, surely wished him dead.

"I felt that most acutely for those closest to him — Clarice, Teddy, Jack, and even you, the only one enough like Ben to stand up to him. But somehow he found a way to damage even you." Leaning forward, Gold looked intently into Adam's face. "I don't know how, and I'm not asking. Instead, I'm imploring you — whatever you've made of your life since then, don't let him damage you still more."

A moment passed before Adam could speak. "Avi," he said, "he's already done all he can. The only harm he can do me now is through my mom or Teddy."

"You're too smart to believe that," Gold objected. "If you keep conducting your own investigation, or get drawn back into the past, you could become entangled in Ben's web in ways you can't imagine. Go too far — talk to too many witnesses, find out too much you shouldn't know — and you could find yourself charged with obstruction of justice. The psychic prison Ben put you in is bad enough. Don't let him consign you to a real one."

Adam felt a moment of deep fear. Covering this, he said lightly, "Believe me, I'm happy where I am."

"In Helmand Province?" Gold shot back. "I don't know what kind of bullshit you tell Clarice. But I do know people who serve there. Whatever you actually do, there are no safe places, or safe jobs." He spoke more quietly. "But that's not my problem, is it? My concern now is trying to keep you safe on Martha's Vineyard. I'm giving you the name of the best criminal lawyer in Boston for Teddy, and suggesting you resign as executor. Your father has laid too many traps already."

In that moment, feeling the kindness beneath Gold's acuity, Adam did not wish to answer. "True enough," he said. "But for which one of us?"

Gold shook his head — a little sadly, it seemed to Adam. But when Adam stood, Gold clasped him by the shoulders. "I always liked you, Adam, and admired your promise. If you need me again, please call. This time I want you to escape this place unharmed."

When Adam arrived home, the light in the guesthouse was on.

Adam found Teddy painting something new — the still life of a fried egg in a pan, perfectly rendered, the illusion of dimension lent by a shadow beneath the yolk. Without looking up, Teddy said casually, "I was cooking the other morning, and this came to me. Breakfast as art."

His brother had such gifts, Adam thought, and deserved so much better than life had given him. "You shame me, Ted. Until now I thought breakfast was food."

Teddy laughed. "You always were a philistine, Adam. Though you were good at sailing boats." He turned to look at his brother, and then his face changed, reflecting what he saw on Adam's. "Isn't this past your bedtime? It's morning in Afghanistan."

"That's why I'm up." Adam sat across from him. "Tell me what happened that night."

Teddy's careless voice did not match the wariness in his eyes. "Dad fell off a cliff. I thought you knew."

For a moment, Adam felt the undertow of Gold's all-too-good advice. Then he said harshly, "Enough fencing, Ted. Tell me what I don't know."

Teddy's forced smile stopped at the corner of his mouth. "That sounds like a riddle, doesn't it? Only you can know what you don't know."

"Then I'll tell you what I do know." Adam's speech became staccato. "The cops believe you were there that night. They also know about the call to your ex-lover, who revealed that your childhood fantasy of giving Dad a shove persisted well into adulthood. He seems to lack our bond of loyalty. But then he never met our father, did he?"

Hunched on his stool, Teddy had turned pale. "How did you learn all this?"

"That's my concern. I've got the name of a lawyer, and you damn well need to hire him."

"With whose money?"

"Mine, for now. No matter how this mess turns out, one of us will have some." Adam lowered his voice. "You're my brother, Ted. I don't know what our mother knows, but she won't hear this from me. For everyone's sake, don't tell her anything more than she knows already. If it helps, you can pretend she's me."

Teddy stared at him. "What's happened to you, Adam?"

"Life."

Teddy shook his head. " 'Life' is what you used to be full of — our father's energy, our mother's core of optimism. Now you're watchful, and cold as ice. So you tell *me* something for a change. What the fuck is it that you do when you're not with us?"

Even while fearing for himself, Adam saw, Teddy also feared for him — why he seemed so different, and what might happen to him now. Expelling a breath, he said, "All right, Ted — the truth, between brothers. It's true I work for Agracon. It's also true that I ask farmers who grow poppies for the Taliban

212

to grow something else. What I've lied about is that my work isn't dangerous. It could get me killed or kidnapped in a heartbeat. Knowing that will change you quick enough.

" 'Watchful'? You bet. The Afghans suspect any American — no matter how well intended — of being a spy. That means the friendly tribesman you meet may be setting you up for decapitation. I like my head right where it is. So I take nothing on faith, and believe nothing and no one completely. In that sense, our father trained me well. As for 'cold,' " Adam finished evenly, "in my work that's a synonym for 'nerveless.' To survive, you have to divorce your brain from your emotions. So if you don't like who I've become, too bad."

To Adam's surprise, tears sprung to Teddy's eyes. "That's not what I'm saying, you fucking moron. I'm afraid for you."

Adam touched the bridge of his nose. "That makes two of us, Teddy."

"So don't go back there, for chrissakes."

"I have to," Adam responded. "Survive for six more months, and I'm out. I plan on leaving upright. Good enough?"

Slowly, Teddy nodded.

Adam looked him in the face. "There's also something about an insurance policy. Whatever it is, tell your lawyer."

Teddy's eyes went blank, and then he nodded. "I promise I'll call him, Adam. All you have to promise in return is to get out of Afghanistan alive."

"Don't ask for much, do you?"

"Seems like a lot to me," Teddy replied. "Six months from now, I want to be sitting in Mom's house, looking at you across the dinner table. That'll mean that we've all survived him."

There was nothing more for Adam to say.

That night he awakened from his nightmare, sweating, still seeing his father's face on his shattered body. He could not escape this, Adam realized, nor did he believe that he could keep his promise to Teddy. All that mattered to him now was that Teddy keep his.

At dawn, Adam took the first Cape Air flight to Boston, and met Dr. Lee Zell for coffee at the bar of the Taj hotel.

The two men sat at a table by the window. Across Arlington Street, students and tourists and nannies with strollers wandered through the Public Garden or sat beneath willow trees enjoying the flowers, the lush green grass, the swan boats on the pond. But the specialist Ben's doctor had referred him to seemed edgy. Though esteemed as a neurosurgeon, Zell looked younger than Adam expected, with thinning brown hair and dark liquid eyes that conveyed a nameless discomfort with the man across the table — perhaps, in part, because he so deeply resembled the doctor's now-dead patient. Abruptly, Zell said, "I know you're entitled to ask about your dad's treatment. But I'm not anxious to be sued."

"I'm not here for that," Adam said flatly.

"Still, let's be direct. Given that he's disinherited your mother, her quickest route to financial recovery is a wrongful death suit against his doctors —"

"Wasn't he a dead man?" Adam interrupted. "No matter what you did?"

"I believe so, yes."

"Then you can relax, Doctor — dead men lack earning potential. My father's demise didn't prevent him from writing another ten novels, or even one. Just how long did he have?"

Zell bit his lip. "With the most sophisticated treatment," he said slowly, "thirteen months or so. But that's not the path your father chose."

This surprised Adam. He sipped his coffee, then said, "I'm chiefly interested in how the disease affected his cognition and mental acuity —"

"Can I ask why?"

"As executor, I'm charged with carrying out his wishes. That will is being contested — by my mother, as it happens. I'm obligated to find out why he concealed his cancer, behaved bizarrely, and left his estate to a woman he'd just met."

Zell seemed to relax a little, and his expression changed from wariness to regret. "I saw him only twice — the first time six months ago, the second two weeks later. He'd complained to his doctor on Martha's Vineyard about migraine headaches that impaired his ability to write. So I checked his reflexes, which were normal, and determined that his physical condition was that of a man twenty years younger." Zell smiled a little. "Your father said he wasn't interested in dying. So he'd worked like hell to keep himself vital."

Adam could imagine this; even in his forties, his father could hear death's footsteps. *The thing about dying,* he told Adam once, *is that there's no future in it. I mean to live a crowded hour until I drop.* Softly, Adam said, "Death terrified him."

Zell nodded. "I saw that after I reviewed the MRI on his brain and called him in again." The doctor paused, recalling the moment. "I told him he had a brain tumor. Your father sat back, closing his eyes. Then he said, 'This is the end for me, isn't it?'

"I conceded that it might be, but that the next step was to drill a hole in his skull and remove a sample of brain tissue. That would tell us whether, as seemed likely, the tumor was malignant. Then we could decide what to do."

Looking out at the brightness of a summer morning, Adam imagined his father in this doctor's office, realizing that the world outside — his life of joys and conquests, adventures and adulation — could be taken from him by an enemy lodged within the brain that made him who he was. "How did he react?"

Zell paused again, searching for words. "The haunted look seemed to vanish. Then he said, 'I can't die.' As though the thought of dying was foreign to him, and he refused to allow it."

"You describe my father as I knew him," Adam observed. "Some people assess the facts confronting them and adjust their behavior accordingly. My father focused on what he wanted and willed it to be so."

Zell stirred more sugar in his coffee, his long, graceful fingers holding the stirrer as though it were a scalpel. "I know. I damn near had to challenge his manhood to make him sit and listen to his alternatives."

"Which were?"

"One was radiation to shrink the tumor. That could at least relieve the symptoms." Zell looked up at Adam. "But radiation would be palliative, not curative, and could also dull cognition. And no doctor would prescribe radiation until there was a biopsy."

"He never had one, did he?"

"No," Zell answered flatly. "He said there

was no way anyone was drilling a hole in his head. He didn't want to walk into a room, he said, and have people seeing a dead man —"

"Without treatment, they'd be seeing one quick enough."

"Maybe so, but on your father's terms. That's why he ruled out the second alternative — surgery followed by radiation. One risk of surgery is that it might impair vision, impacting his ability to write. Worse, it could inflict serious damage on his cognition, comprehension, and speech. Worst of all, it could cause strokes or excessive bleeding, both potentially fatal. And the follow-up treatment — chemotherapy — could impair his mental and physical functioning. 'In other words,' your father interrupted, 'you could gain me three months as a vegetable who can't find his own limp dick. Unless you kill me outright.' "

Despite himself, Adam laughed briefly. "I feel for you, Doctor. I can see this all too well."

Zell nodded. "The atmosphere between us was visceral. This man lived through his mind and body, and I was trying to steal them both. Then he said, 'There's a woman, Doctor. So tell me this — if you buy me a few more months by invading my brain with knives and chemistry, will I be the man I've been?' "

Adam tried to grasp what had terrified his father more: struggling to comprehend his world — or, fully cognizant, to look at Carla Pacelli knowing that he could never have her again. "Death may have no future," he said, "but you forced him to imagine a living hell."

"By his lights, yes. I told him that sexual function would likely be over. He looked me in the face and said, 'It will be over when I'm dead.' As though we were enemies, and I was bent on stripping him of every scrap of his being."

"So he decided against treatment."

Zell's gaze at his coffee was thoughtful. "No. Instead we entered into a negotiation over the nature and extent of your father's remaining time on earth. At length, we decided on oral chemotherapy. Prednisone and Temador."

"Why that?"

"Because it might bring him a couple more months while being virtually undetectable — no hair loss, no hole in the skull, and, most important, no loss of sexual potency. In turn, I made him sign a letter stating that he was rejecting all other treatment options with full knowledge of the consequences."

Reaching into his sport coat, Zell took out a copy of the letter and laid it on the table. Adam stared down at the signature that had graced countless books — "Benjamin Blaine." The bold letters, slanting forward, bespoke vigor and aggression, as distinctive as his father's face in profile. For an instant, Adam saw him piloting his sailboat, as clear as though it were yesterday. "Were there side effects?" he asked.

"A few. A potential drop in white blood cells, weakening the immune system. They also would have caused him to bruise more easily — not to the touch, but if he bumped into something or someone."

At once, Adam thought of the pathology report George Hanley refused to give him. "So if someone struck him, or gripped him with any kind of force, bruises would reflect that?"

The look Zell gave him was curious. "I'd think so, yes."

"How long did you expect him to live?"

"At a guess? About as long as he *did* live, deteriorating steadily toward the end. All of which I told him."

"Then let me ask you a critical question. In discussing his refusal to seek more aggressive treatment, did my father seem rational to you?"

Zell folded his hands in front of him, gazing at a slice of morning sunlight that had appeared on the corner of the table. "It's not the course I'd take, but I can't say that it's flat crazy. He wanted to be the man he was for as long as he could. 'If I get to the point where I'm not,' he told me, 'I'll know what to do.'"

Surprised again, Adam asked, "Suicide?"

"He wasn't explicit. But that was implied, I thought."

Adam tried to imagine his father, powers flagging, deciding to end his life in his favorite place and on his favorite day, the summer solstice. Then he gazed at the date of the letter, a little over five months before. "By the end, how would you expect this disease to affect him?"

"There are a variety of possibilities. Worsening headaches. Problems speaking or remembering words. Visual deficits. Impaired coordination —"

"Could it have caused him to fall off that cliff?"

"Might have. His balance could have been compromised. He might have had a seizure, or blacked out. He could even have had a stroke."

"My mother says he'd stumble, or forget

222

words. She thought it was drinking."

"Maybe," Zell allowed. "But just as likely it was the tumor spreading. Did your mother mention mood changes?"

"Yes. That he was much more volatile and erratic."

"No surprise. As it grew, the tumor could affect areas of the brain that govern reasoning, self-control, and comprehension."

Adam looked Zell in the face. "And the capacity to execute a will?"

"It could," Zell said, with obvious reluctance. "But a medical opinion requires 'a reasonable degree of medical certainty.' Without having seen him further, all I'd have is the MRI and, eventually, the pathologist's report. Only a charlatan would opine on his mental fitness to execute a valid will."

Adam felt discouraged and angry at once. "There's an irony here, Doctor. It seems likely that, by refusing treatment, my father increased the likelihood of mental impairment. Even as he made it impossible for you to ascertain that."

Zell gave him a sympathetic look. "I understand. For my own part, having Benjamin Blaine as a patient was one of the most disheartening aspects of my career. I'm confronted with this vigorous, talented man, and all my training tells me I could extend his life, and its quality. But he focused on the possible effects of treatment, not the inevitable effects of the disease. And, of course, on secrecy."

"How so?"

"One of his imperatives was that I tell his doctor nothing. Your father shared Dr. Gertz with your mother, he told me, and he didn't want to burden Gertz with keeping secrets. He said he'd tell her when it was right."

"He never did," Adam said bluntly. "Instead, he stole her future."

Zell tilted his head. "I have to wonder if he told Carla Pacelli. Of all people, she might be the last person he'd want to see him as a dying man."

Adam considered this possibility, trying to fit it into the puzzle of Carla's involvement in the will. "Then let me ask you something else," he said. "Was my father as you perceived him capable of ending his own life?"

Zell gave an incredulous smile. "You tell me."

"That would be difficult," Adam replied. "I hadn't seen or spoken to him in a decade. To borrow a phrase, having Benjamin Blaine as a father was one of the most disheartening aspects of my life."

Zell stared at him. "As an amateur psychologist," he said at length, "I think your father was capable of anything he set his mind to. If he thought living a day longer would diminish how people saw him, he might have thrown himself off a cliff." He paused. "Your father had an elemental force, and palpable strength of will. One thing I'm pretty sure of is that I'd never want to be in his way."

"You wouldn't, Doctor. That much I can tell you."

Quiet, Zell gazed out the window, watching the hotel doorman hail a taxi. "Your father had a very strong idea of himself," he said at last. "Maybe, as you suggest, he lost his powers of reason. But it's at least as likely that the last months of his life — Carla Pacelli, the will, his haste to finish a book, even his final moments — had to do with how he accommodated his self-concept to the reality of imminent death." Zell paused, then concluded simply, "Your father finally met something he couldn't beat. But that doesn't mean he wouldn't die trying."

EIGHT

A bumpy flight later, at twelve fifteen, Adam entered the law office of Ted Seeley on Main Street in Vineyard Haven. Unlike Edgartown, this had always been a place for working people, full-time residents of the island, and taking an office here seemed a shrewd choice for a newly arrived practitioner. But the office itself, on the second floor above a defunct restaurant, suggested a threadbare practice — the reception area was cramped, with cheap furniture and cheaper wood paneling; a fiftyish receptionist perched by a phone that did not ring; a cubbyhole where a younger woman perused a paltry selection of legal documents; and a closed door, slightly warped, behind which Ben's lawyer was doing something or nothing. Adam tried to imagine seeing the office through his father's eyes.

The receptionist buzzed Seeley. When he burst through the door with an aura of energy and goodwill, Adam formed a first impression — a slight, thirtyish man with flaxen hair, a too-eager smile, and small, calculating eyes. Adam sensed his calculations were short-term. From Seeley's offices, the wolf was pawing the door.

Seeley gave him a firm handshake. "Great to meet you, Adam. Can I get you some coffee?"

The fervor of this greeting, Adam thought, was pitched too high: no doubt this man was chary of the missing son who, in the words of his father's will, "had the courage to hate," and whose mother Seeley had helped to disinherit. "No, thanks," Adam said coolly. "Let's get to it. Do you have the time sheets I requested?"

Seeley's smile faded. He ushered Adam into his office, shut the door behind him, motioned Adam to a wing chair with faded upholstery, and handed him a pile of documents purporting to show the time spent preparing Benjamin Blaine's last will. Adam took brief stock of the windowless office, the shelves holding treatises on the staples of a small-town general practice: divorce, real estate, wills and trusts. Then he perused the lists of activities — client meetings, document review, legal research, drafting, execution — Seeley had undertaken to cement Clarice's ruin. The name Carla Pacelli appeared nowhere.

Looking up, Adam asked, "Is this everything?"

"Absolutely." Seeley fidgeted in his chair. "You had questions about the will?"

Adam considered his aims in coming here. One was to gauge Seeley's skills as a lawyer, another to determine the facts behind the will, still another to determine how formidable Seeley might be in opposing his mother's challenge. None required excessive courtesy. "A few," he answered. "You took the gifts to Carla Pacelli and Jenny Leigh out of the estate and put them into trusts. Aren't there questions under *Sullivan v. Burkin* about whether such a trust is valid? And, if it isn't, whether this device exposes the gifts to massive estate tax?"

As Adam had intended, Seeley looked surprised. In a different tone, he said, "I took *Sullivan* into account. I believe the will and trusts can hold up."

Adam remained expressionless. "Then you've tried this before."

"Not personally, no."

"Can I ask how many wills you've drafted?"

"A few."

"More than one?"

"I haven't counted," Seeley replied, then leaned forward to fix Adam with a look of deep sincerity. "I did my best to carry out your dad's wishes. Whatever his reason for these bequests, or for choosing me as his lawyer, I was honored to represent him. From all I knew of him, and all that I experienced, Benjamin Blaine was a truly great man."

"He certainly left a hole," Adam replied. "Including in my mother's finances. You're aware that Matthew Thomson was his lawyer for almost forty years."

"He told me that." Seeley's tone grew firmer. "Obviously, someone helped him draft his prior will, and the postnuptial agreement with your mother."

"Did he tell you why he'd decided to change lawyers?"

Seeley's face closed. Cautiously, he said, "I think we're getting into areas covered by the attorney–client privilege."

"I'm sure we are," Adam went on. "Just as I'm sure that as executor, I stand in my father's place. I'm not only the son of a great man but effectively your client. Given that my father is dead, I'm the Blaine you have to please."

Seeley placed his palms flat on the desk. "What he said," he answered stiffly, "and what I told the police, is that he wanted to start fresh. New estate plan, new lawyer. Then he told me what he wanted."

"The validity of which depends on the postnup. Did you call Matthew Thomson for insight into whether it would hold up?"

Once again, Seeley looked off-balance. Crossing his arms, he said, "I told your father that your mom was certain to challenge the will, and that I wanted Matthew's advice. He instructed me not to contact anyone and said that it was my job to make this will ironclad. He wasn't the kind of man you challenge."

"Did he also mention that he was dying?"

Seeley stared at him. "Of what?"

"Brain cancer." Adam waved at the time sheets. "According to these, he came to you four months ago with cancer eating his brain. Makes you wonder, doesn't it?"

"About what?"

"Whether this will was my father speaking or the cancer. Or, for that matter, Carla Pacelli."

Seeley sat straighter. "I only met your father three times, the last when he signed the will and trust documents. But he seemed sharp, determined, and very clear on what he wanted and who he meant to benefit. I didn't know he was dying, and he sure as

230

hell didn't seem deranged. So my job as a lawyer was to make his will stand up in court. Period."

"Was anyone with him at these meetings?"

Seeley fidgeted with his pen. "Do you mean Carla Pacelli?"

Adam shrugged. "Or Jenny Leigh."

"Neither."

"Did you ever speak to Carla or Jenny?"

"No." Seeley seemed to have recovered his poise. "In fact, your father instructed me not to tell any of the beneficiaries that he was leaving them money. First and foremost, that meant Carla Pacelli."

Surprised, Adam said sharply, "That makes no sense to me. Why would he keep a bequest worth at least ten million dollars secret from his mistress?"

"I don't know that he did," Seeley said slowly. "All I can tell you is that he made a joke of it with me. Something about liking it when women loved him for himself."

What must have happened came to Adam suddenly — if everyone thought the gift to Carla was a surprise, her hand in seeking Ben Blaine's money would remain hidden. Someone — maybe Carla, maybe his father — had been more clever than Seeley knew. "So much to love," Adam said. "So many to love him. Did he explain why he was showering his largesse on these two women?"

"No." Seeley's shrug came with a knowing look. "I live here, so I'd started hearing rumors about him and Carla. But that was all. Other than that he wanted to make her his principal beneficiary, he never said a word about her — not their relationship or why he was leaving her money. Zero."

"Did he ever say she'd asked for anything?"

"Never." Seeley paused. "In the will he gives the reasons for his bequest to Jenny: to help her succeed as a writer. He even had me put in that sentence about you. But all he did was leave Carla millions of dollars. He never said why, and I never asked." He smiled sheepishly. "I mean, that would have been a stupid question, right — a woman who looks like that? With all respect to your mother."

"In other words," Adam said evenly, "you figured the privilege of sleeping with Carla Pacelli was worth millions of dollars. Sounds reasonable to me. Especially given my father's scant experience with women."

"Maybe he'd lost his mind, all right? I know you'd like to think so. But he didn't seem like a man who'd be led around by anyone or anything — including his own dick, if you'll excuse my frankness. So

232

maybe it's possible your father really loved her."

"That *would* be a novelty," Adam replied. "Didn't you think his bequest to me — 'To Adam, who has the courage to hate' — was also a little bizarre?"

Seeley seemed to consider this. Then he said, "Only until I met you."

"Meaning . . ."

"That you seem so much like him." Seeley paused. "You did hate your father, didn't you? And you impress me as a very determined man."

Seeley was sharper than Adam had thought. Softly, he replied, "You have no idea."

For a moment, Seeley looked away. "While we're on the subject," Adam continued, "why did he leave me an album of old photographs from Southeast Asia? He must have had a reason, however strange."

In profile, Seeley nodded. "I assume so. But he never said."

Adam waited for the lawyer to meet his eyes again. "So let's sum this up," he said succinctly. "My father canned his longtime lawyer, changed his will entirely, disinherited his wife and oldest son, gave millions to his thirtysomething girlfriend, and left me — who despised him — a hundred thousand dollars and a bunch of yellowed photo-graphs of a trip I wasn't alive for and don't give a damn about. But none of that struck you as peculiar."

For a moment, Seeley took him in. "Maybe it's not what I'd have done, or you'd have done. But I've got no doubt whatsoever that Benjamin Blaine knew exactly what he was doing."

A few hours ago, Adam realized, Dr. Lee Zell had spoken of his father in almost the same words. "Anyhow," Seeley continued, "he signed those documents in the presence of two witnesses — my receptionist and my legal assistant, who doubles as my wife. You can step outside and talk to them both. They can tell you what he was like."

"Not really."

"They can for the purposes of the will. They spent a half hour with your dad, wait-ing for the accountant next door to free up and notarize his signature. He was com-pletely charming — telling stories about the places he'd been and the people he'd met. All of us found him fascinating —"

"And sober?"

"Definitely. His speech was clear, and so were his eyes. He seemed like a man taking a weight off his shoulders. Settling your af-fairs can do that for you. Especially if you're dying —"

"And screwing your wife in the bargain," Adam cut in. "Your obligation wasn't just to him, but to draft a will that acknowledges her interests under the law. *Sullivan* suggests that you didn't, and the postnup is shaky at best. Surely you told him that."

A feral look flickered through Seeley's eyes. "You're questioning my integrity as well as my competence as a lawyer. That cuts pretty close to the bone, all right? You can think whatever you want — about him or about me. But there's no way you'll ever prove your father had lost it.

"I did what my client wished. Now it's your turn. You're the executor of his estate, not your mother's lawyer. If you're pissed off about this will, blame him; if you're pissed she signed the postnup, blame her. Frankly, signing it was crazier than anything your father did. I don't have a clue why she would have, or any obligation to find out. So ask her — better yet, let her lawyer ask her." Abruptly, Seeley tempered his voice. "Sorry if I went off on you. I know this is emotional, okay? But you can't stay as Ben's executor and try to undermine his estate plan. When he signed that will three months ago, under the law he was as sane as you or me. Understand me?"

Adam stared at him. Should he try to waive the privilege to help his mother, Adam now knew, Seeley would make a formidable witness against her. "Well enough," he answered. "Including the things you don't yet understand."

Adam got up and left, feeling Seeley's look of doubt follow him out the door.

NINE

On the sidewalk, Adam paused to gaze at the waterfront — in high school, his point of embarkation for athletic contests on the mainland — taking in the sailboats at mooring as they bobbed in the water, the three-decker ferry from Woods Hole laboring toward the cement and steel pier. Then he drove the length of the island to a white frame house overlooking Menemsha Harbor.

Charlie Glazer sat on the porch. Standing, he greeted Adam warmly, his smile filled with pleasure and curiosity. An eminent psychiatrist who also taught at Harvard, Glazer had spent all sixty-nine summers of his life on Martha's Vineyard. For fifty of those he had known Benjamin Blaine from the cycle of sailing, fly-fishing, and socializing in which both men partook. In Adam's life between fifteen and twenty-three, Charlie had been an amiable presence, chiefly because of his dogged but fruitless efforts to best Ben Blaine in the summer races on Menemsha Pond. Glazer was a bright-eyed man with white hair and mustache: instead of the mandarin gravity common to his profession, he combined a certain restless energy with an air of sweet-natured good humor that at times concealed the tough-minded psychoanalyst beneath. Adam had always liked him.

As they renewed their acquaintance, Glazer recounted his last and most vivid memory of Adam. "The racing season of 2001," he said. "You against your father — I'd never seen anything so intense as that last race. Then you just disappeared. All of us wondered why, and Ben would never discuss it."

Once again, Adam felt the familiar stab of pain and loss. "Then I should honor his wishes."

Glazer tilted his head. "Nonetheless, he seems to have brought you back."

Adam nodded. "Ostensibly, to carry out a will that destroys my mother's life. I'm trying to figure out if he had the mental capacity to do that, or to resist pressure from this actress. So far I'm not having much luck."

Glazer gazed past him, seemingly absorbed in the waters of Menemsha Pond, sparkling with afternoon sun. At length, he said, "Armchair psychiatry is an iffy exercise. Ben was never a patient of mine or, I'd have to guess, anyone's — the last thing he'd have wanted is to let anyone pierce that carapace of confidence and swagger." He turned to Adam. "So I can't say anything about his last six months. But whenever I looked at him, I imagined a deeply frightened man peering back. I'd guess fear was at the heart of everything Ben did."

" 'Fear,' " Adam repeated. "Of what?"

"The black hole at his core." Glazer gathered his thoughts. "At the risk of sounding portentous, I'd say that Ben suffered from a poverty of spirit. Only the admiration of others could slake his hunger. But there was never enough. So he kept reaching for the next achievement — a woman, a race, the accolades of fans or critics — and whoever stood in his way got hurt. Beginning with your uncle Jack."

The summary was so concise, yet so devastating, that it left Adam speechless with surprise. At length, he said, "Sounds like you gave him a great deal of thought."

"Oh, I did. Your father was an extremely interesting study, as well as a man to be wary of." Glazer sat back in his rocking chair. "How much do you know about his childhood?"

"Only what he told me, plus a few scraps from Mom. The father he described was barely human — coarse, brutal, and drunk — and his mother seemed like a shadow."

Glazer nodded. "That may be more accurate than you know. My understanding is that Nathaniel Blaine was a limited man who seethed with resentments, and was given to violent rages that reduced his wife to a timorous cipher. Both were alcoholics, so there was no safe place for either boy. Since then, I think, everyone else has paid for the damage they did Ben in childhood."

Adam shook his head, less in demurral than confusion. "I was too close to him, Charlie. How did that boy become the father I knew?"

Glazer nodded. "A good question. No one on earth is Adam or Eve — our parents had parents, too. So here's how Ben lays out for a psychiatrist. As a child, he had no love from either parent: his father beat him, and his mother couldn't protect him. That led to a terrible narcissistic injury — Ben's lifetime quest to heal the wounds to his own sense of manhood." Smiling, Glazer stopped himself abruptly. "Am I making sense, or does this sound like total bullshit?"

Adam stared at the deck, not answering.

"Hardly," he said at length. "In fact, you just surfaced a memory. My father and me, just the two of us, standing on the promontory after his own dad's funeral."

Glazer eyed him curiously. "How old were you then, Adam?"

"Not yet ten, I think. But suddenly I remember it all too well."

His father stared moodily at the water, falling into a silence that Adam feared to break.

"It's so strange," Ben said at last. "The death of a father is a profound thing, I'm finding, no matter how great a sonofabitch he was. I don't know why I should feel like this. It's pathetic to be the slave of archetypes."

His father's voice was low and soft, as though he were speaking to himself. Curious, Adam asked, "How come we never saw him?"

"Because I could never forget who he was." For a moment, Ben studied him. "Be grateful I'm your father, Adam. Mine used to get drunk and slap us around, then beat up my mother for sport. The only way I survived was to make myself tougher than he was."

"What did you do?"

"Read book after book on boxing. Then I

hung up a heavy bag in a neighbor's barn and tore into it every day after school. Not to let the anger out, but to train it." Ben turned to his son again. "I punished that bag until the stuffing bled through the canvas. A sign from God, I thought." Adam heard Ben's reflective tone transmute to something harder. "That night, at dinner, my father slaps my mother — there's something about the stew he doesn't like. She is cowering in a corner with that same look of incomprehension, a small animal petrified of a big one.

"I get up from the table and grab him by the wrist. 'You're a pussy,' I tell him. 'Good only for drinking and beating up women and small boys. You're just smart enough to know I've gotten way too big for that. But too stupid to know what that means.' "

Listening, Adam felt his heart race. "The bastard's eyes get big," his father continued. "Suddenly, he takes a swing at me. I duck, like I've taught myself, and Jack tries to step between us. 'Get out of my way,' I bark at him, 'or you'll come next.' " Ben's speech quickened. "Jack backs up a step. Before my father can move I pivot sideways and hit him in the gut with everything I've got. He doubles over, groaning. As he struggles to look up at me, I break his nose with a right cross." Ben's voice was shaking now. "His blood spurts on the floor. I'm breathing hard, years of hatred welling up. 'Remember hitting me?' I manage to say, and send a left to his mouth that knocks out most of his front teeth.

"My father starts blubbering, and he looks like Halloween. I pull him up by the throat and press my thumbs on his larynx till his eyes bulge. 'I run this house now,' I tell him. 'You just live here. Hit her again, and I'll cut your balls off with a butter knife.' "

As Adam watched him, frightened, Ben's barrel chest shuddered like a bellows. Tears began running down his face. "He's dead now," he said in a choked voice. "Thank God it won't be like that for us."

Not knowing what to do, Adam took his father's hand and felt Ben squeeze his in return.

Finishing, Adam felt the dampness in his eyes, a grief too deep and complex to express. For a time, Glazer let him be, scanning the horizon. "Do you remember what you felt, Adam?"

"Terrified," Adam murmured. "Of both men in the story, the father and the son. And of being like either one."

Glazer nodded. "That makes sense, and

not just because they fought. The forgotten person in that scene is the mother — whose passivity helped make Ben who he became. Among other things, a serial pursuer of women, scarred by neglect from the first woman in his life."

"Too many parallels," Adam told Glazer. "My father never beat us — or, to my knowledge, her. But all of us lived in his shadow. My mother deferred to him, and couldn't protect us from the psychic damage he inflicted. Like Jack, my brother stood aside. And, like Ben, I broke with my own father."

The look in Glazer's eyes combined compassion and deep interest. "You think you're too much like him, is that it?"

"That's all I ever heard," Adam said in a low voice. "Not just to look at, but to be with."

"Then bear with me for another moment. Because the father you knew was his own singular invention. No doubt you've heard of narcissistic personality disorder."

Adam searched his memory. "As I recall, it involves an insatiable need for attention and admiration. Plus a tendency to see others in terms of those needs."

Glazer nodded. "At the positive end, you find someone like John F. Kennedy, a high-functioning leader who's rewarded for his gifts. Or you get someone more malignant, seeking dominance by subjugating or destroying others — taking their jobs, stealing their women. Does that sound much like you to you?"

"Not as I imagine myself. Though I'd be the last to know, wouldn't I?"

"You're very much like him, it's true. But the person you're most likely to damage is yourself. Your father's efforts were far more comprehensive. Regrettably for Clarice, however, narcissistic personality disorder does not disqualify someone from executing a valid will." Glazer paused, reflecting. "What I can't know is how the course of his disease, and the fear of imminent death, affected your father's mental state. Or how Carla Pacelli fits into the puzzle."

"Really?" Adam said tartly. "Everyone else tells me it's obvious. My mother is sixty-five. Carla Pacelli is half that age, and known for her remarkable face and figure. Seems like enough for Dad, they tell me."

Glazer's face was skeptical. "But why leave her all his money? Ben was far too conscious of how the world saw him to play the besotted old fool." Glazer looked at Adam intently. "Granted, sleeping with Carla Pacelli fit Ben's need to prove his own superiority.

But psychologically, his hunger for transcendence involved concealing his 'true self' — the wounded son — behind a 'fake self' who was omnipotent, omniscient, and invulnerable. He needed to risk death because he feared it so much. But the last thing he'd do is risk appearing to be controlled by a younger woman — even this one. That's why I find Ben's relationship with Carla so completely enigmatic. As, I sense, do you."

"True enough," Adam conceded.

"I don't know this woman at all," Glazer cautioned. "But you don't either. So don't respond to stereotypes, no matter how tempting. She may be more complicated than you think."

Adam gave him a dubious look. "I'll hold the thought."

Glazer read his expression. "Sorry I can't be more help. But while I've got you here — for the first time in a decade, at that — there's one more subject worth discussing further."

"Which is?"

"Your own family, Adam. Starting with you and Ben."

TEN

The two men leaned on the railing, the blue panorama of Menemsha Pond before them, the images of a long-ago racing season ghosts in Adam's mind. "To escape his inner self," Glazer observed, "Ben needed to write bestsellers, face down danger, and eviscerate anyone he saw as a rival. That came to include you, didn't it?"

Adam did not answer. "And women?" he asked. "What were they to him?"

"Mirrors in which he saw himself — or the man he wished to see. Until Pacelli, and with the partial exception of your mother, I read him as the classic sexual narcissist: insatiable, emotionally cool, and incapable of love." He glanced at Adam. "I remember a cocktail party one summer, watching him charm my college-age daughter — hopefully just for sport. I wasn't amused: it was one thing to enjoy Ben as the compelling and often generous figure I'd known well since we were young, and another to want him near the daughter I loved dearly. So I took her aside, told her Ben was the most dangerous man on the island, and spelled out why. I don't think she ever spoke to him again."

There was no humor in Glazer's eyes or voice. Quietly, Adam asked, "Was he capable of sexual violence?"

Glazer gave him a dubious look. "I never heard that he was, and it runs contrary to his self-image. But if some woman challenged his vanity? Wrong time, too much to drink, and who knows. Do you have something in mind?"

"No." Adam paused. "I keep thinking of my mother. What kept that going? I wonder — at least until Carla Pacelli."

Glazer's gaze at him was ruminating. "Growing up, it must have seemed mysterious to you. But in certain ways they were a match — for reasons functional and dysfunctional. Your mother was lovely, aristocratic, socially skilled, and, beneath the surface, deeply dependent. From what I could grasp, her parents raised her to be an asset, rather than an independent being. Damaging to her; perfect for Ben. She became a badge of honor for a young man who started with nothing but ego." Glazer paused, amending his remarks. "They did have things in common. Both were articulate, smart, and charming. Your mother was made for the outdoors, as was he. She could ride or swim or play tennis with the best of them."

Adam nodded. "Sometimes they seemed most compatible in motion. When they were still, they had to face each other. Or, in my mother's case, work overtime to avoid facing unpleasant truths: the latest woman, the indifference with which he sometimes treated her. I always wondered what she got from being with him."

"That's not hard," Glazer said crisply. "In his own way Ben had need of her. In return she got Benjamin Blaine, the preeminent American writer — a high achiever, unlike her father, with all the access and cachet she'd been accustomed to since birth. I always sensed her comfort in that amused him."

Adam smiled without humor. "It did. I remember her lobbying to attend an annual Fourth of July party given by some guy who'd call the *Boston Globe* to list the celebrities attending. It was part of the Vineyard social season, she told him — everyone they knew would be there. 'Society,' he retorted, 'was invented by

people with no actual talent. Without orna-
ments like us to get their names in the
paper, and the lemmings who envy them
for it, they'd shrivel up like salted slugs.' "

Glazer laughed aloud. "That's so like Ben
— I can even hear his tone of voice. How
did your mother react?"

"Not well. All the more so because his
penchant for publicly speaking unpleasant
truths ran so contrary to her nature. She
had opinions for sure — some caustic —
but few outside the family ever heard them!"

"That's one aspect of your mother, Adam.
But she also survives by avoiding dark
nights of the soul. If a fact was painful, she
would do her damnedest to repress it. For
the sake of others, I'm sure, but also her
own."

"But now she can't," Adam shot back with
sudden anger. "In death, my father set out
to crack her facade in the cruelest and most
public way, turning forty years to ashes. It's
more than callous — it's an act of hatred
meant to ruin another human being, poison-
ous and inexplicable. It's like he set out to
destroy all of us, and she was the last one
standing. I used to think there was nothing
else he could do to me. But I was wrong.
Watching her now is painful beyond words."

"And so you mean to fix that for her."

"Who else will?" Adam turned to him. "There's also Teddy. He got the shaft from the beginning. Not only did my father prefer me, but I think my mother did, too. And now Teddy's got nothing because my father left her nothing. I'm the only one who escaped."

"If so," Glazer replied, "it's for reasons embedded in your family. In her way Clarice loved your father deeply; Ben loved his idea of himself. And there you were. The one who looked like him; the great athlete; the young man who attracted women easily. In short, the one who reflected the Benjamin Blaine he needed others to believe in. But a gay son? Never. So he spat out Teddy like a piece of bone. Cutting him off was Ben's final rejection."

Silent, Adam watched a trim sailboat skitter across the surface of the pond. At length, he said, "If the purpose of this will was to destroy his wife and son, maybe Pacelli was just a vehicle. Is that what you're suggesting?"

A corner of Glazer's mouth pinched in a dubious expression. "I'm not sure. The idea of Carla Pacelli as Ben's weapon makes more sense to me than imagining Ben as hers. But as hard as this is to envision, suppose he saw Carla as his equal? If his intention was simply to ruin your mom and Teddy, he could have found a hundred other ways. Why this woman, and why now?"

"Maybe he was afraid of dying," Adam rejoined sharply, "and she was smart enough to exploit that. Even ruthless enough to see the benefits of a long fall off a cliff."

Slowly turning, Glazer stared at him. "Be careful where you go with this, Adam."

"Meaning?"

"You've drawn a target on Ms. Pacelli's forehead. But if your father was afraid, so was your mother — of Ben, and his new lover. Clarice survives by compartmentalizing. That stopped working with Carla Pacelli." Glazer drew a breath, speaking gently but succinctly. "Imagine how much she frightened your mother. All the property was Ben's. What if he decided to spend his golden years seeking youth in the bed of this new woman? Not some anonymous arm piece, but a celebrity in her own right who, despite her public downfall, seems to have considerable resilience. Clarice couldn't just wish her away."

With willful calm, Adam asked, "And so?"

Glazer fell quiet, and then answered with palpable reluctance. "Your mother may not be quite as hard as Ben was. But she may be tougher than you think, and her instinct for self-preservation much keener. She'd invested a lifetime in preserving her identity as Mrs. Benjamin Blaine. Imagine the void she saw opening up before her. The most unlikely people, if desperate enough, can muster an astonishing resourcefulness and force of will, and a depth of hatred few who know them can imagine. Even your mother."

Or brother, Adam thought. But he could not speak of Teddy. With an edge in his voice, he said, "What are you saying, precisely?"

"Just that. Your father had a gift for creating hatred within any family he was part of — first in his brother, then in his wife and sons. As a matter of literal fact, you're the only one who couldn't have pushed him off that cliff." Glazer held up his hand, willing Adam to listen. "Instead, you're still competing with him, just like you did that final summer. No matter where it leads."

"That's a little deep for me, Charlie. No one in my family killed him. And all I'm trying to do is get their money back."

Glazer shook his head. "Too deep for you?" he repeated. "I doubt it. So tell me this — why did you sail against him all those summers ago, knowing he cherished the Herreshoff Cup as much as any woman?

And what price did you end up paying?"

Ten years later, Adam knew, the fateful skein of cause and effect still tormented him. With feigned carelessness, he answered, "Sometimes a cigar is only a cigar, and a trophy only a trophy. There's less to it than you think. But for whatever it's worth, our final test of wills started with a game of golf."

As with anything involving nerves and sinews, Ben Blaine was a natural at the sport. Born without privilege, he had picked up the game late. But within a year, and without lessons, he had mastered the subtle nuances of swinging a golf club that most men found counterintuitive. And as in all else physical save firing a gun, he had passed those skills on to Adam.

Beginning in the summer of Adam's sixth year, Ben had gotten him up before dawn, spending hours on the practice tee at Farm Neck. No golf pro gave him lessons; in Ben's eyes, no tutor but he would do. No detail of Adam's swing was too minute; no choice of strategy on the course beyond challenge. By the time Adam was fifteen, he, like Ben, shot close to par. The lead in any given round went back and forth between them; if victory lay in the balance, they played the eighteenth hole in taut near silence. Ben had created his own rival.

This was true on the final hole they ever played. It was just before the summer solstice. Adam was twenty-three, and they had not resumed their running battle in several months. Ben's drives were a few yards shorter, Adam noticed, his swing a bit less fluid. But on the eighteenth hole, with the two men tied, Ben uncorked an epic drive that propelled the ball ten yards past his son's.

Smiling to himself, Ben said nothing as they strode down the fairway.

They had started the round at six; it was not yet ten. The morning sun left a sheen on the pond guarding the green, still two hundred yards distant. Or, for Adam, a little farther.

Hands on hips, Adam considered his choices, then the man he planned to defeat. The tactics were simple enough — Adam could hit the ball safely short, hoping to follow with a chip shot near the hole. Or, far more risky, he could try to attack the pin with the 3-wood shot of his life and, should he carry the water, dare his father to follow. That was where his bone-deep knowledge of Ben led him. In golf, as in writing, his father took risks; perhaps he had yet to face the fact that in six months' time his son's strength had surpassed his own.

Without glancing at his father, Adam took the 3 wood from his bag.

Addressing the ball, he felt Ben watch intently, grasping the choice his son had made. Then Adam cleared his mind of any thought but the mechanics of a flawless swing, any image but the red flag that flapped above his target. As he raised his club in one fluid motion, twisting sideways as his father had taught him, Adam's eyes remained fixed on the white ball.

His downward swing was vicious yet smooth. The club head as it struck the ball produced the hollow sound of a perfect shot, and the follow-through raised Adam to the tips of his toes without throwing him off-balance. Only then did he watch the ball in flight.

It rose like a laser, becoming a dot against the horizon of grass and sky as it strained to cross the pond. Taut, Adam watched it descend, drawing slightly, unsure of whether it could reach the other side. A matter of feet or inches.

No splash. The ball bounced just clear of the water, kicking in the air, then dribbled onto the green. Adam watched it die ten feet from the pin.

Neither man said anything.

After a moment, Ben took out a 3 wood. Closely, Adam watched him, like a cat eyeing its quarry. His father's first practice swing was too savage for total accuracy; his second, smoother and more confident, bespoke his self-control, the mental toughness of a born competitor. As Ben stood over the ball, Adam watched him marshal his strength of mind and body. His downward swing was much like Adam imagined his own, a smooth but strong uncoiling.

But not quite.

The ball rose a little higher, and its downward arc began a hair sooner. The fateful splash, perhaps a foot from the bank, marked Ben Blaine's defeat.

He stood there, motionless, his face without expression.

After a moment, Adam approached him, then placed a consoling hand on Ben's shoulder. "You're fifty-five," he said in a solicitous tone. "You're supposed to lose strength, and gain wisdom. A wise man would have played it safe."

Ben barely smiled. In his eyes Adam read the awareness of time, the first faint shadow of mortality. "A wise man," he answered coolly, "knows the grace of silence. Too bad you don't have your own boat. We could see how you'd do on the water."

Glazer listened intently. Without smiling, he said, "Beware of what you wish for. He forgot buying Jack that Herreshoff."

Lost in memory, Adam stared out at the windy sweep of Menemsha Pond, saying nothing.

"Why don't you stick around," Glazer suggested after a moment. "Rose and I have enough salmon for three."

Adam glanced at his watch. "Thanks," he said. "But I've already got dinner plans, with someone I've been avoiding. Seems like it's time."

ELEVEN

When Adam entered Atria restaurant, pausing on the screened porch surrounding the main dining room, Carla Pacelli was already there. At first she did not notice him; seated by a window, she looked out at the side garden with a reflective smile, watching a small boy and girl play on a swinging chair suspended from a willow tree. She wore little makeup, Adam noticed, and a loose, flowing dress that concealed, rather than accented, what he knew to be a remarkable figure. He paused, hands in his pockets, until she noticed him. The instant of wariness in her eyes was succeeded by another smile, this one suggesting curiosity and a hint of welcome. Then she stood, extending a warm, dry hand.

"You surprised me," she said.

"By being early?"

"By inviting me here at all," she said as he sat across from her. "Being early is ingrained in me. I went to UCLA on a scholarship, with no money or margin for error. So I never missed a class. When I entered the business, I was determined to make every audition on time, or be on the set at whatever ungodly hour they wanted." She gave a fleeting ironic smile. "I was the most reliable, least temperamental actress in Los Angeles. Until I wasn't."

As before, her voice, familiar from television, underscored for Adam the strangeness of encountering her. But she seemed bent on reducing their awkwardness; from what he understood of celebrities, including his father, one technique was offering up small pieces of themselves, self-flattering but not deeply revealing. Then their waitress, a young woman in her twenties, reminded Adam of the detriments of being, as Ben had put it, "face famous." "I just have to tell you," she told Carla, "how much I loved your show."

Carla smiled. "I'm glad you did."

The young woman hesitated, encouraged. "You're so much more beautiful in person. Do people tell you that?"

A hint of amusement danced in Carla's brown eyes. "That's nice of you," she said pleasantly, and then ordered a mineral water before Adam requested scotch. When the waitress left, Carla remarked, "I've never known how to take that particular compliment. On the one hand, she could be saying I look surprisingly good for a drugged-out has-been. On the other hand, she could mean that every Monday night I looked like hell — which, by the end, was true. I guess I can take my pick."

"What would my father have said? I wonder."

The light in Carla's eyes dimmed. "I'm not brain-dead," she said bluntly. "I understand that you're her son. But you're also the son of a man I cared for deeply. Whatever your motives, and however you must feel about me, I'd never have refused to see you. So let's make the best of this."

"You weren't afraid to come?"

Carla shook her head. "I'm not afraid of *you*, if that's what you're asking. And the truth about Ben and me won't change, whether I'm in court or we're having dinner." Carla hesitated, looking directly into his eyes. "Besides, you're the only member of your family I can be certain didn't murder him. That gives us more in common."

This remarkable statement left Adam without words: if this woman knew how Ben had died, she was not simply a gifted actress, but utterly without nerves. "My other reason," she continued in the same level tone, "concerns your mother. As I already told you, Ben's bequest was a complete surprise to me. But just this morning I found out about the postnuptial agreement, and that she has no money of her own. All along, I thought she was born into wealth. I never dreamed Ben would leave her with nothing."

Adam gave her a sharp, skeptical look. "No? Then that's something else we have in common. Though I feel much more strongly about it than you do."

"I'm sure you do," Carla said calmly. "But this morning I felt sick to my stomach. I don't like being in this position, and didn't need for Ben to put me here."

"So give up the money," Adam rejoined.

Carla met his eyes. "That's for the lawyers, and it's not as simple as you think. For now, let's leave it there, all right?"

He could not shake her self-possession, Adam saw. But beneath this he sensed a watchfulness. Part of her agenda, he felt sure, involved assessing the man who might stand between her and ten million dollars. Abruptly, she asked, "So what is it you want from me? Other than to renounce Ben's gift and vanish from this island forever."

It was best to keep her talking, Adam judged. "Maybe you can satisfy my curiosity. Beyond money, what did you see in him?"

Carla sipped her mineral water. "A different man than you saw, I'd imagine."

"Maybe we just have different standards. Or different needs."

A corner of her mouth upturned in a puzzled smile that did not change the coolness in her eyes. "You really did hate him, didn't you? Would you mind telling me why?"

"I would, actually."

Carla seemed to inhale. "Then I'll tell you why I was so drawn to him and what, by the end, Ben meant to me. Assuming you can stand to listen."

Adam took a swallow of scotch. "Try me."

Carla hesitated. "At the risk of sounding self-absorbed, the story starts with me. Or, more accurately, the person I was before I met him — or wasn't. Stop me if you're bored."

"I doubt I will be," Adam said crisply. "Go ahead."

"All right. I got out of UCLA at twenty-two, with a major in drama, a minor in psychology, and not much life experience beyond working pretty damned hard to get

263

there. For the next four years I kept on like the Energizer Bunny — failed auditions, failed relationships, aborted movie projects, pilots no one wanted. All I could think to do, like your father told me he did, is keep striving to become the person I imagined — an actress people cared about." Her voice became rueful. "And then, before I could absorb what had happened, I became the lead in *Deep Cover*."

"More than the lead. As I recall it, you were in every scene."

Carla laughed in surprise. "You actually watched it?"

"A few times. Not for you, of course. I consider myself a scholar of espionage."

Her eyes glinted with amusement. "Then I guess it escaped you that we were all about cleavage."

All at once, imagining himself as Ben, Adam grasped what his father must have found appealing — not just her appearance but a keen intelligence accented by humor and vitality. "True enough," he said. "I'm one of those guys who reads *Playboy* for the articles."

"Don't they all? Anyhow, despite the fact that I was the centerpiece of a male fantasy, I found myself nominated for an Emmy, then another. People kept on watching; I kept filming season after season, shooting thirty shows a year while transitioning into movies during the summer hiatus. First, a gross-out film where I played the unattainable love object, then an okay romantic comedy —"

"*As the Romans Do.* I remember it."

She gave him a mock-incredulous look. "You saw *that,* too."

"On an airplane to Karachi. It was a very long flight."

"It must have been. But at least you could get off in Karachi." Her smile faded. "I was working all the time, trying to become the great actress of my generation. But I was living life in the third person. The real Carla was like a gerbil on a wheel, becoming even more lonely and anxious, yet going faster all the time. And so the gerbil started needing stimulants."

"You could have stopped," Adam said evenly. "Or at least taken a summer off."

For a moment, Carla closed her eyes. "That seems so obvious, doesn't it?" she said, then looked him in the face again. "Later, when I talked to Ben, I understood it better. He was always running scared, he admitted, afraid the past he was trying to escape would grab him by the collar —"

"He said that?" Adam inquired.

"He said many things, some of which I know were hard to admit. This one struck me. Like Ben, I'd had two uneducated and inattentive parents — not as cruel, I'm sure, but hardly nourishing. I left home without having any concrete sense of who I was. Seeing myself in the eyes of others was the only way I felt real." Carla paused, her voice dispassionate, as though pronouncing judgment on the woman she had discovered. "Having drive and talent is different from having character. When the pressures of celebrity and constant work started to overwhelm me, I had no self to fall back on. Just a shell."

"Hence cocaine."

"And bourbon." Her voice became raw. "Throw in cigarettes to keep me way too skinny and help accelerate the aging process. At first all that propped me up. Other people had done it, I told myself — Dick Van Dyke and Robert Young went through their hit shows drunk from noon to night. But it became the same old tired story — the more cocaine I snorted, the more ragged and paranoid I got. I started showing up late and blowing lines. But I was the one on whom everyone else's jobs depended, so the producers covered for me. You know the rest," she finished. "Another haggard actress in a mug shot, tossing her career in the trash with both hands. 'The End.' ”

She said this wearily, Adam thought, but without self-pity. “There was a little more to it, I thought.”

Carla raised her eyebrows. “Which part? Where my show was canceled? Or where it turned out my financial manager had embezzled all my money?”

Their waitress interrupted them, taking their dinner orders — a green salad and seared ahi for Carla; calamari, swordfish, and a glass of chardonnay for Adam. Looking at her across the table, he said, “Maybe the part where you triumphed over drugs, moved to the Vineyard, and discovered my father.”

She ignored the sarcasm in his tone. “A long journey,” she said. “It began when I woke up at Betty Ford. It came to me that I might have filmed my last scene as an actress and couldn't even remember what it was. When I told your father that, I could read it in his face: I'd become what he feared most — a failure, an object of pity. But instead of despising me, all that mattered to him was that it never happen again.”

Adam struggled to imagine this. “That's more compassion than he ever showed my mother about anything."

"Maybe so. But Ben was closer to the end of his life than the beginning — too late for failure, but with time to reflect. Maybe I got the best Benjamin Blaine there was."

Adam wondered if any part of this was true. But with her story of ruin and redemption, and her claim to be innocent of Ben's intentions, Carla might well make a compelling witness on her own behalf. Probing this, he asked, "What was treatment like?"

"I had to take what they call a 'fearless moral inventory,' " Carla answered dryly, "and found out how much I had to fear. It's no fun to discover you've lived a wholly self-centered life without developing any sense of self. Or to find out you've got no money to fall back on, and no career that would be healthy to resume. So I threw myself into therapy and exercise with the same single-mindedness I'd put into acting. That's what addictive personalities do."

The waitress brought their appetizers. As the rhythm of their conversation slowed, Adam felt acutely conscious of how strange it was to be with this woman — his father's lover, the cause of his mother's humiliation. Over coffee, she finished quietly, "Coming to the Vineyard was a fluke — a fateful one, I know. I needed a place to get stronger, and my actor friends Ted and Mary knew someone with a guesthouse. The last thing I imagined was meeting Ben."

The phrase contained the hint of an apology. "But you did," Adam said, "and quickly, too."

"Not for months, actually. My life was the daily AA meeting in Vineyard Haven, the yoga studio in West Tisbury, a little painting, and reading more books than I had in years — many on psychology. I began to wonder if counseling was a possible career. I'd learned what genuine therapy can do."

Once more, Adam felt skeptical — a Hollywood ending, he thought, contrived by a woman who had Hollywood in her bones. "Not acting?" he prodded.

Carla sipped her coffee, seeming to weigh her response. "I don't think so," she said. "I'm getting used to being a private person, not depending on celebrity to fill the void inside me. One challenge is letting go of who people expect me to be. That's why I began avoiding the social scene, especially in Chilmark. Too many of those people are insecure, self-referential, and reflexively unkind. Ferreting out intimate facts about others becomes their coin of exchange."

"You sound like my father," Adam said. "I remember him saying 'a more secure bunch would have bored each other to death. Only gossip keeps them going, and gossips make lousy friends.' "

Carla smiled at this. "Ben and I were attracted for a reason, after all. Several, in fact. But celebrity wasn't one of them." Her smile vanished. "The last thing I wanted was a return engagement with the *National Enquirer*. Not that I didn't know better. But our time together will stay with me, money or no money."

For a moment, Adam remembered Carla in the light of her kitchen, washing dishes alone. No doubt she was trying to persuade him of her story. But sometimes even calculation could feed a larger need. Perhaps this woman, however beautiful, was lonely; perhaps, whatever her reasons, she mourned the loss of Adam's father.

At once, he shrank from the thought of their intimacy. Carla studied him across the table, as though reading his thoughts. Then a middle-aged woman stopped by the table until Carla looked up. "Excuse me," she said, "but could you autograph a menu for our daughter? She idolized you."

The look Carla gave her was pleasant without being welcoming. "Then I'm sure you also know what happened to me," she said politely. "Everyone does, and that's fine. But I'm just not that person anymore."

Confused, the woman stared at her. "I hope you have a good vacation," Carla finished, and allowed her a moment to withdraw. Adam gave her points for quiet grace.

"We're through with dinner," he said. "But I think you have more to say, and so do I."

Outside dusk had fallen. For a long moment, Carla gazed out the window. "That swing chair seems to be empty," she said. "Why don't we sit there."

TWELVE

They sat at the opposite ends of the swing, sheltered from view by the branches of the willow, Carla with one hand on the rope as she watched Adam's face. Even here, her posture was straight, that of a dancer. In a low voice, she said, "I want to tell you about your father. Not the one you've hated for ten years, but the Ben I knew in the last months of his life."

Adam felt bitterness seep into his speech. "There's nothing different about cheating on my mother. What's novel is the damage he inflicted on your behalf."

Carla gave him a level look, her eyes somber in a slice of moonlight. "If you don't want to listen, I can leave. We don't need to torment each other."

Either she meant it or, as Adam suspected, knew that he needed to hear her story for reasons of his own. "Go ahead," he said evenly. "I've got a strong stomach."

Carla ignored this. Instead, she seemed to gather herself, gazing at the grass. "We met when I was walking on the beach, alone," she finally said. "I knew who he was, of course. I'd met men like Ben before — all that charm, all that self-involvement, though usually with much less talent. But I was lonely, and your father never lacked for interest —"

"I'll give him that."

Carla smiled faintly. "For several days running, we just talked. No harm in *that*, I told myself. So I learned a little about the history of the island, his family, his life here. But he seemed more intent on getting me to open up —"

"Of course," Adam interrupted. "You were the only person in the world, a woman of unique value."

Carla stared at him. "Do you think I hadn't seen that one before? But I'd been alone for a long time, in some ways all my life. He had a gift for making me feel that I *did* have value, that I *could* get better, that I had the resources to redefine my life in whatever way I chose.

"Because of all he'd done, I believed him. This man had taken a life that was going nowhere — his own — and turned it into one of richness and accomplishment. And he had an energy and conviction that moved me more — or at least in a different way — than a year of speeches at AA." Her tone assumed a smoky intensity. "You'll never know what that meant to me."

Adam paused a moment, listening to the crickets, remembering those quiet summer nights on their porch when, still a boy, he sat beside his father as Ben wove a future in which Adam would achieve great things. Pushing this away, he said, "So somewhere amid this uplift, you stumbled into an affair."

Carla brushed back a tendril of hair from her forehead, a distracted gesture that, to Adam, was nonetheless strangely sensual. "I didn't stumble," she said. "The first night he wanted to make love to me he'd been drinking. I told him that was not just insensitive but insulting, and pushed him away." Her tone softened. "I expected that would be it. Instead, he apologized and asked if I would stay with him while he sobered up in the night air. We sat on my porch for an hour, saying very little, gazing at the stars and the moon. At the end he said he had a problem with alcohol — that he'd always used it to chase away the demons, and it had led to one of the worst moments in his life."

For a moment, Adam felt a shudder go through him. Then he saw that Carla was watching him closely. "What is it?" she asked.

"Nothing. Go on."

Carla turned from him, staring down. "I said that I'd keep seeing him, with all that implied. But never when he was drunk, and only on certain conditions. Before he came over, he was to call — if I felt like being with him, I'd say so. But not if he wanted to show up for an hour, sleep with me, and leave. And no talk to anyone else about our relationship." Carla paused, adding tartly, "For whatever devalued male coinage that might be worth. But when you've hit rock bottom, I told him, you don't ever want to be there again. And you don't want anyone to act as if you are.

"He just listened. At the end, he said, 'You're not that person anymore, and neither am I.' Then he left. Two nights later, he returned." She turned to Adam again. "I don't expect my sense of ethics to impress you. I entered an affair with a married man, which I'd never done before. The rules I imposed on Ben didn't change that. They just helped me live with myself."

They were also clever, Adam thought. Ben would admire her core of strength — real or feigned — and the dignity she had salvaged from the ashes of her life. "What about my mother?" Adam asked. "How did you rationalize that part?"

"Not well. Although that was less about your mother than who I wanted to become. Adultery wasn't on my checklist. And my psychoanalyst asked whether my personal stations of the cross should include stealing someone else's husband. An excellent question." Carla exhaled. "So I decided to break it off. The night I planned on doing that, Ben told me he had cancer."

Adam felt the jolt of real surprise. "When?"

"The day he came back from the neurosurgeon." She paused, her voice thickening. "He sat there, tears streaming down his face. For a long time I listened and held his hand. Then I made him walk me through his options. After he was done, I begged him to have surgery."

Reviewing his conversation with Dr. Zell, Adam knew that this part of Carla's story must be true. Nor was this account to Carla's advantage — with exclusive knowledge of his fears, and of his inevitable deterioration, she was uniquely positioned to influence Ben's decisions. Adam tried to imagine this woman occupying the role of helpmate that by rights belonged to Ben's wife of forty years.

"How did my father respond?" he finally asked.

In the silver light, Adam saw a brief pulsing in Carla's throat — remembered sadness, or grief mimed perfectly. "Ben was too frightened of the consequences — physical or mental incapacity. He asked me to help him live a few good months, then to have the best death he could." Carla bowed her head, folding her hands in her lap. "I promised I would. After all, I was used to loss. And I knew now that our affair would end without me ending it. But I never imagined how he'd die."

Unless you pushed him, Adam thought. With a slight edge in his voice, he said, "When did you last see him?"

Carla turned to him, her tone suddenly resistant. "That afternoon — as I told you at his grave. I also told you that what we said and did is personal to me." Her voice changed again. "He was dying, and knew it. In weeks, or even days."

"And you were helping him make a graceful exit."

"Actually," Carla rejoined with a trace of anger, "I felt cheated. But I also thought I'd become strong enough to face whatever came once he was gone. Thanks in part to him." She paused, then spoke with calm and directness. "You may think he'd lost it, but that's not true. To the end he was a source of strength, tenderness, and advice. And painfully lucid. Ben admitted that he'd lived a careless life, not caring about the broken china he'd left behind —"

"Broken people," Adam corrected sharply.

"He knew that. However it happened, he had deep regrets about losing you."

"A little late. As for his so-called lucidity, you never saw any symptoms of the disease?"

This was a critical point, Adam knew — Clarice, Teddy, and the neurologist could offer a persuasive catalog. "Some," Carla answered. "Ben would stumble, or slur his speech, or grope for the word he wanted. He said that he was butchering his novel, that the language wouldn't come to him —"

"Did he tell you it was about hatred between a father and son?"

Carla lowered her eyes. "I'm not surprised," she said at last. "It would have been kinder if his mind was going. Instead, Ben saw himself with merciless clarity — his present and his past." She smoothed her dress, an absent, nervous gesture. "I hadn't planned on telling you this. But that last afternoon he asked if he could live with me. Even though he was dying, I knew it was a lot for Ben to leave his home and marriage. But I said that he could come to me. Instead, I never saw him again."

"Never?"

"Meaning never. This may sound like a funny scruple. But I never set foot on your parents' property, because I knew it had been your mother's home since birth." Carla's tone hardened. "You'd like me to have pushed him, I know. That would cure your mother's financial problems, and end the police investigation of your family. But why would I kill Ben? And why would he ask to live with me, then leap to his death hours later?" She looked Adam in the face. "Someone took a dying man, unable to defend himself, and threw him off the cliff. Maybe someone in your family. No matter what else you feel, I hope that makes you as sick as it makes me."

With startling suddenness, Adam saw another building block of Sean Mallory's case against Teddy: Carla's account, if believable, made suicide seem far less likely. And it undermined Clarice's claim to have seen a woman standing on the promontory with Ben on an earlier evening — or, at least, the inference that it was Carla Pacelli.

"Let me get this straight," he rejoined. "My father told you he was dying, but failed to mention that he was leaving you ten million dollars."

Carla nodded. "Ben said that he'd take care of me. But he didn't say what that involved, and I didn't feel like interrogating a dying man."

Adam leaned forward. "Then how do you explain his bequest?"

"I don't try," Carla snapped. "At least not to you. I've told you I'm uneasy with Ben's will, and that the rest is for the lawyers to sort out. But you know better than most that their marriage was a sham."

Abruptly, Adam stood. "Not to my mother," he said with suppressed fury. "All my life I heard about my father. Right up until I left, she was worried about him and other women. And she was right to worry."

Impassive, Carla gazed up at him. "You were there. I wasn't. I apologize for insulting her." She stood to face him, placing a light hand on his arm. "I don't know how or when the court will resolve her petition. But if she fails, she can stay in the house for as long as she needs. I don't cherish the idea of being her landlord, or serving up eviction notices."

"But that's where my father put you."

"Not because I asked him to, or because he was insane." She paused, then finished in the same even tone. "If you'd still been speaking to him, you'd understand that the last few months were the sanest of his life. Cancer allowed Ben to see himself whole, and hope that some good lived after him. Whether or not you think that I bewitched him, how else do you explain his gift to Jenny Leigh?"

"I have no idea," Adam retorted. "Do you?"

"I think so. Ben read me one of her short stories in a literary magazine, and told me she had talent. His career had been a lucky one, he said — these days a writer's life is even harder. Especially for a young woman from the Vineyard who'd had even fewer breaks than him." Carla's voice softened. "I thought he might do something to help her. Maybe he imagined that a piece of him would live through her. But if that impulse was in any way selfish, Jenny was the beneficiary."

A crosscurrent of emotions silenced Adam. One clear, cool thought emerged — this account of his father's generosity, the act of a sane and compassionate man, strengthened Carla's case for upholding the will. And the intensity of her gaze, the light touch of her fingers on his arm, suggested how deeply she wanted him to believe this.

"I know what you're thinking," she told him. "But I've only lied to you once, for reasons of my own, and not about Jenny or the will. Even by the standards of a 'fearless moral inventory' I can live with that." She removed her hand, drawing back a step, still looking into his eyes. "Good night, Adam. Thank you for dinner."

For a moment, he was frozen there. Before he could respond, Carla turned and left.

THIRTEEN

Leaving Atria, Adam drove down Water Street and parked in the shadow of the Edgartown lighthouse. The image of Carla Pacelli lingered in his mind.

I've only lied to you once, for reasons of my own, and not about Jenny or the will.

Refocusing his thoughts, he watched the porch of the Harbor View Hotel. Forty minutes passed, time dragging in the darkness. Then the woman came through the door, glancing at her watch, and walked swiftly toward the parking lot. As Adam had instructed her, she was alone.

Starting his car, he turned into a side street and waited. In minutes, her car passed along the only route toward Chilmark. Adam turned in the same direction as though by coincidence. For twenty minutes, he trailed her until she reached the cemetery where his father lay, satisfying himself that she would not pick up anyone else. Then he slowed, watching her taillights vanish around a curve, and pulled onto the dirt road toward his home.

It was nearly midnight; no lights came from the house or guesthouse. Parking on the gravel driveway, Adam hurried in the darkness toward the promontory, recalling the shadowy presence that had followed him on the evening he had met with Nathan Wright. On the cliffside, the night was dark and cool and quiet, the only sound the susurrus of waves on the rocky beach below. For a second, he imagined himself as Benjamin Blaine.

Someone took a dying man, unable to defend himself, and threw him off the cliff. Maybe someone in your family. No matter what else you feel, I hope that makes you as sick as it makes me.

Slowly, Adam climbed down the stairs toward the place his father had landed. The distance his father had fallen in the darkness made his skin feel clammy. He imagined the last seconds of Ben's life, as he hurtled through the night toward his doom.

You might ask Teddy, Bobby Towle had told him, *the last time he was at the promontory.*

Reaching the bottom, Adam turned from the site of his father's death, walking toward the water. Here the tide was a continual low rumble, punctuated by the deep echoing surge of six-foot waves striking land. Thick clouds blocked the moon. His surroundings were monochrome — starless sky, dark water, darkened beach. Briefly, Adam took out the night vision goggles he used in Afghanistan.

Walking toward him along the shoreline was the lone figure of a woman. He waited, shivering in the chill wind.

Spotting him, she briefly stopped, then closed the remaining distance. Only when she stood before him could Adam see her features.

Amanda Ferris looked into his face. "Why are we meeting like this?" she said. "At midnight, in the loneliest place on earth. I keep wondering if you're a serial killer."

The reporter's voice was slightly louder than required to carry over the pounding surf. Perhaps it was nerves, Adam thought; perhaps not. Calmly, he said, "First take out your tape recorder. I'd guess it's in the pocket of your blouse."

Her face and eyes became immobile. "What do you mean?"

Now Adam was quite certain. "Do it," he snapped. "Or go back to the swamp you came from."

Ferris's shoulders turned in, as though she were hunched against the cold. Then she reached into her pocket and held out a digital tape recorder in the palm of her hand. "Erase my voice," Adam ordered. "Then throw it at the water."

Ferris stiffened. "Take it, if you like. Then give it back when we're through."

"With my fingerprints on it?" Adam said coldly. "Quit playing with me. You're not qualified."

Ferris stared at him. Then she erased the tape and flung it into the surf with an angry underhand motion. "Who *are* you?" she demanded.

"You've already researched me on the internet," Adam replied. "Not to mention calling Agracon. As to why I'm doing this, you'll understand by the time we're through. But 'off the record' doesn't cover this encounter. Except for the benefit to your career, the next half hour never happened."

Watching her eyes, Adam took stock of her once again — bright, determined, and aggressive, with a good measure of cupidity and amoral curiosity. Her job was not about anything save the public desire to pick the bones of celebrities like Carla Pacelli and his father — or, perhaps, become one. At times, Adam was glad that he no longer lived in America.

"All right," Ferris said sharply. "Let's talk about what both of us want."

"I already know what you want," Adam replied. "You think someone killed my father — that's why you're still here. But you're getting nowhere with the state police." Adam glanced up at the promontory. "Like you, I'm curious about how my father fell from there to here. Unlike you, I can't pay people to find out. But I do know who might take your money."

Shifting her weight, Ferris studied him with narrowed eyes. "Explain to me what you get from this."

"First let's talk about what you need. To start, you want the complete autopsy report, focusing on the marks on my father's body or evidence on his clothes — rips, mud, hairs or saliva that weren't his. The report is under wraps, so that's a bit of a trick —"

"In other words," she interjected, "someone will have to sell it —"

"Next you'll want the evidence they found on the promontory, including footprints and any signs of a struggle. Beyond that, you'll need the witness statements — especially from my family, Carla Pacelli, and Jenny Leigh."

"That's a lot to get."

"You're a clever woman, and money will make you smarter. As for me, I want copies of everything — starting with the autopsy report. And I expect to hear what you know before you print it." Pausing, Adam spoke slowly and deliberately. "Don't even dream of holding out on me, Amanda. If you do, I've already figured out how to get you indicted for obstruction of justice —"

"You're joking."

"Hardly. You've got three choices — failure, a career-making story, or a potential stretch in prison. The risks you should be taking aren't with me. From what I've learned, your career is on the bubble. So how badly do you need this story?"

Almost imperceptibly, Ferris seemed to recoil. In an undertone, she said, "You're a very strange and scary person. It's pretty much common knowledge that you couldn't stand your father."

"I'm rethinking our relationship. So how much nerve do you have? I can always go to TMZ.com."

Ferris clamped her lips, then nodded.

"Good," Adam said. "While you're at it, check out Carla Pacelli. From the rumors I've picked up, she claims to have known nothing about the will before he died. Prove that false, and her entire story unravels.

That would interest me."

"And the *Enquirer*," Ferris agreed. "So tell me where I start."

Feeling the tug of conscience, Adam hesitated. His deepest loyalty, he told himself, must be to his mother and brother. When he spoke, his mouth felt dry. "There's a policeman in Chilmark," he answered in a monotone. "He can't ever know I've given you his name, and, as best you can, I want you to protect him. But he's in desperate need of money."

After she had gone, Adam remained on the beach, his soul leaden. His mind framed useless apologies to Bobby Towle.

How did I get here? he thought. *How did all of us get here?* He did not want to face the world, or himself.

At length, he found a familiar patch of sand in the shadow of the promontory. Ten years ago, at night, he had picnicked here with Jenny.

How else do you explain his gift to Jenny Leigh?

A central question, Adam knew. But now he could barely stand to look at her. He sat back, envisioning her face before time had poisoned his memories.

That evening, the air had been balmy,

dusk peaceful and enveloping. The surf was a whisper, not a roar; the cloudless night when it came distilled light from a full moon. Listening to Jenny, Adam had loved her as only a young man could love.

It was just after she invented Celebrity Pac-Man. Wrapped with Adam in a blanket, she explained the scoring system for social avarice in Chilmark. As her inventiveness grew, her voice filled with wonder at the hungers of the human psyche. Finishing, she said, "It's sort of sad-funny, isn't it. Funny because of the way these people scheme to drop the name of someone like your dad, sad because their relationships aren't real — even with themselves. It must be terrible to feel so empty."

She sounded like his father, Adam thought, but far kinder. "You have the soul of a writer, Jenny. To me, the worst books are those where you feel nothing for the characters but pity or contempt, and wind up depleted at the end. But even your sharpest observations are leavened with compassion."

Impulsively, Jenny kissed him. "How do you know if you've never read my writing?"

"And how can I read your writing," Adam replied with humor and frustration, "if you won't let me?"

"It's a problem," Jenny said blithely, and then her voice became quiet. "I'm sorry. But so much of it is personal to me."

And painful, Adam suspected. "Lovemaking is personal, too," he answered lightly. "And we do that all the time."

Only when he said this did he connect her writing to Jenny as a lover, both of them elusive in different ways. He could know her body and yet, in their most intimate moments, there was something beyond his grasp. But now she was snuggling against him. "If that was a hint," she murmured, "I just might be available. But only if I'm on top. This sand's a lot harder than the bed in your parents' guesthouse."

Adam felt his body stir. With feigned casualness, he replied, "Oh, all right. As long as you let me try something first."

"Such as?"

"It's a surprise. The only clue is that it requires an absence of clothes."

"I think we've already been there," she said reproachfully.

Adam grinned. "I promise you we haven't."

When she was naked, Jenny straddled him. But instead of slipping inside her, Adam grasped her hips and lowered the moistness between her thighs onto his warm mouth. "Oh," she whispered in surprise, and then said nothing at all.

Eyes closed, Adam could feel her body quiver as, gently and without hurry, he brought her to the edge. Then she cried out, the spasm running through her.

"Now me," he said, and lowered her toward his hips. When he entered her, he gazed into her face, and saw that her eyes had closed, her face frozen in a blank mask. "Look at me, Jenny," Adam urged.

But she did not. Only after she came again did her face soften, and then tears ran down her cheeks. "Lie down beside me," Adam requested softly.

She curled with her back to him, wordless for a time. "It's not you," she said in a muted voice. "I go somewhere else."

"Tell me, Jen."

"I can't yet." Her voice became broken, bereft. "We'll be all right, I promise."

FOURTEEN

Just after dawn, Adam and his uncle met at the trailhead to Sepiessa, walking in first light through the trees and brush along the Tisbury Great Pond.

This had always been Jack and Adam's favorite hour, when the natural world of the Vineyard seemed as new as creation. The grass glistened with dew; the water shimmered with shards of light; birds called from the branches of oaks; the air, scented by foliage, cooled Adam's face. But today his thoughts, and his conscience, were weighted by his pact with Amanda Ferris. At length, his uncle asked, "Feeling life's burdens?"

"Burdens," Adam said simply. "And confusions."

He felt Jack's gaze as they continued along a path dappled with light and shadow. In the same reticent tone, Jack said, "Your thoughts are your own, Adam. But if there's some way I can help —"

He let the question hang there. All at once, Adam recalled how straightforward their relationship had always been — by comparison with Ben, to be sure, but also his mother and Teddy. As before, he felt the comfort of Jack's company, redolent of the times when Adam had failed at something, and Jack had offered consolation and perspective instead of Ben's razor-sharp critiques. Talking with Jack was safe.

"It's about Dad's death," Adam said at length. "I'm pretty sure someone killed him."

Face creased with thought, Jack gazed at the trail in front of them as it wound deeper into the woods. At last, he said, "Why does this have to be murder? Granted, it's hard to imagine Ben tumbling off the cliff by accident, even sick as he was. But ever since I learned that he had brain cancer, I've thought he might have jumped."

"That's hard for me to accept."

"Because you remember Ben as he was. It seems like this disease was stealing his identity, piece by piece — he couldn't write, couldn't sail, maybe could no longer make love to Carla Pacelli. He could have looked at what he was becoming and figured it was time." Jack slowed his steps, turning to face his nephew. "No one saw him die. Even if

294

you're right, this may be a case where someone literally gets away with murder. I wonder if you can live with that."

Suppose, Avram Gold had said, *you find out your father was murdered by a member of your family. Is that something you really want to know?* "Without knowing who did it," Adam replied, "I can't say."

"But you do know the four people most impacted by the will. Two of whom are Teddy and your mother."

Edgy, Adam wondered if Jack — like him — knew something about Teddy neither wanted to say. "And your point?"

"That both of us may never know, and the police may never solve this. What matters most is helping your mother gain back what Ben took."

There was wisdom in this, Adam conceded. But he knew too much, including about Teddy, and Jack's way was not his. "Anyway," Jack concluded, "you've spent more time worrying about Ben's death than being with your living mother."

His comment was typical of Jack, Adam thought, and fair enough. "I'm still too much like him, aren't I?"

"Maybe so," Jack answered. "But life is long."

Perhaps not mine, Adam thought, and

continued walking with his uncle.

Wondering if this were the last time, Adam steered Ben's powerboat from its mooring near their home, taking his mother for lunch along Edgartown Harbor.

It was a crystalline day from his youth, evoking again how deeply he had cherished Vineyard summers — a cloudless blue sky, temperate air, a cool breeze, spray thrown up into his face by the knife edge of the prow. Through some trick of the mind, Clarice looked as he remembered her — younger, her eyes brighter, a half smile on her face as she let activity dull her worries. Taking a course along the North Shore, Adam recalled similar outings with Teddy and his mother, their destination the street fair in Vineyard Haven; or Oak Bluffs with its crowded waterfront and gingerbread Victorians; or the Old Whaling Church to hear some local musician of their acquaintance. It brought back how spirited Clarice could be — always up for an adventure, with an energy and a spirit that lightened the burden of Ben's imperious nature. The thought summoned a fleeting smile of his own.

Clarice seemed to understand this. "We had fun then, didn't we?"

"Yeah, Mom. We did."

Rounding Cedar Tree Neck, Adam saw the low hill above the beach where, that summer, Jenny and he had watched the sun die, turning the water a muted blue-gray. "A promontory of our own," Adam had told her wryly. Perhaps his mother read this thought. "Have you seen Jenny yet?" she asked.

"No time," Adam said, then decided to cut to the quick of this. "You keep mentioning Jenny, and I keep wondering why."

As Clarice appraised him, he sensed her avoiding confrontation. "I love Jenny," she said simply. "Whatever happens with this will, she's been like a daughter to me. Wonderful as you two boys may be, I needed a young woman on whom to inflict my good intentions."

Beneath its surface, Adam knew, the remark was laden with a significance he was meant to grasp. "When we were seeing each other, you barely knew her. What changed that?"

Struck by a wave, the powerboat jolted, knocking Adam off-balance as it threw up spumes of white. Righting himself, he saw Clarice grasping the arm of her deck chair, her lips compressed, her blue eyes reflecting her reluctance to answer and her need to do so. "In a way, Adam, it had to do with you. Even though you were gone."

Adam felt his exasperation warring with the instinct that he wished to hear no more. "For godsakes," he said at length, "are you going to be passive-aggressive all the way to Edgartown? Please put this verbal pas de deux out of its misery."

Clarice's countenance took on a determined air. "All right," she said in her flattest tone. "Two days after you left, Jenny tried to kill herself."

Adam felt the shock run through him. But all he could say was, "How?"

"She overdosed on Quaaludes. Your father found her on our beach and carried her up the stairs on his shoulders. She was limp, her face as white as china. But for Ben, she'd be dead."

Half-conscious of doing so, Adam throttled back the motor, dreading the answer to the question he must ask. "Did Jenny ever say why?"

"Never. Nor did she scrawl a suicide note in the sand." Clarice lowered her voice. "We *were* your parents, Adam. Perhaps she didn't want us to know."

"God damn you, Mother," Adam burst out. "Hearing this is bad enough without you blaming me. No matter how much pleasure you're taking from it." Seeing her blanch, he muted his tone. "Why didn't you tell me?"

"How?" Clarice snapped. "You didn't exactly leave a forwarding address. We didn't even know where you were. So forgive me if I sound bitter." She crossed her arms. "In any event, Jenny swore me to secrecy. Especially from you."

Killing the motor, Adam let them bob in a cone of silence. At length, he said, "I take it you got her help."

"A great deal of help. For two months she was hospitalized at Mass General. Your father paid for everything." Clarice paused, then spoke in a different register. "Despite what he's done to me, Ben saved her life. I expect that explains his bequest."

Carla had proposed one theory, Adam thought, his mother another. And neither of them knew. "Other than my departure," he inquired, "did you divine any reason why a twenty-year-old girl would decide to end her life?"

Reproach resurfaced in Clarice's eyes. "Not to a certainty. Medically, her doctors at Mass General proposed bipolar disorder, or schizoaffective disorder — which is far more dangerous. Or even post-traumatic stress disorder —"

"The trauma being?"

"Nobody knows. And Jenny couldn't — or wouldn't — help." Clarice's tone became less harsh. "Bipolar disorder tends to surface between sixteen and twenty-two. Did you see any signs of it?"

Remembering Jenny as she was, Adam felt a deepening sadness. "Looking back, her moods would shift abruptly. The swings could be pretty wide."

"That's what the doctors said. At first they kept her in lockdown, then heavily medicated. Her mother was working, and not much help. So I stayed there for days at a time."

Adam felt obscurely shamed — not just about Jenny, but that he had known nothing about such a central piece of his mother's life. "Now I understand why Jenny is so important to you."

"Do you?" A film of tears appeared in his mother's eyes. "Ben dominated our lives. First he'd driven Teddy away, and then you simply vanished. But now I had Jenny. Every day I watched her coming back to life. Sometimes we'd talk, and sometimes she'd let me brush her hair." Clarice's voice thickened. "When at last she was better, Jenny's mother drove her home. But by then we were bonded in a way more profound than blood. My husband was unfaithful, my sons missing. But Jenny helped fill my life.

"She still does. Sometimes we fly to New York, shopping or going to galleries or the theater. Every few days we'll meet for lunch or dinner, or just go for a walk. The thing she rarely does is come to the house. She says it reminds her too much of you."

Once more, Adam felt a wave of guilt and anger. "After all these years, why should I still matter?"

"My theory? To Jenny, you represent an ideal. When you left, she lost the one man she'd ever loved." Clarice leaned forward, as if to reach him. "You're not a woman, so you may not understand this. But I think that Jenny is capable of loving you, and hoping you'd return, for the entire decade you were gone. Some women are like that, no matter how little encouragement they get."

In the crosscurrent of his emotions, Adam felt sadness prevail. "Tell me what her life is like."

"She's had some success getting her stories published. Day to day, she works mornings in an art gallery and spends time with women friends like me. Romantically, she's had a series of unsatisfying relationships, often with older men." Clarice paused. "Jenny has come to believe she's been trying to replace her father, who abandoned them when she was eleven. She's ready for something deeper."

Adam gazed out at the water. For a while the boat drifted, rudderless, mother and son sharing long moments of silence. Then Adam started the motor again, remaining quiet until the boat rounded West Chop, the estates of WASP families as privileged as Clarice's once had been. "I have an awkward subject of my own," he said. "Last night I saw Carla Pacelli."

His mother's eyes widened in hurt and dismay, as though Adam, like Ben, had betrayed her. "For what earthly reason did you do that?"

"My duties as executor, an excuse for helping you sub rosa. But something strange came up."

"Which was?"

"Apparently, my father suggested to her that your marriage was a 'sham' — quote unquote. I took it to mean that you were no longer intimate. Or perhaps that you were unfaithful, too."

Clarice's jaw clenched in anger. "How pathetic," she said scornfully. "That Carla believed it, or that you believed Carla. Even men like Ben make excuses for infidelity. It only surprises me that he bothered."

"So it's not true."

"Hardly. Though at times I wished it were. Feeling alone in a marriage is worse than *being* alone." She shook her head, as if at her wasted years. "On the subject of solitude, let's get back to Jenny. No matter what you feel now, there's no harm in being kind to her."

Silent, Adam tried to imagine how it felt to prefer oblivion. Then another memory came to him, more telling now than then.

They had taken North Road to the entrance of a hiking trail, Alicia Keys on his CD player, then climbed through woods and fields until they reached Waskosims Rock.

They sat at the crest of the hill, looking out. Even at this elevation, they could not see the water; the scene before them, miles of woods and farmland and stone walls, was rolling and pastoral, a portrait of New England. "At moments like this," Adam said, "I want to live here all my life."

Jenny kept watching the horizon. "How long will that be? I wonder."

Adam smiled. "I'm planning on forever. I'm too afraid of dying. Like Dad, I guess."

Jenny considered him. "Not me," she answered softly. "From what I've read, it's just as well. Often people like me don't live past thirty."

Troubled, Adam grasped her hand. "What 'people like you'?"

Jenny gazed down and then, quite suddenly, conjured her brightest smile. "Brilliant, of course. It's such a burden being me. So much talent, so little understood."

But Adam was not mollified. He kissed her gently, then looked into her face. Impulsively, he said, "I won't let anything happen to you, Jen. I promise."

Closing her eyes, Jenny rested her head on his shoulder.

Ten years later, Adam remembered the catch in his throat. "I'll go see her," he told his mother. "I promise."

FIFTEEN

Late that afternoon, Adam climbed into his father's truck and took South Road to the intersection crossing over to Menemsha. The lawn of one of several great houses overlooking the pond was covered with tables beneath umbrellas, the scene of a wedding or fund-raiser or dinner party, reminding Adam that he was moving through this summer season without taking any note of it. His family's past and present had consumed him; the summer most vivid to him had happened years ago.

Reaching Menemsha, Adam walked along the dock. Charlie Glazer was tending to his Herreshoff, *Folie à Un,* the boat he had raced against Ben for many seasons. The psychiatrist waved Adam on board, fixing him with a bright, inquisitive expression as his visitor sat across from him. "Sorry to trouble you," Adam said, "and so soon at that. But things have started crashing down on me."

Glazer's eyes became graver. "Concerning Ben's death? Or your relationship when he was still alive?"

"Both."

Glazer nodded slowly. "Yesterday I felt this coming. It seems we have a lot to cover, much of it painful. So you can start this any way you like."

Adam bent forward. Closing his eyes, he was barely conscious of the cries of gulls, the great pond flecked with boats, the gentle rocking of the Herreshoff in its slip. "Let's begin with that summer," he said.

For over an hour, Adam talked, gazing at the shoreline he barely saw. He felt Glazer watch him fixedly. But except to clarify a point, the psychiatrist said nothing. Only at the end did he permit himself an audible intake of breath. "That's a lot to carry around, Adam. And to conceal. I suppose your work helps you compartmentalize."

"More than that. I have an existence no one in my family can imagine. I've developed this distance — physical and emotional." Adam paused, trying to explain a sensation foreign to almost everyone he encountered. "I've learned to split off from the past, or even what's happening to me in the moment. In effect I've become a differ-ent person, who can stuff even the worst experience until it's time to face it."

Glazer regarded him closely. "And now your father's dead, and you're ten years harder. And coming back has forced you to confront the reasons that you left."

"So it seems. I'd like to exhume the past, then bury it for good. At least to the extent I can."

Glazer hunched in his chair, blue eyes fixed on Adam. "And that racing season was the catalyst, you believe."

"For both of us. Without that, I'm certain, I'd have gone back to school and become a lawyer."

"And married Jenny?"

Adam closed his eyes again, his voice lower and quieter. "I'll never know, will I? All I'm sure of is that one summer on this pond changed everything."

In Adam's understanding now, the annual competition for the Herreshoff Cup caught the primal essence of his father: a ruthless competitive drive, an ineradicable class envy, the lust to subordinate other men. The novels, the accolades, the women — none of that was enough. There was also the bat-tered silver trophy with a half century of victors engraved on its side. By 2001, Benjamin Blaine had stamped his name on it seven times; this summer, as before, the cup sat on their dining room table like a prize of war.

From his father's earliest memory, Adam knew, he had been captivated by the sight of these gaff-rigged boats, so perfect in design, racing one another on the pond from which his drunken father had extracted lobster — at once a wondrous spectacle, a privilege of wealth, and a contest between competitors stripped of all excuses. As a youth, Ben had begged his way onto the boat of a wealthy man, Clarice's father; as a man, he had bought her father's house, then his Herreshoff — the boat he had always craved, a wooden-hulled classic from the early 1900s, as beautiful as it was balanced. With what seemed an act of fraternal generosity, but which Adam now perceived as malignant perversity, his father had purchased a companion boat for Jack. So that every summer, on these same waters, Ben could remind his older brother of which man had transcended Nathaniel Blaine.

The occasion was the summer races sponsored by the Menemsha Pond Racing Club, a preserve of skilled sailors who, quite often, were also celebrated as actors, writers, musicians, and lions of industry or Wall Street — or, for several seasons, a scientist and a doctor who had both won the Nobel Prize. As a teenager, Ben had crewed for affluent Brahmins; in adulthood, he had recruited Adam to race with him against Jack and Teddy. The stated reason was to give Jack the oldest and most experienced son. But, again and again, Ben and Adam prevailed. Against his deepest inclinations, Teddy sailed on with great determination, unwilling to beg off. Perceiving his brother's silent humiliation, Adam understood Ben's real purpose — to show Teddy that, like Jack, he did not measure up to his younger brother. So it was Adam who, at twelve, had refused to extend the fraternal rivalry.

After this Ben had sailed alone. It became his pride that, without Adam, he could outrace men who had devoted their lives to sailing. Not until 2001 did Adam sail again — this time against his father.

On the surface, this had come about by accident. Adam had gone on one of his uncle's practice sails, two weeks before the racing season began and a day after he had played mind games with his father on the eighteenth hole at Farm Neck. The story had reduced his uncle to laughter, eyes bright with merriment and a rare touch of malice. "Wish I'd been there," Jack remarked. "His face must have been a study."

Adam grinned. "In granite. I'm afraid I didn't let the moment pass without remarking on the aging process. All he could do is express the pointless wish that I'd race him in a boat that I don't have."

Glancing at the mainsail, Jack adjusted the tiller. At length, he said, "There's always this one, Adam. Maybe you should take my place."

"Why?" Adam asked in surprise. "You've been racing this forever."

"And losing. It's pretty clear that I can't beat him. Now it's your turn to try."

Adam felt a stab of doubt. "I'm not sure, Jack. You know how he always needs to be top dog — even within this family. Won't that create another problem for you both?"

Jack shrugged. "Maybe for him. But what can Ben say? That he's afraid you'll beat him for the Cup?"

"I can't beat him," Adam said flatly.

"You can, though." Facing him, Jack said with quiet conviction, "I've watched you sail, summer after summer. You've learned more from him than either of you know — and a bit from me as well. Now you can teach him how to lose."

■ ■ ■ ■

Listening, Glazer touched a finger to his lips. "Did you understand how provocative that was? Your father buys Jack a boat so that Ben could keep on beating him. And instead your uncle enables Ben's own son to compete with him as Jack's surrogate."

"I understood. Not as well as I did later, but well enough."

"But still you competed," Glazer probed.

"Yes," Adam responded. "I wanted to beat him. Jack knew that as well."

In the first race in July, Adam climbed into Jack's boat.

Since Jack had recruited him, Adam had sailed *Sisyphus* for days. To his surprise, piloting the boat felt like second nature. The Herreshoff sailed easily, rudder instantly responsive to the tiller in Adam's grasp as his free hand gripped the mainsheet, pulling or releasing the rope to control the sail. The real challenge was presented by the pond itself — the currents were tricky and the winds capricious, often shifting at ten-second intervals to blow *Sisyphus* off course. And Adam's practice runs, however disciplined, were nothing compared to the races as he remembered them: forty-five minutes so intense they felt like hours — an unremitting war of nerves and concentration and the iron will to win, competitors fighting to stay closest to the wind, to divine its shifts in seconds, to seize the right-of-way from boats a few feet distant. His father was the master.

Cruising toward the starting line, Adam saw Ben to his left, narrowed gaze focused on the course before them. The thirteen boats around his made a stunning armada, their sails swelling in a stiff breeze. By tradition, the commodore of the club, Paul Taylor, had the power to design the race course for each challenge, altering the location and sequence of the six numbered markers as he saw fit, his sole guide the weather conditions and the velocity and current direction of the wind. That afternoon a hazy sun filtered through a fog creeping in from the south; the prevailing winds blew twelve knots from the southwest: the tide, rushing in, created enough chop to wet the sailors before they started. Not the worst of days, Adam thought, but test enough for his maiden race.

Ignoring each other, father and son forged on toward the starting line.

The commodore had laid it east of the

channel from the Vineyard Sound at a 90-degree angle to the wind, one end marked by a bright orange buoy, the other by the committee boat. Sailing by the committee boat, Adam saw the commodore holding up the course he'd crayoned on a waxed whiteboard. Taut, he heard five blasts of the air horn that announced the minutes left until the race began.

As he edged toward the line, Adam's stomach felt empty. Four blasts, then three, then two. Fourteen boats converged in the mist, jockeying for the ideal spot to start, the air filled with skippers shouting at one another — "Come up — don't try to fit in there, you've got no rights." Adam angled for a starboard tack without fouling Charlie Glazer. Noting this, the psychiatrist smiled, waving in acknowledgment.

The pace of the air horn quickened. At one minute and thirty seconds, Adam heard one long and three short blasts; a single blast marked one minute. Ben's boat, the *Icarus,* sliced in near Adam on the starboard side.

Thirty seconds — three short blasts. Ben was beside him now. Two short blasts at twenty seconds, a single sharp blast at ten. A chill spray dampened Adam's face. Five quick blasts marked the last few seconds.

In unison, Ben and Adam crossed the starting line.

Adam grasped the tiller and mainsheet, straining to catch the wind. With mixed tension and exhilaration, he felt the two boats beginning to clear the fleet. Already their contest felt visceral — they raced in parallel, a mere twenty feet apart, Ben barely ahead of his son.

For an instant, Ben glanced at Adam, then bent all his efforts to seizing each shift of wind. The fog kept lowering, obscuring the water ahead. At the first marker, then the second, Ben maintained his lead. Looking back, Adam saw that this race belonged to the two of them. For the first time, he sensed that he could match his father.

Another marker, then another, the two men battling the wind and each other. Gusts of air buffeted Adam's face. He bent at the knees for balance, muscles aching, his palm chafed by the mainsail he gripped too tight.

At mark five, the wind shifted abruptly.

Ben saw this first. Sailing into the wind, he began switching his mainsail, first to starboard, then to port, then back to starboard as he beat toward the finish line. Sinews burning, Adam fought to catch him, but Ben sailed closer to the wind, gaining precious feet on Adam. Then Adam caught a wind shift before Ben did and surged within a half-length of his father.

Just ahead, Ben peered at the misty surface of the pond. Abruptly, he changed course, his bow cutting across Adam's. At the last minute, Ben veered away. Suddenly, Adam saw the lobster pots ahead concealed by his father's ploy. As Ben cleared them, Adam fought to change course — five feet, then four, his mainsail luffing. Then Adam felt the sickening, unmistakable sensation of the pot's warp scratching along his wooden hull, *Sisyphus* lurching as the pot's line snagged between her rudder and keel.

Squelching his fury, Adam leaped into the pond, diving under *Sisyphus*'s stern to free the rudder. Deftly, he untangled the line, then clambered back into the boat soaking wet. No more than a minute lost, but enough. Helpless, Adam watched his father's back as *Icarus* tacked toward the finish. Ben had stolen his victory.

Teeth gritted, Adam felt his father's hatred of quitting swell within him. In some crevice of his mind he knew that in the total of points for a season, he must stay within striking distance of the only rival that now mattered. For bitter moments, he battled the elements and Charlie Glazer for second place. With a last shift in the wind, he reached the finish a boat's length ahead.

Easing toward the dock, Ben circled. The two men passed in opposite directions, Ben smiling slightly without acknowledging his son.

A wise man knows the grace of silence, his father had told him. Suffused with anger, Adam silently promised that the race would go on.

Listening, Charlie Glazer looked somber. "I remember that day very well," he told Adam. "But until today I never knew what it meant."

Adam felt drained. "How many times, I wonder, have I wished that I'd never stepped back inside that boat. But I did, and everything followed."

"You couldn't have known," Glazer consoled him. "In a few days let's talk more."

SIXTEEN

Jenny Leigh lived off a rutted dirt road hacked through the woods in the middle of the island. The rough-hewn cabin she rented sat on a glade surrounded by trees, its deck sheltered by a grove of pines. It was a place of quiet and seclusion and, to Adam, isolation — though reachable by all-terrain vehicles in the summer, the cabin could be sealed in for days by a winter snowstorm. As he took the gravel driveway rising to the cabin, a deer skittered across his path. This time, preoccupied with Jenny, Adam did not flinch.

He parked, walking across the grass to her cabin in the soft light of early evening. He paused there, conflicted, then rapped softly on the door.

Through the screened windows he heard a stirring, then footsteps. He felt a tightness in his chest. The door cracked open; in the space she peered through, Jenny's expression changed from wariness to surprise, and then she managed a smile that did not erase the caution in her eyes. "I'd hoped you'd come," she said. "Then I was afraid you would. Or wouldn't."

"Can I come in?"

"Of course."

Inside was a small living room with a table and two chairs, a single place mat marking where Jenny ate alone. The décor was simple — a couch, two wooden chairs, pieces of driftwood in one corner, and bright abstract paintings offset by one of Teddy's stark winter landscapes. There were dishes in the sink, an open book on an end table, and a jacket on a hook beside the front door. It was neater than he had expected from a woman who, when younger, could within hours turn any space she occupied into something that, Adam had told her, evoked the contents of a madwoman's brain.

"Would you like to see the rest?" she inquired awkwardly. "It won't take long."

Adam followed her, surprised further by the neatly turned bed, the papers carefully arranged on a blond wooden table larger than the one at which she ate. Even her clothes seemed to be in drawers and closets instead of strewn on chairs. Looking about him, Adam inquired, "What on earth did they do to you?"

At once, she grasped the reference. "I guess you were expecting chaos?"

"At the least." He turned to her, adding softly, "My mother told me, Jenny."

She glanced at the floor, then looked directly at him. "That I tried to kill myself, you mean."

"And nearly succeeded. She rebuked me for my lack of grace."

Her eyelids lowered. "Is that why you're here?"

"I might have come without that." Unsure what else to do with them, he put his hands in his pockets. "I wish I'd known."

She looked up at him with new directness. "About my pitiful attempt at suicide? I didn't want you to, Adam. That was all I had left."

"What, exactly?"

"My own dignity."

Adam regarded her, unsure of what to say. "Sit with me," she said. "Please."

He sat on the couch. Jenny settled beside him, neither too close nor too far away. For an odd moment he thought of Carla Pacelli, regarding him gravely from the other end of a chair swing. "Tell me how you are, Jen."

"I'm all right." Smiling briefly at herself, she amended this. "You could say I'm even. At whatever cost to artistic inspiration, the meds seem to level me out." Her tone was factual and resigned. "With lithium, they tell me, I've got a better than fifty-fifty chance of remaining stable. But I'll be on it for the rest of my life."

Or my life may be shorter, she did not need to add. Tentative, Adam remarked, "It's quiet here. That must help your writing."

She seemed to read his expression. Adam, whose work rewarded inscrutability, realized that he had not become opaque to Jenny Leigh. In the same flat voice, she said, "If I don't try it again, you mean."

"The thought struck me, yes. It seems lonely here."

Jenny shook her head. "To me, it seems peaceful. And safe. I've come to realize that I'm better at perceiving life than living it. I'm afraid my stories reflect that."

Between them, Adam knew, was a constraint she felt as deeply as he. But she also seemed more self-aware, less prone to moods. Watching him closely, she said, "Your mom says you're working in Afghanistan."

"Yes. As an agricultural consultant."

"For which crops? Is there anything there

320

besides opium?"

"Not much. Taken all in all, it's the worst job in the firm. But I'm single, and someone had to go."

Jenny's eyes became questioning and a little sad. "You were going to be a lawyer, Adam."

He did not wish to pursue this. "And you were going to be a writer — and are. I've read some of your stories."

"You have?"

"Uh-huh. Once you began to be published, you couldn't hide them from me. They're good."

Jenny gave him the same ghost of a smile, probing his eyes for the truth. " 'Good'?" she repeated.

Adam marshaled his thoughts. "I think you have great talent. The stories are observant and precisely written, with every word the right one." He paused. "Also a little detached. Like you're holding back from expressing pain."

To his surprise, Jenny nodded. "So my therapist tells me. But he seems to think I'm creeping forward — in art and in life. So I'm trying to integrate all that into a novel."

"Your first?"

"And maybe my last." She paused, then

added, "This one hurts."

The way she said this made him wonder why. "But you're keeping at it."

"I have to," she said with quiet resolve. "In that sense your father's advice had value. One key to writing is to show up every day. A good reason to stay alive."

Adam felt a stab of pain. Softly, he said, "I hate what happened. To both of us."

To his distress, Jenny's mouth trembled, and then tears sprung to her eyes. She looked away, mutely shaking her head.

He moved closer. "You're doing better, Jen. I can see that."

Crossing her arms, she gained control of herself again. "Then I'm glad."

For several moments Adam was silent, still sitting beside her on the couch. In a reluctant voice, he asked, "There's something I need to ask you, Jenny."

Still unable to look at him, she said miserably, "What?"

"Did you know about his bequest to you?"

Silent, Jenny shook her head again.

"Do you have any idea why my father did that?"

With seeming effort, she straightened her body. In a voice etched with irony, she said, "He liked my story, remember?"

"I remember it well. Now he's left me with

another poisoned chalice." Adam's tone grew firmer. "This isn't about you — or us. But if I can help my mom and Teddy break that will, I have to."

She squared her shoulders. "I know. What he did to your mother was incredibly cruel."

"And so perfectly in character," he responded bitterly. "His final touch was pitting you against my mother with me in the middle. This particular act of cruelty has a certain geometric elegance."

Jenny closed her eyes, speaking in a near whisper. "After I tried to kill myself, Clarice treated me like a daughter. But for her —"

She could not finish. For one moment, a reflex, Adam wanted to take her hand. Then he recalled his mother's warning that he still occupied psychic space in Jenny's life — too much, he alone knew, given all that had happened to them. She had come this far without him; whatever affection he still felt, he could not, would not, act on it. Instead, he fell back on the distance that had become his last defense. "I know how terrible this must be —"

"You can't." Fresh tears sprang to her eyes. "You'll never know how sorry I am. And how ashamed."

"It's done, Jen. There's nothing left but to let it go."

Jenny bit her lip, a wet sheen in her eyes. "Can you?"

Adam felt a constriction in his chest. "No."

Turning, she looked into his face and then, gently, put her hand behind his neck, pulling his mouth to hers. For Adam, that summer became yesterday, before everything changed, and the warmth of Jenny's lips was once again a preface — not just to their lovemaking, but to a life. Then he pulled a few inches back, resting his forehead against hers.

"We can't," he murmured. "You know that."

Her throat pulsed. "Will I see you again?"

"Yes. At least before I go."

Gently he withdrew, then left, wishing it were not so.

When he got to the car, Adam found a message on his cell, relayed through a ghost phone no one could trace.

Stopping at the foot of Jenny's driveway, he tried to shake off the last hour, then listened to the message. The voice belonged to Amanda Ferris. She was making headway with her new source, she told him, though it was clear that the man had no access to the coroner's report. But she had learned that the report was crucial to a web of evidence — including the crime scene report and statements extracted from Adam's family — that could lead to Teddy's indictment for the murder of Benjamin Blaine.

Struggling to detach himself, Adam weighed his choices. He could walk away from this, hoping that Jack was right. But if he wanted to warn Teddy of the case against him, then work to alter the course of events, he must place himself at risk. His advantage was that no one on this island knew what he was capable of doing. In many ways, if not all, this was still an innocent place.

He started driving again. By the time he reached his family's home, his plan was fully formed. But then, he had started on it the day he saw George Hanley.

SEVENTEEN

To assure his solitude, at dusk Adam took the stairs down to the beach below the promontory. Pulling out his cell phone, he called a former colleague for the second time that week.

"Other than you," Adam said, "I'm out of answers. How do you get me in?"

"Not sure I can," Jason Lew replied laconically. "Even the standard system you describe is difficult to beat. Cut the power, you trigger the alarm. And you're also dealing with cameras, right?"

"Yes. I've got the locations memorized. I also know where the control panel is — a room just off the entrance."

"That's what I need." Lew paused, signaling his reluctance, then said more slowly, "I'd have to pose as a service guy and insert a receiver. That will connect to a switch that shuts the system down from the outside. Pushing the switch is your job."

"How long do you need on your end?"

"Two days to build the receiver, then a day trip to the Vineyard. Say three nights from now you can go in. Assuming they don't spot me as an imposter and arrest me on the spot." Lew's chuckle became the phlegmy rumble of a smoker. "Funny work for an old guy. But fifteen thousand in cash would send me to Costa Brava."

Adam felt the night envelop him. "I'll have it for you by tomorrow."

"Deal." Lew's speech slowed again. "This kind of service doesn't come with warranties. You could hit the switch and find yourself on candid camera, with a shriek alarm for a laugh track. Instead of Afghanistan, you'd wind up in jail."

How had he gotten here? Adam wondered again. "If you'd screwed up on the job," he said, "the guys relying on you could have been killed. They tell me no one was."

"Different times," Lew said. "The obstacles are greater now. We'll see if I still have it. Otherwise, you're fucked."

That night, Adam twisted fitfully in bed, unable to find sleep.

Again and again, he saw the Afghan reach for the gun hidden beneath his robes. For a split second, Adam imagined the consequences of failing to react — instant death or, more likely, kidnapping followed by torture no normal man could endure. At the end he would become a mutilated body by the side of the road, or the centerpiece of a videotaped beheading he prayed his family would never see. The lies he had told them would cause suffering enough.

He jerked the wheel abruptly, throwing Messud sideways as he pulled the gun concealed beneath his seat.

Righting himself, the Afghan perceived that he was speeding down an empty road at night with an American who was exactly what the Taliban suspected, and knew Messud's true loyalties very well.

"I never trusted you," Adam told Messud in Pashto, and shot the Afghan between the eyes.

For fifty miles, Adam drove with Messud's body slumped beside him. Dumping it by the road, Adam hoped that someone would blame an Afghan. Then he drove to Kandahar and learned that Benjamin Blaine was dead.

Adam closed his eyes, and tried again to sleep.

Early the next morning, he took a flight to Washington, D.C.

There was a Vineyard sunrise of heart-breaking beauty. Looking out the window as the plane climbed higher, he saw Cuttyhunk Island on the edge of the blue horizon, and thought of his last sail with Jenny Leigh.

They had rented a sailboat. Though not an experienced sailor, Jenny was eager to learn. She took the helm, holding the tiller in one hand and the mainsheet in the other. Adam sat beside her, noting subtle shifts in the wind. A stiff breeze blew the blond strands of hair across her smiling face.

"Good," Adam said. "Now let out the mainsheet a little."

She did this, tentative at first, then grinning as the mainsail caught the wind. The sailboat gained speed. Satisfied, Adam slid forward on the port side, balancing the boat to help her. Even when sea spray splashed her face, Jenny's eyes were bright. Adam could feel her exhilaration.

After an hour, her mood still elevated, Jenny began to talk about her writing. "For me," she explained, "it's partly about why we are the way we are. But it also means I feel safe." Hand on the tiller, she gazed ahead, face solemn now. "In my stories, I control what happens. There's no experience I can't use. But it can't hurt me anymore. Instead, I can understand it, then change it to be more the way I want."

As more often lately, Adam sensed that Jenny was dealing with a pain she refused to reveal, perhaps did not fully understand. "So do you write for other people, Jen, or for yourself?"

"Both." Suddenly, she was animated again. "I don't just want to be a writer, but a great one. I want to be on an airplane, or on a beach, and see someone so enthralled by what I wrote they don't notice me at all."

This was Jenny at her emotional peak, her ambitions boundless and romantic. To Adam, three years older, she seemed touchingly, almost heartbreakingly, young. He hoped that life would not give her more hurt than she could endure. "I like the part of being anonymous," she explained, "where the reader's only idea of me comes from what I write. Did it ever feel strange to read your father's books?"

"In a way." Adam paused, trying to express what he had never told anyone. "I admired his talent, and also felt sad. The man who wrote those books was larger in spirit than the dad Teddy and I knew. 'If you can be that way on the page,' I wanted to say, 'why not with us?' "

As Jenny adjusted the tiller, Adam felt her mood change. Pensively, she said, "Maybe

I'm like that, too." Heading for Cuttyhunk, the idea seemed to consume her, rendering both of them silent.

On the way back, a fierce current along the Elizabeth Islands caught them up.

Adam took the tiller, fighting stiff and erratic winds as the current increased to twenty knots. The jib became snagged. When Jenny scrambled to free it, a sudden wave knocked the boat sideways.

Adam saw Jenny lose her balance, suspended in slow motion above the side before pitching into the chill waves of the Vineyard Sound. Turning, he spotted her bobbing in the water as the current swept him away.

She was not a strong swimmer, Adam knew. Quickly, he wrenched the boat in a circle back toward her. Jenny's arms began thrashing, her eyes wide with fright. Only the life jacket kept her head above water. He fought the wind, his progress toward her agonizingly slow.

Minutes passed. Her face was waxen now, her mouth shut tight. Desperate, Adam tacked to reach her. At last, he came close enough to toss her a line knotted at the end.

She clutched the line with both hands, hope and panic etched in her face. The wind shifted. Abruptly, the mainsail filled, propelling the boat forward at startling speed. The rope snapped taut in Jenny's hands, the forward motion of the boat dragging her through rough waters like a rag doll. Adam heard her scream. In seconds, she would release the line, falling back as the boat sped away, or keep swallowing water through her mouth and nose until the sensation of drowning forced her to let go.

Jerking the tiller, Adam steered into the wind. The boat slowed abruptly, forging back toward Jenny. At last, the line went slack, and Jenny began bobbing again. Tiller in one hand, Adam pulled her toward him with the rope. As she came close, he reached out, risking his own tumble into the water. The instant his hand clasped hers the boat rocked again. The fierceness of her grip was all that linked them.

With desperate haste, Adam pulled her into the boat. Still gripping the tiller, he hugged her. He felt her trembling with relief and fear.

"Strange," she murmured after a time. "Suddenly, I was just so scared of dying."

Adam kissed her forehead, felt cold skin and damp tendrils of hair. "Now you're like me," he said gently. "But it's like I promised at Waskosims, Jen. I'll never let anything happen to you."

In late afternoon, they spotted Menemsha Harbor. Though warmed by the sun, Jenny still leaned against him. "I've never talked to anyone about my writing," she said. "At least not like I do with you."

"Do you know why?"

She hesitated. "I'm afraid of rejection. Both of my stories and of me. Sometimes I'm too scared to show them to anyone, especially someone I know."

A new idea struck him, a way to encourage her. "Suppose my dad wanted to read one of your stories, Jen. Could he?"

She stared at him in wonder. "Do you think he would?"

"I could always ask." Still watching the current, Adam considered how much this might appeal to Ben's idea of himself. "He just might give you feedback, and he knows damn near everyone in publishing. Maybe you should come to dinner." Pausing, he smiled at another thought. "Actually, you'll be a welcome distraction for us all. Given that we're close to the last boat race, and I've nearly caught him in the standings, Dad's a little short with me right now."

The wheels of the plane touched down, jolting Adam back to the present.

EIGHTEEN

In the next three days, Adam met with his superiors, transferred money to Jason Lew through two separate bank accounts, and returned to the Vineyard. On the day following, Lew called him to report. "I got by with it," Lew said. "I don't think the security guys suspected me. If you're feeling reckless, you can find out if my technical gifts survive."

That evening, at twilight, Adam told Clarice he was going fly-fishing and drove to Dogfish Bar.

Several men were already there, spread like sentries along the surf. Spotting Matthew Thomson, Adam stopped to chat, then took his place among the others. For several hours he tried to clear his mind of tensions, focused on his casting. Only as the rest began drifting away did Adam's thoughts turn from the water.

Shortly after midnight, he found himself alone.

Edgier now, he made himself remain for one more hour. Then he returned to the dirt patch where he had parked his truck, changed into jeans and a dark sweater, and made the forty-minute drive to Edgartown.

He parked on a residential lane two blocks from Main Street. The town was dark and quiet, the last of the drunken college kids cleared from the sidewalks. Sliding out of the truck, he walked near the shade trees lining the road.

Headlights pierced the darkness, coming toward him. Swiftly, he slipped behind the cover of a privacy hedge, kneeling on the lawn of a darkened house. Peering through its branches, he saw that the lights belonged to a patrol car from the Edgartown police. This much he had expected; what he could not know was whether the cop at the wheel would continue on his rounds.

Standing, Adam looked in both directions, then continued past more white frame houses in a circuitous route toward Main Street. Then he veered again, quietly but quickly crossing a yard before concealing himself behind a tree next to the court-house.

Its parking lot was empty, the rear entrance lit by a single spotlight. Putting on his father's old ski mask and gloves, he took Lew's device from his pocket. It was no larger than a car fob, with a simple switch that would disarm the security system. Unless the device was defective — in which case arrest was the least of Adam's worries.

He paused, envisioning the challenge ahead. A sheriff's deputy would monitor the surveillance screen in the room near the main entrance, watching images sent by cameras in the hallway and just above the rear door. Assuming that the shriek alarm did not go off when he opened the door, any one of the cameras could reveal his presence inside the courthouse, bringing a swarm of cops and deputies. His choice was to back out or trust in Lew's skill.

For a moment, recalling the young man he had been, Adam was paralyzed by disbelief. But since then he had learned to ignore boundaries and to mold events to his purposes. Stepping from behind the tree, he felt the coldness come over him, his heartbeat lowering, his breathing becoming deep and even. His footsteps as he crossed the parking lot were silent.

Nerveless, he pushed the button.

The first test would be the door.

Adam inhaled. The door had unlocked; so

far, Lew's bypass had worked.

Slowly, Adam edged inside. Dim light illuminated the hallway. A camera aimed down at him from the ceiling, meant to reveal his presence at once. But if the device functioned properly, the monitor would show the empty space that had existed a moment before Adam filled it. No one inside seemed to stir.

With painful slowness, Adam crept down the hallway toward the stairs to the second floor. As he reached them, he glanced into the security room and saw the broad back of a sheriff's deputy gazing at a TV monitor, watching the door through which Adam had entered. The intruder was safely inside.

Catlike, he started up the stairs. He willed himself not to look back at the deputy who, simply by turning, would catch him. Reaching the top, he turned a corner, out of sight once more.

The second floor was quiet and still. If he got in and out without being seen, Lew had promised, no one would ever know he had been there. But Adam had more complex plans. Reaching the door of George Hanley's office, also wired to the system, he turned the knob.

Once again, Lew's device had disarmed the lock. Slipping inside, Adam softly closed the door.

Through the window Main Street appeared dark and silent. Using his penlight, Adam scanned the surface of Hanley's desk.

Nothing of interest. Kneeling, he slid open the top drawer of a battered metal cabinet, then another, reading the captions on manila folders. Only in the bottom drawer did he find the file labeled BENJAMIN BLAINE.

Taking it out, he sat at Hanley's desk.

The sensation was strange. But for the next few minutes, Adam guessed, he was safe. The danger would come when he tried to leave.

Methodically, he spread the contents of the file in front of him. Hanley's handwritten notes, suggesting areas of inquiry. The crime scene report. Typed notes of the initial interviews with his mother, brother, and uncle — as well as Carla Pacelli, Jenny Leigh, Nathan Wright, and Adam himself. And, near the bottom of the file, the pathologist's report.

For the next half hour, he systematically photographed each page, blocking out all thought of detection. He had no time to read. But once he escaped, and studied them, he would know almost as much as George Hanley and Sean Mallory — and, unlike them, would know that. Especially advantaged would be Teddy's lawyer in Boston, who would receive them in the mail from an anonymous benefactor, and who, himself innocent of the theft, would have no ethical duty to return them.

Finishing, Adam reassembled the file and placed it in a different drawer. This last was for Bobby Towle — Hanley would know that someone had rifled his office, but not who, creating a universe of suspects who might have sold out to the *Enquirer*. A gift of conscience from an old friend.

Opening the door, Adam left it ajar.

At the top of the stairs, he stopped abruptly. The deputy was padding down the hallway, perhaps sensing that something was wrong. If he glanced up, Adam was caught.

Utterly still, Adam watched him. The man disappeared, the only sound the quiet echo of his footsteps.

Adam stayed where he was.

Moments crawled by while the deputy inspected the first floor. At last, Adam heard more footsteps, and prayed that the deputy would not come upstairs. Back toward Adam, the man plodded to his station and sat before a monitor Adam knew to be disabled.

With agonizing care, Adam walked down

the stairs. With each step the distance between him and the deputy lessened. As Adam reached the bottom of the steps, it narrowed to ten feet.

Head propped on his arm, the deputy gazed at the frozen screen.

Turning down the hallway, Adam passed beneath more cameras, still unseen. A few last steps, swifter now, took him to the entrance.

Slowly opening the door, Adam reentered the night.

As he stepped onto the asphalt, headlights sliced the darkness. In an instant Adam grasped that the patrol car was arriving. As its lights caught Adam, the driver hit the brakes.

Whirling, Adam sprinted down Main Street, footsteps pounding cement. In one corner of his mind he gauged the time it would take the patrolman to swing back into the alley toward the street, picking him up again.

Suddenly, he swerved, cutting back through the lawn of the Old Whaling Church and then a stand of trees bordering a neighbor's backyard. Behind him he heard brakes squealing, a door opening, the footsteps of the cop scurrying from his car.

Adam had little more time to run; in

minutes more police would converge, on foot or in patrol cars. Nor could he drive away. His last hope was to hide.

Bent at the waist, he crossed another yard, heading for his truck.

It was parked in a line of cars along the crowded lane. As headlights entered the lane, Adam reached his truck, sliding to his stomach at the rear. Clawing asphalt, he pulled himself beneath it, invisible to anyone who did not think to look.

He heard the patrol car pass, then his pursuer, still on foot, reaching the lane near Adam's truck. Listening to the man's labored breathing, Adam imagined him looking about, mystified by the absence of sound, the sudden disappearance of his quarry.

Move on, Adam implored him.

Another car passed without stopping, and then the man's footsteps sounded again, fading as he moved away.

Adam removed his mask and gloves. Damp face pressed against the asphalt, he glanced at his watch.

Three twenty. Two hours until dawn. Head resting on curled arms, Adam waited.

First light came as a silver space between the tires of his truck. Sliding out, Adam looked around him, and saw nothing but the still of early morning.

He climbed into his truck, started the motor, and drove out of town at a slow but steady pace. Glancing in the mirror, he saw that no one followed. As had been his plan, he headed back toward Dogfish Bar.

The beach was empty, the only sign of human existence the footprints left by fishermen. Satisfied, he changed into his fishing gear and drove to a restaurant overlooking the Gay Head cliffs. He ordered breakfast amid the tourists and tradesmen, a nocturnal angler as determined as his father, refueling after hours of solitary fishing. He made a point of joking with the waitress.

On the way home, he tossed the garbage bag filled with his clothes in a pile of refuse at the Chilmark dump, and dropped Lew's device in its incinerator. Parking at his mother's, he saw Clarice drinking coffee on the porch. "You look terrible," she observed.

Adam fingered his dark stubble. "The price of watching the sun come up. All that's left when you catch no fish."

"Get some sleep," his mother suggested with a smile. "You're not twenty anymore."

Climbing the stairs, Adam closed himself in a room that still held the artifacts of his youth. For a moment, he contemplated Jenny's photograph. Then he downloaded the images he had taken into his computer, reviewing the documents he would provide to Teddy's lawyer.

The process took two hours, more disturbing by the minute as the mosaic of evidence began forming in his mind. He found no reference to the insurance policy obliquely mentioned by Bobby Towle. But the witness statements conformed to what he knew: the Blaines, Jenny, and Carla Pacelli all denied knowing about the will, and his mother and Teddy's central assertion — which, in his brother's case, Adam no longer believed — was that neither had seen his father once he left the house. Far more lethal were the crime scene and pathology reports. He was not surprised that someone besides his father — no doubt Teddy — had left distinctive boot prints at the promontory. But there had been drag marks in the mud as well, mud on the heels of the dead man's boots, suggesting that someone had dragged him, perhaps struggling, through the wet earth near the point from which he fell. Worse yet, there were circumferential bruises on Ben's wrists, no doubt heightened by his regime of chemotherapy, appearing to confirm that a murderer had grasped him by both arms. It was plain that the police and prosecutor believed, as Adam did now, that someone had thrown Benjamin Blaine off the promontory.

Suppose you find out that your father was murdered by a member of your family.

Adam felt a coldness on his skin. His next task was to print these pages, mail them to Teddy's lawyer, then erase the images from his camera and computer before getting rid of both. But he paused to absorb what he and the authorities now further believed in common — that Teddy had killed their father. The job Benjamin Blaine had left him was not just to execute a will, but to save a guilty man, his brother.

■ ■ ■ ■

Part Three
The Executor

■ ■ ■ ■

ONE

Four nights later, Adam again met Amanda Ferris beneath the promontory.

On the surface, little had happened since the break-in. Whatever inquiry Hanley and the police had launched — an exhaustive one, Adam was certain — they had suppressed any news of the incident itself. The previous day Teddy had flown to Boston to buy art supplies; only Adam knew enough to guess he had been summoned by his lawyer. No one had questioned Adam about anything: with the security cameras disabled, all Sean Mallory had was a faceless man, swift and resourceful enough to vanish, thereby eliminating a host of potential suspects while creating a dead end. Unless someone checked his bank accounts, Bobby Towle was in the clear.

Knowing all this, Adam had the familiar sense of having set events in motion without leaving any trace. But he also continued to parse the varied narratives surrounding the will and his father's death, including those from his family, sensing that none of them was truthful or complete. And now he had the problem of Amanda Ferris.

As before, he had followed her from Edgartown; as before, he wanted no evidence that they had met. But the woman was no fool. Now he would learn how fully she understood their chess game.

The air was balmier; the seas calm. She had not brought a tape recorder. By now she grasped that their conversations were damning to them both.

"Too bad I couldn't get the pathologist's report," she said with quiet acidity. "But you may not have to wait long. Only until Hanley indicts your brother."

Hearing this made Adam cringe inside. "Tell me about that."

Ferris shifted her weight, adding to the restlessness animating her wiry frame. "First, there's the evidence at the scene. A footprint matching your brother's boot. Plus skid marks suggesting someone dragged your father toward the cliff."

And mud on his father's heels, Adam thought, but Ferris did not know this. "What else?"

"There's a button missing from his shirt,

suggesting a struggle —"

"Have they found it?"

Ferris hesitated. "No."

"Then it means nothing."

"There's also the neighbor who was walking along the trail. He thought he heard a man screaming, then saw a figure leaving the promontory —"

Nathan Wright, Adam knew. Feigning curiosity, he asked, "Man or woman?"

"He couldn't say." Ferris's tone became more assertive. "But the crime lab found a hair on your father's shirt that matches Teddy's DNA."

This Adam had not known. "Anything more?"

"Your brother's cell phone records. About eight fifteen, well before sunset, he received a call from the landline in the main house — no doubt from your mother. At nine fifty-one, after the neighbor saw this unknown figure, Teddy left a message on an ex-lover's voice mail —"

"Concerning what?"

"It wasn't specific, though he sounded distraught. But the time between calls leaves an hour and a half for Teddy to go to the promontory and push your dad off the cliff. Maybe in response to something your mother told him."

"Or," Adam interjected, "maybe she and Teddy gave him a shove together. He was pretty big, after all."

For an instant, Ferris was silent. "You see my point," Adam said with the same indifference. "You're still awash in 'maybes.' So are the police."

Ferris crossed her arms. "Then why did Teddy lie? Not only did he say he hadn't gone there that night, but that he never went at all. Just like he claimed not to remember Clarice calling him at eight fifteen. How could *that* be?"

"Maybe because the phone call was so ordinary. And even assuming the footprint was Teddy's, we don't know whether he left it before eight fifteen or after — or any time near the time my father died. You haven't given me a murder, let alone a murderer."

Once more Ferris hesitated. But she did not know, as Adam did, about the bruises on Ben's wrists. "Let me ask you this," he pressed. "Did the crime lab find any DNA under Teddy's fingernails?"

"No."

"So let's catalog what you don't have. First, definitive proof of a murder. Second, a murderer. What you do have is this boot print, the drag marks, the shadowy figure, the phone records — all subject to multiple interpretations. A first-year lawyer could defend Teddy in his sleep." Adam paused, then prodded, "So now that we've acquitted my brother, what do you have on Carla Pacelli?"

"Her DNA on your father's clothes and face. But is she strong enough to throw him off a cliff?"

Adam flashed on Pacelli at dinner. "She looks pretty fit to me."

"So I hear," Ferris answered pointedly. "I understand you made quite the couple at Atria, too intent on each other to notice anyone else. And those tender moments on the swing chair — oh my. People will say you're in love."

For a moment Adam was stung, then grudgingly gave Ferris points for tenacity. "Actually," he said, "we're running away to Portofino on the old man's money. But you'll have to pay for the wedding pictures." His voice became sharp. "On the question of strength, my dad was dying. He might even have had a stroke — in which case, an average woman could have tossed him overboard. That would explain the drag marks. So we can add Carla to the suspects, I suppose."

Ferris shook her head. "She's a dead end. I can't find anyone she told about the will.

All I've got on her is trivia — an occasional trip to Boston, one dinner with you, and a real effort to withdraw from public view. Present company excepted, she's the most guarded person in America. You tell me what *that* means."

I've only lied to you once, Carla had told him, *for reasons of my own, and not about Jenny or the will.* "Maybe she's in mourning," Adam rejoined. "But every instinct I have says she's hiding something serious. According to my mother, a few nights before he died she saw my father on the promontory with a woman. Who else but Pacelli?"

"Quit trying to divert me," Ferris said in a relentless tone. "I've got more than enough for a story. We're going to print that Edward Blaine is the prime suspect in his father's murder, and spell out the evidence against him."

In the half-light, Adam looked into her face. "Actually," he told her softly, "you're not."

Ferris gave a short laugh. "Can I ask why?"

"Several reasons. Unless Teddy's indicted, he'll sue you and the *Enquirer* for libel —"

"Don't try to threaten me," Ferris shot back. "We have lawyers for that."

"I'm counting on it. So you should confess to bribing a cop, then obtaining documents and information critical to a murder investigation. Then ask how long it will take the police to indict you for obstruction of justice. Because if you print another word about my brother, I'll make damn sure they do."

"That's bullshit." Suddenly her voice was shrill, uncertain. "Do that, and you'd go down with me."

"Would I? You're the one who passed the money, not me. You have no evidence we've ever spoken. And if you try to trace your calls to me, you'll find out that you can't. That also goes for the anonymous call I'll place to the police." Deliberately, Adam muted his voice. "You lose, Amanda. All you can do is leave this island for good. But before you go, you're going to give me the piece you're still holding out. Something about an insurance policy."

She looked away, caught, then met his eyes again. "If you already knew, why ask?"

Ask Teddy about the insurance policy, Bobby Towle had said. "Because you're telling me what *you* know. So that you remain in my good graces."

Ferris's face twisted, a study in stifled anger. "Four months ago, according to your

353

friend, your mother took out a one-million-dollar insurance policy on your father's life, with her and Teddy as beneficiaries. They collect unless Ben committed suicide, or one or the other killed him. Or," she added spitefully, "if they knew he was terminal and bought it to cash in."

Jarred, Adam mustered an air of calm. "From which you conclude —"

"That they knew about his will, and lied to the police. And that one or both knew that he was dying, and lied about that, too." She gave him a sour smile. "Any comment?"

Adam shrugged. "So many questions, so few answers. The only person who knows what they knew is dead."

"Conveniently so." Ferris's tone became chill. "Your brother will be indicted by summer's end. Then I'll print my story, and there's not a fucking thing you can do. Especially from Afghanistan."

That much was true, Adam realized. "We're through now," Ferris finished with palpable bitterness. "I don't need a lawyer to know that you poison anything you touch." She laughed. "Poor Carla."

She turned from him, walking swiftly away as though fearing for her life. A good thing, Adam supposed.

■ ■ ■ ■

He found Jack and his mother on the darkened porch, sitting in Adirondack chairs beside a radio tuned to the Red Sox game. "I thought they'd invented television," Adam remarked.

This drew a wispy smile from Clarice. "Memories," she answered. "When I was a little girl, I'd sit here with my father listening to the games. We had Ted Williams then, and always finished behind the Yankees. But it felt magical — just my dad, me, and the crickets, the announcer's voice in the darkness and the sounds of a game far away. This may be the last summer I can relive that."

Turning, Jack regarded her with avuncular concern. "It'll work out, Clarice. This place is meant to be yours."

There was something old-fashioned about this scene, Adam thought — not just the radio, but that the two of them seemed like actors in a play from another era. Perhaps he should have found this more affecting. But Amanda Ferris had curdled his mood.

"I need to talk with you," he told his mother.

As she looked at him in surprise, Jack

regarded him more closely. Then Clarice said, "You can help me make fresh coffee."

He followed her into the kitchen. Stopping by the sink, she poured out the scalded coffee, then carefully ladled more beans into a grinder. "What is it?" she asked.

"The insurance policy."

Glancing up, she asked in a thinner voice, "Where did you hear about that?"

"Not from you. Or Teddy, for that matter."

"Don't reprimand me, Adam." She paused. "The police know, of course. But it isn't that important. After all, it won't let me keep the house, and with Ben having cancer, I don't know that I'll collect. At least that's what my lawyer tells me."

She made not telling him sound innocent enough, Adam thought, but this was not the real problem. Evenly, he said, "The police must wonder why you took it out. So do I."

Clarice put down the bag of beans. "So now you're looking at us like you're Sean Mallory?"

"Please don't try guilt, Mom. I outgrew it. What concerns me is the answers I'm not getting. Did you expect that something would happen to him?"

"Not anything specific. But when you've lived with someone for forty years, you notice not-so-little things like drinking too much, or losing one's balance for no reason. Or Ben's indifference to being caught out with this actress." She paused, as though finding her own answer. "I didn't imagine him falling off that cliff, or changing his will. Except for worrying he might drive his car into a tree some night, it was nothing that concrete. More a sense that the ground was shifting under us in ways I couldn't identify. When you're as afraid as I was, and as defenseless, you become good at reading tea leaves."

"Did you discuss this with Teddy?"

"In a general way, yes. But the initiative was mine." Her voice became clipped. "Are we quite done with this now? We've left your uncle sitting there."

"One more thing," Adam said. "Why did you call Teddy the night he died?"

Clarice cocked her head. "Did I? When?"

"About eight thirty."

"I really don't remember. So it can't have been important." Clarice frowned. "I certainly didn't call him to predict your father's death. Which leaves me wondering why you seem to know more about me than I can remember."

"Because Teddy's in trouble," Adam said curtly. "Do you recall anything else about that night? Specifically, anything that would make it harder for the police to suspect my brother?"

"I know this much," Clarice responded firmly, "as a mother. No doubt Teddy feels protective toward me. But he's the last person on earth capable of killing Ben. You're imagining Teddy as yourself."

Turning from him, Clarice foreclosed any further discussion.

Two

When Adam stepped outside, he saw light coming from Teddy's studio.

His brother painted up to fourteen hours at a stretch, Adam knew, working at night under 200-watt bulbs. But this was late even for him. Walking to the guesthouse, Adam could see Teddy through the window, seated at his easel with a glass of red wine beside him. The stillness of his posture suggested a trance.

When Adam entered, pulling up a stool at Teddy's shoulder, his brother's only movement was to pick up a brush. This canvas was abstract, with garish colors to which Teddy began adding slashes of bright red. He worked with what seemed a terrible intensity, the sheen of sweat on his forehead; but for the obstinacy of his brother's concentration Adam might have believed that Teddy did not notice him. For an instant, he recalled watching Teddy as a youth as he

359

painted — Adam at twelve, Teddy at four-teen or fifteen — and how magical it was to see his brother fill a blank canvas with such startling images. Calmly, he said, "Any time you're ready, Ted."

After a moment, Teddy turned to him, his smile guarded. "What is it, bro?"

"I know you were on the cliff that night. I don't mind that you lied. But Hanley and the cops mind quite a lot."

A shadow crossed Teddy's face. "How do you know all that?"

"That's irrelevant. All that matters is that they're preparing to indict you."

In the harsh illumination from above, Adam saw the first etching of age at the corners of Teddy's eyes, and, more unset-tling, the deep vulnerability of a man who felt entrapped. Teddy lowered his voice, as though afraid of being heard. "My lawyer says not to talk about this."

"Good advice for anyone but me." Adam's tone became cool. "The first thing I ask is that you listen, then tell your lawyer what I've said without disclosing who said it. That conversation is covered by the attorney-client privilege. Understood?"

Silent, Teddy nodded.

With willed dispassion, Adam recited all that he had learned: the unknown person

Nate Wright saw at the promontory, Teddy's boot print, the drag marks, the bruises on Ben's wrists, the mud on his boot heels, Teddy's hair on his shirt, Clarice's call to Teddy, Teddy's call to the ex-lover, Teddy's fantasies about killing their father, the insurance policy on Ben's life — all rendered more damning by Teddy's lie. "I'm sure your lawyer knows most of this," Adam concluded. "But not all — unless you've told him more than I think you have. If there's anything you've left out, tell him now. Then start perfecting a story that covers all this and still makes you out to be innocent."

Teddy flushed. "So you think I killed him?"

"I don't give a damn. You've paid too big a price for him already."

A brief, reflexive tremor ran through Teddy's frame. "And if I tell you what happened?"

"It never leaves this room."

"It can't," Teddy said with sudden force. "This involves more than me. You'll have to be every bit the actor I've come to think you are."

Adam felt a stab of dread, a sense of coming closer to a reckoning with the truth. "Go ahead."

Teddy bent forward on the stool, hands folded in his lap, then said in a husky voice, "We didn't tell the truth — not all of it. Mom called me that night, close to frantic. Dad was drunk and rambling, she said, not really making sense. But the essence was that he was leaving her for Carla Pacelli."

Adam felt the jolt of revelation run through him: first that his mother and brother had lied to him and to the police, then that — at least on this point — Carla Pacelli had told the truth. "Why didn't you tell that to the police?"

"Because I knew that Mother hadn't. She told me she was afraid that could make his death look different from what it was — an accident."

Adam tried to envision Clarice suggesting this, further complicating his sense of who she was. Quietly, he asked, "Because she believed that? Or because that's what she needed other people to believe?"

Teddy rubbed his temples. "I can't be sure. See, I concealed the truth from her as well. She still doesn't know that I went to the promontory."

"This family certainly has a gift for candor, doesn't it? Tell me when you went there."

"After she called me." Teddy's voice

became harder. "That sonofabitch had tormented me for years, and now he was humiliating our mother. So I decided to confront him." His words came in a rush now. "He was standing there like he had a thousand nights before, staring at the fucking sunset like it was the last one in human history and he was there to bear witness."

I can't imagine not looking at this, Ben had said to Nathan Wright. *Can you?* "Maybe he was," Adam said. "After all, the man was dying."

"I didn't know that. All I knew was that he treated her like dirt." Teddy shook his head, voice thickening with emotion. "God help me, I wanted to push him off that cliff, just like I'd imagined ever since I was a kid. Instead, I just stood there waiting for him to notice me.

"When he finally did, he gave me this look — not disdainful like normal, but more puzzled. 'What are you doing here?' he asked. 'You hate this place.' It threw me off guard — suddenly he had the tone and manner of an old man, and his face looked ravaged. My idea of him was so strong I hadn't seen that he'd become his own ghost.

" 'I'm here for my mother,' I told him. 'For years I've watched you degrade her in private, humiliate her in public, and exploit her fear of being abandoned. She's the only parent I ever had. You were only a sperm donor, and even that makes me want to vomit.' He tried to muster that supercilious smile, but even that was a ghost. 'Then go ahead,' he told me. 'Just keep it off my boots. They're new.' "

Adam tried to imagine the ferocity of will that made his father, dying, still prefer hatred to pity. But Teddy seemed transported back in time. " 'Maybe I'll push you off this cliff,' I told him. He just kept looking at me, almost like he was curious what I'd do. Then he spoke in a strange new voice, tired but completely calm, 'If you hate me that much, do it for your mother. Or better yet, yourself.'

"He sounded like he didn't care, that he'd be willing to die if that would make me feel better. All at once I saw him as he was, this aging husk of a man. I couldn't move, or fight back the tears." Briefly, Teddy closed his eyes. "Looking back at me, he seemed to slump. 'Jesus,' he said in this heavy way I'd never heard before. 'What have I done to you, Teddy? Did I make you like this?'

"I don't know whether he meant gay or too weak to act in my own behalf. Then he finished, 'To come to the end, and face this. It's not your fault you could never be like

Adam. It was foolish of me to want that.' "

For a moment, Adam could say nothing. Then he said softly, "He certainly had a gift, didn't he? Only he could issue an apology meant to cut you to the quick."

Teddy continued as if he had not heard. "I started toward him. He just watched me, not moving, when suddenly his eyes rolled back in his head. Then he kind of collapsed, like he was too tired to stand, and sat there in the mud near the side of the cliff, his eyes as blank as marbles." Pausing, Teddy looked into Adam's face, as though recalling he was there. "He was utterly defenseless. But killing a helpless man is what he would expect from me. So I grabbed him by the wrists and dragged him to the rocky area, where at least it wasn't muddy. Then I sat there, studying his face as though he'd gone to sleep, trying to remember when I'd loved him.

"Suddenly his eyes snapped open. He looked at me, surprised, then said, 'I passed out, didn't I? It's happening more often.' Then he asked in this quiet voice, 'Why didn't you kill me, Teddy?' I gave him the only answer I could think of: 'Too easy.' "

Someday people won't read you anymore, Adam remembered telling his father. *You'll be left with whoever is left to love you. It's not too late for Teddy to be one of them.* Finally, he asked, "How did he react?"

Teddy swallowed. "His eyes seemed to focus, like he'd never seen me before. Then he sort of croaked, 'I'll change things, Teddy. At least those things I still can help.' "

"The will?"

"Maybe," Teddy answered. "But I didn't know about that, and I'm sure Mom didn't either. So what I imagined him saying was that maybe he wouldn't leave her.

"Suddenly, I felt exhausted — not only by what happened between us, but by being in that place. Without saying another word, I left him there. I never saw my father again." Teddy looked at Adam intently, finishing with lacerating bitterness, "For all I know, he jumped or fell. Whatever happened, the sonofabitch fucked me one more time. Instead of fixing the will, he made me the prime suspect in a murder I could only fantasize about."

For a moment, Adam struggled to distance himself from Teddy's story, and his desire to believe it. Finally, he asked, "Why did you call your ex-friend?"

"Jesus, Adam — wouldn't you call someone after an experience like that? Or would you just pour yourself a drink and switch on the Red Sox game?"

"I really don't know. But I might have told Sean Mallory what you just told me, instead of framing myself for murder. Assuming, of course, that anything you've told me is true."

A moment's anger flickered through Teddy's eyes, and then he looked away. "You've met Mallory," he said in a dispirited tone. "I took one look at him and knew he wouldn't believe me. All I'd do is get myself and Mom in trouble."

"Instead of just yourself," Adam rejoined. "But now you're right to protect her, I suppose, given what you say she doesn't know. A sudden recollection of her phone call might not help either one of you."

Looking up, Teddy met his brother's gaze. "Do *you* believe me, Adam?"

Adam weighed his answer. Too much of Teddy's story was implausible. But it had the virtue, at least, of accounting for the evidence Adam had siphoned to his lawyer — suggesting its essential truth, or, more likely, his brother's considerable ingenuity. A jury might not — probably would not — believe him. But Adam could not bring himself to reject the story outright. Then it struck him that if Teddy's account was true, and Ben had resolved to revise his will yet again, Carla Pacelli might have had reason to kill him. But this assumed that Carla had come to the promontory, and that Ben had told her. An assumption that, as of now, was as unprovable as the other indispensable assumption: that Carla had known about her inheritance.

"It doesn't matter what I believe," Adam said at length. "Your story covers the evidence as I know it — except for the button. Tell me how that came off his shirt."

"I have no idea," Teddy insisted. "I never touched his shirt. For all I know the button was already missing."

Adam considered this. The button had not been missing; Adam had found it at the scene, and the hair on Ben's shirt suggested closer contact than Teddy admitted. But if his brother were telling the truth, then someone else — perhaps Nathan Wright's elusive figure — had ripped the button off. And only Adam knew that.

Watching his face, Teddy said, "You don't believe me, do you? I'm pretty sure my lawyer doesn't either. I guess that's what happens when he gives you a lie detector test and it comes out inconclusive. All I could tell him is that my fantasy was so strong that sometimes I *feel* like I killed him. Doesn't inspire much confidence, does it?"

Adam did not answer. "Just keep our mother out of this," he instructed. "Including what I know about her not-so-small lapse of memory. At least until I figure out what else to do."

Teddy stared at him. "You sent my lawyer those documents, didn't you?"

Adam stood. Then he smiled a little, placing a hand on Teddy's shoulder. "What documents?" he replied, then returned to their mother's house, his expression as he said good night to her placid and untroubled.

THREE

On the way upstairs, Adam paused in the dining room, placing a hand on the Herreshoff Cup. The name Blaine was now engraved on it ten times, with the year of triumph beside it, the last victory occurring the summer before his father's death. Now, perhaps like the house itself, someone else would claim it. But on the long-ago night Jenny Leigh had come to dinner, the cup was on this table, Ben's prize from the previous year, the only question which Blaine — father or son — would claim it at summer's end.

That night, however, Adam had other worries, principally about his mother. The evening before, with his father out, he had found her on the porch. The bottle of Chassagne-Montrachet at her side was almost empty. Adam understood that, at times, his mother would dull some unspoken worry with an extra glass of wine, drifting into a space where she seemed untouchable. At these times, she spoke sparingly, careful to conceal whatever troubled thoughts were roiling beneath the genteel veneer. But tonight, she seemed almost stupefied, and her belated greeting to Adam was delivered in a slurry voice he had never heard before. This slippage, startling in a woman so self-controlled, had caused Adam to sit beside her, though tact kept him from asking questions.

Finally, she said in a low voice, "You're a kind person, Adam. Not like Ben at all."

To someone accustomed to hearing how much he resembled his father, this remark was troubling. Trying to delve into its cause, Adam inquired, "Are you angry at him about something?"

Clarice inclined her head and propped her chin with one hand, the posture of inebriation or despair. "More angry at me," she said haltingly. "So many compromises, so much hurt."

Adam leaned close to her. "Maybe to you, Mom. You haven't hurt anyone else."

"Haven't I?" She peered out, as though the answers existed somewhere in space. "I've certainly hurt myself. I only wish I could confine the damage."

Adam waited for a moment. "Is this about

Teddy?"

"Teddy?" Her laugh, though quiet, startled him. "You would think that. I wish it were so simple."

Surely this was about his father, Adam thought, perhaps another woman. But he had not seen the restless, predatory look that suggested Ben was on the hunt, or the complacent air that went with some new conquest — this summer, Benjamin Blaine's ego seemed preoccupied with besting his younger son in sailing. Watching Clarice in profile, Adam had the tantalizing, disturbing sense that he was closer to penetrating the inner life she tried so hard to mask. Gently, he said, "Talk to me, please. You're the most loving mother on the planet, but I'm not always sure I know you."

A mist appeared in her eyes. "Then I've succeeded, haven't I? Who really wants to know their parents? And what 'loving mother' would inflict that on her children?" She faced him, her need to restore self-discipline showing in the tightness of her jawline. "I'm sorry to be so delphic. As you can see, I'm drunk, babbling about nothing. I'll behave myself for Jenny."

To Adam, the last phrase was freighted with meaning — not about dinner with Adam's girlfriend, but as the credo for his mother's life. In seconds the wall between Clarice and the world had reappeared. "Go on," she said in a brittle voice. "I'm sure she's waiting for you, as I once waited for him. I'm fine here by myself and fine tomorrow night."

There was nothing he could do. Touching her hand, he left, trailed by the shattering sense of a long-ago psychic explosion, its damage concealed by a shell.

Ten years later, with his mother facing ruin, the memory seemed oddly prescient. But now, as then, its deeper meaning eluded him. And on the night Jenny had come for dinner, his father and mother were the parents he wished for.

Looking about her, Jenny had seemed in awe of the size of their house, the artifacts of privilege and travel. To his surprise, she accepted a glass of wine, a sign of nervousness that put Adam more on edge. But Clarice, an expert hostess, engaged Jenny with what seemed to be genuine interest, while Ben presided with avuncular good humor. "Is it true," he asked, "that Adam is trying to make a sailor out of you?"

To Adam, the trill of Jenny's laugh suggested a paradoxical emotion — the determination to relax. "Did he also say he was trying to drown me?"

Ben grinned at Adam. "Another failure on the high seas."

"A small setback," Adam interjected airily.

Jenny sipped her wine, glancing nervously at Ben. "Actually, I was terrified. You know how they say your whole life flashes before you? *This is ridiculous,* I thought. *My life isn't even a short story, let alone a novella. I've hardly left Massachusetts.*" Glancing at Clarice, she said, "You've been everywhere, right?"

Clarice smiled at her. "Ben's been everywhere," she answered with wry self-deprecation. "He takes me to the nicer places, like Tuscany and the south of France. But I get to skip Kosovo and Darfur." More seriously, she added, "It's a terrible character defect, I know — one Ben as a writer can't afford. But I've learned that human ugliness is hard for me to witness."

Jenny nodded. "I know it would be for me. Still, I'd like to see everything I can."

Ben regarded her with curiosity. "Why is that?"

"Because writers shouldn't protect themselves. I want to know the truth, whatever that is, then write about it in a way that causes other people to see." She shook her head. "My problem is how little I've experienced."

"Oh, you'll catch up," Clarice assured her. "At this age, you and Adam have barely nibbled around the edges."

With a dubious smile, Jenny looked around her at the polished antiques, the ornate Persian carpets, the African masks, and Asian tapestries on the Blaines' spacious walls. Adam could follow her thoughts — Clarice's remark, though intended kindly, reflected an ease of access to the world Jenny Leigh had never known. Judging from his observant look, Ben saw this as well. "I know what you're feeling," he told her. "I remember having nothing, and wondering if my ambitions were delusional. Like you, I'd barely been off this island. But for all its faults, this is a meritocratic country. A smart young woman like you has the power to create her own future. But you have to want that with every fiber of your being."

This, Adam knew, was the heart of Ben's code — that the world was a malleable place for those with the will to make it so. Pleasantly, his father said to Jenny, "Tell me about your family."

Briefly, she averted her eyes. "Not much to tell. My father's long gone. There's only me and my mom."

There was a great deal of meaning, Adam knew, in these few words — abandonment, struggle, an adolescence without nurturing. "My father was a vicious drunk," Ben responded bluntly. "I used to wish he *had* taken off. But not all of us can be so lucky." He paused, moderating his tone. "I don't mean to make light of it. Drunk or absent, we both wanted the father we didn't have."

From Jenny's expression, open now, Adam perceived that his father had succeeded in disarming her. "It's all I know," she told him. "In some ways, I guess I raised myself."

Ben smiled at this. "From what Adam tells me, and from meeting you, I'd say you've done just fine." He turned to his wife, including her. "Wouldn't you say so, Clarice?"

"I would," Clarice said firmly. "On that point, at least, it seems that the Blaines are unanimous."

Turning from Ben to Clarice, Jenny gave them both an incandescent smile. Relieved, Adam began to hope that the evening would go as he had planned.

At dinner, his biggest concern was for Jenny herself, nodding each time Ben offered to fill her glass with wine, chilled on ice inside the Herreshoff Cup — an act of proprietary lèse-majesté that, Adam suspected, was calculated to remind the son that this prize belonged to his father. Though he rarely saw Jenny drink, Adam could anticipate the changes in her behavior — by dinner she was vivacious, even charming, but poised on the brink of unpredictability. "If you had your choice of travels," Clarice asked her, "where would you go first?"

To Adam's mind, Jenny considered the question too long, as though wine had altered the chemistry in her brain. "This may sound strange, but I don't really care. I'd like the experience to pick *me*, then let me be surprised by how I've changed. Sort of like going in the Peace Corps, and winding up somewhere you've never imagined."

"A fair response," Ben answered. "Only my Peace Corps was the army. I learned about cowardice then, and cruelty, and nobility. And I was forced to look inside myself — the best of me and the beast in me." His tone became insistent. "Good writing takes courage. You have to see the truth about other people, and about yourself. Often, it's not pretty. But after Vietnam I couldn't read novels that sugarcoated the human condition, and it's good you don't want to write them." Glancing at Adam, he said more easily, "My son says you brought a short story. If you don't mind, I'd be pleased to read it."

Jenny flushed. "I'd love that," she answered, her voice laden with humility.

Ben took the story to his den, closing the door behind him.

Minutes passed, with Adam and Clarice trying to keep Jenny at ease. Adam knew that what was happening behind Ben's door must feel momentous — a verdict not just on her writing but on Jenny herself. Adam understood the feeling all too well.

Suddenly, Jenny covered her face, a comic pantomime of apprehension. "God," she told them. "I feel like I'm sitting outside the emergency room and someone's operating on my baby."

"Well," Clarice ventured with a hopeful sigh, "maybe they can save him."

Jenny managed to laugh. "In all seriousness," Clarice went on, "Ben's an honest critic, but not a cruel one. Whatever he says, he'll mean it to be helpful."

Slowly, Jenny nodded. "I know he will. And I wanted so much for him to read it. It's just that I've never shown my work to anyone but my teachers, and all of them consider Benjamin Blaine one of our greatest writers. Now I'm sitting here wondering what he thinks of me."

"Your story," Clarice corrected. "Not you. After all, your life is subject to many more revisions —"

Ben's door opened abruptly. He emerged with a snifter of cognac, his thoughtful gaze directed at the rug, then sat in his chair across from Jenny. Looking up at her, he raised his eyebrows in an ironical expression. "I suppose you're curious what I think."

Jenny laughed nervously. "A little."

"All right," he responded briskly. "For openers, you can write. Your imagery is strong, though strained at times. I've scribbled some notes in the margins, and underlined passages I particularly liked or questioned. I wouldn't have bothered if this story were no good." His voice became stern. "Just from reading it, I'd have known you were young. Too often you try to kill your readers with sentence after dazzling sentence, until you're all too likely to succeed. You want to write simply and clearly, so that the reader sees and feels what you're describing rather than stopping to admire the brilliance of your prose." He leaned forward, looking at Jenny with deep seriousness. "That said, you've written a number of passages with real clarity and grace. But there's also a depth to the writing, a genuine grasp of character."

Watching Jenny sag in relief, Adam felt this, too — his father would not have delivered this speech unless he meant it. In a lighter tone, Ben told her, "I particularly like the young woman in the story. She's so uncertain of herself, yet so clear about what she sees around her." Smiling, he added, "You probably know that girl, too."

"As well as I can," Jenny confessed. "Sometimes she confuses me."

"Then try to get her figured out," Ben urged. "The talent is there. The only question is whether that same young woman is tough enough. And only you can answer that."

Jenny cocked her head, her eyes filling with doubt. "What do you mean?"

"Several things. Tell me when you write."

Jenny moved her shoulders. "In spurts, I guess. When I'm feeling creative."

"That won't cut it, Jenny. Writing, like life, is showing up every day." Animated by his own passion, Ben stood and began pacing, seeming to fill the room. "Make a deal with yourself — ten hours of writing, every week, or maybe five good pages. Then stick to it." He took a deep swallow of cognac. "Life is choices. You can go to a movie or you can write a chapter. So ask yourself this: Would you rather watch someone else's creation or create something that's yours alone?"

Listening, Adam was struck by his father's elemental force, seldom quite this naked. Suddenly, Ben pointed. "See that chair, Jenny? Jack made it with his own hands. It's perfect in form, at once elegant and simple. A novel is like a chair — a tangible thing, with a distinctive shape and design." Turning, he waved to a shelf filled with his work. "And *I* made these. Everything they are comes from me. And yet, unlike Jack's chair, millions of people have held them in their hands and in their minds."

Adam noticed Clarice look down. For the first time, a discordant note had entered the room, Ben's denigration of his brother. But Jenny did not seem to notice. "Too many writers," Ben went on, "lack the guts and drive to take their talent all the way. Don't let go of a sentence or a scene until it's the best you've got inside you. You have to be ruthless with the people who distract you, and even more ruthless with yourself. If you can do that, Jenny, I'll read your second draft. Do we have a deal?"

Jenny looked stunned. Belatedly, she gave Ben her brightest smile. "Definitely."

"Good." Pausing, Ben seemed to step out

of his own spell, then looked from Adam to Jenny with a smile that seemed to mock his own passion. "So go have fun, the two of you. You've spent enough time with pontificating elders."

Adam and Jenny drove away, headed for the beach at Dogfish Bar, Jenny glowing with wine and elation. "He was so amazing," she exclaimed. "When you're with him, you just know why he's so great. It's unbelievable that he liked my story."

Adam felt the tug of jealousy. "True enough," he allowed. "But what's even more unbelievable is that I've never read it."

Jenny gave him a sideways look. "Don't confuse things, okay? This is about my writing, and between me and your dad. You and I are separate."

"Not if you're anything like him, Jen. What he writes is all about who he is." Adam paused, trying to unravel his emotions, then cautioned, "He's admirable and selfish in equal measure. You don't need to be exactly like him to succeed."

Receding into her thoughts, Jenny did not answer. They headed down South Road toward the Gay Head cliffs, perhaps a hundred feet from the lighthouse that marked the turnoff to the beach. Suddenly, impulsively, Jenny said, "I want you, Adam. Right now."

Adam laughed, startled by her change of mood. "Where?"

Smiling, Jenny gazed out the windshield. "Don't you have a passkey to the light-house?"

"My dad does. They gave him a key for helping save it."

"Then find the closest parking place. You and I are standing watch."

She was pretty drunk, Adam knew, but also high on excitement, feeling reckless now and looking for an outlet. He could either resist her, deflating the moment, or go along for the ride.

Braking, Adam parked, snatching his father's key from the glove compartment. "Come on," Jenny urged. As they left the car, she tugged at his hand, pulling him in her wake. Together they ran across the grass to the lighthouse.

Taking out Ben's key, Adam jerked open the metal door. They darted inside, slamming it behind them, Jenny scurrying up the twisting steps, her footsteps and laughter echoing as he followed.

Panting, he reached the top. Jenny looked out the aperture, eyes fixed on the water. Her dress was on the floor.

Adam stared at her. Still watching the sunset, Jenny unhooked her bra and stepped out of her panties, arching her back toward him. "This way," she instructed. "Hurry."

Astonished and aroused, Adam stripped, entranced by this new Jenny. Bracing her hips, he gently began to enter her, and discovered she was wet. As he slipped inside her, she leaned her torso out the window. "Touch my nipples," she implored him.

He did that. "Harder," she demanded, and then Adam was caught in the frenzy of her desire. When he placed his head beside hers, he saw the orange light spreading on blue water. Then Adam closed his eyes, his thrusts from behind her swifter, deeper. Suddenly, she cried out, the shudder consuming her body in a way he had never felt. When he joined her, Jenny laughed in delight. "Stay inside me, Adam, as long as you can. This is my favorite sunset ever."

Once it had been Adam's, as well. Now, ten years later, he sat at his old desk, studying their photographs — his father, dead; Jenny, gazing at him from a time before she tried to end her life.

FOUR

Unable to sleep, Adam felt his thoughts drifting from Jenny to Carla Pacelli.

I followed Ben on one of his nightly jaunts, his mother had said, *and saw him standing with a woman on the promontory.*

In the morning, he went there, barely cognizant of a day ironic in its warmth and brightness. Again and again, his mind returned to whether Carla had known about the will and, as Teddy's account might suggest, had come to fear that Ben might change it back. He tried to imagine his father and Carla standing here together as dusk enveloped them, Ben blurting out his misgivings, Carla facing the loss of ten million dollars — a combustible moment between a dying, weakened man and a newly desperate woman. A split second of calculated fury, with Benjamin Blaine sent hurtling into the void.

If that were true, his brother was paying

for a lethal combination of ill luck and a stupid lie that rendered his story unbelievable. But in turn this thesis required Carla Pacelli to have lied about every key element of her narrative — her ignorance of the will, her refusal to enter Ben's property, his father's decision to live with her, her belief that he was murdered by a member of his family. Unless Adam could prove all this false, and Carla a murderer, Clarice faced losing the only life she knew, and Teddy faced a life in prison that, for him, might be worse than dying. He could not let this happen.

Reining in his emotions, he walked toward Carla's cottage.

The sun grew warmer, the breeze light. Still, he hardly noticed this. He was too intent on forcing some telling mistake from a woman whose intelligence and self-possession seemed a match for his own.

Crossing the grassy field toward the guest-house, Adam saw the deck, sheltered from his view by pine trees, on which Carla and his father had sat on the first night he had come to her. From this angle all that was visible was one corner, with a book and sunglasses on the railing, suggesting that she was nearby. But only when he passed the tree line did he see her.

She was lying naked on a chaise longue, sunbathing. Her eyes were closed, her robe draped on a nearby chair. Adam froze, mute. She was stunningly beautiful, her body ripe but slender save for the incongruous roundness of her belly. In the moment it took him to comprehend what he was seeing, Carla opened her eyes.

She looked startled, and then her face set, her eyes ablaze. "Don't you ever call first?" she said with tenuous calm. "Even your father learned to do that."

Adam willed himself to see only her face. "I apologize," he managed to say.

"Too late for that now — or for modesty." She got up, walking over to retrieve her robe. Adam could not make himself turn away. Then she covered herself, facing him with a cool, angry look. "What is it you want from me, Adam? Though maybe now I can guess."

Adam could not respond to this. "Why didn't you tell me?"

Carla crossed her arms. "Would it have made any difference? Or would you have thought I was playing another card?"

Adam still felt the dullness of surprise. "I can't answer that," he said, then glanced at the swelling beneath the robe. "Do you know if it's a boy or a girl?"

"A boy. Benjamin Blaine's last son."

Once again, Adam was jarred; for better or worse, he had always been the younger of Ben's sons. Then he realized how much this new child might explain, and remembered what his father had said to Matthew Thomson: *Carla has promised to make me immortal.*

"Did he know?" Adam finally asked.

"Of course." Carla sat in the chair, her tone still cool but quieter. "I found out shortly after Ben got his diagnosis. He begged me to keep the baby. And, yes, he promised to support us. Though not by cutting off your mother."

I've only lied to you once, she had said, *for reasons of my own, and not about Jenny or the will.* Adam glanced at her stomach again. "How far along are you?"

"Four and a half months." Carla paused, then added tonelessly, "If you're hoping for a miscarriage, I'm sorry. My doctor in Boston says that we're both fine."

Adam flushed. "I'm not quite that cold-blooded. Whatever you and I feel about each other, I wish your son well. I wouldn't have wished my father on him, or anyone. Nor would I wish a child to be without a father."

He could read the doubt in her eyes. "I'm sure you think I tricked him," she said in

388

the same flat voice. "The surprise was mine — I thought I was infertile. So did my doctor in L.A.; you can call him if you like. But I don't know when, if ever, I can have another child."

He should have guessed, Adam thought. He recalled her asking to sit at the grave site, the loose-fitting dress she had worn to dinner, her expression as she watched the boy and girl on the swing chair. But sooner or later the will contest would have surfaced her pregnancy. Then it hit him that Carla had made every effort not to seek his sympathy, perhaps from some stubborn perversity of character, perhaps for fear of provoking his cynicism or contempt. At length, he asked, "Mind if I sit?"

Carla shrugged. "You've just seen me naked. I minded that a good deal more."

Adam sat on the edge of the chaise longue. After a moment, he said, "I can only imagine what this baby meant to him. A last chance to replace two disappointing sons."

Carla met his gaze, unflinching. "Perhaps he felt something like that," she responded evenly. "After I learned about his will, I wondered if he were trying to redeem himself in some skewed way — through Jenny, through me, and through this child. A literary heir, and a son who would idealize his imagined father."

Adam felt his anger return. "It's a narcissist's fantasy — living on in the hearts of his grateful beneficiaries while taking his revenge on those who didn't worship him in life. A last protest against the dying of his light."

Carla shrugged. "Have it your way. At least you understand why I'm not willing to sign away this inheritance. Though I'd have been happier if Ben hadn't tried to make us into adversaries." She paused, giving Adam a thin, ironic smile. "Of course, he knew you. So he must have known you'd try to dismantle all his plans."

Studying her, Adam tried to sort through the kaleidoscope of inferences derived from Carla's pregnancy, their patterns and relationships shifting by the moment, complicated by what surely was Ben's certainty that Clarice would challenge the will. But Carla's pregnancy provided a rational basis for Ben to revise his estate plan, refuting the idea that he was his lover's docile tool. And it argued against Carla as a murderer, at least if she understood the law — even if Clarice invalidated the will, Adam guessed, a child born after Ben's death was entitled to some share of his estate. Watching him, Carla asked, "What's bothering you?"

"There's something you're still not telling me. Something important."

Carla shrugged again. "If so, don't expect to hear it. I've told you the truth about Ben's will, and that's all you need to know."

"Not quite. What happened between the two of you that day?"

Adam imagined a trace of sadness in her eyes. "Why is that any business of yours?" she demanded. "Or do you have some prurient interest in the details?"

Adam tried to imagine his father at the promontory as Teddy had described him — barely able to stand, susceptible to changes of heart and mind, fearing death and yet fatalistic in the face of Teddy's threat to kill him. Calmly, Adam said, "Whatever our relationship, he was my father. I'm trying to imagine the last hours of his life."

Carla looked past him, then down, her face shadowed in the late morning sun. Finally, she said, "I told you Ben was dying. In one way, he already had."

"Meaning?"

Still Carla did not face him. "He was very afraid of knowing, yet not knowing, that any moment could be his last. Including his moments with me." Her voice became low, almost inaudible. "That afternoon Ben wanted to make love, perhaps for the last time. But he discovered he no longer could. So I just held him, and stroked his hair, and told him it was okay." Looking up at Adam, she added, "I don't expect you to feel sorry for him, or to be anything but disgusted. But to watch Ben feel the life force drain from him was unspeakably sad to me."

"Did he say anything about it?"

Carla closed her eyes. "Only that he wanted to die here, with me."

Again, Adam felt the stab of resentment — not because he thought she was lying, but because this sounded like truth, all the more toxic because it was so dismissive of his mother. Detaching himself, he compared this account to Teddy's unsettling description of his father on the promontory, a chastened man indifferent to his fate. "Then why are you so sure he didn't jump? Given how he saw himself, impotence must have been devastating."

Carla sat straighter, pride showing in her eyes. "We were more than that," she insisted. "He wouldn't have done that to me, and he didn't. Someone murdered him."

There was no place left to go with her, Adam perceived, and he had no heart to try. "So now you're alone, and about to become a mother."

Her look of pride became resolve. "As I

knew would happen. But this child is more than a surprise — he's a gift. I mean to put everything I've learned into making my son as strong and secure as he deserves."

After a moment, Adam nodded. "So what will you do?"

"As I told you at dinner, I'm done with acting. I keep thinking about getting an advanced degree in psychology. If I'm a decent mom, and do something useful with my life, I'll have Ben to thank."

Adam could not restrain himself. "Not to mention ten million dollars."

She stood abruptly. "Damn you," she snapped, her voice filled with an anger that startled him. "I don't need that much money, and I didn't ask for it. This is the last time I'll bother telling you that. You're obviously set on believing what you want, and I don't know why I even care."

Adam stood, facing her. In that wordless moment, he grasped how alike they were. She was an actress, he told himself yet again. But he had never been dispassionate about her, he realized, and was not now. Except that this time he wanted to believe her.

Still no one spoke. Carla's smile, fleeting and enigmatic, did not change the intensity of her gaze, as though she, like he, was at last perceiving in the other something neither could say. "I know," she said simply. A world of possible meanings in the words.

Unable to answer, Adam walked away.

Sitting back in his chair, Matthew Thomson emitted a bark of incredulous laughter. "That's certainly a rude surprise."

"I thought so," Adam said. "I assume this changes things a little."

"More than a little," Thomson answered briskly. "This child will become what the law calls a pretermitted heir, born after execution of the will. Even if Clarice reinstitutes the prior will in her favor, your little brother-to-be is entitled to what he'd receive if there *was* no will: an equal share with Teddy and you in one half of Ben's estate. Close to two million dollars, give or take."

"To be managed by Carla Pacelli."

"Of course. If Pacelli didn't know that before Ben died, she certainly does now. Two million is her starting point, and she can only go up from there."

Adam thought of Carla again, gazing back at him in a silence neither could break. "Then why conceal her pregnancy?"

"Who knows? Maybe to ward off the *Enquirer,* or as a tactic. Or maybe, for whatever reason, she didn't want to further humiliate your mother. From what you say, Carla's not an easy woman to read."

You're obviously set on believing what you want, Carla had said, *and I don't know why I even care.* "Unless she's extremely easy to read," Adam replied, "and I've complicated her by assuming everything but the obvious — that she's essentially honest."

Thomson smiled. "Maybe you *should* have finished law school, Adam. What you're describing is a lawyer's syndrome."

No, Adam thought, *it's my syndrome. Compared to me, lawyers are the kind of people who cry in movies.*

FIVE

Driving away from the lawyer's office, Adam wrestled with an image he could not shake — Teddy pushing their father off the cliff; Nathan Wright hearing Ben scream as he fell, then seeing his attacker vanish in the darkness. Whoever the shadow had been, Adam now believed, it was not Carla Pacelli.

He headed up-island, without a destination, testing assumptions based on stories he did not wholly accept. Though he doubted his mother's claim to have seen a woman on the promontory, he had thought that — were this true — Clarice had seen Ben with Carla. Now he considered that both his mother and Carla might have told the truth. Given what Carla had said, Adam doubted that Ben had pursued other women on the eve of his death. But there was another woman on the island who knew his father well.

So long ago, Adam thought, yet like yesterday. Inexorably, he headed toward the dock on Menemsha Pond where Ben had kept his sailboat. Within an hour, he was sailing in the sunlight of early afternoon as though into another such afternoon, its twin, and a son's final race against his father.

The night before, against his better judgment, Adam had allowed Ben to buy him dinner at the Beach Plum Inn.

They sat at an outside table overlooking the pond, the site of their climactic contest. After fifteen races, Ben led Adam by a single point; to win the cup, Adam had to beat him by two spots. Given his father's skills, he could not imagine Ben coming in worse than third. This meant that Adam must finish first: even at that, he was hard-pressed to name another sailor — including Charlie Glazer — who could surpass Ben on a day so central to his need for mastery.

The summer season was at its height, the restaurant packed. Though Menemsha was dry by law, diners could bring their own liquor, and Ben had supplied a full bar — a fifth of single malt scotch, a bottle of excellent Meursault, and several snifters' worth of Calvados. Content, he filled two tumblers of scotch on ice, and settled back to survey the gentle evening sunlight on the lawn, the grassy hillside, the softening blue of the pond. "The best of all possible worlds," he remarked, "for the most worthy of competitions — men pitted against one another and the caprice of wind and water. I pity anyone who'll never know the feeling."

"Can I quote you?" Adam inquired. "I'm thinking about an article for the *National Geographic*. Something about primitive folkways among the residents of provincial flyspecks."

Ben laughed aloud, eyes glinting. "Already discounting its significance, are you, so that losing won't matter quite so much? Then why bother borrowing Jack's boat, instead of letting my brother fail on his own?" He took a deep swallow of scotch, adopting a tone of mock nostalgia. "It takes me back thirteen years — Jack and me, the last race, his one great chance to wrest the cup from my grasp. Two boat lengths ahead, the final leg, and then he judged the wind wrong. It was over before he knew it. Guess that still must fester."

Adam grinned across the table. "You know, Dad, you really *are* a prick."

Ben gave another whoop of laughter. "Takes one to know one, Adam. But you're still on a journey of self-discovery." His tone became consoling. "It's no disgrace to finish second, son. Jack did it his whole life. You can draw on his experience."

"Not my plan," Adam countered evenly. "You're out of lobster pots."

His father's smile was tighter. "Live and learn," he replied, and filled their tumblers again. Raising his glass, he said, "To fathers and sons."

"And mothers and brothers and uncles," Adam parried. "The kinder, gentler Blaines." But he had already begun matching his father drink for drink.

By the end of a rich dinner — with the fifth half-gone, the Meursault consumed — Adam vaguely perceived that Ben might have preempted their competition with a contest he could not win. "Have some Calvados," Ben prompted. "It'll cut through all this food."

His voice seemed to come from some great distance. Rashly, defiantly, Adam said, "Pour away."

He could not remember the ride home. As he climbed the stairs, he heard his father say, "Good night, son," the trace of a chuckle in his voice. Adam's first stark moment of clarity was spent vomiting into the toilet. He imagined his father laughing in the darkness.

The next morning, Adam's temples throbbed. He rose unsteadily, dressed with clumsy fingers, and sat drinking black coffee at the dining room table, transfixed by the Herreshoff Cup. Ambling in from breakfast on the porch, Ben gave him a small, appraising smile. "Ready for our race?"

Unable to look at him, Adam shrugged. Then he forced himself to put on shorts and tennis shoes, and ran ten miles along South Road to sweat the poisons out. Returning home, he took a cold shower and dressed for the race, refusing Ben's offer of a ride.

Driving to Menemsha, Adam smiled grimly to himself. He had let Ben seize the advantage, a costly and stupid error. But there was one thing about their final contest his father did not yet know.

When Adam sailed out onto the pond, Jack was already in the boat he had borrowed from Charlie Glazer.

Together, uncle and nephew ran wind shots in *Folie à Un* and *Sisyphus,* repeatedly turning their bows to gauge patterns of gusts and breezes. Today the wind was tricky, shifting as much as 25 degrees from south to southeast and back again. To seize the advantage from Ben, Adam must anticipate the timing of each shift, tacking into a wind that propelled him toward the next marker. Gliding across his stern, Jack called out, "Which side of the course?"

"I'll take the right. The wind seems stiffer."

Nodding, Jack turned back to running wind shots. By two thirty, twelve other boats had joined them, headed for two orange buoys placed by the commodore near the creek flowing out to the Vineyard Sound. From his observation boat, the commodore, Paul Taylor, hoisted the order of the markers that defined the course, calculated to accent sudden changes in the wind.

Glancing over his shoulder, Adam saw his father in *Icarus,* tacking back and forth behind the starting line, angling to seize the best position when the final horn blasted. When he saw Jack at the helm of Charlie's boat, Ben's face hardened. But today his goal was brutally simple. It did not matter if he won; all that counted was beating Adam. If Ben could cover his son throughout the race, blocking his path, the cup would remain his; Adam's only chance was to break free of his father and never look back. His temples still throbbed, and his stomach felt raw and empty. He was grateful for the wind and water in his face.

Five blasts of the horn marked the last

five minutes. Fourteen boats kept tacking; with a minute left, Ben knifed in beside Adam, catching the wind his son needed. As Jack found his place just behind Ben, Adam felt the tightening of his neck and jaw.

With a final blast of the horn, the race started.

The boats headed downwind, taking a 30-degree angle into a southwest wind. Looking from Adam to Jack, Ben crossed the line on a starboard tack seconds ahead of his son, forcing Adam to give way. Tacking into the wind, they fought for advantage, muscles straining, Ben leading by seconds as they reached the first marker. The one boat ahead was *Folie à Un.*

In the distance, Adam saw his mother and Jenny in Ben's powerboat, watching what was becoming a three-man duel. But for the next thirty frustrating minutes, Ben ignored Jack, intent solely on staying between Adam and the next mark. Taut, Adam calculated their shifts, fighting to catch a gust that would erase the narrow lead his father had seized at the outset.

For one leg, then another, Ben blocked Adam's path.

They reached the final leg with Ben two boat lengths behind Jack, both tacking upwind, forced to adopt zigzag courses as they struggled to catch the next shift. The only choice left to Adam was whether to follow his father on the right side of the pond, fighting to pass him at last, or to break to the left behind Jack, hoping that a wind shift would allow him to beat *Icarus* and *Folie à Un* to the finish line. But with the tide swifter on the right, Adam decided to stay where he was, still locked in a tacking duel with Ben. Muscles aching, he sailed furiously, salt spray in his eyes and mouth.

But his father would not give up his lead. Suddenly, Adam felt as if he could watch the race from above. With the finish line in sight, and Ben seconds ahead of him, Adam saw that there was no way for him to edge Jack, leaving Ben in third — his only hope of taking the cup.

Suddenly, Jack tacked toward the right.

Glancing over, Ben saw *Folie à Un* slicing toward his bow. *"Starboard,"* he cried out — a demand that his brother yield the right-of-way. The three boats converged, seemingly headed for a collision.

"Starboard," Ben yelled again.

In a sudden, perfect maneuver, Jack tacked again, cutting off Ben from the wind and causing him to abruptly lose speed. Suddenly, Jack had reversed the dynamic of the race, blocking his brother as Ben had blocked Adam. At this moment, Adam saw his chance.

Marshaling speed, he tacked to the left, catching a lift that brought him surging closer to Jack. Fifteen feet, then ten. A hundred feet to go.

Jack was still in the lead, tacking to block Ben's way, Adam to the left. Five feet behind Jack, Adam passed his father.

He was alongside Jack's stern now, running with the wind. Angrily, Ben strained to pass his brother. Alongside one another, the two brothers and Adam fought for position, the commodore waiting at the line to call out the order of finish.

Thirty feet from the line, Adam was three feet behind his uncle, the wind still at his back.

Two feet from Jack, then one.

Adam had no time to see if Ben was catching up. One foot closer to Jack, and then the uncle and father and son were bunched so tightly that no one seemed to lead.

Ten feet to go, vanishing in seconds.

As the three boats crossed the finish line, three blasts sounded in succession, though for which boat Adam could not tell. Then the commodore called out, "*Sisyphus* first, *Folie à Un* second, *Icarus* third."

Adam Blaine had won the Herreshoff Cup.

In unison, he and his uncle turned, smiling and waving at Ben. But his father did not catch the spirit of the race, or the irony of its final moments. Expressionless, he sailed on toward his mooring, acknowledging neither his brother nor his son.

For an instant, Adam felt deflated, uneasy at his triumph and Jack's help. Then his uncle called out, "I guess we made up for those lobster pots," and Adam began laughing, the shadow on his victory passing from his mind.

This season was his now. For as long as the cup existed, ADAM BLAINE — 2001 would be engraved on its side. Like his father, he would bring it home and place it in the center of the dining room table. He thought of John F. Kennedy, one of Ben's heroes, and imagined raising his glass to his father, uncle, mother, and brother. "The cup has been passed," he would intone, "to a new generation of Blaines."

He never did. Before the engraver had finished, Adam had left the island and his family. Now, ten years later, he moored a dead man's sailboat and went to surprise Jenny Leigh.

Six

When Adam knocked on her door, Jenny did not answer.

He glanced at his watch. It was two fifteen; by now her shift at the gallery should be over. He tried the doorknob.

Like many people on the Vineyard, Jenny did not lock her house. Stepping inside, Adam glanced around, acting on an instinctive fear that she might have harmed herself once more. Instead, he found himself alone.

For an instant, remembering the night he had broken into the courthouse, Adam felt like an intruder. But now, as then, he had good reason to be alone here. He considered where to start, then walked into her office and began opening drawers.

He found little — no legal documents, nor anything suggesting that she had expected her bequest. The calendar on her wall, on which she had penciled in doctors' appointments or lunches and dinners with friends, contained no mention of his father. Nothing seemed to mar the innocent surface of Jenny's life.

All that was left was her stories.

Drafts of several were arranged neatly on her desk. The thickest stack of papers, Adam discovered, was her novel-in-progress. Like his father's last, aborted work, Jenny's had a title page: "No One's Daughter."

She had a series of unsatisfying relationships, his mother had told him, *often with older men. Jenny has come to believe she's been trying to replace her father.*

Uneasy, Adam flipped the page.

"To Adam," the dedication said.

He felt his skin tingle. Then he sat at her desk and began to read.

As with his father's manuscript, each page increased a sense of dread that nonetheless impelled him to continue. Shortly after the hundredth page, he stopped abruptly, feeling his face go white.

"Oh, Jenny." He said this softly, aloud. "Why did you never tell me."

He sat back, eyes closing, beset by images he could no longer push aside.

In early September, the contest with his father won, Adam drove to New York.

His second year of law school started in

two weeks. In the spring he had found a new apartment in Greenwich Village with two friends from his class; he moved his stuff — PC, television, CD player, winter coats and jackets — looking forward to another year in the city on the way to his career. His mission completed, he met up with Teddy and took in Village life.

Teddy was living with a guy, and seemed to be pretty good — Adam had missed him, and was glad they could spend time outside Ben's shadow. But after a couple of days, he found himself looking forward to Jenny's first visit, and then thinking about her pretty much all the time. On impulse, he decided to return to the Vineyard, intent on spending his last free days with her. His life in the law would resume soon enough.

He drove back in five unbroken hours, high on images of the time ahead. He loved the Vineyard and, he decided, loved Jenny Leigh. Whatever she struggled with, they would be okay.

This is my favorite sunset ever, he recalled her saying. Smiling to himself, Adam knew he would remember this moment for the very long life he imagined sharing with her.

Driving fast, he caught the noontime ferry from Woods Hole to Vineyard Haven, then sped down State Road toward his parents' place. His mother was gone, visiting a cousin. But if his father were not writing, he would share with him some stories of the Village, renewing a bond frayed by competitive tension and Ben's hatred of defeat. Then he would shower and go find Jenny.

The house was empty, including his father's study. But Ben's truck and car were there. Perhaps he was on the promontory, or walking the beach below. Eagerly, Adam went to look for him.

His path took him past the guesthouse. Through its open window he heard a male voice. Though he could not make out the words, they carried a rough sexual urgency that stopped Adam in his tracks.

For a moment he stayed there, torn between anger and revulsion. The man could only be his father, once again slaking his restless, relentless desire for other women. But this was a terrible violation — a betrayal of his mother committed within sight of the house she had loved since childhood, the home they now shared as husband and wife. Inexorably, Adam found himself drawn to the window, his footsteps silent on the grass.

There was a bottle of Montrachet on the bedside table, Ben's signature. Adam turned his gaze to the bed and saw his father's naked back, the woman beneath him lying on her stomach, moaning as he thrust into her with brutal force. Then Adam took in her long blond-brown hair and long slender legs and felt himself begin to tremble.

Harder, she had implored him.

An animal cry erupted from his throat. Wrenching open the door, he saw blood on the sheets. Not even her period would stop them.

His father turned his neck, eyes widening at the sight of him. As Adam grabbed his hips and wrested him from inside her, Jenny Leigh cried out in anguish.

With a strength born of adrenaline and primal hatred, Adam threw his father on the stone floor, the back of Ben's skull hitting with a dull thud. Gripping the wine bottle by the neck, Adam mounted his father's torso, knees pinning the older man's shoulders as Ben's eyes rolled, unfocused by shock and blinding pain. Then Adam clutched his throat with his left hand and shattered the wine bottle on stone. Holding its broken shards over Ben's eyes, Adam saw the wine dribbling across his face like rivulets of blood.

Shuddering with each convulsive breath, Adam lowered the jagged points of glass closer to Ben's face. His stunned eyes widened, the look of a trapped animal. Adam could smell the alcohol on his breath.

He raised his weapon in a savage jerk, prepared to blind this man for whom no punishment was enough.

"No," Jenny cried out.

His hand froze. Beneath him, Ben began writhing in a frenzied effort to escape.

Adam dropped the bottle, glass shattering on the floor. Then he took his father's head by the hair and smashed it savagely against the stone. The groan that escaped Ben's lips made Adam slam his head again, the other hand pressing his Adam's apple back into his throat.

"Please," his father managed to whisper.

Adam forced his own breathing to slow. In his own near whisper he spat, "I could kill you now. Instead I'll spend my life regretting that I didn't. And you'll spend yours remembering that I know exactly what you are."

Legs unsteady, Adam stood. He stared at his naked father, then faced his girlfriend as she knelt on the bed, tears running down her face, hands covering her breasts as if he were a stranger.

Turning his back on both of them, Adam walked blindly from the guesthouse. By the time he heard its door closing behind him, he knew that he would never speak to his father as long as they both lived, or disclose his reasons to anyone. Only the three of them would know.

Without leaving a note for his mother, Adam left the island the way he had come — Vineyard Haven, the ferry, the long drive back to New York. But he did not go to law school; never again would he take money from Benjamin Blaine. Adam Blaine, no longer his son, would find another life.

Ten years later, Adam forced himself to keep reading until he discovered the deeper meaning of what he was never meant to see. Then he heard another door open and close, and knew that Jenny had come home.

SEVEN

Starting at the sounds of his footsteps, Jenny whirled to see Adam emerging from her den. "What are you doing here?" she blurted.

He paused in the doorway. "I read your manuscript."

It took Jenny a moment to grasp this, and then Adam saw her blanch. "All of it?"

"Every word," he answered softly. "Is that what happened to you?"

Drawing a breath, Jenny briefly closed her eyes. "Yes."

He crossed the room, standing in front of her. "Why didn't you tell me?"

"When?" she demanded. "Even if I could have faced you, I couldn't find you. And why make excuses?"

"What about the part when she was a child? If it's true, that's much more than an excuse."

Without looking at him, Jenny walked over

to the couch and sat, staring into space. "That girl is me," she said in a lifeless voice. "From when I was nine until he left, my dad molested me."

Adam felt a moment of sickened anger, then only sadness. "Like you describe in the manuscript?"

In profile, Jenny nodded. "When it was happening," she managed to say, "all I could do was dissociate. At least that's how I understand it now. But I couldn't talk about it then."

Adam sat beside her. "Not even to me?"

"I didn't want you knowing I was defective." She hesitated, her eyes lowered in shame. "As a child, I discovered that my body was a source of power — if my father wanted these things, so would other men. But it scared me, and I was completely helpless. To survive him I just numbed out." She hunched forward, tears wetting her lashes. "The numbness kept on happening, no matter who I slept with. But it was so good with you, and I loved you so much. Instead I let your father destroy us."

Once more, Adam tasted ashes in his mouth. With quiet bitterness, he said, "He didn't destroy us, Jen. All he did was transform our lives."

Jenny's throat pulsed. At length, she

asked, "Do you care why it happened?"

Silent, Adam fought to erase the image that filled his mind, two bodies glimpsed through a window. "I don't see how it matters now."

"It does to me."

He did not want to relive this, but had no right to stop her. In his silence, she spoke in the same bereft tone. "After I came to dinner, I worked so hard to make that short story better. I was afraid to have him see it, but even more anxious to know what he thought. So I brought it to him." She closed her eyes again, voice drained of feeling. "You were gone, and so was Clarice. But we needed our own workplace, he told me. Then he took me and a bottle of wine to the guesthouse, saying he'd take the time to read each sentence carefully, and that a little wine would help me feel less anxious."

Adam felt a visceral hatred for his father, and for Jenny in her naïveté. As though in a trance, she continued, "He sat beside me on the couch, reading my story in utter silence. By the time he was done I had drunk half the bottle, trying not to become a nervous wreck. When he took my hand, I thought it was out of compassion. Then he smiled and said, 'You really *did* listen to me, didn't you?'

" 'Of course,' I insisted. Suddenly I was grinning like an idiot, filled with this crazy kind of joy. With persistence and a little help, he said, I could make it as a writer. Then he poured us another glass and went over my story with me, line by line, until his face and voice seemed to fill my consciousness."

He had a gift, Carla had said, *for making me feel I* did *have value.*

"Didn't you wonder about him?" Adam asked sharply.

"What I remember is feeling mesmerized." Looking down, she shook her head. "Suddenly, he was staring into my face like he'd just discovered who I was. 'It's so hard to believe,' he told me, 'because you're so young. But I've never shared writing like I have with you —' "

Do you think I hadn't seen that one before? Adam remembered Carla asking. But Jenny's experience was of her father, who had violated her, and of Adam, who had loved her. "I was just so stunned," she said in a broken voice. "It was the recognition I'd always wanted from my father, this time from a man who was all I ever wanted to be. When he began to undress me, I just went somewhere else, like always. The next day I came back, and the next." Abruptly, her speech became dispassionate, almost clinical. "After I was institutionalized, a psychiatrist said I was replicating what happened with my father, hoping I could master it. This time I'd be in control; this time I wouldn't be hurt. I thought I could walk away from him. But I couldn't." Her tone changed yet again, etched with quiet horror. "Before you found us, he'd taken me in the normal way. But I'd left my body, as always, and this time he must have felt it. He looked into my eyes and asked if sex with him was as good as it was with you —"

"Jesus Christ —"

"Please, Adam." Face still averted, Jenny groped for his hand. "I remember staring at him like I'd awakened from a coma, shocked to find out where I was and that this man wanted me because of you. I sat up and said, 'It's different with Adam.'

" 'Different?' he repeated.

" 'Because I love him.' " Jenny bowed her head, seeming to force the words out. "We'd both drunk way too much. He got very quiet, not like himself. Then he said he'd make me feel different, too. His voice had changed — it was colder and harsher." She inhaled, shivering. "When he rolled me on my stomach, I flashed on us in the lighthouse. But it wasn't like that at all. Not what he did or the way he hurt me. Then you came through the door, and all I wanted was to die."

With a visceral shock, Adam grasped what he had seen and heard — Jenny moaning, her blood on the sheets. She sat straighter, as though determined to finish. "After you left, Ben got up off the floor, wine streaking his face. He looked at me with a kind of horror, like he realized what he'd done. Then he left me there, as you had." Jenny's fingers interlaced with Adam's. "It was my childhood again," she continued in a brittle tone, "but so much worse. That day was like another message from my father: 'You'll never be important enough to care about, just to use.' So I overdosed on your beach, praying that I'd die there. Then Ben would have to look at me, and you'd have to come back.

"Instead, he saved my life, having destroyed my desire to live. But then Clarice took over, and helped me heal without knowing what we'd done." Jenny paused, her voice filling with shame. "Suddenly I had a mother who loved me, and who I couldn't bear to lose. That's why I let her believe you'd driven me to suicide. And now you're helping me do that."

Adam struggled to respond. "I was convenient," he answered. "And what good would my telling her do now?" Suddenly, he felt the balance of his thoughts shift, becoming analytic. "Have you told anyone you're writing about this?"

Jenny looked away. "No one. Including your father."

Adam watched her. "But you did meet with him, didn't you? You're the woman my mother saw on the promontory."

Jenny withdrew her hand. "When he called," she said at length, "he begged to see me, saying it was important to us both. Even the sound of his voice made me sick." Pausing, she looked back into Adam's face. "But I thought — or hoped — that it was about you. So I said I'd meet him somewhere I felt safe."

Still appraising her, Adam sat back. "Tell me about it, Jenny."

At first he was not there.

Alone, Jenny stared down at the beach where she had tried to kill herself, feeling all the hatred she had struggled to transcend. Then she heard his footsteps behind her.

"Hello, Jenny."

His voice was older now, and his face

seemed gaunt and worn. Jenny was silent. It was enough that she could look him in the face.

His somber gaze betrayed the loathing he saw. "I guess you're wondering why I called."

The loathing in Jenny's voice surprised her. "Only until you roll me on my stomach."

Ben looked away. "I'm dying, Jenny."

Startled, she scoured her emotions, finding everything but compassion. In a quiet voice, he continued, "I've put you in my estate plan. On my death you'll receive a million dollars."

Disbelieving, Jenny crossed her arms. "If you're looking for forgiveness, it's not in me. I can't even forgive myself."

Ben shook his head. "I'm not so deluded as to hope for absolution, and it's way too late for that. But I do respect your talent. I don't want the worst thing I ever did to be the only way I touched your life." Briefly, he looked away. "I've also found a way to bring Adam back to the island, then keep him here for a while. That way you can tell him how it was. For whatever good that does."

Jenny's stomach twisted. "What makes you think I'd take your money?"

Ben looked into her face. With an air of

sadness, he said, "Because you need it, and the chance to write is all I can give you now. Make the best of it, please."

Without saying more, he turned and walked toward the cabin where Carla Pacelli lived.

Listening, Adam wondered whether to believe her. But the story had the same quality of regret Carla ascribed to him, and it was just strange enough to be true. Finishing, Jenny said, "He was trying to live with what he'd done to us."

"He was trying to buy you," Adam retorted curtly. "For a million dollars, he hoped you'd keep his secrets. Even from beyond the grave he cares about how people see him."

Doubt clouded Jenny's eyes. "I don't pretend to understand him. Then or now."

"You're not twisted enough. Did he also mention he was cutting off my mother?"

"No. Or anything about Carla."

Pausing, Adam reviewed his memory of Sean Mallory's interview notes. "You never told the police about this meeting, did you? Let alone about what my father did to you."

Shaking her head, Jenny turned away. "What I couldn't conceal, I lied about. I couldn't destroy my relationship with

Clarice."

But there was more to it, Adam perceived — once again, he was caught in his father's vise. The sexually avaricious writer in the manuscript was unmistakably Benjamin Blaine, and his mistreatment of Jenny could serve as a motive for murder, especially in light of her instability. Given what Adam knew, the best way to divert suspicion from Teddy was by exposing her lies to the police. And should George Hanley indict his brother, a good defense lawyer would surely exploit her trauma: even if a jury did not think Jenny a murderer, Ben's actions might render him so despicable that no one would care who killed him.

But his betrayal could destroy her, Adam knew, and devastate his mother. And on a coldly practical level, casting Jenny as a potential murderer would not help Clarice at all. Her problem was Carla Pacelli, not Jenny Leigh.

"What are you thinking?" Jenny asked.

"That I forgive you," he said. "And that you may have killed my father."

Jenny flinched. "Are you going to the police?"

Adam could not answer. Instead, he touched her face with curled fingers and left.

Eight

Too much had hit him too quickly.

Shaken, Adam parked at the side of the road, sorting the lies and deceptions that bound them all — Jenny, Clarice, Teddy, and himself — to a man who, even in death, continued to control their lives. He did not yet know how, if at all, Ben's will was linked to his murder, and what truths about his family he had yet to grasp. The only person he credited with candor, however tentatively, was Carla Pacelli.

I've only lied to you once, for reasons of my own, and not about Jenny or the will.

Whatever it was must concern his father, and perhaps his mother.

So many compromises, Clarice had said to him long ago, *so much hurt.*

Which compromises, he wondered now, and whose hurt? The more threads he pulled, the more Adam sensed that the damage Ben inflicted, including Jenny's and his own, stemmed from something still concealed from him. More deeply than before, he had begun to fear the truth. And yet he had to know it.

I thought Grandfather went bankrupt before I was born.

No, his mother had replied. *After.*

Switching on the ignition, Adam headed for Edgartown.

It was a quarter to five, near closing time at the Registry of Deeds. But a jovial gray-haired woman who recalled Adam from high school pointed him to the index that listed buyers and sellers of real estate back two centuries and more. Clarice's father and his own were linked by a single line.

It took forty minutes more, the clerk waiting patiently. At last, Adam found the deed that passed title to his mother's childhood home to Benjamin Blaine. The document which, combined with the postnuptial agreement, had empowered Ben to give it to his lover.

Pensive, Adam stared at the date: February 16, 1974. A schism in the lives of his family, capping the financial ruin that had stripped Clarice's father of everything. A date three years before Adam was born.

Adam thanked his helper for her patience

and drove to Matthew Thomson's office.

The lawyer was still at his desk, scanning computerized time sheets he would turn into billings. "I hate this part," he told Adam. "Measuring my time in tenths of hours. Makes me feel like a damned accountant." He paused, gauging Adam's expression. "This is your second visit of the day, and you're looking even grimmer than before."

"Just curious. I'm wondering if you have the postnuptial agreement at hand."

Thomson's expression became probing. "Ordinarily, something that old would be in a warehouse. But your mother's will contest with Ms. Pacelli has given it fresh currency. Still, I'm wondering why you need it. You're well aware of its parlous effects on Clarice, and I'm sure she has a copy at home."

"True. But it's a sensitive subject with her. I'd rather review it in the serenity of your office."

Thomson raised his eyebrows, then took a file from a desk drawer and handed it to Adam. "My proudest moment in the law," he said wearily. "Let me show you to the conference room."

They went there, Thomson closing the door behind his visitor. Sitting at a mahogany table, Adam began to read.

Thomson had done the job Benjamin Blaine had paid him for. The document was detailed, precise, and draconian, destroying his mother's rights with chilling thoroughness. None of this surprised him. Nor, to Adam's profound unease, did the date — October 11, 1976. Over two years after his father had bought their house.

There's something else I'd like to be clear about, Adam had told his mother. *When you signed the postnup, you believed you'd still inherit from your father.*

Yes, she had said brusquely. *As I recall, this is the third time you've asked that.*

And each time Clarice had lied.

Chin propped on balled fist, Adam stared at the table.

I asked Ben, Thomson had told him, *why the hell she'd sign a document consigning her to economic serfdom, and why he'd want her to. His response — delivered in his most mordant tone — was that this was personal between husband and wife.*

Between February 1974 and October 1976, something had happened.

Standing, Adam returned to Thomson's office, placing the document on his desk. "Satisfied?" Thomson asked.

"Completely. As I read this, Carla Pacelli

has every reason to be grateful for your efforts."

Thomson considered this with a frown. "An odd thought," he replied. "Considering that she probably wasn't born yet." His frown deepened. "I remember thinking this was a time bomb I devoutly hoped would never go off. Thirty-four years later, it has."

Troubled, Adam drove home for dinner with the mother and brother who had lied to him, pursued by thoughts of Jenny.

The dinner hour was subdued. Adam had little to say, less he could tell them, and too many questions it was not yet time to ask. The unspoken knowledge he shared with Teddy, withheld from their mother, burdened them both.

At length, she looked from Teddy to Adam. In a sharp tone that hinted at her tension, she said, "What is it with you two?"

Teddy's belated smile was more a tic. "It's just hard, Mom. Both of us miss Dad such a lot."

And maybe you killed him, Adam thought. Then Teddy caught his eye, and Adam understood that there was something his brother wished to say to him alone.

"I wish his death were that amusing," Clarice rebuked her sons. "You can't imagine how it feels to begin a family with such hope, then see it deteriorate so horribly, with Ben delivering his final judgment on us all."

But why? Adam wanted to ask, and could not.

Afterward, the two brothers sat on the porch gazing at the woods and grass, a soft green in twilight. It reminded Adam of their youth, the many days and hours when, chary of their parents, they had taken refuge in each other's company. But by this time next year the house might be Carla Pacelli's, and Teddy might be in prison.

"Do you have something to say?" Adam asked.

Teddy eyed him. "I was thinking you look like hell."

"So I'm told. It's been a bad day."

"Seems like an understatement," Teddy said pointedly. "The light in your eyes is gone."

He could have been describing himself, Adam thought — he looked haggard, as though sleep had eluded him for nights on end. "My problems are yours," he countered. "I sense that something more happened since our last frank and candid exchange."

Teddy glanced over his shoulder, ensuring that their mother could not hear. Under his breath, he said, "George Hanley told my lawyer he's impaneling a grand jury. I could be indicted within days."

Gazing at the lawn, Adam absorbed what this could mean: the machinery of justice switching into gear, slowly but inexorably grinding forward until it delivered his brother to a life of torment and confinement for a crime that, to Adam, was less a crime than an act of cosmic justice. "What's your strategy?" he asked.

"I've got two choices," his brother replied in the same near whisper. "Take the information you gave us and try to give George Hanley a story that creates enough doubt to slow him down. Or accept that indictment for Dad's murder may be inevitable, and save my version of events until Hanley puts me on the stand. If there were a third choice, I'd take it."

Adam felt leaden. Once Teddy's fate was in the hands of a jury, it might be sealed by his lies to the police. And all that Adam could offer him was Jenny.

That day was like another message from my father, she had told him. *"You'll never be important enough to care about, just to use."*

Watching his expression, Teddy regarded

Adam with tender gravity. "Don't take it so hard. You've done all you can. As only I know."

But Adam had not. As only he knew.

Touching Teddy's shoulder, he stood, went to the kitchen for a bottle of Ben's scotch, and then locked himself in his room.

For an hour, Adam sat drinking scotch, the window a dark square, the chirring of crickets evoking nights spent with his father on the porch.

Who had killed him, he kept asking, and why?

Most likely Teddy; least likely Carla — with Jenny in the balance. Someone for Adam to sacrifice in the hope of saving another of Ben's victims, his brother.

At midnight, the bottle half-finished, Adam fell into a broken sleep.

The nightmare came swiftly. Hellfire missiles rained down on a village controlled by the Taliban. Adam watched the carnage from the edge of a cliff, surrounded by other Taliban with rifles. Their leader spoke in the tones of a judge passing sentence. "You are responsible for the death of our brothers." As his followers aimed their rifles at his head, Adam leaped off the cliff, a vertiginous fall toward the beach where his father died and Jenny had tried to kill herself —

He snapped awake, sweat dampening his face.

There was no point in asking what this meant. The meaning of Afghanistan was simple enough. He had six months left to serve, and an excellent chance of dying. It would be easier to accept his fate, whatever it was, if he left his brother and mother better off for his return.

Stumbling to the bathroom, he splashed cold water on his face, then resumed sitting at the end of his bed.

Why did my mother lie to me? he silently asked his father. *And what secret did you entrust to Carla Pacelli?*

The answer, if Adam could find it, must lie in the will Benjamin Blaine had left them.

By now he could divine, however imperfectly, the workings of Ben's mind. He had left money to Carla because of their son; to Jenny less out of guilt than shame, the hope of burying his seduction of a young woman and the betrayal of his son. But his motive for making Adam executor was more obscure. Though this ploy seemed likely to keep Adam on the island, he rejected the notion that Ben had done this for Jenny's sake, or that his father imagined that Adam's hundred-thousand-dollar inheritance would

431

keep him from undermining the will. Father and son had known each other too well; Ben could not have doubted that Adam would act to protect his mother. So Ben's treatment of Clarice remained the heart of the unknown, revealing a depth of malice unexplained by anything Adam knew. And the gift of an old photo album, one among so many, made no sense at all.

Once again, Adam picked up the album.

It contained photographs of Ben in Cambodia, meticulously dated, covering a two-and-a-half-month period in that country's terrible history, including atrocities committed by the Khmer Rouge in the spring and early summer of 1976. His father had dared much to go there, and documented it all. There was page upon page of photographs of Ben with soldiers, guerrillas, doctors, and guides, or on a sampan or in some temple destroyed by war. Were another man featured in these photographs, he would have drawn Adam's admiration — he knew very well how it felt to put his life at risk. As it was, given that this bequest accompanied the ruin of his mother, Adam wondered at the vast reserves of narcissism that had caused Ben to think his son would give a damn.

Suddenly, he stopped, staring at a date on

one page. Then another.

I think he loved your mother once, Jack had told him. *At least as much as he was capable of love.*

When? Adam had asked. *Before I was born?*

Ben had hidden their secret in plain sight, knowing he would come to it in time.

Adam began shaking.

"You bastard," he said aloud. Said this in grief and hatred and wonder. Said this with a crushing sense of solitude that was too much to endure.

His entire life had been premised on a lie.

NINE

Still and silent, Adam rethought the past, willing himself to feel nothing.

But dispassion was beyond him. A single fact had transformed the meaning of his life, and his relationship to its central figures — from the first moments of his existence, he had been the catalyst for a web of hatred and deception that had enveloped them all. He would not come to terms with this in an hour, or a year. But there was too much at stake not to start.

With deliberate calm, he dressed, walked down the hallway, and knocked on his mother's bedroom door. She answered too quickly to have been sleeping.

Cracking open the door, she stared at him. "What's wrong?"

"Please come downstairs," Adam said. "There's something we need to discuss."

For the first time, Clarice looked haggard, almost old. "Can't it wait until morning?"

"No. It can't."

The look of alarm in her eyes was replaced by a fear that seemed years deep. In a weary voice, she said, "Give me time to dress."

He went to the living room, turning on a single lamp before sitting in Ben's chair. For what seemed endless minutes, he waited there, the room quiet, the cool night air coming through an open window. He had never felt more alone.

His mother's footfalls sounded on the wooden stairs. Then she appeared, dressed in jeans and a sweater, a semblance of her usual calm slipping into place. But her posture when she sat across from him was taut, her hands folded tightly in front of her. The pale light made her face look waxen, accenting the apprehension in her eyes. "What's so urgent?" she inquired.

Adam composed himself. "Tell me about you and Jack. Everything, from the beginning."

She was quiet, her eyelids lowering. He watched her contemplate evasion, the habit of years. Then she said simply, "It started before you were born."

"That much I've worked out. The question is why all of you perpetuated such misery."

His mother searched his face, as though

trying to gauge what he knew. "More than I'd understood, Ben was a selfish man. His early success made him hungry for more — more adventure, more accolades, and, I suspected even then, more women. For weeks on end, he left me here alone with Teddy."

"And Jack?"

Reluctantly, she nodded. "It happened over time, without us fully realizing how we'd come to feel. But he was everything Ben couldn't be — gentle and reflective, more inclined to listen than talk about himself." Emotion made her voice more throaty. "He *valued* me. With Jack I was never an accessory."

"Isn't that the life you signed on for?"

Clarice flushed. "I suppose so. But it seems I needed more. Jack provided it."

"By sleeping with his brother's wife," Adam rejoined. "A landmark in their rivalry. Imagine my surprise at discovering where I fit in."

Her eyes froze. "I'm not sure what you mean."

"That since I was young, I always felt that something wasn't right. I'd like to have known when it still mattered who Jack really was to me."

For a telling moment, Clarice looked

startled. "Your uncle," she parried. "A man who cared for you."

"Give it up, Mother. From the May through July before I was born, Benjamin Blaine was in Cambodia. But I look too much like him for that to be coincidence." Pent-up emotions propelled Adam from his chair. "Once I grasped that, it explained so much. Jack's kindness toward me, and Ben's ambivalence. Their lifelong breach. The warped psychology of that last racing season, Jack pitting me against his brother." *And,* Adam thought but did not say, *Ben's desire to sleep with Jenny Leigh.* "Most important," he finished in a lower voice, "the truth behind Ben's will and, I believe, his murder. That when he presented you with the postnuptial agreement, you were pregnant with Jack's child. I'm the reason you agreed to it, aren't I?"

Clarice sat straighter, marshaling her reserves of dignity. "Yes," she said evenly. "In legal terms, you were the 'consideration' for everything I signed away."

Hearing this said aloud made Adam flinch inside. "But why agree to all that?"

A plea for understanding surfaced in her eyes. "Is it really that hard to grasp? I did it for Teddy, and for you —"

"For me?" Adam said in astonishment.

"Do you really think making Benjamin Blaine my father was a favor? Then let me assure you that I'd pay any price to go back in time and stop you from making this devil's bargain. For Teddy's sake even more than mine."

Clarice turned white. "Do you think I have no regrets? What you've just discovered has haunted me for years. But I had no choice —"

"Would it have been so terrible to be the wife of a woodworker?"

"Please," his mother said urgently, "consider where I was then. I had no money or skills of my own, and was pregnant with another man's child. The price of being with Jack would have been penury, a bitter divorce, and scandal — with me exposed in public as the slut who slept with two brothers, and you stigmatized as the product of an affair. My choice was wrenching for me, and humiliating to Jack. But with Ben as your father, both of my sons would have the security you deserved —"

"And you'd go on being Mrs. Benjamin Blaine."

To his surprise, Clarice nodded. "Whatever you may think, I'm not a mystery to myself. My upbringing was a tutorial in dependence — on men, money, and the security of affluence and status. Whatever his weaknesses, I loved my father dearly. But what I understood too late was that to him a person was who he or she appeared to be. And when that was taken from him, Dad withered and died — figuratively at first, then literally." Her tone grew bitter. "But not a man like Benjamin Blaine. I came to wish my father had one-tenth of his strength. Ben started with nothing, took what he wanted, and made sure he kept it. I might have been afraid of him, but not once did I fear that he would fail. I'd never be poor or desperate like my mother became. And, yes, I enjoyed the reflected glory of being his wife, and all the privilege that came with it. That was part of the bargain, too."

"What was in it for Ben?"

His mother seemed to fortify herself, then spoke in a reluctant voice. "Beneath the surface, Benjamin Blaine was a very frightened man. One night early in our marriage, he got terribly drunk. He came to bed and suddenly started rambling about Vietnam, this man in his platoon. He'd been exhausted and afraid, he said — that was why it happened. I realized without him saying so that 'it' involved another man. What tortured Ben was that it might be fundamental to his nature." Pausing, Clarice inhaled. "The next day he carried on with false bravado, like he hadn't told me anything. He never mentioned it again. But on a very few occasions, when he was drunk, Ben's tastes in sexual intercourse didn't require me to be a woman. A brutal instance of *in vino veritas.*"

When he rolled me on my stomach, Jenny had said, *I flashed on us in the lighthouse. But it wasn't like that at all. Not what he did or the way he hurt me.*

Sickened, Adam said, "And the others?"

"Weren't enough to banish his fears." Turning from him, his mother continued her painful narrative. "That I was pregnant by Jack made him all the more insecure. But I couldn't bear the thought of aborting Jack's child, and Ben was afraid of anyone knowing he'd been cuckolded by his brother. By exacting the postnuptial agreement as the price for keeping you, he kept Jack and me apart. His ultimate victory."

"Hardly," Adam said. "After that, he tormented all of us for years. I'll never fathom why Jack stayed."

His mother faced him again. "Because he loved me. And you."

"But not enough to claim me," Adam retorted. "I should be relieved that Benja-

440

min Blaine wasn't my father. But now I'm the son of two masochists-for-life —"

"You don't know what it was like for me," his mother protested. "Or for Jack, waiting for whatever moments we could steal, the times he could watch your games —"

"I know what it was like for your sons," Adam shot back. "I always wondered how a father could demean a boy as kind and talented as Teddy. Now I understand — Ben's only son held up a mirror to his deepest fears." He stood over her, speaking with barely repressed emotion. "I became the 'son' he wanted. I can imagine him trying to believe that my achievements came from him, not from Jack's DNA. But he could never resist competing with me, just as he competed with my father." He shook his head in wonder and disgust. "Even now you have no idea how much damage you inflicted, or on whom. But knowing what you did, how could you stand to watch it all unfold?"

Clarice stared at him. In a parched voice she said, "I watched Ben raise you to be the person *he* wanted to be. By accident or design, he made you enough like him to be strong. So strong that you can live with even this."

"In a day or so," Adam responded sharply,

"I'll work up the requisite gratitude. But not before we talk about the night Ben died. This time I want the truth."

Clarice met his eyes. "As I told you, Ben locked himself in his study, brooding and drinking. When he came out, he was unsteady, almost stumbling. Alcohol had never done that to him before. But it was his words that cut me to the quick."

She stopped abruptly, shame and humiliation graven on her face. Sitting beside her, Adam said more quietly, "Tell me about it, Mother."

Ben's face was ravaged, his once vigorous frame shambling and much too thin. He stared at his wife as though he had never truly seen her. "I'm done with this farce," he told her bluntly. "Whatever time I have left, I'm planning to spend without you."

Facing him in the living room, Clarice fought for calm. "You can't mean that, Ben. We've had forty years of marriage."

The light in his eyes dulled. "God help me," he replied with bone-deep weariness. "God help us all."

Clarice could find no words. In a tone of utter finality, her husband continued, "I'm going to be with Carla. If there's a merciful

God, or any God at all, I'll live to see our son."

Clarice felt bewilderment turn to shock. "Carla Pacelli is pregnant?"

Ben nodded. "Whatever you may think of her, she'll be a fine mother."

The implied insult pierced Clarice's soul. "And I wasn't?"

"You did the best you could, Clarice. When you weren't sleeping with my brother. But please don't claim you stayed with me for our son, or for yours. Your holy grail was money and prestige." His voice was etched with disdain. "You'll have to live on love now. The money goes with me, to support Carla and our son —"

Startled, Clarice stood. "You can't do that," she protested.

"You know very well that I can. That was the price of Adam, remember? For what little good that did any of us." Ben slumped, as though weighed down by the past, then continued in a tone of indifference and fatigue. "I'm going to admire the sunset. When I return, I'll pack up what I need. You can stick around to watch me, if you like. But I'd prefer you go to Jack's place, your future home. Maybe you can start redecorating."

Turning from her, he left.

Clarice stared at the Persian rug, unable to face her son. "I never saw him again."

Adam wondered whether to believe her. "How did you react?"

Clarice swallowed. "I was frightened and humiliated. He'd never threatened me before, and this child made it real. To think I could lose everything was devastating."

"But you didn't just sit here, did you? You called Teddy and told him what Ben had said."

"Yes," Clarice admitted. "I've been lying to protect him."

"But not just Teddy," Adam continued. "First, you called Jack."

Surprised, she glanced at him sideways, then turned away. "He didn't answer," she murmured. "So I left him a message, telling him what Ben had said and done."

"And where he'd gone," Adam said crisply. "Then you lied to the police about both calls. Do you realize what trouble that caused for Teddy?"

Clarice straightened. "What on earth do you mean?"

For the first time Adam was surprised. He gazed into her eyes, and saw nothing but confusion. "What do you suppose he did that night?"

"Nothing." Clarice paused, eyes filling with doubt. "Isn't that what he told the police?"

Adam weighed the possibilities: that she knew nothing of Teddy's actions, or that she had caused Ben's death — or both. "Maybe he thought he was protecting you. But here's what I think, Mother. You couldn't reach Jack, and felt certain that Teddy couldn't help you. And you were ignorant of one crucial fact — that Ben had already changed his will." Adam forced a new harshness into his tone. "In desperation, you went to the promontory. You found him weak and drunk and disoriented, like a man who'd suffered a stroke. So you pushed him off the cliff, hoping to preserve the prior will. The one that gave you everything."

"No," his mother cried out. "I never went there, I swear it. As far as I know, Ben fell."

"True enough. But one of you helped him." Abruptly, Adam stood. "Call Jack," he finished. "Tell him to meet me where Ben went off the cliff."

TEN

Adam stood alone in the darkness. The moon was full, and a fitful breeze came off the water. For a half hour he thought about his father.

From behind him he heard footsteps on the trail. Turning, he saw the outline of a man for whom, Adam realized, he had been waiting all his life. Then Jack stepped into the pale light.

"Hello, Jack," Adam said with tenuous calm. "Is there anything in particular you'd care to say?"

Jack's face was worn, his eyes somber. "That I'm sorry," he said at last. "I always loved you, Adam. For years my reason for staying was to watch you grow."

Abruptly, Adam felt his self-control strip away. "As Benjamin Blaine's son?" he asked with incredulity. "You and my mother trapped me in a love–hate relationship with a man who resented me for reasons I couldn't know. Then you pitted me against him in that last racing season. Do you have a fucking clue what came from that? Or do you give a damn?"

Though shaken, Jack refused to look away. "I never thought you'd leave," he said in a low voice. "I still don't know why you did."

"The reasons are my own, and you've got no right to know them." Adam caught himself, voice husky with emotion. "There were times, growing up, when I wished you were my father. Now I wish you'd been as strong as the man who pretended I was his son. But for better or worse, I absorbed Ben's will, his nerve, and his talent for survival. Along the way I learned to trust absolutely no one. A useful trait in a family like ours." Adam paused, then finished with weary fatalism. "On balance, I suppose, I'd rather have you as a father. Yet right now I look at you and Mother, and all I want is to vanish off the face of the earth. But I can't, because the two of you have created a mess I plan to straighten out."

Jack cocked his head. "What do you have in mind?"

"We're starting where you and Ben left off," Adam responded coldly. "Tell me how you killed him, Jack."

Jack hunched a little, hands jammed in

his pockets. "So now you're the avenging angel, or perhaps the hanging judge. You seemed to have developed the soul for that."

"No doubt. But not without help."

Jack seemed to flinch. "Maybe I deserve that. But before you judge me, listen."

He found his brother sitting slumped on the rock, his eyes bloodshot, his gaze unfocused. With terrible effort, Ben sat straighter. "I'm taking a rest," he said tiredly. "I can only assume she called you."

Jack knelt by him, staring into his face. "You can't do this to her," he told Ben. "Not after all these years."

Ben's face darkened, and then he bit off a burst of laughter. "So I should leave everything to Clarice? Then you could move into my house, claim my wife, and take the fruits of all I've done. You may have lived for that, Jack. But by God, I did not." Ben lowered his voice. "I've found someone who loves me, a woman with grace and grit who'll give me a son that's actually mine. They're what my life comes down to, and where my money is going. You and Clarice can do what you please."

Filled with anger, Jack leaned forward, his face inches from Ben's. "This is her home, Ben. You can't take that from her."

Ben smiled a little. "I already have," he answered calmly. "I gave you a home, Jack — our parents' cracker box. Ask Clarice if she wants to live there with you. But I suppose you learned her answer long ago. All these years she preferred to live with me than in the mediocrity that is your birthright —"

Filled with hatred, Jack grabbed his shirt. "She can file for divorce, and challenge the agreement you forced on her."

Despite the violence of Jack's actions, Ben's face revealed nothing but mild interest. "Not a bad idea," he remarked. "That's what I'd have done in her place, many moons ago." He paused, gathering strength. "Unfortunately for you both, I'm dying. She can't divorce me fast enough. So unless she wins a will contest, which I believe she can't, she'll have nothing but the deathless love you've imagined sharing. She'll be looking for a rich man by Thanksgiving."

Overcome by rage, Jack wrenched him upright, ripping a button off Ben's shirt. In two steps he held his brother over the edge of the cliff, staring into the face he had always loathed. "I can kill you now," he said in a strangled voice. "I've wanted to for years."

Ben stared at him with contempt. "So did

Adam. But even he couldn't, and I don't think you have the guts for it. He got all that from me."

Jack thrust his brother forward, his grip all that kept Ben from falling over the precipice. Ben looked back at him, speaking with his last reserves of will. "You're a loser, Jack. And you're about to lose again."

Jack held Ben's face an inch from his. "Do you think I can't do this, Ben?"

Smiling with disdain, Ben spat into his face.

Jack felt the spittle on his cheek. A surge of insanity seized his body and soul. He stared into his brother's adamantine eyes, then felt his hands let go.

Frozen in time, Ben filled a space above the void. Then he hurtled toward the rocks. For an instant, Jack swore that his feeble cry turned into laughter. Then a distant thud echoed in the dark, marking the death of his brother.

Facing Jack, Adam felt his skin crawl. Perhaps, as Ben had implied to Teddy, he might have provided for his family had he lived a day longer. Perhaps the laughter Jack imagined hearing had been real.

"You held him over a cliff," Adam managed to say, "then let him fall. Murder, plain and simple."

Jack's voice shook. "He'd been spitting in my face ever since he learned to walk. For that one instant, I could do what I'd imagined all my life."

"And save my mother from humiliation in the bargain. Or so you thought." Adam heard the horror in his voice mingling with despair. "You helped him commit suicide and lock in the new will, putting yourself at risk. No wonder he died laughing."

Jack closed his eyes. Watching him, Adam was overcome by the tragedy of all that he had learned, the incalculable damage to so many lives. Quietly, he said, "You've been worried all along that you'd get found out. It was you who followed me here, wasn't it?"

Drained, his father could barely nod. "I wanted to see what you were doing. From the start, you were sure that someone killed him."

"What does my mother know?"

"Nothing. When I came back to the house, I told her I couldn't find him. By morning, I'd figured out a plan. Incinerate the boots I'd worn, then stumble across his body on the beach, as though his death were an accident." Jack paused, touching his eyes. "It almost worked."

"Not for Teddy," Adam retorted. "They're about to charge him with killing Ben."

Jack stiffened. "How can *that* be?"

"Doesn't matter. The point is that I know you're a murderer. But if I turn you in to the police, they may think my mother's an accomplice. On the other hand, there's Teddy to consider. I can't let him take the fall for you."

Jack straightened. "Do you think *I* can? After I tell Clarice what happened, I'm going to the police."

"Don't overdo it, Jack. There's been heartache enough, most of it Ben's doing." Adam paused, finding a calmer tone. "You *are* my father, after all. So I'd prefer that you not pay for getting Teddy off the hook. And given that you're a reasonably accomplished liar, why not make that work for you?"

"What the hell are you saying?"

"You'll have to improve your story, merging it with Teddy's. In my version, Ben never threatened my mother with disinheritance. Because he was drunk and abusive, you decided to confront him in your role as her protector." Adam looked into his father's eyes. "You found him here, and asked him to stop mistreating her. A quarrel ensued. Suddenly, he took a swing at you and lost

452

his balance, the victim of alcohol and disequilibrium caused by his tumor. When you reached for him, it was too late."

Jack stared at the place where Ben had fallen. At last, he said, "Still more lies, after so many. Do you think they'd believe me now?"

"Not really. They'll also think you're protecting Teddy. But I've become familiar with what the police know and don't know. They have no witnesses to the murder. Teddy's account will cover all the physical evidence, leaving them with nothing to refute your latest story." Reading Jack's doubt, he added, "Granted, telling it will take some nerve. But once you do, it creates reasonable doubt in Teddy's favor, and he'll do the same for you. George Hanley is nothing if not practical. He'll see the wisdom in letting go of the death of a dying man."

Jack studied him, then shook his head. In a tone of sadness, he asked, "When did you become so cold-blooded? I wonder."

"The day I left here. All I've done since is refine my talents." Adam paused, struggling with emotions he refused to show. "But that's for another day — if ever. This family has one more thing it needs to settle."

ELEVEN

"You can practice on my mother," Adam had told Jack on the way to the house. Now, as the first light came through the window, he watched her face as she listened to Jack's carefully crafted falsehoods.

In rapid sequence, her expressions betrayed surprise, bewilderment, anger, horror, and, at length, deep anxiety. Unless she and Jack were extraordinarily accomplished actors, Adam concluded to his relief, their unrehearsed interaction suggested that Clarice knew nothing about Ben's death. That Jack had planted another lie at the heart of their relationship was the price of saving him.

Clarice took Jack's hand, shedding the pretense of years. Worriedly, she asked, "Do you really have to tell them?"

"He does," Adam broke in flatly. "What the police have on Teddy could convict him of a murder he didn't commit."

Clarice turned to him. "How can you know all that?"

"Just trust me that I do." He paused, then said, "Like you, Teddy lied to the police about your phone call. That was your idea, wasn't it?"

Slowly, Clarice nodded.

"I assume you were trying to protect him," Adam continued, "and not just yourself and Jack. But I know that Teddy was protecting you." Turning to Jack, he finished, "I'm sure that Avi Gold would represent you, and work with Teddy's lawyer. That'll help everyone keep their lines straight."

Staring at him, Clarice said, "This is a lot to absorb, Adam." Seeing his expression, she added softly, "For all of us, I suppose."

"Then brace yourself, Mother. Because there's more." He sat back, speaking in the same clipped tone. "The will contest has become more complex than you know. Thanks to me, you won't get caught trying to pass off the postnup as misplaced self-actualization. On the other hand, I'm now aware of the truth — that you got plenty of 'consideration' for signing it, from continuing to live here to concealing the messy facts surrounding my birth. And I suspect that Carla Pacelli knows that, too."

Clarice looked stricken. "Ben told her?"

"I'm pretty sure he did. If so, I can't lie about it. Right now you've got a decent shot at overturning Ben's will. But between Carla and me, you could wind up with nothing. So here's what you're going to do.

"First, your lawyer will offer Carla a settlement of three million dollars, on which you're also paying the estate taxes —"

"No," Clarice protested. "I refuse to treat her as an equal."

"You've got no choice," Adam said coldly. "So feel grateful to get by with that. Carla's got a real chance of walking off with everything; at a minimum, she'll get almost two million for her son. Who, by the way, is Teddy's brother, Jack's nephew, and my cousin. All of us need to see to his well-being. This family has inflicted enough misery on its own."

He paused a moment, allowing Clarice time to absorb this. "Next, Jenny gets her million, also tax free. That leaves you with roughly seven million dollars, of which you should give Teddy one million for himself." Adam looked from his mother to Jack. "The two of you will have more than enough to live here. Though if I were you, I'd sell this place. The karma leaves a lot to be desired."

Clarice seemed to blanch. "How do you know that Carla will agree?"

"Because I'm developing a sense of her. In fact, despite my best efforts, I may have a better grasp of Carla Pacelli than of either one of you. That'll give me food for thought on the flight back to Afghanistan." Briefly, he paused, watching the stunned look in his parents' eyes. "For now," he told them, "I plan to shower, drink several cups of coffee, and then call Avi Gold. After that Jack should meet with Avi, and I'm going to see Carla Pacelli. If she consents to this, as I think she will, we're settling Ben's estate. Are all of us agreed?"

Clarice looked at Jack, who nodded. Facing Adam, his mother retrieved some of her composure, accenting the sadness in her eyes. "I still look at you, Adam, and see him. The same iron will, the same belief that you can bend the world to your ends."

Despite himself, Adam discovered, comparisons to Benjamin Blaine still pierced him. "Better ends, I hope — especially yours and Jack's. But I'd appreciate it if both of you disappeared for the next few hours. I really do need to be alone."

At ten o'clock, Adam went to see Carla Pacelli.

She was waiting for him on the deck, a light breeze rippling her hair. Smiling a little, she said, "Thanks for calling. It gave me time to dress."

Then I regret that, Adam might have said in another life. But he felt way too tired, and even more confused. "I had to see you."

It came out sounding wrong, not as he intended. Carla regarded him gravely. "You really do look awful."

"And feel worse," he admitted. "How long have you known that I wasn't Ben's son?"

Briefly, she looked down, then met his eyes with new directness. "For months now."

Adam shook his head in disbelief. "And yet you had the grace not to tell me. Even though we were enemies."

"It wasn't my place," she answered in a level tone. "And you were never quite my enemy. It was a little more complex between us, I thought."

This was true, Adam realized. "Still, you could have warned me off any time you wanted to. All you needed was to tell the truth."

"And tamper with your life?" Carla asked with quiet compassion. "It was clear that you loved your family, despite all you'd gone through. I couldn't know how revealing the truth might change that. Once I realized that you knew nothing, it seemed best to keep Ben's secret. At least for as long as I could.

"But there's something else I can say now. Whatever her reasons, the affair between Clarice and his brother caused Ben terrible anguish. That's why I never considered his marriage sacred ground." She paused again. "At least that's my excuse."

"No help for it now," Adam said wearily. "I came here to resolve the future." He paused, searching for the proper words. "There needs to be an end to all this sadness. If I can guarantee you three million dollars, would you take it? That would spare you a will contest, and help both of you quite a lot."

A moment's surprise appeared in Carla's eyes, and then she gazed down at the deck with veiled lids. "More than 'a lot,' " she finally answered. "My lawyer won't like this, I'm sure. But if your mother can accept that, so will I. I don't have the heart for any more of this." She gave him an ironic smile. "As if I'm being so beneficent. I grew up without a dime, made millions as an actress, and blew it all because of my own failings. Now I can give my son the security I lost. That's what Clarice must have thought before you were born."

The comparison — and Carla's honesty

— gave Adam pause. "Maybe so," he replied. "But she was also in love with someone else."

"Then accepting this money is easier for me, isn't it?" Carla looked into his eyes. "You persuaded her, I know. But why?"

Adam managed a shrug. "It's simple, really. As I recalculate my genealogy, you're carrying my cousin."

For another moment, Carla gazed at him, then patted her stomach. "Actually, I thought I felt him move this morning. A mother's imagination, probably. But at least I'm not sick anymore."

Adam shoved his hands in his pockets, quiet for a time. "I'm not sure how to say this without sounding stupid. But you're a far better person than I took you for."

Another smile surfaced in her eyes. "I suppose I could return your backhanded compliment. But you're exactly who I took you for, though you did your damnedest to conceal that." Carla paused, then said in a reticent tone, "You're leaving soon, I know. But once you're back, you can come to see us if you'd like."

Adam searched her face, trying to read what he saw there. "Perhaps I will," he told her. "After all, every boy can use a man who cares for him. No matter who."

"Then we'll look forward to it." She hesitated, then added, "Be safe, Adam. Despite everything, Ben worried for you. Now I do, too."

Adam fell silent, unsure of what else he wished to say. Then he felt the weight of what he could never tell her: that his father had killed the father of her child. "I'll be fine," he promised. "Take care, Carla."

Turning from the doubt he saw in her eyes, he left without looking back, still followed by the shadow of Benjamin Blaine.

Alone, Adam walked in the Menemsha hills, too exhausted to absorb what he had heard, too shattered by the truth to seek refuge in his mother's home. Again and again, he was beset by images of the last few days and hours, questioning his choices, yet he was unable to imagine what else he could have done. Then he grasped the moment that, more than any other, would trouble his conscience until he acted.

Before he could rest, there was one more person he had to see.

He met Jenny on the pier at Edgartown. For a time they sat together, silent, gazing at the sunlit water, the sailboats at mooring, the great houses surrounding the harbor.

"I came to tell you something important," he finally said. "I know you had nothing to do with his death. I'm sorry for ever suggesting that you might have."

Jenny turned to him, a deep sadness in her eyes. "It was because of what I did with him. The gift that keeps on giving."

"No more, Jen. That was another life."

Jenny drew a breath. "But we can never go back, can we?"

This simple question, Adam found, deepened his sadness. "No," he answered. "We're different people now."

Jenny looked down, as though trying to decipher what that meant. "There's something else," Adam told her. "My mom and Carla Pacelli are settling his estate. Which means that your bequest is safe." His tone was quiet but insistent. "Keep it, Jen. If not for him, for me. You've got all that talent. Take it as far as you can." He took her hand. "I've also been thinking about your manuscript, and wondering if you should turn the page. My father's posthumous reputation means nothing to me. But for your own sake, maybe you need to let him go."

Jenny searched his face. "You still haven't told Clarice, have you?"

"And never will. It would be no kindness to anyone."

Slowly, Jenny nodded. "And you? What will you do now?"

"Go back to scenic Afghanistan, where simple farmers tend their poppies." Seeing her anxiety, he added, "Only six months more, and then they'll send me somewhere else. Wherever that is, I'll keep in touch."

Tears welled in Jenny's eyes. "Will you?"

"I still care about you," Adam assured her. "I always will. Whatever his motives in bringing me back, Ben helped me rediscover that. I wanted you to know that, too."

She forced herself to smile. "But do I have to let you go?"

Gently, Adam kissed her. "Never. I'll always need to know how you are."

It was true. But in that moment Adam realized that the woman he was drawn to, more by instinct than by reason, was no longer Jenny Leigh.

TWELVE

When Adam arrived home, no one was there.

Tiredly, he climbed the stairs, his thoughts jumbled, certain only that he had reached the end of his string. It was safe to sleep, he realized; this was not Afghanistan. Stripping to his shorts, he took a trazodone and fell into a darkness that, for once, was dreamless.

A knock on the door awakened him. He sat up, disoriented, unsure of where he was until he looked out the window. It must be morning, he realized; the sunlight was gentle, and dew glistened on the grass. And Benjamin Blaine was not his father.

"Adam," his brother called. "Are you all right?"

They could be boys, Adam thought in his confusion, Teddy come to get him for an early morning sail. At once, the pieces of his new reality fell into place.

"Just tired," he answered, and went to open the door.

Teddy looked at him, and then comprehension stole into his eyes. "You must have heard about Jack."

"I have. A lot to take in, isn't it?"

His brother closed the door behind him. Quietly, he asked, "Do you really think it was an accident?"

Adam shrugged, then wiped the sleep from his eyes and sat on the edge of his bed. "To me, the important thing is that you're off the hook. So I guess I don't much care. One way or the other, our father was a dead man. All Jack did is advance the date."

Teddy sat in his brother's desk chair, regarding Adam with deep curiosity. "Mind telling me what you had to do with all this? I'm already sure that you're not who you say you are."

Adam managed to laugh. "Who in this family is?"

Though Teddy smiled a little, his eyes were still grave. For a moment, Adam considered telling him that they were half brothers, and half cousins. But Teddy had always been his brother, and always would be. He thought of Carla, deciding that, for Adam, the truth was not hers to tell. It would do Teddy no good, he reasoned, to

465

know that he was Ben's only son, or that, despite this, his father had chosen to claim Adam as his own. And the burden of protecting Jack was Adam's to bear, not Teddy's. Some family secrets needed to be kept.

"Anyhow," Adam said. "It's done."

"Not for me." Leaning forward, Teddy regarded his brother with new intensity. "Ever since you got here, you've been looking out for me. How did you find out all the stuff about the police?"

Adam considered his answer. "As a favor to me, please be a little less curious about what I've been up to, and focus more on what our uncle did for you. He couldn't stay quiet with you in trouble —"

"I understand," Teddy interrupted. "Now tell me what you had to do with that."

"Next to nothing. All Jack did was use me as a sounding board. So leave it there, all right? Just remember that there are few surprises in life as good as avoiding indictment." Briefly, Adam smiled. "Or escaping homelessness."

Teddy studied him. Then, at length, he nodded his assent. "Life feels different this morning, doesn't it?"

"Yes, and no. You're still my brother, and there's no one in the world I love more. Now that our father is gone, it's really just the two of us. That suits me just fine."

"Me too." Teddy glanced at Adam's open suitcase. "Does that mean you're leaving?"

"Yup. Frankly, I'm a little burned out. I hope our next reunion bores us all to death."

Even as he said this, Adam wondered how coming back would feel. Lonely, he realized. The pathology of the Blaines would persist in all that Adam must conceal from Teddy, the person to whom he felt closest — that Ben was not Adam's father, that their mother's poise concealed tragedy and deceit, that ignorance of a murder separated Teddy from Adam and his parents. However deeply he wished otherwise, there was nothing Adam could do to change this. Whenever their family was together, Adam, like his mother and father, would become an actor in a play whose author was a dead man.

He could say none of this to Teddy. Instead, reaching out, he held his brother close, mutely apologizing for the silence that would always lie between them.

Suitcase in hand, Adam found his parents on the porch.

Lines of pain and weariness were etched in his mother's face. Halfheartedly, she asked, "Do you really have to go?"

To his own surprise, Adam emitted a joyless laugh. Not unkindly, he said, "It's not the time for party manners, Mother. There's no etiquette for this one."

Jack reached for his mother's hand, a gesture meant to comfort. As their fingers intertwined, Clarice smiled wanly. "I suppose not."

"So I'm off. I've done what I needed to do, and all of us need some distance from that." He paused, looking from one parent to the other. "In a while, maybe this will seem better. But I've been too busy dealing with the consequences of what happened years ago to absorb how it's affected me. Only time can help."

Suddenly, Clarice fought back tears. "I'm sorry, Adam — for everything. Please know how much we love you."

"And I love you." Turning to Jack, he said, "I don't know if I'll ever stop seeing you as my uncle. Whatever comes to me, I suspect, will happen far away from here. There's really nothing you can do."

There was a brief silence, then both of his parents stood. Adam kissed his mother's forehead, then gave Jack an awkward hug. "Will you be all right?" Adam asked him.

Jack gave him a wan smile. "So Avi tells me." Except, Adam supposed, in his heart.

Saying good-bye, he picked up his suitcase

and left, walking toward the taxi parked beside his father's — his uncle's — truck.

In time, Adam reflected, Clarice and Jack might marry. It depended on whether they could live with what they knew, and still live with each other. But they lived for years with everything but murder, and perhaps Jack could deal with even that. Adam himself had lived with worse.

Climbing into the taxi, he asked the cabbie to head for Menemsha Harbor.

Together, Adam and Charlie Glazer sailed out onto the pond, Charlie at the helm.

The day was warm, the breeze fitful, the water dotted with sailboats and powerboats and kayaks. For an hour, as Charlie piloted *Folie à Un,* Adam told him everything he had learned and done. All that he omitted was that an accident was murder.

When he finished, Charlie bent his head, stroking the bridge of his nose as he somberly regarded Adam. "That's a lot to do," he said softly. "And even more to endure."

Adam felt the salt spray on his skin. "So how do I live with this?"

Reflective, Glazer considered him. "Here's where I suggest you start. Whatever your methods, you seem to have restored some semblance of moral order. You kept Ben from disinheriting your mother and brother. You protected his unborn son, and his bequest to Jenny Leigh. You kept your brother out of prison. And you were strong enough to do all that despite discovering some very hard truths most people would find crushing. All in all, a decent two weeks' work. Forgive yourself for feeling tired."

As Glazer must have intended, the laconic understatement drew a smile from Adam. "Still," the psychiatrist continued in a serious tone, "there's Ben, the father who wasn't yours. The man who exploited Jenny's weaknesses, and drove you from the island. And Jack, who never acknowledged you as his son, but deployed you in their rivalry. And Clarice —" Pausing, Glazer asked, "Would you prefer never having learned all this?"

Adam pondered the question. "In some ways. But by bringing me back here, Ben forced me to understand the past, and enabled me to limit its impact on the future. I guess that's something."

Glazer adjusted the tiller, fighting headwinds. "It may not feel this way, Adam. But in a certain sense, you were lucky. Of all the members of your family, you were the one who got the resilience gene, while Teddy got the shaft. Jack loved you as his son; Ben wished you were his son. All that helped give you the strength to break away." Glazer shot him a keen look. "On that subject, would you mind telling me what the hell you do in Afghanistan? Last time I checked, Johnny Appleseed didn't specialize in burglarizing courthouses."

Despite his mood, Adam laughed. Watching a young boy piloting a Sunfish, he weighed how much to say. "I'll skip the details," he said at length. "But the short is that I work for the government, recruiting double agents among the Taliban in the most treacherous part of the country. The goal is to identify their key military leaders, then target them for assassination."

The psychiatrist stared at him. "Dangerous work, it sounds like."

"Dangerous enough. If you misjudge someone, he may well kill you. Then your best hope is dying quickly. Knowing that makes you watchful, resourceful, duplicitous, and accustomed to working outside the rules. Useful skills on Martha's Vineyard, I discovered. At least if you're a Blaine." Adam caught himself; for once, he would not try to conceal his feelings. "Know what's funny?" he asked. "Three weeks ago I killed a man while driving at warp speed down some godforsaken road. I had no choice — he was about to shoot me. But the worst part is that I still don't know how I feel about it, except in nightmares where I wake up sweating." He stopped, shaking his head. "What am I becoming? I wonder."

Glazer regarded him gravely. "And yet you're going back."

"That's the life I chose when I left here. Maybe I had a death wish. But for the next six months, Afghanistan is part of that commitment."

Glazer sat in a deck chair beside the tiller, deliberately allowing the Herreshoff to lose speed. "What will you do if you get out of there alive?"

"A pretty thought." Adam paused, trying to imagine a future beyond survival. "Who knows, Charlie? Maybe I can reclaim my life — whatever that is." He laughed without much humor. "I could even go to law school, I suppose. Though I've lost count of all the laws I've broken in the last two weeks."

"A trifle," Charlie replied. "At least you're not a tax evader." Once more his tone became gentle. "And Carla?"

Adam shook his head. "She was his lover, Charlie, and this family is incestuous enough. Like it or not, I'm drawn to her, for reasons I can't yet explain. But I'd

472

always remind her of him, and vice versa. It's all too weird."

"You could certainly argue that," Charlie replied with a trace of arid humor. "I suppose it depends on how weird you want it to be. She was only your uncle's girlfriend, after all, and the boy is only your cousin. Though I grant you that a Blaine family Thanksgiving might be a little fraught." He paused, adding mildly, "But then it would be anyhow, wouldn't it?"

Adam faced him, trying to gauge what this man was saying. "Weird," Glazer continued in an emphatic tone, "is using Carla as a way of getting back at Ben. If it's anything like that, please don't go near her. But if you genuinely care for her, then other questions arise. Is it best to deny your feelings, as your mother did? Or to ask if Benjamin Blaine is still making choices for you, and instead find out what you and she can offer each other. Assuming, of course, that you can also care about her son." Glazer paused, then finished, "Whatever the case, Adam, this may be important to you and others. Take your time to sort it out."

Silent, Adam gazed out at the pond where he, Jack's son, had raced against Ben, ignorant of what this had meant to both of them. There was something terribly wrong,

473

he knew, when sons paid for the sins of their fathers. "I'll hold the thought," he told Glazer. "Right now, it's time to get off the water. I've got a plane to catch."

That night, Adam flew to Boston, as he had told his family he would. But before returning to Afghanistan, he caught another plane to Washington, D.C., then headed for the headquarters of the Central Intelligence Agency. No doubt, he reflected, his gift for keeping secrets — even from his employers — was hereditary.

Alone in his car, he pondered this. He could live in the past, he concluded, or outrun it. Perhaps when he got to Kandahar, he would call her.

AFTERWORD AND ACKNOWLEDGMENTS

I've long wanted to write a novel set on Martha's Vineyard, my summer home for almost two decades now. When several strands of thought coalesced into a psychological novel about a domineering writer, a missing son, and their complex and tormented family, I knew that I'd found the narrative I wanted. After that, and with some crucial help from others, *Fall from Grace* seemed to flow.

Critical to its story was an understanding of psychology; as in other novels, Dr. Rodney Shapiro and Dr. Charles Silberstein helped me probe the endless complications of human behavior, as well as the treatment of addiction and personality disorders. Marjorie Suisman and Tom Frisardi generously helped me with the essentials of the will contest, and Marcia Cini helped explain the system of records regarding land transfers. As to painting and fly-fishing, Kib

Bramhall — a man gifted in both — helped give the Blaines his skills. And Brock Callen was kind enough to help turn them into sailors.

Others helped in critical ways. Howard Hart, a man revered within the intelligence community, helped sketch Adam's perilous life in Afghanistan. Judge Jim Collins, a former defense attorney, helped me assess Teddy Blaine's dilemma, as did District Attorney Laura Marshard from Martha's Vineyard. Teddy's legal plight owes much to pathologist Dr. Terri Haddix and homicide inspector Joe Toomey, with advice on Massachusetts procedures from Jeff and Peggy Stone. My smart and observant daughter Katie Patterson, while still a teen, invented the concept of Celebrity Pac-Man. Laura Roosevelt helped me with various aspects of Vineyard life, and Dr. Maureen Strafford explained the symptoms and progression of brain cancer. And I could not have buried Benjamin Blaine without the services of Father Rob Hensley. While I could not have done without the help of all, any errors are mine alone.

As always, the manuscript benefited from the close attention of my assistant, Alison Thomas; my beloved and much-missed friend and agent, the late Fred Hill; and my wife, Nancy Clair. And I'm deeply grateful for the help and support of my publisher, Susan Moldow, and my editor, Colin Harrison.

Two friends deserve special mention. While Dr. Bill Glazer was endlessly patient in enriching my knowledge of my characters' psychology, that was just the beginning. By introducing me to the Herreshoff racing season, and — with Brock Callen — imagining two races, he provided the central metaphor for the rivalry among the Blaines. This novel is far richer for Bill's wisdom, generosity, and friendship.

Finally, there is Al Giannini, to whom this book is dedicated. Among lawyers, Al is known as a peerless homicide prosecutor; to me, he has been not only a dear friend but a source of brilliant advice since the time I wrote *Degree of Guilt.* I would not be here without him.

ABOUT THE AUTHOR

Richard North Patterson is the author of *The Devil's Light, In the Name of Honor, The Spire, Exile,* and fifteen other bestselling and critically acclaimed novels. Formerly a trial lawyer, he was the SEC liaison to the Watergate special prosecutor and has served on the boards of several Washington advocacy groups. He lives in Martha's Vineyard, San Francisco, and Cabo San Lucas with his wife, Dr. Nancy Clair.

CPSIA information can be obtained
at www.ICGtesting.com
Printed in the USA
FFOW051455120113
683FF